LIGIA DE WIT

BRADAÍS PLEDGE

CORRUPTION OF FAETE

Cursed Dragon Ship Publishing, LLC

6046 FM 2920 Rd, #231, Spring, TX 77379

captwyvern@curseddragonship.com

This books is a work of fiction fresh from the author's imagination. Any resemblance to actual persons or places is mere coincidence.

Cover © 2025 by MiblArt

Developmental Edit by Kelly Lynn Colby

Proofread by S.G. George

ISBN 978-1-951445-92-8

ISBN 978-1-951445-93-5 (ebook)

To all the readers who can't live without their glossaries, Gaelic Irish translations, and pirate lingo cheat sheets... and who might need a gentle nudge to remember what happened last time.
You're welcome.

The Story So Far

IMPORTANT DETAILS TO REVIEW BEFORE
DIVING INTO BOOK THREE

Titus has fallen from grace in the eyes of Anord, the godlike, powerful creature from the dark dimension who created him. Nearly killed by Peter, Titus was stripped of his coin—the magical spell Anord uses to control all bradaís. Without it, Titus is free from the gold lust that once consumed him and now remains hidden from Anord's gaze.

Yet his beast is not gone. It still whispers to him, though its influence is dulled when he is with Ryanne. Her growing fae power has a unique effect, numbing the beast's hold over Titus.

Ryanne has grown stronger, overcoming some of her greatest fears— confronting nymphs and standing against Edward. Edward, determined to kill Titus now that he is no longer useful to Anord, seeks to recover the coin so he can claim Titus's power for himself. However, Ryanne's and Titus's combined cold fae power is enough to thwart Edward, allowing them to escape.

But their respite is short-lived. The fae find them and demand that Titus be the one to kill Edward, claiming that Edward is the key to defeating

Anord. As the only one capable of bridging their worlds, Titus holds the potential to defeat the Alpha.

Torn between their own desires and the fae's demands, Titus and Ryanne refuse to be pawns in anyone's game. The fae insist on keeping Ryanne safe behind their walls, but she and Titus choose their own path, defying both Anord and the fae in their fight for freedom.

Part One

ONE

Titus

The Morrigan take all relatives to hell and leave them there.

On second thought, she could take all relatives *and* bloody ridiculous neckties.

I shifted the tie's knot, uncomfortable like a man about to be hung, while sweat condensed at my armpits. We were supposed to be in the middle of Autumn. Instead, a too-warm sun in a bright blue sky shone over this boring Seattle suburban neighborhood where we both stood like gobshites before a white wooden door with a brass handle.

"Too hot," Ryanne mumbled, squinting at the bright sun. Beads of sweat covered her forehead.

"If I recall, sun is usually absent from Seattle's sky."

"Yeah, shouldn't be so sunny in November. Highly unusual weather."

My discomfort faded at her own nervousness, and the bloody heart thumped fast. What an annoying thing to have, this heart. Yet, the feeling that it gave me when I held her in my arms at night was nothing I'd ever felt before.

Feel.

A bradaí like me should not be able to develop deep emotions

1

besides anger, lust, and hate. We were supposed to be empty like a can of beer on St. Paddies' day. And yet, here I was, feeling and bubbling.

"I bet Dad's in his basement," Ryanne mumbled, "and Mom's in the kitchen. I can't believe it's taking them so long to open this damn door."

I seized her hand and squeezed it, making certain *dorcha* remained within my body since my dark oily energy desired to burst into her and corrupt her own. Barely glancing at me, she gave me a half-hearted smile. I stroked her short chestnut hair that brushed her shoulders in a heavy cascade.

I was unaccustomed to being without a beard for so many weeks, and I hadn't left my hair long in the past century. Now it matched her length.

She let out a long sigh and again rang the bell at the side of the elegant white wooden door that stood before us like the mouth of a wolf.

"Easy, Titus, they won't eat you," she said without taking her eyes off the door.

"I still think this is a bad idea," I grumbled loud enough for her to hear me. "I feel too exposed here."

I observed the street with narrowed eyes for the umpteenth time, full of gabled houses with gardens and leafy trees, typical of a suburban Seattle neighborhood. Humans with their noisy kids had taken over the street, but my senses weren't screaming a warning. We hadn't had any odd encounters either with my kind or any of the fae while looking unsuccessfully for Homkar, my loyal first mate and friend.

"It's been two weeks," she said wearily. "I think we can come to see my family without yours bothering us."

"A fortnight is like a second for my kin."

"Then a few hours are a fart. A bradaí fart. Figure that."

I chuckled. I liked that we could be so comfortable around each other and not pretend. I didn't like that we had to see her parents though.

That'd been her condition: she'd follow me to the end of the world, but she needed to see her parents first. I exhaled loudly, trying to relax.

I'd rather have a good fight with any of my kin over getting stuck in a room with these strangers.

Ryanne needed to ground herself though. Her fae power had grown too much, too fast, and she needed human touch, a concept as foreign to me as a catgut scraper was for her.

I checked my texts once again. While I'd changed my number, Homkar and I shared a secret code.

Catgut scraper, slang for the ship's fiddler, and any number combination including 18 and 05—1805 had been the year Homkar and I met. No one, not even Ryanne, knew about that. My loyal first mate deserved his privacy.

"Nothing?" she asked after a quick glance at my phone.

"No. Silent as a dead man."

"Don't say that!"

"It's so unlike him, not only this silence but his absence."

"Then let's look for Quintus first. If he's as powerful as you claim, then he might know something."

"Quintus is a nádhúrtha, and his realm is here, in the human realm. He wouldn't know about Homkar's whereabouts."

We'd looked for him in the three spots Homkar and I had used in the past. It was unnerving. And there was Ryanne's powerfully bizarre highs and lows. She'd finally begged—nay, demanded—to see her family.

The door clicked open.

"Ryanne!"

"Mom, I thought you'd never open!"

The older brunette woman standing before us looked like she'd won the bloody lottery by the way her smile widened and how her eyes shone. She hugged Ryanne as though she hadn't seen her in years. Why the hell all this fuss? I rubbed the back of my neck and refrained from looking over my shoulder yet again.

"What poor timing! A few days more and you'll be in for Thanksgiving," the woman said.

"Sorry it didn't line up," Ryanne said, releasing the woman. "Titus, this is my mother, Harriet."

"So he *is* real. We were starting to think he was like your pretend friend Bricius." She winked at me.

"Mother!" Ryanne chided.

"Oh just a bit of a joke. Nice to meet you, Titus." Harriet offered her hand.

I arched my eyebrow. Ryanne didn't resemble her at all. Harriet was of a delicate constitution and shorter than Ryanne. Her clear eyes reminded me of the fae. The association made me frown; they must be looking for us. If I were them, this would be the first place where one of them bloody daighs would be stationed.

Bad idea. Why did I agree to this?

Ryanne nudged me, discreetly nodding at her mother, still with an outstretched hand and a forced smile on her delicate face.

Not having a choice, I grabbed her hand. She was fully human, not a hint of fae power at all, forty-eight or so, and liked to cook, based on the smell of fried potatoes and raw fish. Her rough fingers told me she didn't shy away from manual labor either. Gardening, perhaps? Aye, she had grass stains at knee level.

"Come in, come in," she said, waving inside the house. "Such a shame you're coming for lunch instead of dinner. I'd make something more spectacular!"

"Fish is perfect, Mom," Ryanne said with warmth. "I've missed your cooking."

Harriet beamed.

I looked to the street again, expecting to see a flaming-orange-haired daigh hidden behind a bush. My kin would have hit, so they weren't around.

Ryanne took my hand and pulled me into a spacious place. The inside of the ordinary house looked spotless, and the care Ryanne's mom put into the house showed, though it was too feminine for my taste. Obviously, the father didn't have a say in the design. Family photos littered the shelves like a bunch of apelings on tree branches. This woman loved her family.

Family, a concept once mystifying for me, but now it had a face. Several, actually: Kara, Sergei, and Homkar, even Stephen and Mouse.

Ryanne and Harriet were engaged in conversation away from me.

Before me was a door with old, chipped paint: her father's hiding place, surely, so then this should lead to the basement. As though answering my thoughts, the door swung open and gave way to a man with a hair color similar to Ryanne's, though the chestnut was sprinkled with gray, especially at his temples.

Gray eyes behind his glasses constantly moved, unfocused. The man seemed to be distracted by thoughts in his mind instead of noticing anything in front of his nose. He walked on without even addressing me.

The corduroy trousers were frayed on the hem. I looked at Harriet's perfect pants, except for those grass stains. The man's shirt was buttoned wrong and had two dark smudges under his right pocket. Blood? No, sauce, possibly barbecue. The crumbs on his shirt and in the corner of his mouth gave away his snacking.

"Dad!" Ryanne shouted while throwing her arms around his neck and kissing him on the cheek.

The man thumped her back twice, smiling nervously and arranging his lenses. "We have a pending chess game, Ryanne. Do you want to continue it?" he said without preamble.

"Later, Dad. Here, meet Titus." She gave me a smile, but her beautiful moss-green eyes darkened.

Hell, she'd learned well from me.

"Nice to meet you, Ditus," the man said, offering his hand.

"Titus."

He was slightly taller than Ryanne and smelled of expensive lotion that Harriet must have bought. If he spent so much time on his lab as Ryanne said, he couldn't be the type of man who bought his own things.

"Titus also likes to play chess, Dad."

"Fantastic! Maybe you're interested in a game later, Ditus?"

"Titus." I doubted he'd heard me. His eyes were unfocused, possibly thinking of a chess move, as Ryanne had told me he often did.

"Want something to drink?" Harriet asked me.

"Whiskey."

"Oh dear," Harriet said. "I fear we're not whiskey drinkers here, but how about Baileys?"

"Hell, no! Who drinks that shite?"

Ryanne gave me a nudge. I opened my mouth to ask why she'd done so, when I remembered her warning. Harriet had left her smile plastered on her face, but her eyes registered shock. Ryanne's father—what did Ryanne say his name was?—James was also looking at me, now attentive.

"No, Harriet, thanks," I said with a forced smile. I glanced furtively at the door. How long does one have to do this? Twenty minutes should be enough for Ryanne to root herself.

"We have red wine," James offered.

Wine was not of my liking since it was Edward's favorite drink, but I acquiesced. Anything to get through this nightmare.

With the glass in hand and sitting in their living room, I glanced up to the ceiling for what felt like the millionth time while Ryanne and her mother talked. James was now completely immersed in a book, completely oblivious to the prevailing conversation. Thank the Morrigan for small favors.

The nagging to-do list ate at me: find Homkar, find Quintus, hide so neither fae nor bradaís could find us. Quintus could help us train and enhance our combined powers and remain undetected. Perhaps once Ryanne's power strengthened, she could nullify the beast as well.

Instead of completing our quest, we'd returned to Seattle and to visit Ryanne's bloody family. The waste of time bothered me so much I had trouble keeping my human face in place.

The doorbell rang, and Harriet went to answer it.

"Why can't you be friendlier?" Ryanne hissed from the corner of her mouth.

I had no idea how she could talk like that, but I understood her perfectly though she hardly moved her mouth. Experience, I supposed, after speaking for years with a pixie no one could see except her.

I leaned toward her, inhaling her flowery aroma that reminded me of a misty morning in a forest in Tír D'aois. "I'm being incredibly friendly. My old self would have taken off from here in two seconds."

Perhaps even killed them all.

She snickered. I slid my hand over her cropped silken hair, wishing she would grow it again.

"We should go," I said. "We're not safe here."

"You know why I need this. Have patience."

"Patience? That's what I—"

"Ryanne!"

The shrill cry came from a woman who resembled Harriet but younger and curvier.

Ryanne exchanged a warm hug with her sister, their laughter weaving into the din of family chatter, before drifting back to my side. Her sister turned to embrace their father, leaving me rooted in my chair, counting the seconds until this familial circus gave us an exit.

I wasn't one for begging, but I whispered to Ryanne, "Please. Tell your mother we're starving."

"Not yet," Ryanne hissed. "I haven't seen Evelyn since you tried to kidnap me."

"How long?"

"Until lunch's over. Chill."

I pulled out my phone from my pocket. Besides Homkar's number, I'd also saved Stephen's, the ship's helm, and the only human I'd trust my ship with. Albeit Homkar was the one who'd usually contact Stephen.

And there was Kara's. But I couldn't cross that bridge, not when she might be under surveillance. After our attack on Edward where she was left wounded, she must be flying low.

Frowning, I placed the phone back, patting the chair with both hands, shuffling my feet.

I heard Ryanne calling me. "Well?"

She stood before me and had a weary expression. Everyone was watching me.

"What?" I exclaimed.

Ryanne reached out and forced me to stand. Bloody hell, what a man had to do for the woman he loved.

You do not love, you destroy, the voice inside me whispered. My beast.

Préachta, that energy that came from the fae, drowned my beast's thoughts.

The object of my confusion pulled my hand again, and reluctantly I shook the outstretched hand of Evelyn and her fiancé Tim. I didn't bother to evaluate them. My attention was fixed on the door, hoping for Ryanne to say the magic words.

"So you're the famous Titus," Evelyn said, drawing my attention to her.

"Famous? Hell no." I sincerely doubted these vanilla humans had heard of my business before.

The father looked up from his book.

"She means I've told them about you, Titus." Ryanne's smile didn't reach her eyes. Those drew sparks and promised me she'd give me hell later.

I grinned and bent to kiss her; I could feel her body tense at my proximity, how her breathing quickened. Satisfied with her reaction, I placed my lips on the sensitive skin of her neck, knowing it excited her.

She attempted to push me. "Remember what we talked about," she hissed, pushing harder.

I lowered my eyes to her modest cleavage. By the Morrigan, she was right, I should stop behaving like a bloody teenager.

Ryanne pulled me to the couch, where we sat again. I brought her closer to me to better inhale the eucalyptus with the subtle touch of jasmine.

"So what do you do, Titus?" Harriet asked, bringing me back to reality. "We just found out about Ryanne's plans with you and that sadly, you won't be staying for Thanksgiving."

Something in her voice sounded like reproach. Ryanne hadn't kept in constant contact with her family with fae and bradaís at our heels, and apparently, they didn't like it. James, her father, hid it well, though, and kept his attention on his book.

"I'm a merchant," I said. It sounded better than mercenary, or so Ryanne had said.

"Really?" Tim asked politely. "What do you trade?"

There was something agreeable about him that didn't bother me. "Oh, a lot of things. I have my own clients." That was how I met Ryanne. I'd kidnapped her to sell her to a laboratory that would test her because Ryanne was special. So special that my first attempt had been thwarted by one of the Guardians of the Hawthorn himself named Gallchobhair. Though Pretty Boy suited him better.

The fae had given her a touch of fae energy when she was eight, although her family was unaware of that fact. Having visions of the future was something they couldn't understand, nor having their precious daughter exchanging polite commands with ogres.

"So you're independent." Tim smiled and linked his hand with Evelyn's. "That's great, not to depend on a boss."

"Oh, Tim, what are you saying?" Evelyn straightened and looked at me proudly. "He's a Sales Manager for Delaware Northwest Region."

Like I cared.

"And you travel a lot?" Tim asked.

Ryanne squeezed my leg.

"All the time."

"Where to?" he insisted with genuine curiosity.

"All over the world. There's no country I haven't visited. My clients are varied." Sheikhs, peace groups, members of cartels, the mafia, and politicians, among others. Anyone who could afford my higher rates. Ryanne didn't want me to say that though.

There were many things Ryanne didn't want me to say.

Mostly everything.

"Wow." Tim shook his head. "That sounds fantastic. I wish I could do that."

I doubted it. He'd need a ship but not any ship. It had to be built from dragonwood to be invisible to the international police. Plus, the materials from Tír D'aois could take you anywhere through a special portal. Of course, to really do what I did, Tim would have to be a bradaí, something not easy considering there had not been more of us created for over three hundred years. The fae had stopped our creator, Anord, from producing more. And our Alpha Edward had killed two of us, something unheard of since we were supposed to be immortal.

I shook my thoughts, not wanting to deal with their deaths right now—or rather the cause of them. Those thoughts took me directly to my own near death at the fae's hands. Without thinking, I pressed a hand on my left side, where I'd been skewered and left for dead.

"That is nice, isn't it, dear?" Harriet said to James, who gave a noncommittal grunt then kept on reading. "Traveling around the world!"

"Speaking of traveling . . ." Evelyn's pitch was high. She wriggled her left hand, on which shone a diamond ring. "We booked the honeymoon in Bali." She beamed at everyone. "The hotel . . ."

"Let me see your ring," I said, reaching out.

Confusion reflected in her eyes for a moment. With a big smile, she approached, placing her hand on mine.

"Hm. Round cut, three-quarters of a carat, has many flaws but it's not bad. Its current value would be about four thousand dollars. At least the band is platinum."

I raised my head to silence. Evelyn's jaw hung open, and Tim chuckled nervously.

Ryanne pulled me toward her.

"Wow, you know a lot about diamonds," Tim said, shuffling in his chair.

Like you have no idea, mate.

"And where exactly are you flying tonight, Ryanne?" Harriet asked.

"Prague, Mom."

We weren't, but they didn't need to know that.

"So far away! Do you have wedding plans?"

"Mom!" Ryanne exclaimed, shocked.

"Hell, no! Why?" I cried at the same time. Anord's balls, what was that about?

Ryanne chuckled. "Titus and I have been dating for just a few months. It's not in our plans." She shrugged.

"It's not something we'll *ever* do," I said, bringing her into my arms with a smile, hoping to please her. "At all."

Her body stiffened, and a look of annoyance crossed her moss-green eyes, eyes that shone emerald for a moment as brief as lighting striking on the ocean.

Anord's balls, had I say something wrong?

Evelyn whispered to Tim, while Harriet brought more drinks. Thank the Morrigan.

I scratched below my chin, wondering what had upset Ryanne. Then it clicked—there was no future for us while Edward lived. Did she think we did have a future?

The idea of staying with her forever sprouted in my mind and made me smile. A smile that withered as fast as powder spent from a cannon. With Edward on our trail, forever could mean a few hours or weeks.

No one from Ryanne's family seemed willing to keep talking to me, to my relief.

"You're not mad at me, are you?" I whispered.

"No," Ryanne said. Again that brief emerald shine crossed her eyes.

The heart—*my* heart—clenched. As did my jaw. How inconvenient to acquire a new organ after more than three hundred years of living without.

Now that I had a heart, would I bleed to death? That moment when I'd been in the void all bradaís belonged to was not something I relished. The fae-spirit had brought me back with Ryanne's help, albeit that didn't mean she could save me again.

With bradaís chasing us like pirates after pieces of eight and fae wanting us to drift apart, nothing was certain.

I lifted a hand and watched the veins beneath tanned skin. Either faction could take me out if I was mortal.

The Morrigan take bradaís and fae to hell.

TWO

Ryanne

Could you give me a hand, Ryanne?"

My sister practically dragged me into the kitchen. Which wasn't surprising. When I lived here, Mom would cook and Evelyn and I would set the table, while Dad worked in his basement.

Work or hide—he preferred to do both in solitude. And read in solitude too.

Préactha stirred and it peeked its head in my mind, an awareness that was ever present. I'd never thought about it like that until recently, but besides its many other features, it also acted as a defense system.

"Is the food ready?" I asked her while the aroma of oven baked fries and pan-seared fish—my childhood favorite—reached my nostrils. I hadn't realized how hungry I was. My fae power scoured my body, and I felt it like a hose of cold water on a hot day.

She closed the door of the kitchen and stared. "You're upset."

"Me? No, I'm hungry, not hangry. Why do you ask?" I hunched down to look inside the oven. "Looks delicious."

"About Mom asking about marriage. She can be a bit tactless but—"

"That?" I laughed merrily while I opened the oven to snatch a fry.

"You sure?"

Concern reflected in her eyes. She could be a little pompous, but deep inside she was a good sibling who loved me.

"Oh, yes," I said nonchalantly, then blew on the steaming fry before biting into it. "It's not on my bucket list. C'mon, Eve, I'm a few weeks away from turning twenty-three. Basically a child." I winked at her.

The fae might have treated me like a child until recently, but Evelyn took the joke and grinned.

My own grin faltered, remembering Titus said it would never happen. *At all,* he'd said. But then, he was no regular boyfriend material. *At all* might very well be what it would be.

"Good," Evelyn said, "because I was starting to worry. He's scrumptious, but you guys aren't serious, are you?"

Again that worry in her eyes. I guessed she didn't want me to fall for the first guy that I finally could date more than once. Ironically, besides that date on the ship right before he sold me to that Japanese lab, we hadn't had any dates at all.

So that second date still eluded me—not to mention Paris, a destination that had slipped through our fingers ever since he promised to take me on a tour. A tour that never happened because a hideous man named Sanders kidnapped and tortured us. *Préachta* stood by, like an ogre ready to strike, but I forced it to relax, not wanting to worry Eve further.

"Nah, marrying's for old people like you."

She swatted my arm playfully. *Préachta* reacted and stood by once again. Did it think my sister was a threat?

"I asked Tim, and we'll take you to the airport tonight. What time are you guys leaving?"

Shoot. But I smiled and said, "The flight leaves at six p.m." She didn't need to know we were using a magical portal to Rome, not Prague.

She glanced at her watch. "We have plenty of time! We can leave at three to get your suitcases from your hotel. Prague," she sighed, "I'm dying to go there too."

Double crap. I should have said earlier! It'd be more difficult to open a portal in such a crowded place. Well, we'd make do.

We returned to the living room, and I helped her to set the table.

Then I glowered at Titus, who was comfortably sitting on the couch, so he would move his ass and help as well.

But the darned pirate didn't take the hint. Which wasn't surprising since his crew did all the cooking and he only sat prettily like the captain he was.

One of the many things I had to teach this deluded pirate. "Titus, can you bring the forks please?"

"Why?"

I had to refrain from throttling him and remind myself again he was a pirate who'd never ever been to a family dinner. The type of dinners he attended were the kind where the other diners might stab or betray him.

"Because I asked?" I said with a sweet fake smile, my own Ryanne Trademark Smile.

Comprehension dawned in his eyes, and he whispered, "How long?"

"Just go," I said in my pixie voice.

And my mom had suggested marriage? Yeah, right. With Titus being a bradaí and danger hanging over us, it hadn't even crossed my mind.

Staying safe and staying alive was all that mattered.

I felt terribly happy for Evelyn's marriage. But like I'd said to her, marriage wasn't on my bucket list. Stabilize my fae power while rooting my humanity, otherwise, I'd remain unstable with those weird mood swings. *Let it take roots,* Cuidi had said. Yes, I'd let it root, while hanging out with Titus.

Now that was a goal I wanted to achieve.

Nullifying Edward while avoiding blood spill came next.

In his magic dragonwood ship, Titus would show me the world—first stop, Paris—and that was what came next after Edward.

Fingers crossed. Maybe then I could have a true second date with Titus. And then some.

At all, he'd stressed.

I shook my head and glanced at my distracted father, who was chatting with Tim, and then at my sister and mother, talking animatedly among themselves. They always did that, Eve and Mom.

Anger swelled up inside me. They were excluding me as usual.

Titus returned and placed the forks in a pile on the table.

I blinked, then shook my head and placed them correctly at each plate.

"Come, Ryanne, let's eat," Eve said cheerfully. "I'm so happy that you're here."

"She is," Tim said in the same tone. "She was excited to see you today."

"We all were," Mom said, taking her place and lifting a hand toward Dad. "Darling, please help me serve."

They weren't excluding me as I thought. I used to get out of their way to talk to Bricius because it was more fun. Maybe I'd been excluding *them*.

But as I watched my family gather, *préachta* attempted to pull me away from them. They were humans after all, so I glued my back to the chair and—what was I doing? I came here to be *near* them, to anchor me. I tried to *feel* that coveted warmth in me, but cold filled me instead. I felt detached, faraway. And I didn't like that. That upturned-nose cold feeling crept inside me, around me, like a gilded cage with flowery bars. A cage that reeked of fae power.

I clenched my fork.

"Are you well?" Titus whispered at my left side. He looked like a man about to be hanged.

"Yeah." I released the fork and snatched his hand. He squeezed my fingers, and my *préachta* relaxed. It was so easy now with his own fae power; both acted like longtime friends.

"I love you," he whispered in my ear, his nose tickling my skin in a wonderful array of emotions.

Since he learned to say it, he kept repeating it, though most often while in bed.

"You look so cute together," Evelyn said, winking at me.

I sighed, if only *préachta* would relax here. I couldn't act like a fae in my own house.

No. As much as I loved the fae, I didn't want to become one, not entirely. And I needed my roots, my family, to be me.

So I talked to everyone and laughed out loud while we ate the fries and the pan-seared fish that I loved so much as a child.

Since my daunting attack on the Alpha, my *préachta*, that power of the fae we both had inside us—mine as a gift and his to numb his darkness—was unbalanced. Sometimes it morphed into an ogre. Sometimes it made me act like a fae without any control of my own emotions.

And I was going away to learn how to neutralize a bradaí who wanted to kill Titus and me. To learn under a nádhúrtha called Quintus if and only if we were able to find him. I couldn't let my humanity slip away, so I had to do something else.

Humanity felt cozier than the cold fae power.

There was nothing else I wanted but to balance myself again.

And *préachta* was inevitably inside me. I kept expecting it to send me images of the taigh to return, as it did after I found the first sign of the spark in Titus. When it didn't despite the fact that Titus and I escaped from the taigh against the fae's orders, I thought it had to be because I'd outgrown the *cailín*—child—moniker. Bricius had said when fae became adults, they took to quests even if against their elder's orders.

And I was certainly on a quest against my elder's orders—to learn how to defeat a bradaí.

Dad stood next to me while everyone cleared their dishes. Titus didn't bother and sat with his brow furrowed while checking his phone for the umpteenth time. I was tempted to send him to wash dishes but one step at a time.

Dad adjusted his glasses and smiled almost shyly. *Préachta* attempted once again to take over, and I almost took a step back to put some distance between us. Just like Peter had done so many times when I attempted to embrace him.

The heck with that.

I reached out to Dad, who welcomed me with a warm hug. As soon as my arms enclosed him, that warmth seeped into me like a blanket on a winter evening.

"I missed our games." He sighed.

"I missed them, too, Dad."

I then went to hug Evelyn, even Tim, tighter, warmer. Their hugs fed me their humanity, and my own took a deep breath, as if it'd been drowning and now it felt safe.

That detached cold feeling flew away. I was me again.

"This feels so good," I said while hugging Mom.

"Oh, dear! I'm so happy you're here with us. Are you sure you're okay?" she whispered, casting a worried glance at Titus, who'd remained sitting and with the expression of a man about to be hanged.

"More than okay."

"Don't get mad," she chided, "but there is something about him that doesn't feel right."

I almost choked. *Mom, your instinct is right. He's a killer. A murderer. And I'm helping him out because I believe he can change. Well, his inner self must change because, you see, he was created for evil. But there is a spark in him that I helped ignite, so yeah, he is able to change. I'm not delusional!*

Yeah, I could see how that would make her feel at ease.

"He's . . ." I choked this time for real while *préachta* filled me up. I couldn't lie. That was not right. But I couldn't tell her the truth either. "He's okay. But, Mom, I'm going away for a long time, and I'll miss you."

Couldn't lie outright. Just like the fae.

She gave me an extra warm hug that felt even better. It was like this affection, this human, motherly affection, encased my fae power and neutralized it.

"I wished I could wrap your hug and carry it with me," I whispered, knowing that wasn't possible.

"Hang on," she said, and went upstairs.

My skin tingled, like when I lay on the grass back at Tír D'aois, watching the myriad of stars next to Bricius, and my heart swelled in happiness.

Happiness that morphed into guilt. I'd left Bricius behind, and there hadn't been a day where I didn't miss the bug. He'd understand. He knew I was on a quest, but he'd been present in my life for most of it. His absence was heartbreaking. I'd make it up to him.

Peter? He'd drag me back to the taigh and put daighs on me to ensure my fae power rooted according to *their* rules.

But I didn't need fae rooting. What I needed was human warmth. I needed my human family. Screw the fae rules.

Mom returned in no time.

"Here," she said, placing a silver necklace in my open palm, one I remembered quite well.

I lifted it in awe, my gaze tracing the rectangular-shaped links down to the tiny flower with petals barely open, from which a silver round locket hung. The pretty flower engraved on its surface brought back childhood memories. Bricius used to love it and would open and close it many times just to see my grandma's picture inside. We even played games, hiding the locket in the garden and seeing who could find it first. We did that even in Tír D'aois, where gnomes would join in our game. How could I have forgotten it?

"I kept it in my drawer after you left it here. I thought you'd like to have it again. Now I hope every time you see it, you remember us, wherever you are."

The necklace that my grandmother gave me as a child felt heavier than it looked, and I relished its comfort. I put it on, the silver locket warm on my chest.

"Thanks, Mom, for keeping it safe all these years." I hugged her tightly again, and I knew how a cat felt when it purred.

Then that tingling took over again, and I felt even giddier without understanding why.

The doorbell rang. My ears pricked. My rounded ears felt different than before, as if they were pointed and I could swivel them. I reached out and touched them, almost sure they were indeed pointed.

"Are you expecting someone else, Mom?" I asked, releasing myself from the embrace.

"No," she answered. "Let me get the door."

My body felt light, and it tugged me toward the door, vibrating.

I swiveled on my heels to Titus, who'd leaped to his feet with rigid arms.

"Sure, she's here." Mom's voice intoned clear. "A friend of Ryanne, you say?"

Fae, I mouthed. Peter!

THREE

Ryanne

My hands clenched into fists. My fae mentor had come to take me back to the taigh. Without Titus. Without me having a say.

Titus stepped closer to me, his body shielding mine.

"Come," I breathed, tugging him along toward the kitchen. Before stepping through, I caught sight of Bricius.

My darling friend! My friend, who had come to take me back to the fae prison despite the fact he knew I was on a quest. *Traitor.*

He hovered near the door and shouted, "*Mo thiarna*, here they are!"

Behind the group that had gathered near the door, a tall fae with reddish brown hair in human glamour stepped forward.

The bug flew to us. "Ryanne, wait!"

I'm sorry, Bug, I mouthed while I shut the door closed. "Portal!" I hissed to Titus. The door wasn't even locked, but it might throw Peter off for a second, which was all we needed.

Titus was already opening his portal, a trail of blue sparks following his fingers. Night showed from the other side, and we stumbled through the portal.

"Ryanne!" Bricius almost reached us.

"Wait!" Peter shouted, then the portal closed with a zing.

Bitter wind goose-bumped my arms, and I started to shiver. "Where are we? It's too cold!"

Before I knew what was going on, Titus opened another portal and dragged me through it.

"What are you—?"

"To throw the fae, in case he can follow us."

I faced a dark street where Mom's kitchen stood a moment ago, heart thumping fast. Bright lights ahead signaled we were in a city.

Titus scanned the area. "*Acushla*, those were incredible reflexes."

"Give me a sec. Please." I lifted a hand as if to touch an imaginary door. *I'm sorry, Bug. I'm so, so sorry.* I'd just run away from my best friend. I'd turned my back on him.

Would he be mad? Would he resent me? Or would he understand I had to take my own quest as we discussed back at the taigh. A quest that didn't include him, but I knew he respected that. If only he had come alone, maybe we could have talked at least.

"*Acushla?*"

Some loud people were laughing across the street, and I thought I heard them speaking Italian. "So, finally, Rome."

"Aye. Come."

We walked toward the lights and reached an avenue, a popular one by the open bars and restaurants and the melee of people crowding the street. Well, there weren't as many as I thought at first, but somehow it felt like that. Weird.

I rubbed my forearms. Darling Bricius, surely he was worried about me. But he should know I couldn't go back to the taigh. Not now.

Maybe not ever.

While we were on the run, looking over our shoulders for bradaís and fae, I hadn't had a minute to think. But I missed the weight of my friend on my hair or on my shoulder. If I was honest with myself, I also missed Peter.

But neither of those fae had a place on the path I was taking. While it was necessary to exclude them, it hurt.

"Let's warm you up," Titus said, jutting his chin toward a busy bar with a green awning.

"Coffee would be better," I mumbled.

"Whiskey will do the trick. Or we could get you an Irish coffee."

"That sounds much better," I said as I followed him into the charming bar, antique furnishing and decoration making it cozy. Warmth seeped into my numb limbs, and I let out a sigh of relief. We found a table, and soon Titus ordered drinks.

"My family will think something's off," I said, raking a hand through my short hair and making an attempt to smooth it out. I hadn't had this length since I was a kid. "Damn Peter."

"Call them later and make up something about Pretty Boy being a stalker and you needed to get out."

"I'll do that now." I fished out the brand-new cell we bought, location disabled of course, and texted Evelyn. She texted back in no time that everyone was puzzled since not only had we disappeared, but "that guy" had as well. I texted back to assure her we'd make it to the airport in no time and sent her our love.

"Bricius." I sighed. "He surely misses me." And my skin had tingled because of him, I knew.

Titus reached out and covered my hand with his. "Were you able to root yourself? With your family?"

"In that short time?" I scoffed. "Just enough, I guess." I seized the locket, its warmth reaching out to every corner of my limbs.

Silver lockets were usually cold, but there was a power in this one—the power of family, of history, of happy memories that my fae being recognized.

Fae *being*, not fae power. It hadn't been just power for some time now. But the locket grounded me, and I silently thanked my mother for keeping it all these years.

He squeezed and let go when the waitress came with our drinks. If it weren't for the constantly looking over our shoulders, Titus and I could have enjoyed our time as if we were on a date, a real second date. Something that sounded like heaven at the moment.

"Do you think we can be together without danger if we nullify Edward?" I asked, taking a sip of the Irish coffee. Piano notes took over laughter and the clinking of glass.

"Not nullify. We must kill him." Titus clenched a fist and pumped it.

I cringed. "Must we? Can't we just tie him up after removing his darkness and throw him to the Erlking as a present?" A nice, dark present. Surely the Erlking would love it.

"Nay."

Of course. What would be the point of having something easy if things could be complicated to the extreme? If Titus and I could ever have something like a future, Edward couldn't be up and swaggering about. But I hated the idea of more blood, especially if it'd be on our hands.

I scrunched my nose. An itch that I'd dreamt something about blood on our hands bothered me.

"But aye, he must be terminated. Otherwise, we'll be hunted down until he kills us both." He tightened his hold on his glass. "I don't like that."

"I don't like that either."

He had a point, of course, but couldn't there be another solution? Maybe, just maybe, there could be a way to deal with Edward. My eyes strayed toward the crowd in the bar, a place I used to love to hang around with my friends. My older self would have loved it here.

Now, I found it too noisy and crowded. I found myself missing the forest and the taigh. That was such an alien feeling—fae alien.

I'd been with the fae off and on since I was eight, granted without understanding my power until Titus came into the equation. And lately, especially since the Edward confrontation, my *préachta* acted weird, like I was losing myself in a sea of fae energy.

I liked old Ryanne, human Ryanne. And being with my family for that short length of time had cured my heart, if temporarily. The locket on my skin was a connection to my old self, the human rooting I had so longed for.

Thank Cuidi for moms and their love of their daughters.

Titus scrunched his brow as he checked his phone.

"Still wondering if they're going to track us if you call her?" I asked between sips of my coffee.

"Edward found us at my place because he was following Sergei. Anything is possible, *acushla*."

I wondered how Kara was faring. Edward had threatened to cut off her limbs and dump her in the ocean. Titus had explained that she had to stay on the move and not remain in one place for too long. Edward could find them quickly in the ocean, but it was harder to find them on land, though not impossible.

Kara was smart. She knew how Edward operated after centuries of experience, so Titus was certain that, despite the fact that Edward could find her, the possibility was low with her knowledge.

And I was certain that Edward had bigger worries than Kara at the moment.

Hopefully, we would find out if Homkar was all right. And Kara. And Sergei. Our friends who had taken a shot for us and we had no idea how they were faring.

"So what?" I said. "Are you going to stare at the phone until she calls you to this new number she doesn't have?"

"It could be like that nádhúrtha said. *De fumo in flammam.*"

I'd forgotten about Amriel after all we'd been through. An angel. A true angel Titus and I met in a church after the cave, after Minho had tried to kill Titus. "What did that mean again?"

"Out of the smoke and into the flame."

"I don't think Edward was the smoke and fae the flame." I winced.

"That's what you think, *acushla.*"

Acushla, an Irish endearment that means "darling," and according to Titus, paired with another word it means, "vein of my heart," but he liked the simple *acushla.*

I wanted to pull Titus to me and kiss him silly, especially after he finally was able to feel love.

But it wasn't time to get cozy with bradaís, even if I loved said bradaí and he loved me back. The dimmed lights in the bar grew brighter, the sounds louder. Suddenly dizzy, I snatched my hands back as if something in our touch caused the uncomfortable sensations.

"You good?" Titus laid a hand on my forearm, his warmth helping me to feel a bit like my old self.

"Yeah. Cuidi warned I'd been using too much *préachta*, so I might stop using it for a while. Root it." I clenched the locket again, and its warmth reassured me.

"Aye, sounds good."

"Should we find Quintus instead of Homkar then?"

"Not yet. I will call Stephen tomorrow about Homkar's whereabouts. If he doesn't know, then aye, Quintus."

Quintus. Another nádhúrtha. They were the equivalent of the fae in the human realm, but unlike fae, who only had one tone, nádhúrthas were more complicated and nuanced. Some were what we called angels, like Amriel, but this Quintus was more on the darker side if he was able to command shadows.

It said a lot that I was actually looking forward to that meeting.

We had escaped from Cuidi's taigh, escaped from the fae's rules and their desire for Titus to kill Edward on their own accord, by their rules.

We didn't want that.

Titus swigged the rest of his whiskey, thoughtful. The appetizer remained mostly untouched.

"Cuidi and Peter believed I wasn't ready," I said, mulling over that time in the taigh before we escaped, barely a couple of weeks ago. "Perhaps we should have told them about how we defeated Edward."

"We didn't defeat him. We only put him in a muzzle he removed in no time. And no, remember how your precious fae want to dictate things on their own."

"They should have trusted me," I mumbled.

Instead of having me prisoner in the taigh because they didn't trust my fae power at the moment. Yeah, I felt dizzy, but I knew the answer was for Titus and me to practice with our powers. Fae would never understand that.

I nodded to myself as I guzzled the rest of the Irish coffee. We had successfully thwarted the most dangerous bradaí thanks to our *préachta,* if only momentarily.

"What success rate did you give us? With Edward."

He scoffed. "With our *préachta* at this level? Ten percent, if we're lucky."

"Your mission, if you choose to accept it, is to kill the Alpha." I gave him a small smile. "And we've accepted our impossible quest."

"It's not impossible, just difficult."

"It's a shame Peter burst in." I placed the mug on the table and looked around. "I was enjoying my family. That cozy feeling they brought in."

Titus looked thoughtful for a moment, then seized my hand. "Why were you upset? When we were with your parents."

"It's the fae power acting, well, fae, you know that."

"No, no. Before that."

I shrugged. "Don't worry about it."

"I won't learn if you don't tell me."

I let out a sigh. In the two weeks we'd been running away, he'd been adamant to learn how to be selfless in order to get rid of his beast. The first thing on the agenda? Being a proper boyfriend.

"Tell me what it is. It's not about us getting hitched, is it?"

"Titus, are you *nuts*? We're being chased by a mad pack of hyenas and we're trying to find a nádhúrtha who may or may not help us."

"So I didn't say anything wrong."

"No. Chill, okay?"

He lifted my chin. "You say no, but it's upsetting you. If it's important to you, we can get hitched. I'm willing to make the sacrifice. That's selfless, aye?"

"Oh, for the Erlking's horns! You're making a fuss out of nothing. We must go now."

I stood to my feet and stormed out into the street.

Titus reached my side, his hand capturing mine while looking around as he constantly did since our escape.

"I don't want you to be upset by anything I do," he said.

"Let's not discuss my family or anything of the sort then." I sighed. "I need to relax."

"You need the sea. It crashes and sweeps, but there's peace within."

He smiled, that loving smile he gave me more of late, one that proclaimed his love more than anything.

I pulled him to me and kissed him, my hands caressing his back. Warmth reached to my body, and I kissed him harder, wanting more of him.

This was just not enough.

"We should find a room. Soon," I breathed.

My body tensed as if suddenly pulled by a chord and cold swirled in me. "Something's wrong."

A tug, and the locket was gone.

"Hey!" I snapped.

At our left, there was a boy in rags, leaning against a tree. The boy grinned mischievously, locks of dark hair partly covering his eyes. From his raised hand, my locket dangled.

Despite the fact it was night and he was about ten feet away, his eyes shone yellow.

The pooka! The one changeling who had thwarted my attempt to escape from Peter, that time when Peter had been able to kill Titus. Well almost kill him.

I let go of Titus's hand and dashed after the boy.

"Wait! No, Ryanne, he's a pooka. Get away from him."

"I know that. Hey, you!"

I almost reached the boy, whose eyes were a fiery gold. The pooka grinned in that feral way those creatures did, tucked the locket into his dirty rags, then turned and ran away.

"That's mine!" I yelled.

"Ryanne!" Titus seized my arm.

I shook his grip. "He was in that clearing where you almost died. And now he took my necklace. I need to know who sent him."

Things didn't just happen in that land. He knew something, and it was high time I knew why. And I also needed to recover my locket.

I frigging *needed* that locket.

Without waiting Titus to decide, I darted across the sidewalk. He followed close behind. My fae power stirred in me, the cold expanding and attempting to reach out.

"Wait!" Titus yelled.

But I'd been faster, focused on reaching the pooka. I didn't recognize the feeling until it was too late. Millions of bubbles exploded around me, like that portal I crossed when I was eight. Then I staggered into pitch-black darkness.

"A portal," I breathed.

"Aye, we crossed one. Bloody trickster!"

We'd crossed right into Tír D'aois. Could fae be behind the pooka?

Could Peter? But there was no sign of my fae mentor or my beloved pixie guardian. Instead of tingling in my skin, dread covered me.

The air was chilly, soaking through to my bones. Bright orange-red lava swirled beside the blackened soil near us. Dark caves loomed in front of us, their entrance even blacker than the moonless, starless sky.

"This is not a good place." Titus lifted his hand to open a portal.

I frantically searched for the pooka. And there it was, a few feet away from us. Yet he'd changed forms.

The pooka had transformed into a jet-black horse with the same gold fiery eyes. My locket dangled from his thick mane.

"Give it back!" I clenched my fists.

It neighed in triumph and kicked the air with its hind legs, then galloped away.

I stood in the dark, missing the warmth of the locket. Something pricked at the back of my neck, and I turned around.

And that was when I saw it. A creature perched atop one of the caves, humongous wings stretching like a bat out of hell. A dragon stared at us, yellow eyes bright in the night.

A vision flashed of a dark cavern and red eyes in a mist.

Dainséar, the power in me whispered.

Danger. I shuddered at an unknown energy, pulsating with a power that made my legs wobble.

"Titus—"

"*Welcome, bean.*" The voice calling me was powerful.

Benn? The way the voice said it, that accent . . .

A burning sensation spread on my neck like the sting of a poisonous bug. I slapped my hand to it, trying to ease the itch.

"By the Morrigan!" Titus had his hand on his neck too, and he staggered. "Ryanne . . ." He fell to the ground.

My vision blackened, and I slumped too.

FOUR

Titus

The smell of urine and raw meat clung to my nostrils. The Morrigan take me. I slapped a hand to my scorched throat. Hurt drilled my head from within, so I covered my ears to dim the loud ringing.

Where were we?

It took a lot of effort to open my heavy eyelids and get an understanding of the place we were in—a cell of sorts, with a floor, ceiling, and walls made of dirt. A sickly orange light came from a small, barred window in the door.

"Titus?" Ryanne's voice pierced the rotten stench like a breath of fresh air. "What happened? My head hurts like the worst migraine ever."

"We were drugged." I stood and reached out for her hand to give her a reassuring squeeze then extended my senses. Dormant yet powerful energy hit me with force. It was familiar and alien at the same time.

"This reeks of goblin." I stared at the window, attentive to any sound outside while attempting to open my portal. The energy in my fingers froze as if I'd tried opening it through a cement wall, just like at the spirit-fae's cave.

Anord's balls. Every bloody creature wanted a piece of us.

This devilish place throbbed with dense energy that stuck to my skin, making my breathing difficult. Even the air felt thick.

"Where are we?" she asked, lowering her voice to a whisper. "I need to find that damn pooka."

At least she sounded fine.

"We're underground," I said. "In a goblin's lair."

"I saw a dark place like this one when I was riding a dragon."

"What do you mean?"

"When Peter separated us, after Sanders." Her voice took on a hard edge. Not surprising after Sanders tortured me and weakened her. "There was lava swirling around that dark place, and it gave me shivers. A goblin's, you say?"

"It's their standard operating procedure: drug your prey to incapacitate them."

My beast stirred. It seemed to try to reach out for the thick energy looming in every breath of air.

"Not good news anyway." Or that my beast awakened with it.

"I'm sorry," she said, hugging me. "The pooka. He's been appearing to me since Peter captured you. I thought it a coincidence then, but he was also in that clearing where Peter killed—*tried* to kill you. And Fé Erie didn't send him to stall me."

The spirit with the fire-red curls. The one holding my coin—the physical manifestation of the closest thing a bradaí could call a soul. If someone were to touch said coin with bare hands, I would be blasted into oblivion. "A fae machination, but not from her part."

"Exactly. Who then? One of yours?"

"No, pookas don't like us at all. As a matter of fact, we bradaís rarely use creatures from Tír D'aois as allies." I glanced at the only source of light—if you could call it that—and hugged her tighter. "Occasionally goblins and, in my own particular case, Homkar." Though that was certainly fortune's favor.

The warmth of her body pressed against me, and I could feel her *préachta* intertwining with mine as it had been doing in this crazy escape.

It was an energy circuit that started to feel as familiar as breathing.

Ryanne grumbled, "Ugh. This is a mess. And it's my fault."

I kissed the top of her head. "Not your fault; we've been played." Again.

"It *was* my fault. When we arrived, someone called me in my head and welcomed me." She shivered.

"In your head? That's not good news."

"We need to get out." She walked to the entrance and tiptoed to look outside. "I can't see. The light is terrible." She placed a hand over the door.

It opened without a sound.

I pulled her behind me. Carefully, I peeked outside to find a tunnel on both sides. Empty. I clasped her hand and walked out.

"What happened there?" I whispered as quietly as I could.

"I only thought about going out," she answered in the same hushed tone.

The tunnel had torches on the wall. Everything around us was dirt. Twisted, bare roots broke the terracotta monotony.

"Stay close to me," I said.

"It's not like I'm going to scurry away like a brownie," she said, annoyed.

I smirked. I'd rather have her annoyed than terrified.

We crept forward, muscles tense and ears at the ready. Every few feet there was a door with a barred window like the one we left. Skulls and bones were scattered on the ground. The stench grew thicker, making the stale air almost unbreathable.

How could she open a door here? It shouldn't have been possible. Her energy was akin to the bloody fae, and whoever's lair this was, it was certainly not akin to them.

Feet stomped the ground behind us. We hastened our steps in unison.

The tunnel led to a cave darker than the tunnel. The dense energy was thicker yet still dormant. Waiting.

Deep laughter erupted, followed by peals of higher-pitched laughter, bristling the hairs on my neck and arms. The pooka had led us right into the shark's jaws. Ryanne stuck to me, silent but shivering.

"*De fumo in flamman*," I said, sucking in a breath. This was what the nádhúrtha had meant.

"You could not have said it better, pirate," said a cavernous, powerful voice. Two red spots floated in the darkness. "Although the fire would have been preferable to stepping into my den. Don't you think so, my loyal subjects?"

The peals of high-pitched laughter echoed around—goblins.

"The Erlking." I swallowed, frustrated to be weaponless in front of the most dangerous and powerful being in this land.

Ryanne gasped in shock.

"Indeed, pirate. Kneel before me, kneel before the Erlking!" thundered the mighty voice.

A yellowish dimmed light illuminated the immense cavern where dozens of goblins smirked. Serrated teeth graced their mouth; a pointed chin, nose, and ears deformed their oblong heads. Their wrinkled foreheads were coated with a thick, viscous liquid that dripped over their oversized nose. Beady red eyes watched everything with malice.

While I didn't fear any of these annoying creatures, in this quantity they were certainly a power to be reckoned with, even for a bradaí. Even if the Erlking weren't here. The Erlking could do what only Eadroms could: defeat us in any situation.

Three Eadroms, the Guardians of the Hawthorn, against only one Erlking to balance the land.

Some goblins hooted, jumping in place. Others watched us with glee.

The Erlking stood from his wood-and-bones throne. As tall as Homkar, he had a leather mask partially covering his face. Huge stag antlers sprouted out of each side of the mask. The visible part of his face showed sharp yellowed teeth and a thick beard that reached mid-chest. His strong legs were encased in snow boots. Two dire wolves flanked him, hair ruffled and teeth bared.

A tall woman with thick dark ringlets stood by him, face shrouded in shadows. Yellowish light gleamed from her eyes as she assessed us. I couldn't pinpoint her odd energy nor why she was with the Erlking. A prisoner, perhaps. A toy.

"Well, well," the Erlking boomed. "A bradaí and a human-faeling, together. What a find."

Ryanne released my hand and sank her knee on the ground. "Oh, great Erlking! We ask for your hospitality and your safe conduct out of your lair and to direct us to our destination, if that pleases you."

The Erlking stared, an ogre watching his lunch. "You know your words, human-faeling." His forest-green coat waved as he stalked toward us.

I followed the example of Ryanne and knelt—pride had no space here. The Erlking smirked at my action and stopped in front of us. There was nothing to do but hope her words worked.

"Great Erlking," she continued, her voice amazingly steady. "I am a protégée of Lady Cuidigtheach. Let us leave here, I beg you."

Hell. Wrong thing to say. The Erlking disliked the Eadroms or anything that smelled of fae.

The Erlking gasped and placed the tips of his fingers over his lips. "Oh, she's a protégée of the queenie faerie!"

Mocking laughter erupted from the goblins' throats.

"My humble apologies. Arise, protected of the fae," the Erlking said with a benevolent wave of his hand.

I rose with her, aware of the goblins around us. Their red eyes shone, their lips snarling back and revealing pointy teeth. The woman with the thick ringlets cocked her head and grinned, shadows dancing across her face.

The Erlking lifted a hand and made as if to touch Ryanne.

I placed myself in front of her. "Don't even try," I said with a sharp tone. I might not be able to reach my bradaí pocket and retrieve my sword, but the Morrigan can take me if he hurt her, Erlking or not.

Not even the dozens of goblins closing on us would make me move.

"I applaud your noble intentions, pirate," he answered, expression unfathomable under that mask. "Although I merely want to sense her fae power. I've never met a human with such a concentration. May I?" He waved a hand, his eyes now intent on Ryanne.

Ryanne placed a hand on my arm. "It's okay, Titus."

Nay, it wasn't, and my body tensed like an anchor thrown to sea.

He placed a beringed finger on Ryanne's forehead. "Yes, I can feel the fae touch on you. It's quite strong. Interesting." He stroked his long beard. "Well, human-faeling, you may leave."

I clenched my fists, weary.

"Thank you, great Erlking."

"Just because the lady protects you, and I feel generous, I'll give you a twenty-minute advantage. What say you, pirate? Will you join me?"

"What does he mean?" she whispered to me.

My beast awoke with a roar.

Join the Erlking.

The Erlking raised his hands. "Let the *Wilde Jagd* come!"

By the Morrigan, we were doomed!

The goblins burst into wild cries, hooting.

Accept it. It is your nature.

"Join my Hunt, pirate! You're a predator, like us. You will have fun. After all, she must be someone *special* if the queenie faerie has her under her wing, is she not?"

Ryanne's huge eyes looked purely innocent in that moment. "Titus?"

Every cell in my body wanted to take a step forward and join him. The call of the Erlking prompted my beast, crying for blood.

Do not resist. Join the Erlking.

With all my self-restraint, I stood taller, seeking comfort in Ryanne's hand. I wouldn't give in.

"Pity," he said with a contrite voice. "Some of your kind joined before. You have twenty minutes." He raised a massive hand, and an hourglass appeared in midair, grains falling rapidly. "Off you go."

He pointed to an opening in the wall. The goblins parted and cleared the path in front of us.

We dashed for it. The opening led to another tunnel that ran straight as far as the weak light let me see.

"What's the vilder-whatever?" Ryanne asked while running.

"*Die Wilde Jagd*. The Wild Hunt. Nothing good for us. We must find a way out." Before the worst predators of Tír D'aois obeyed the Erlking's call and butchered us limb by limb. Not even I was sure to get away from them. I could be mortal now. I could die.

The tunnel turned right and then left. How to get out of the underground? The dirt tunnel stretched in front of us, sickly light barely letting us see. Ryanne stumbled on a root but regained her footing quickly.

"You did a good job handling the Erlking," I said to motivate her. "You spoke well."

"Did I? I almost peed. If I had nightmares before . . . Who was that woman? The one beside his throne. She looked at me weird."

"I couldn't get a good look at her." She seemed like a prisoner, yet her confidence made me doubt it. But then again, what creature could be here in the Erlking's lair other than his own? None that I could think of.

"Hey, lady, over here," called a youthful voice, coming from one of the doors.

Ryanne approached the door where a dirty boy peeked behind bars. Despair and terror reflected in his face.

"We don't have time. We must go," I said, looking behind us.

"We should help him. He's trapped."

"Yes, help me," the boy said, clinging to the bars. "Get me out of here, I'm afraid." His voice broke.

"We don't have time; let's go."

"But he's just a boy."

"That I am!" the boy shouted. "I'm scared."

"Please, Titus, let's get him out of here."

He wasn't fae, and he looked human, yet I couldn't feel him, just like that strange woman. It might be that the Erlking's energy was numbing mine.

"Remember the pooka," I warned.

"I'm no pooka!" the boy shouted, indignant. "I'm from Tír na Donna."

A human, then.

"He's one of mine! The door looks solid, and there's no lock," Ryanne said. Her desperate look made the pesky heart twitch.

I slid a hand over the rough door. "Think about letting him out, then."

My palm tingled with energy, then she placed her hand next to mine. As if our bodies created a circuit, our *préachta* mixed with the door's energy, and it clicked open. We both stepped aside just as a ragged flurry burst from the cell.

Before my eyes, the grimy boy transformed. His willful and suffering expression evaporated, replaced by a simper that put me on edge. A smile that screamed for me to use caution.

"I'm free!" he shouted in a obnoxious voice. "Stupid Cow Head won't catch me again. Take that, you maggot-faced moron!" The boy jumped in his place, waving a fist.

"Come," Ryanne said. "We're getting out of here."

The boy thumped fists on his waist. "Are you demented, Potato Breath? I can go by myself; I don't need a couple of losers like you."

"Hey!" She straightened and lifted her chin. "We freed you. If you know how to get out of here, you should tell us. You must return the favor."

If the boy belonged to this world, he would have no choice but to obey. Favors must be returned. Ryanne's fast thinking amazed me.

The light of the torches reflected eerily on his eyes. "Do I look like a pig-smelling fae?" He threw his head back and laughed. "Pan needs no one."

Pan. Not a fae, then, but from the human realm as he said.

He ran away in the direction we were going, singing, "Losers, losers."

We dashed after him. Perhaps he knew how to get out.

"It's him," Ryanne murmured. "He's Peter Pan. He's real, Titus!"

"The Peter Pan from the stories you're familiar with doesn't exist as such. Pan does."

"Pan?" she breathed. "As in the god with goat's legs and horns?"

"That might be only mythology. I've never met this moron before," I said as we ran. "Those beings are quite old, and they rarely show themselves to any of us."

"But what if he *is* Peter Pan and you're wrong? Not even the fae know all creatures."

Ryanne and her everlasting confidence.

The tunnel widened, the air grew staler, yet the rotten smell vanished. Three openings appeared in front of us.

"Bloody hell, where to?" I pulled her into an embrace. Perhaps our last.

A shadow jumped in front of us. It was the boy.

"Well, well, the losers are in lo-u-ve." He faked puking and gagging.

"Peter Pan," she said. "Just tell us how to escape from here."

"Ah-ha!" He wiggled a finger. "That is not who the great Pan is. You can call me Your Great Excellency. I'm the greatest Excellency that has ever existed. And I piss on you. And fart."

"That's nonsense," I said, glancing behind me. Hell, this brat was wasting our time.

"That's because I'm an all-powerful king and you're a troll's arse, fart-sniffing maggot." He stuck out his tongue.

"Do you know how to get out of here or not?" I narrowed my eyes at him.

He tapped his chin with a finger. "No. But"—he leaned and pointed at Ryanne's chest—"the answer is within her."

"What?" we exclaimed simultaneously.

Now the foul-mouthed boy was philosophical?

Pan raised an arm and sniffed his armpit. "So much time here has mellowed me, rats! This realm of skunk-piss, pimple-faced fae is already affecting me." His simper matched the mischievous glint in his eyes. "Sayonara, losers."

"Idiot," I said.

Dozens of horns blasted, ringing with the energy that had left its dormant and soporific state and turned into predatory power. The hunt had begun.

We were lost.

Pan scrunched his nose. "Don't tell me you losers caused the *Wilde Jagd*. Are you a pair of maggot-brained morons? Okay, Potato Breath, use your fae-stinking vision and pick a tunnel quickly before Cow Head takes us apart piece by piece."

"I thought you were a powerful king." I arched my eyebrow.

"And you're now my maggot-brained lackeys. I'll let you lead the way." The little brat snapped his fingers. "Chop, chop!"

FIVE

Ryanne

Okay. No pressure. Use my vision—which had never worked in Tír D'aois—to take us out of the Erlking's lair before he disemboweled us.

"You can do it," Titus whispered, lacing his fingers with mine. The trembling in my hands stopped.

Pan gagged.

Closing my eyes, I willed *préachta* to respond. It covered every part of me, tugging at my skin like dozens of miniature fireworks.

Feihnum, it sang.

Feihnum, the walls around us responded in harmonic vibration.

I felt the energy around us, and I glanced at them, expecting awe, but found unawareness. Powerful, ancient, it wasn't evil, not like what I felt with Edward. It just was. The three openings that had looked the same before changed. I could sense with subtle energy each one's different personality.

"Let's take the left one." It beckoned me.

"Are you sure, *acushla*? It looks darker and smells worse."

"I'm sure," I said with a cold tone. The fae energy swirled in me. "It should be left."

"Listen to her, Maggot Brain," Pan said with a serious countenance.

Titus nodded, jaw clenched.

We ran through it. The tunnel shrank, and Pan had to run behind us. It descended in a gentle slope, and my hands turned clammy. Had I been wrong? As wrong as following the pooka?

But who'd called me? It couldn't be the dragon because, well, dragons don't speak!

Do they?

No, a little voice came from me, a voice fueled by the fae power. *You are not wrong.* Coldness washed over me, one that felt right.

After the next turn, the tunnel widened to an antechamber and forked into two again. I chose the left opening again based on their energy. Neither Pan nor Titus complained, and my nerves exploded. What if I was leading us to our deaths?

Préachta assured me I was doing fine.

"Oops!" Pan exclaimed. A thump.

I whirled while Titus cursed something about brat kings. Pan was sprawled face-down.

"Well, Maggot Brain, what are you waiting for? Pick me up!"

Titus grabbed the dirty boy by the neck and made him stand. "There, now run," Titus said.

"I was doing that! Not my fault this tunnel is defective." Pan kicked the root on which he'd undoubtedly tripped.

The horn blasted, and the energy around us responded. It felt like an ogre raking my skin with wicked claws.

"Where are they?" I asked, frantic.

"It takes them a while to gather up," Titus said. "Let's not wait for them to show up before we're outside."

"Then what's up with that darned horn?" I spat, heat displacing the fae coldness as I glowered behind us.

"It serves to frighten their prey."

"Well, it's working," I said, enunciating every syllable, just like a fae.

Without another word, we sprinted. My shoulders tightened, picturing the Erlking breathing behind me.

The Erlking. Dammit! Why did the pooka send us to his lair? And why did he have to keep my locket? I patted my chest where the locket should be, something that could help balance this transformation into fae. Refraining from anxiety, I focused again on the energy and let *préachta* guide me. The light or air hadn't changed.

There was nothing to do but keep running through the dirt maze.

The tunnel widened enough for the three of us to run, and it started going uphill. The sickly orange light gave way to natural daylight, and a stream of fresh air hit us in the face.

By the Hawthorn! I did it. I got us free.

Of course I did.

"Well done, Potato Breath!" Pan yelled, shaking his fist.

I beamed at him.

"Quiet!" Titus shushed.

We stood still. The tunnel took a sharp right turn in front of us. Titus lifted a hand, stole down to the corner, and peeked. He waved us forward. Around the corner, the tunnel ended in an opening where a lava-like rivulet swirled around black rocks. Dawn was breaking over the dreary place.

"Can you use your portal now?" I asked Titus.

"Not during the *Wilde Jagd*. Duh! We need to hide from Cow Head, Potato Breath."

"You're not even funny," I said, sighing. "Cow Head? Potato Breath?"

"Well, then, Pus-faced Pimpled Gnome for you. Better?"

"Moron."

"Slug-eating ogre arse."

"Knock it off, you two." Titus crept outside, tense.

The silly interaction with Pan made me giddy; I was exchanging insults with Peter Pan! Pan. Or whoever he was. We followed Titus until the lava interrupted our advance, burbling with mild *pops*. The coldness inside me helped counteract the heat of the plain, but it felt uneasy—fae power disliked the Erlking's lava.

A large plain lay in front of us. A stale breeze wheezed as if not wanting to blow around this place. On our left, burned trees and stumps grew far apart. On our right, there was a forest of huge, thick-trunk trees.

My vision blurred into sepia. Hounds and horses bolted in mad pursuit through the dead forest. They weren't here yet since there was no red circle in the vision, but it felt like they would be soon. Hellish jet-black hounds rolled their tongues between sharp canines. Huge, hideous riders sat atop the black stallions: phantasmagoric and skeletal humanoids, ogres, and trolls. A familiar pooka shape-shifted into a fox, then into the same hellish stallion, and my locket hung from its neck. They all were armed: large poles, swords, and bloodied daggers.

I swallowed, feeling hot as if the lava covered me. It *was* hot under my feet, and I moved my weight from one leg to another. We needed to keep moving.

"They're coming that way!" I pointed left.

"How long?" Titus asked.

"No idea, but I sense soon. Five minutes, tops."

"We need to hide in the forest," he said.

We jumped over obsidian-black rocks, avoiding the lava stream criss-crossing the plain. Sweat damped my forehead, back of my neck, and armpits. A strong sulfur odor made me gasp for air.

When we left the darkened plain, I sprinted into the darkly brown forest. The energy levels were clear to me now—when to duck and which roots to avoid despite there being no discernible path. My feet were thankful it was no longer hot under them, though it was humid and I was dripping with sweat. Titus's dark hair was plastered to his forehead, and Pan sweated copiously. Sulfur was faint in the air, though not as present as on the plain. The battle horn blasted, closer than before.

"Two minutes!" I yelled. I didn't know how I knew it, but they'd reached the lava plain.

"Are you leading us to a trap, Potato Breath? What farted pixie taught you how to use your power?"

"You are welcome to leave us," I said with that fae cold tone, then shivered.

"Duh! You're my ticket out of this filthy, puke-smelling rat-fae hole."

"Then shut your mouth," Titus said. "She got us out of the Erlking's lair."

We reached a small clearing. The tree trunks were immense, wider than ten people joining hands in a circle. Roots, thick as a man's waist, twisted above the ground.

One of the trees pulsated. The sparse, muted green around it blurred, and I could see it as if my vision tunneled toward it. I felt *préachta* tugging me forward.

"That way." I pointed at the tree.

This was how fae navigated their world, by understanding the energy levels.

You are not only human, Zadora the silver-haired nymph had said. I pushed the cumbersome thought aside and reflexively tried to grasp the non-existent locket.

Damn pooka.

Underneath the roots, there was a hole we managed to squirm through, which opened onto an antechamber beneath the tree, tall enough for Pan to stand, though Titus had to bend. The ground outside peeked through the thick roots, mimicking a prison cell. Humidity was worse here, and the stale air reeked of rotten mushrooms. At least it wasn't sulfury any longer.

Energy rippled across the roots and covered us like a dome. Not unlike the dormant one from the Erlking's lair. I reached out to it. It wasn't against us but protecting us? Under whose orders? Fé Erie? It must be so. I thanked her from my heart.

Titus must have sensed it, too, since he sighed in relief.

"Congrats," Pan said, thumping my damp back. "You managed to take me out of one prison into another. Woo-hoo." He plopped on the ground, as far away from us as possible, brooding. His wet clothes stuck to him, just like ours.

"He's such a charmer. Well done, Ryanne."

I sat next to Titus and leaned my head on his shoulder to connect with him and push that coldness away from me.

"Stinky, maggot-filled place," Pan whimpered. "I'm stuck with you love-sick losers." He stuck out his tongue at me, so I stuck mine out at him.

"Ryanne," Titus warned.

"He's Pan." I clung to that memory of Peter Pan, of listening to my mom telling Eve and me that story, and I smiled warmly. Perhaps somewhere, there would be two stars at our reach and we could fly away to them.

"I feel heavy, bloated." Pan farted. "Now I feel lighter." He picked his nose then swiped his fingers on his damp clothes.

"You're gross," I said.

His face lit up. "Aw, Potato Breath, you're going to make me like you."

Préachta felt icier than ever, and I gave him a leveled look. The kind of look fae gave. I reached out to family memories, how Mom's hug had been so warm and cozy. The icy feeling dissipated, and I let out a shaky breath. It was hard to remind myself not to give in to that cold fae feeling. Fae power was intoxicating, but the consequences were far less appealing.

"You're stronger than you look," Titus whispered to me. "I thought you would collapse, but you kept on going."

"Bricius has trained me for as long as I can remember. Rain or shine, he made me jog every day. Woke me at six, even on weekends." I smiled, remembering his drill-sergeant way.

"Well, it certainly paid off."

Pan sprawled over the ground. Not many minutes passed before he snored and drooled. I bit my lips to contain a smile. As hideous as he was, he was Pan. I wondered where he came from since evidently he wasn't from Tír D'aois. So many questions I wanted to ask him.

The energy crackled like a flash of light across a lake, as if a nymph had just touched the surface. It felt oddly familiar. I stood and reached out toward the energy dome.

"What are you doing?" Titus asked from his spot.

"The energy. It feels similar to—"

The earth shook, and I took a couple of steps back, then retreated to an alert Titus. Pan sprang to his feet, knees bent and pointy ears pricked. His eyes flashed—eyes the color of time, profound and ancient. Titus placed a hand on my shoulder and squeezed softly.

A battle horn blared, resonating in every cell of my body. Dust rose from the ground. Dozens of hounds and horses stomped past us. Titus closed his eyes, his face showing a struggle. I squeezed his hand, and his *préachta* reached out to me. His face relaxed.

Barking, panting, grunts, and eerie yells sprouted goosebumps on my skin. One of the bloodshot-eyed hounds approached the roots, lips curling back and revealing a long set of serrated canines. I held my breath.

The hound sniffed, saliva drooling from the dark-purplish lips. It snarled, its powerful haunches ready to leap. I tightened my hold on Titus's hand, not daring to exhale. The growl intensified, rumbling in its chest.

Pan extended a hand and whispered odd words that held no meaning, like "toto" and "dagaboom." The hound stopped its growling and barked in an astonishingly friendly manner while wagging its tail. Pan wiggled his fingers while a mischievous grin covered his grimy face. He did a weird dance, like a drunken bird. The hound gave a doggy smile, tongue lolling out.

As dire as the situation was, I slapped both hands to my mouth to stifle a nervous chuckle.

"Pan," I hissed. "They'll notice a happy hound. Can you do something?"

"Do you want her caged? Leashed?" His eyes took a hard edge.

"No," I snapped as quietly as I could. "I don't want anyone noticing something's off."

"Ask and you shall be rewarded, Potato Breath." He snapped his fingers, and the hound growled again.

The earth shook, and two ogres crouched, glossy eyes staring where we hid, bald heads sweaty and necks rippling with muscles. The prey's brief respite vanished.

Titus gave a short squeeze, and I ventured a look. The energy rippled while the ogres seemed not to see us. One pushed the other and growled, then suddenly they were engaged in a fistfight. A third ogre shouted, and the pair retreated. The hound barked once more, as if in goodbye, before rushing to follow the ogres.

The procession lasted several minutes, but no other being approached.

I breathed with ease. They were gone. That odd energy had hidden us somehow from the Wild Hunt. The energy zinged, and the dome vanished.

"We're now unprotected," I said. "Time to keep moving."

Not even Pan argued. We squirmed our way out of the tree. As soon as the three of us were free, we ran in the opposite direction of the Wild Hunt.

"*Bean*," the voice called in my head, tugging me.

Bann—"woman" per what Bricius explained back at the taigh. A fae then?

I stopped and turned, unable to do otherwise. There, about thirty feet away, the Erlking sat atop a huge furry four-legged creature with horns. The creature stomped its hooves, dust raising, mist puffing from its nostrils, its fur blacker than the obsidian rocks we left behind.

The Erlking grinned. Not malevolent. Not mocking. Just smiled.

He touched his helmet briefly, then shouted in a language remarkably like German and galloped away from us.

The dormant energy was *exactly* like his lair. He'd been the one who had hidden us!

"Ryanne! Why did you stop?" Titus reached my side and pulled me to him.

"Didn't you see?" I pointed to where the Erlking disappeared.

"Let's go; we don't have time to dally!"

I followed, glancing over my shoulder, puzzled.

Pan stomped his foot when he saw us. "Come on, Potato Breath! Show us the way out so I can kiss this snooty realm goodbye. Can't wait to return home! Woo-hoo!"

I glanced behind me briefly. Why all the drama of capturing us and sending the Wild Hunt if he was going to shield us from them? It made no sense.

The trees bent in an arc as if making a bridge over us. Mist covered the ground, and white clouds reigned above—a ghostly realm. A goblin peeked behind a tree and hissed. Wait, that wasn't a goblin.

Pan stopped in his tracks. "What's that horrible creature?"

"No time," Titus said, grabbing Pan's arms and dragging him along. "Let's get out of here."

Pan and I shared a look. "That wasn't a goblin," I said, panting.

"It looked like an *arae* had a babe with a basilisk," Pan retorted.

"What?"

"*Arae*," Pan shouted while still running. "Don't you Potato Breaths read Greek history anymore?"

"A female demon," Titus answered, eyes focused ahead. "But they don't belong in this dimension. You both saw a goblin, and that's why we need to hurry."

Was it? Pan turned serious, but Titus was right. There was nothing of the sort here. We'd just seen an uglier than usual goblin.

We reached a forked path. The leaves on the right glowed red instead of the opaque orange on the left. The same fog seemed thinner.

"That way," I said, pointing right.

We dashed over the wide path. I searched for differences in my vision to guide me through.

"You're doing great," Titus said. "Carry on."

After what seemed like an eternity, I grew exhausted. As if it guessed, my vision highlighted a tree with small, bright green leaves contrasting in the mist. I wiped the cold sweat beading on my forehead with my dirty blouse's sleeve.

Pan lifted a fist, and his face lit. "Aha! The door is open." His eyes twinkled brightly. "Sayonara, losers."

He disappeared like an old TV monitor turned off.

I gaped at the place where Pan had been. "That's all? That little brat didn't even thank us!"

"What did you expect?" Titus huffed. "We should return to our dimension."

"Okay," I huffed.

Titus opened a portal, and we stepped through, arriving somewhere familiar under a darkening sky.

"The Forum? *Again*?" I snapped. "Titus, last time—"

"Relax, *acushla*. There's no one around, and we'll move somewhere else."

"But that Sanders," I said through gritted teeth. "If I see that fat bastard again, I'm going to . . ." I stopped, shocked at my words. "Sorry, I don't know what came over me."

"He was a jackass for hurting you like that. You're entitled to be angry. Now, let's go."

"Too tired. Give me a sec." I collapsed on the grass, trying to catch my breath, next to stone steps and old pillars. Titus moved warily, eyes darting to every shadow, then sat at my side and retrieved a cellphone from his bradaí pocket.

"Titus," I said once recovered. "The Erlking set us free." I told him about the energy dome and the Erlking's salute. Too much of a coincidence.

"I shouldn't be surprised. Those beings like to play games. They think we're their puppets." He spat the word puppets and clenched his jaw.

"Funny. I fear Edward more now than I fear the Erlking."

"I wouldn't trust either. Let's find Quintus. Homkar is well-hidden, so he must be fine."

"I wished I knew how the others are faring," I said, rising to my feet.

"Aye. I wonder that, too, if Kara's fine, if Sergei's fine."

His eyes shone at the mention of his family. I couldn't return to my human family, not in a while, and my fae family wanted me behind walls. Safe and sound, my hands tied.

Titus opened a portal and beckoned me over. "Let's keep on moving."

Again, I tried to grasp that imaginary locket as we stepped out of the Roman ruins.

I let out a shaky breath. Now that the locket was gone, I needed to find something to help me balance my human nature. While we were on the run.

While we were trying to hide.

SIX

I love this view," Ryanne said, her elbows resting on the modern railing, gaze on the marvelous view in the Altar of the Fatherland, lights twinkling under the velvety night.

The monument to Vittorio Emanuele II was on our left, and the few visitors were already gone. A gorgeous place to admire Ancient Rome. And yet, it was not as popular as it should be.

Which worked in our favor.

"Isn't it a bit hot here?" Ryanne asked while removing her cashmere sweater.

"It's not." Darkening clouds hung above us, the temperature several degrees colder than usual for mid-November.

"Well, I feel hot," she said, annoyance laced her voice while she fanned herself with her hands despite the fact that a cold wind swept across the top.

"Are you feeling okay?" Worried, I placed my hand over her forehead, but she swatted it before I could get a read.

"Yes! No, I'm not . . ." Ryanne closed her eyes, taking deep breaths. "Sorry, I don't know what came over me." She donned her sweater once again.

I reached out and squeezed her hand. By the Morrigan, perhaps

Ryanne, away from the fae influence, was being herself and that was tripping her up.

Or perhaps it was that imbalance.

I glanced around once more, my senses in full alert. I might be untraceable for Anord, but that didn't mean I should lower my guard. We'd kissed outside that bar, and the pooka seized that moment.

"I've always dreamed of Paris," Ryanne said in a whisper, "and look at us . . . Everywhere but there."

I squeezed her hand but kept silent, not wanting to promise something I couldn't fulfill.

"We could flee there for a day," she said, expectant.

"We could, aye, but Paris is special. I do not wish to go there with you and look over our shoulders every bloody minute."

"One day at a time, huh?"

"One day at a time."

I'd finally found someone worth being with, someone who made me feel alive. And yet, it seemed I had to keep fighting to keep her close. So be it. I'd take on the world to stay by her side. Losing her wasn't an option—not now, not ever.

We had no luggage, nothing but the clothes we had on us. I'd managed to stack a few essentials in my bradaí pocket, but it wasn't as big as Ryanne suspected.

My gold account, though, was big enough to support us several lifetimes.

Dusk was on us, a perfect time to slip away unnoticed, but most importantly, to arrive at our next destination under the cover of night.

"So Q?"

"Aye, Q."

Ryanne had come up with that absurd nickname, out of a cheesy James Bond movie, to avoid alerting anyone after the drunken incident in the Forum Romanum back when Sanders trapped us both.

"You're okay?" I asked. The weather had changed again, and it wasn't as cold as half an hour ago.

"Sure," she said absentmindedly.

I glanced around. No drunkards, no one nearby. I slid my hand and opened a portal, right next to our lodgings.

Shadows elongated around us, and my eyes searched for any odd shadow since the Umbra Gente seldom strayed far from Italy.

We waited for a loud couple to pass by before we entered the cozy villa.

Despite the fact I'd spent dozens of years in Rome, I didn't own a place there. I did, however, know where to stay without attracting attention, nothing luxurious but befitting a newlywed couple from Milan.

My Italian was fluid enough to pass as a native with an indiscernible accent. Ryanne, on the other hand, didn't speak a word. She had to exercise restraint to avoid speaking in front of the owners of the little villa-turned-hotel.

I opened the door to our room. A baroque space greeted us, with whitewashed walls and well-maintained, antique-looking chartreuse drapery adorning the windows. The bed, dressed in pristine white linen with a comforter that matched the drapes, stood at the center of the room. Soft light illuminated the space.

"Oh my gosh," she said, turning three-sixty to take it all in. "This is perfect!"

"Best of all no one will be surprised at the time spent in our room instead of enjoying Rome during the day."

She gave me a sultry smile, a newfound confidence in her movements as she sauntered toward me. The way she moved now, there was an allure that hadn't been there before.

"How about we start now?" Her hands rested on my chest, and she tilted her face up to mine, her lips slightly parted, eyes closed.

"You don't have to ask me twice," I murmured, my voice rough as I captured her mouth in a hungry kiss.

"Wait, wait," she laughed, slipping out of my embrace. "First, let's close the curtains. I don't want any peeping Toms."

As she did so, I couldn't help but take in her lithe form, her round arse accentuated by white pants. My heart thudded, a familiar rhythm every time we were together like this. She so bluntly called it sex. I pressed a hand to my chest, trying to calm the storm inside.

"Still not used to that heart, hmm?" she teased, her hips swaying as she returned to me.

I grabbed her hand, pulling her close until she was flush against me. "Don't do that unless you want things to get out of hand."

"I love when things get out of hand," she whispered, her breath warm against my ear. "But right now, I want it slow. Very slow."

"As you wish, *acushla*." My voice was barely more than a growl.

She took her time, torturing me as she peeled off my shirt, inch by agonizing inch. When it finally hit the floor, she stepped back, her hands roaming over my bare chest. Her hand stopped right where the fae had wounded me, back at Tír D'aois, on my left side just above my hip.

"Huh."

"What is it?"

"This area feels different," she mused, her touch lingering over a spot. "Energetically, I mean. Funny, I hadn't noticed before."

"Describe it."

"Thicker. Heavier. Like light doesn't reach here."

"That's *dorcha* for you," I said, my voice low and strained.

"Hmm." Her fingers continued their exploration, and a mischievous glint sparkled in her moss-green eyes. "I wonder if the rest of you feels the same."

"Go on, find out."

I stood still, every muscle tense as she undid my trousers, her touch leaving a trail of fire in its wake. When I was finally standing naked before her, I shut my eyes, trying to keep control.

"This would be even better if you were naked too," I managed to say, my breath ragged.

"Oh, I will be."

She stepped back and, with infuriating slowness, began removing her clothes.

"When did you get so good at this?" I grunted.

"You inspire me," she purred.

When the last of her clothes fell away, she shook out her hair, wild and untamed, just like her.

"You've certainly matured," I murmured, my voice thick with admiration.

"I'm *bean* now, remember?"

"You certainly are."

We reached for each other, our mouths meeting in a fierce kiss, our skin touching with no space left between us. The slow, teasing tempo dissolved, and we stumbled against the furniture, desperate for more, until, somehow, we reached the bed.

She laughed, her glorious chestnut hair splayed on the mattress.

I was in love with this woman, and nothing—no one—would ever take her from me.

We laid in bed, our legs tangled in the sheets. Ryanne pressed against me, her hand caressing my chest.

"I feel so good," she said, happily. "Balanced."

"The sea," I said. "It crashes and sweeps but there's peace within. Remember that when you feel unbalanced again."

"You've become cheesy, Titus." Her laughter was present in her touch and her movements.

"As long as you touch me like that, I'll be whatever you want."

My heart reacted at her loving smile. Inconvenient, aye, and yet I wouldn't change it for a brand-new ship.

What an odd sentiment love was, how profound and enigmatic. It was as deep as Davy Jones's locker, as tempestuous as a raging storm, as calm as my ship sailing under a bright blue sky. Like the sea, it crashed and rolled but peace lay within it.

Bradaís do not love. They hate. You should hate.

Since we left Cuidigtheach's taigh, the beast had been dogging my new heart to forget the lesson of love Ryanne had taught me. But now hate had given way to that marvelous yet bizarre love sentiment.

It was her fault. Since she gave me a heart, it wouldn't stop beating for her.

She squeezed where she found my energy denser. "You're free of that now."

"Not yet. And that's why we need to find Quintus." Much to my chagrin, I removed her hands. "Let's do Shadows."

She sighed. "I'm starting to think Q is a ghost."

"Nádhúrthas are like that. Quite difficult to find if they don't want to be. Hopefully he senses me looking for him and deigns to appear, but I'm starting to believe he doesn't want us to find him.

"All right," she said, stretching her arms above her head. "Let's find Quintus."

We were to move in a couple of days to another hotel, under a different name. Continuous movement was a must while we searched for Quintus, but we also should be able to practice working with our *préachtas*, thus facing Edward should be easier even if Quintus continued to elude us.

And practice we did for days while we roamed the streets of Rome by night. Feeling our own *préachtas* was easier and easier, especially since our bed was not only for sleeping. Making love to her increased my awareness of her fae energy.

Of my own fae energy.

The only real concern was how exhausted she seemed, which wasn't surprising given how much she tossed and turned—and even muttered nonsense—in her sleep.

One afternoon, we'd fallen asleep after spending most of the night searching for Quintus. Her restlessness woke me up. Propping myself up on one elbow, I watched her with growing concern. She was drenched in sweat, and her eyelids fluttered too fast.

"Ryanne," I called softly, careful not to startle her. "Ryanne, wake up."

She bolted upright, her eyes wide and frantic.

"What's wrong?" I asked, my worry deepening. "A nightmare?"

She stared at me for several long moments before finally speaking. "I think I've been having nightmares, but I can't remember them," she said, looking down at her trembling hands. "Just this awful, lingering feeling . . . and something about bloody hands."

"Come on," I said gently. "Let's take a bath and get something to eat."

It wasn't surprising that she had nightmares—not after facing one of her greatest fears: the Erlking. She'd been brave then, but it's always the aftermath that kills us.

After a calming bath, we dressed and went outside to eat. The sun was sinking below the horizon, casting the Eternal City in a dusky glow. Once she'd recovered, we'd continue our search.

"I miss Bricius," she said, eyes sad.

"Don't say his name," I warned. "We wouldn't want him finding us, no matter how much you miss him."

"Don't be silly, it doesn't work that way. I call his name in my head with intent, three times, and it's like I'm texting and sending him my location, but only like that."

"Ah." I clicked my tongue. "The power of three." One thing I'd learned in my trips to Tír D'aois was that names had power and saying them three times exuded power. Although it was never clear to me why.

"Yes. He could help with my changes."

"By yelling at every danger in the street? He can be a bit obnoxious and—"

"He's my friend," she snapped. "I love him, Titus. Can't you understand that?"

The Morrigan take me. Being in a relationship for the first time in more than three hundred years was making me trip like a clumsy lubber on deck. And I wanted to make things right for her. I owed her that, if only because she was in danger with me.

"I love you too," I said, the alien words ringing familiarity the more I said them. They also had power.

You do not love.

The beast had been dimmed by my constant proximity with her and our growing *préachtas*. But the beast hated anything that sang of joy, of love. It kept rearing its ugly head every time love sprung in me, which was mostly every day.

"And I you," she said, her fingertips a brief caress on my cheek, like dove feathers. "And I'm sorry. I'm so snappy. This is not me."

I pulled her to me. "You are you, and that's all right. You make me a better man, *acushla*."

She laughed, her body stuck to mine. Heaven.

The only kind I could aspire to.

"How could Bricius find us then?" I asked.

She shrugged. "It was at home. Not a difficult place to find me. But he can sense me if I'm near, so if we don't find Quintus soon, there's always a chance for the fae to find us as well."

Ryanne stopped all of a sudden and cast worrying glances around. We were outside a *trattoria* and people milled about. But I felt it too. A heat on my arms that only one type of being would produce.

A bradaí.

SEVEN

Titus

"I t's not Edward," Ryanne said, stealing around the corner in a way I'd never seen before: lithe, cautions. Like a fae gliding among trees.

"How do you know?"

"I just know." She scrunched her brow.

"After how you stabbed him, it's no wonder. Though you ought to know how to recognize a bradaí."

"I *know*," she said, annoyed. "I've spent enough time with you, and I feel it, differently from the tingling on my skin or how my chest vibrates when I see a fae, when I *feel* a fae. Here." She lifted a hand for me to stop and peeked around the corner. "He's there. But I don't know him."

She back-stepped for me to see. Tables were scattered outside a trattoria, and many diners chatted the evening away. At one of the tables sat a bradaí I hadn't seen in decades: Cedeño, the Mexican. He held hands with a woman at his table. Now that was weird.

Not that our kind didn't take lovers, but it was never romantic.

The curvy woman had a mess of frizzled red curls that reached her shoulders and wore a strapped green dress that showed her generous curves.

"It can't be another human touched by fae, can it?" I murmured.

"There's only one at a time, so no. She must be human," Ryanne said at my back. "What about him? Is he dangerous?"

"All bradaís are dangerous, even the lesser ones. Though it's odd to see one of mine with eyes filled with admiration, let alone love."

"What do you mean about lesser?"

"We're like sharks."

She gave me a leveled look.

"Not all sharks are equal. A tiger shark feeding on a dying whale would scatter when a great white comes by. Bigger sharks eat smaller sharks."

"Edward is the great white and this guy is the tiger shark?"

"Exactly."

I stepped back and extended my senses, arms slightly raised. But I couldn't feel any other bradaí. Just Cedeño.

"You think there's more than one?" Ryanne asked. "Can we hide?"

"There's only him."

And he wasn't reacting to my proximity. I pondered about that. If Anord still wanted me dead, he would have them on alert.

"I need to get close to him," I said.

"Why?"

"I need to gauge his reaction and find out about Anord's intentions with me."

"I won't stay put." She crossed her arms and gave me a defiant look.

"Wouldn't dream of it." Not to mention if this was a trap, someone might take her while I wasn't looking.

So we stepped into view, although I opted to not take Ryanne's hand in order to appear casual. The ginger lifted her gaze, and I could see her calculating human eyes considering us as I did them. Smart woman.

Cedeño quickly stood, his fierce expression turning into one of apparent joy.

"Doyle! My man!"

Cedeño approached us with the same stealthy cadence and fluid slink I remembered. "Hombre, you look different." He pulled me into a tight embrace before I could blink.

I pushed away from his embrace and instinctively patted my torso. Along with his stealth, he was notorious for his skill as a pickpocket.

He chuckled and returned my watch and cellphone. "You ought to be more careful, my man."

I extended my hand, and he gave an exaggerated sigh as he returned my wallet.

"Fancy seeing you here of all places," I said as I kept my senses alert and gazed around. The woman was still assessing us, but she kept eating her pasta and showing no fear.

Whether she didn't know who I really was or if she was something other than what she seemed was still up for debate.

"My woman loves pasta, and I'd never say no to her." Cedeño glanced past me at Ryanne. "You got someone too! I'm glad. No longer solitary Doyle, my man. Care to introduce us?"

I crumpled his pristine, expensive Italian shirt with my first. Cedeño might have been a lesser bradaí, with not enough power to mess around with me and not one to dare cross my path, still, I couldn't take any chances.

But there was no crazed look in his eyes. No call from Anord demanding my head. Had Anord forfeited the hunt? Was I a free man at last?

No. I would never be free while Edward roamed the Earth.

"Why are you following me?" I deliberately avoided using "us" but at this point everyone knew a human with a touch of fae was by my side. "Who paid you? Edward?"

Cedeño snorted. "I'm having a nice evening with my woman." He jutted his chin toward Ryanne. "Just like you are. Release me, I mean no harm."

I did. "Who's she?" I glanced at the ginger. If my bravado had impressed her, it didn't show. She kept eating her pasta.

"No one you'll care about. My business. Look, man"—he tucked his shirt into his designer pants—"I'm trying to get off Anord's radar, just like you. Follow my own path."

He tried to thump a hand on my shoulder, but I stepped away, my hand already on my dagger's hilt.

"And Edward?" I asked.

"I don't follow Edward. He hasn't been able to snatch me in decades." He tapped his forehead. "I'm clever. So whatever your business is here, it's all right, man. I'll just keep dining with my lovely woman."

I glanced past him. The ginger leaned in her chair, sipping wine and not looking our way.

"You look cozy with her," I said, gesturing to Ryanne it was time to leave. "You say nothing. I won't say a thing either."

"Sounds good to me, man." He gave me a dazzling smile then turned his back on me as if he were dismissing us.

No one gave a bradaí their back. The ginger still hadn't looked our way, but something was definitively off.

I patted my pocket and glared at his back.

He laughed and threw my wallet at me, which I promptly caught.

Not wanting to stay to find what was off, I took Ryanne into the first store we saw, where I opened a portal the moment the clerk was distracted.

It was time to leave Rome.

We toured some of the oldest cities in Italy where Quintus might dwell —Matera, San Gimignano, Siena, Perugia, Civita di Bagnoregio. Ryanne couldn't get enough of these cities and wanted to see more. Her wish to tour Europe had been partially fulfilled, and she acted like a little girl, excited by the sights of the beautiful medieval towns. The weather was capricious and drastically changed even on the same day.

We talked about Cedeño and the mysterious woman. It turned out Ryanne had been trying to feel her but couldn't. It was easy to pin her as human, but something about that encounter didn't feel right. What else could she be? I'd tried to rack my brain about what I remembered about Cedeño, but he'd been like a shadow in the past, always stepping off the bradaís' path.

There was an unspoken bradaí classification, besides the Alpha.

Shen and Cedeño were the second and third created, and seniority fell on their shoulders, though the Mexican had forgone that seniority long ago and seldom did he appear. Somehow I felt he'd always had an agenda of his own.

Those bradaís created after Cedeño and before Kara were called lesser by us. They didn't have as much power, as though Anord couldn't come up with enough black magic to create them. Or so everyone thought back in the day until I recently found, thanks to the Eadroms, that Anord had borrowed—or stolen as Tuiren said—power from other dark beings of Tír Na Vraoichta.

Luckily, there was no other sightings of my kin. We stuck to shadows and nighttime to avoid being detected and made sure to avoid popular places. We chose every off-the-beaten path trattoria to eat at and places to roam about.

Food also kept Ryanne happy: pastas, pizzas, and gelatos were the order of the day. Thankfully we burned enough calories with the constant walking and lovemaking. Albeit if we continued like this, I might end up as some of my kin, with a rounded stomach.

"The sea crashes and sweeps, but there is peace within," I said every morning to Ryanne.

"You miss it, don't you?"

"You have no idea."

Homkar must have anchored her in one of our safe places, but I itched to be aboard her and feel the force of a gale around me, with Ryanne at my side. But the sea was out of our reach. Too dangerous at the moment. Too dangerous until we were free of Edward.

One evening in our room in Bologna, we were practicing with our *préachtas* as we'd been doing every day—hands pressed over the other's chest, eyes closed, and feeling them move between our bodies.

"This is absurd," she suddenly said, rising to her feet in an agitated manner. "We're not getting anywhere, Titus."

"We're practicing."

"And?" she snapped. "It's all the same, every day. Our powers move like eels, but there's nothing more to it. And Quintus is a ghost!" She sat again, hands on her face. "Sorry. My temper is too short nowadays."

I couldn't blame her; we'd been moving around too much and constantly looking over our shoulders.

"Ant's bollock on a beach," I said.

She smiled, faintly. "I'm guessing that's something hard to find."

"Aye. We might have reached the bitter end regarding Quintus, albeit tonight could be the night."

She rose to her feet again, a brightness lurking behind those moss-green eyes. "We need to do something different. Follow me," she said. Her moves were slow and fluid, her lean body wrapped in fashion sweatpants and a white top.

"T'ai chi ch'uan," I said, mimicking her movements.

Her eyes were closed, her face reflecting a peace I was far from feeling. "Yes," she said, a whisper of a voice where the owner was focused on an internal voyage. "Peter practices like this, and it helps. Let it flow."

Her hands gracefully moved, her body an extension of her energy. I felt it stronger in her, mine still dumbed by my own hatred of anything fae.

I started to let go, her own peacefulness proving contagious. Sharing time with her wasn't just numbing the beast, it was making me feel better about myself.

I could be my own man for the first time, even if we were hiding. But best of all, we were together.

"You know," she said, "my birthday is in a few days."

"We must celebrate it, then."

She gave me a tired smile, and I knew where.

"Paris. We can go one night. Only one."

Her face lit up. "Yes! When is yours?"

I shrugged. "I don't even remember which month I came into existence, only the year, 1705."

"We'll set a day for your birthday then."

I pondered about this. "The cave. I came out as a new man."

"That was October, wasn't it?"

"No idea. We were busy running away from my kin and the fae."

"October it is now. And I like number five, so that's your birthday from now on. Let's go out," she said, her body tense with unspent energy. "I need to move."

"And practice the Shadow."

Ryanne and I had been doing that every night in each of the cities we'd been. So far, she'd been a terrible Shadow student, asking questions and commenting on everything instead of being quiet as the Shadow required.

Shadow-walking was an art she'd never master, though our actions might attract Quintus's attention.

As part of the Umbra Gente, Quintus had access to information not even us bradaís knew. He'd been my master and taught me the art of walking in shadows and thus undetected. It was a dangerous thing since if you remained too much in the shadow realm, you could end up as a shadow forever.

We played the part of recent newlyweds while we exited the quaint hotel.

"*Mettiti il maglione, fa freddo,*" the old woman at the reception desk shouted behind us.

"Cold?" Ryanne said once I translated. "The weather's perfect!"

"For them, it is. It's unusual for mid-January."

"Where?" she asked, eyeing the shadowed street, eager to start.

"Wait until shadows cover us completely."

"Yes but—"

"You've asked enough questions to make even the most talkative guy shut up."

"Are you saying I talk too much?" she spat.

"Easy, *acushla*. I was jesting. I didn't say I minded."

"Well don't do that." Her eyes fired up, glowing emerald-green so briefly I would have missed it if I weren't looking directly at her. That was what had lurked before. Fae energy. But then, a fae wouldn't spat.

"Are you feeling hot again?" I asked, concerned.

Her mouth opened, her features disfigured in an angry scowl. Then, her eyes widened and she wriggled her hands. "Yes," she whispered. "My head throbs sometimes. Especially when I have a nightmare."

"Your imbalance." I wondered what should we do to fix that without returning to Tír D'aois or her family. I glanced around. Despite the fact dusk was on us and shadows emerged from the cracks and corners, I felt at ease. Shadows I could count on.

"No, ah, I mean, this feels different. I feel hot all of a sudden, then my hormones fire up, and I want to snap at you. It's like . . ." She rubbed the center of her forehead.

"Your forehead." I placed a hand on her shoulder. "Do you feel the heat coming from there?"

"Now that you mention it, yes."

"Ah. That's not good news. The Erlking touched you there."

"The Erlking!" Her moss-green eyes took on that fluorescent green.

"Aye. I should have seen that coming. He's the master of trickery."

"But what did he do? Mark me like you?" She rubbed her forehead again with her thumb.

"You heard his voice before he touched you, aye?"

"Yes."

"Then no. Besides creatures from Tír D'aois don't do that, only us. I have no idea what he did, but it's not good news, *acushla*." Her eyes were again her own. "Your eyes are changing to bright green, not a human shade but fae like."

"My *préachta* feels icy now. Glacial, even. It's the fae power claiming me." She cursed loudly. "I need to root myself and this damn Erlking comes and messes me up?" She patted her chest as though trying to find something she'd lost. "Damn that pooka too. I need that locket back."

I reached out for her hand and squeezed it. She liked that. "I'll help you. We'll bite this bullet together."

Bloody Quintus. I wondered, not for the first time, if he was avoiding us on purpose. Now we were stuck, since we had no idea where Quintus could be.

Stuck, aye, not only because we couldn't find him, but we were going nowhere with our powers and how to kill Edward. Or even find his Name.

She reached for her sweater, thrown carelessly over her shoulders. Dizziness took her and she stumbled.

"Something's off with you." I looked at her, worried. "Perhaps the Lady was right, and you need to anchor your power to Tír D'aois. We should go there and look for Homkar near the Valley of Dragons, since his kind sometimes dwell there, if we don't find anything related to Q's whereabouts tonight."

Her eyes lighted with power, as though it'd grown too much and was trying to escape her. Aye, grounding her in the fae lands could make that imbalance vanish.

She rubbed her forehead. "I need this *thing* gone."

I pressed a hand over her forehead and felt it, a dark pulsating energy but faint. "Perhaps we could remove it with our energies."

"Yes. Let's try it."

She blinked and her eyes took on her moss-green human tone. Then her mouth made an *O*. "My skin's tingling," she whispered.

That was when I felt it too, and I whipped my head around. The Morrigan take me.

Bloody Pretty Boy stepped out from behind a tree, too close for us to run, the pixie hovering above him.

And my senses hadn't warned me.

EIGHT
Ryanne

Ryanne," Peter said in his marked Oxford accent, "it's nice to see you again."

My fae mentor looked like a normal human, with human clothes. He might be using glamour to hide his true self, yet his reddish-brown hair had its usual length, curving slightly at the base of his neck. Although he was almost as tall as Titus, his physique was leaner.

Bricius hovered behind him, and he gave me a bright smile, obviously not upset that I'd ran away from him. I returned his smile, relieved. Shadows already pooled around us, but a lamppost illuminated the charming old buildings in the quaint, narrow street we stood.

I stepped between Titus and Peter. "I'm not leaving Titus."

"That's right, Pretty Boy," Titus said behind me, "you can go back to that smelly pit you came from and tell Tuiren to look for another sucker."

Peter gave an exasperated sigh. "Neither my ladies Tuiren nor Cuidigtheach sent me this time, pirate. And, Ryanne, while I must express my strong disapproval of your involvement with him, I have not come here with the intention of separating you two."

Fae wouldn't lie. At least not directly and not even when they wore pleated trousers and a cardigan. But this could also mean he planned to put us behind the taigh's walls.

"Bricius can explain this better," he said. "Or so he proclaimed."

My pixie guardian flew to me. "Hi, Ryanne," he said, smiling in such a way that his big orange eyes became small.

"Hey, Bug." That warmth I'd been craving covered me again.

He lifted his little chin to Titus. "Pirate, glad to see you again, yes, yes, yes."

"What in Anord's hell are you wearing?" Titus exclaimed, though at least he didn't sound too upset. Could there be a hint of warmth in this tone?

Bricius looked down at his clothes—which matched Peter's to a T— the gossamer wings beating like a hummingbird. "They're great, yes, yes, yes. Fé Erie sent us to take care of you," he said.

"Then you really didn't come to try to separate us?" I asked.

Titus narrowed his eyes at Peter, his previous warmth dissipating.

Bricius shook her head. "My Lady accepted your decision. She wants us to take you back to Tír D'aois to keep you safe and formulate a plan."

Titus sidestepped me. "Plan? The only plan here is that Ryanne and I are going to be together."

"And how do you plan to do that, pirate?" Peter said, eyes boring into Titus. "By consistently being on the run? Relocating from one town to another ad nauseam?"

"If necessary, yes."

"No, no, no, that's not enough," Bricius said, stroking his chin. "Pirate and fae must work together to eliminate the Alpha, yes, yes, yes."

"Not happening," Titus said, chin high.

Peter took a step forward, and they stood face to face. "You are cognizant of his pursuit of your power. You understand that inevitability. Do you wish to risk her when it occurs?"

"Okay, hang on—" I started.

"You cannot stay here in Tír na Donna," Peter said. "We must go back to Tír D'aois, where we'll formulate a plan. In my taigh. There you shall be safe."

"Wait," I said, frowning. "You want us behind taigh's walls to keep *me* safe? As a prisoner? Answer truthfully, Peter."

"I want you safe, yes, but not captive." His expression suddenly looked haggard. "The situation is escalating beyond control. We are finding fae killed by your kin, more than ever. Fear has seized my own kin, and no one is keen to leave the taighs. But we are not meant to be prisoners. We are meant to roam free, and that is our ruin."

"It is not good, not good at all," Bricius said, his wings downward.

My heart wrenched. More fae killed?

"So what, you two are going to be with us all the time?" Titus all but snapped. "Morrigan's crow. I don't know what fae are into, but this is definitely between only her and me."

I would have chuckled, but the images of those murdered fae still haunted my mind. "Can we have a minute?" I asked Peter and Bricius.

"No," my fae mentor said, his eyes not leaving Titus. "The moment we do, you'll both escape. Again."

"Truce, Peter. Just a minute, okay?" *Préachta* agreed with my statement, and Peter's emerald eyes shone briefly, as if sensing my truthfulness.

Peter retreated to a nearby tree, Bricius zooming after him.

"Great thinking, *acushla*," Titus whispered. "I'm going to open my portal, and we'll leave before they know it." He lifted his hand, and I could feel his energy ready to open one.

I lowered his hand. "No. What Peter says makes sense." Not to mention I must honor my promise. Cold covered me and agreed as before. "We should go to his taigh and review the plan. We must be hidden to avoid any bradaí finding us, or any chance encounter like with Cedeño. I'm tired of changing places every day and looking over our shoulders. Quintus is nowhere to be found, and we could practice in Peter's taigh."

"Do you think that's a good idea?" He cupped my cheek lovingly.

"We need to come up with a better plan, love. What we're doing now isn't working."

His eyes shone as they'd been doing since he'd acquired his heart. He felt love, and giddiness took me over. A bradaí feeling love was unheard of.

It proved anything was possible.

He gave me a soft kiss. "Very well, we'll go with them just because you ask me. But as soon as we can, we're off."

I turned to Peter. "Okay. We'll go with you."

Bricius landed on my shoulder, and I relaxed. His proximity felt as cozy as that coveted human feeling.

Yeah, everything was possible, and maybe it wasn't such a bad idea to balance myself in Tír D'aois.

Préachta swirled and purred.

"I love you, Bug," I whispered out of the corner of my mouth. I felt his *préachta* swirl in happiness. "You have no idea how much I missed you."

"I missed you, too, Ryanne."

"There's a good spot some blocks away," Peter said, pointing ahead. "We'll cross to Tír D'aois there."

Titus grumbled but carried on, Bricius flying to my head and taking two strands as his "reins."

"It's short now," he whined.

"A silly way to avoid being recognized."

"I can recognize you anywhere."

"Sorry I ran away when I was with my family. It was because of Peter."

"I know, yes, yes, yes. I miss your family too."

Sadly they couldn't say the same, since they had never been able to see Bricius.

"They disliked Titus."

"They don't know him, no, no, no."

"Titus can be charming when he wants."

Bricius scoffed.

His "charm" usually hid danger pulsating behind it. But that didn't matter. What troubled me was not being able to find Quintus. During our two-month stay in Italy, Titus had told me more about that time with the Umbra Gente, when he acquired his name back in one-thou-sand-whatever. I would have loved to see more of Italy—or at least been able to enjoy all those wonderful medieval cities and the different flavors of gelato while walking hand in hand with Titus without the rush.

Going to Peter's taigh would be a dream. Getting to know a new taigh? A new Hawthorn? How cool was that? Was his place different? Would I feel it differently?

But it felt like returning to another prison. Peter might not be able to lie but that didn't mean he wasn't withholding the truth. He had been pretty adamant about keeping me "safe" back at Cuidi's taigh while he and Titus hunted Edward.

Edward's black eyes like pits from hell drew me in and made me shudder. We'd been lucky, Titus and I, to have escaped. It seemed we were always running, from Edward, from the fae, from the terrifying and enigmatic Erlking.

My forehead throbbed as it'd been doing, and I stopped near a closed trattoria.

"Peter, can you touch my forehead? The Erlking infused some energy and—"

I hadn't finished talking when Peter slapped his palm to my forehead, the heel right where the throbbing usually was worse. Cold fae power infused in me, not like when he gave me a gift but rather searching, probing.

He removed his hand and took a step back. "When did that occur?"

"Can we tell that story later?" Titus asked, body rigid and scanning his surroundings as he constantly did. A couple walked down the street and grinned at us.

"*Buona notte*," they joyfully said.

Titus gave his customary curt nod while Peter didn't bother to glance at them.

"Ah, *buona notte*," I said back with a terrible accent. I waited until they vanished around the next corner and turned to Peter. "Is it bad? His energy is strong, but he only infused a bit."

"Let's move," Titus said, and we all started walking again.

"Can you remove it?" I rubbed that point with my thumb.

"No. It is bound to its host. However, I believe you can if you concentrate on it."

This must be the same as when Titus marked me and I was able to remove it because it was only a smudge of darkness.

Dark energies might behave the same. Was the Erlking's the same as the bradaís? How different could they be?

Peter stopped and looked confused.

"Are you lost, fae?" Titus smirked.

"Where *is* that park?" Bricius mumbled.

"So many buildings and human energy clog my senses. Allow me a moment." Peter closed his eyes, his arms extended as if to sense energies. He gave a curt nod and, eyes still closed, pointed right. "Not far. We need a good spot to reach near home."

One thing I learned was that it was important to open portals in certain places. A park like the one we were heading to would lead us anywhere safe in Tír D'aois. Understanding your exact landing location within that territory was crucial to steer clear of any significant hazards.

Hazards, like stumbling upon the Erlking. Or Edward.

Having to focus on nullifying Edward was a shame since just before Edward barged into Titus's apartment in West Seattle, Titus, Kara, and Sergei had finally reunited and cleared centuries old misunderstandings. Titus had finally found his family.

Hmm.

"You know?" I said. "We should make one stop before going to your taigh, Peter."

He arched his reddish-brown eyebrows. "Pray tell where."

"Kara." I looked at Titus. "She wants nothing more than to stop Edward, doesn't she?"

"She does." Titus stroked his still shaved chin.

"Who is this woman?" Peter asked. He stopped near a copse in front of a park. We'd arrived at his selected spot.

"Remember when those humans captured me and Titus back in Rome?" I asked. Sanders's mistreatment of me and Titus came to mind, and rage came over me. That bastard! Bricius landed on my shoulder, and his weight calmed me. "The bradaí who rescued us?"

"*That* woman? By the Hawthorn! No." Peter scowled.

"What happened exactly?" Titus asked.

Ah, yes, Titus couldn't remember since he'd been hardly conscious at the time. We'd somehow never had time to talk about it with so much happening. "You know how Sanders had me in that dingy room and was so nasty? Kara came and killed all the guards, but the bastard ran away. She and Homkar, after releasing me from my shackles, helped get you out of there. Then Peter arrived. Then she had a go for Peter."

Titus guffawed.

Peter looked shocked. "She's a pirate. I'd burn my guts before touching one of yours."

"Oh, loosen up, Peter," I said. "She has the same goal as you. She can help."

"Good idea, *acushla*. Maybe we could persuade her to give up her coin. She wants to be freed, after all."

I smiled warmly at Titus. He could say whatever he wanted, but he cared for the bradaí who had raised him. His older sister or so he called her.

"That's not an option," Peter said, not giving space to argue. He lifted his hand to open his portal as I'd seen him do many times.

But not today.

"I thought you said Fé Erie supported us and sent you to *help* us," I said sweetly.

Titus held back a chuckle, and I winked at him, proud that he didn't prod Peter.

"She's a bradaí, and I cannot trust her." Peter clasped his hands behind his back.

"You keep sounding like a broken record, Pretty Boy."

"I don't understand you, pirate *brocach*."

"All right, hold on." I placed myself between them, something that was becoming familiar. "If we're going to do this, then you both say each other's proper names. Titus, this is Peter, not Pretty Boy."

"I'm not calling him by that stupid name." Titus scowled and folded his arms across his chest.

"Gallchobhair is my name, pirate."

"Gally it is," Titus said, showing his teeth in a smile.

I sighed. "And, Peter, this is Titus."

"So I use his first name and he gets to give me a ridiculous nickname?"

Gods, these two were hopeless.

"Call me Doyle then, Gally."

Peter tightened his lips. "I'd rather call you Aodhán. That is your name, is it not?"

"Not a name you should be saying out loud." Titus stepped toward Peter with me in between them like the lettuce of a testosterone filled sandwich. Oh, goody.

"Its purpose is gone, Aodhán. It has no power anymore."

Préachta swirled in me, angry as an ogre, and I pushed them both aside, a task I wouldn't have been able to do before, but both stepped back. "Knock. It. Off," I snarled.

Titus furrowed his brow. "Call me Doyle or the deal's off."

"By the Hawthorn." Peter sighed. "Very well, Doyle *brocach*."

Well that was a start, wasn't it?

"Nonetheless, we are not pursuing that pirate."

Titus opened his mouth, but I beat him to it. "Peter." *You hard-headed fae.* "Think about it. For Fé Erie, the coins are important, right?"

He widened his bright emerald eyes, a shade Titus said I was starting to have. I did the press-imaginary-locket thing.

"Imagine her joy to obtain a second one."

Titus brooded, but Peter nodded. Very reluctantly, but there it was.

"Awesome," I said, clapping my hands. "Now, let's find Kara, shall we?"

NINE

Titus

Kara had been near Oslo when I'd called her, so she took a train, disguised as a tourist, to meet us here. She had arrived at the pub with her usual swagger, and as far as any random observer was concerned, we were three friends hanging out in this noisy local bar. As for Gally, he was in hiding until I deemed it safe. The pixie was our powder monkey and would sit on Ryanne's shoulder or zoom outside to bring tidings to the fae.

The pub felt cozy, with wooden tables and antique-looking wood chairs to match. The lighting was soft, and the music was great, not to mention the drinks: a blood orange gin for Ryanne and whiskey for me.

Still, I glanced around, my senses in full alert. I might be untraceable for Anord, but Kara wasn't.

"Homkar is in Tír D'aois. Are you quite certain?" I asked Kara, fists clenched.

"As sure as Odin is handsome and has one eye," Kara quipped, looking at ease, yet her body was tense, alert. No one but another bradaí would notice that incongruence.

Ryanne leaned toward me. "That's why he didn't answer your calls, or been in any of your safe spots if he's there with his family."

She had a point. Homkar wasn't always with me. It'd been recently when I found out he had a family of his own besides his numerous siblings and spent months in Tír D'aois when I needed my space.

But I'd never been hunted like bloody Moby Dick. Inconvenient to have my reliable first mate away, aye, although it was to be expected. No one found a dannan-dhubb if they didn't want to be found, not in Tír D'aois, though I'd expected him to wait for me in any of our safe spots.

Trouble. He wouldn't have gone in hiding without attempting to contact me otherwise. It wouldn't surprise me if Edward made him run away.

"Why worry about your resourceful first mate?" Kara said, her eyes roaming about the pub, the lines of her mouth hard.

"Isn't it a bit hot here?" Ryanne asked, removing her cashmere sweater.

"It's not," Kara and I said in unison.

"Well I feel hot," she said, annoyance liaising in her voice, while she fanned herself with her hands.

"I only want to make certain he's safe," I said to Kara. "As I'm doing with you."

"By Odin, aren't you sweet, little brother." She winked, an expression out of habit since her eyes lacked her usual luster.

"He doesn't like to be called little brother," Ryanne spat, her face red like that of a hanged man. "Why can't you stop!"

"*Acushla*, are you feeling fine?" Worried, I placed my hand over her forehead but she swat it before I could feel it.

"It's your influence," Kara said with a blithe demeanor.

"No, I'm not . . ." Ryanne closed her eyes, taking deep breaths. "Sorry."

I reached out and squeezed her hand. By the Morrigan, the Erlking's touch hadn't been as easy to remove as the fae had said. Although it wasn't only Ryanne who looked out of sorts, Kara wasn't her old self either.

"I thought you wouldn't be here in Oslo," Ryanne said to Kara, "because this would be the most obvious place to find you."

"Oh love," Kara said, smiling condescendingly, "of course Edward has tried to track me down here before, but I've set up so many traps and security measures that not even the combined efforts of the CIA,

Interpol, or any elite agency could touch me. Besides, I was in Stadt-landet when Doyle called." At Ryanne's look of confusing, Kara added, "Where I was created. Near the sea. Anord always create us near a body of water." She leaned back and gazed around.

"What's wrong?" I asked.

"Nothing." She took another swig, albeit it seemed a movement to avoid my eye.

"Didn't you want us to be like we were before?" I arched an eyebrow. "Talk."

She sighed, the glass in her hand a distraction. "Force of habit, little brother. Edward is what's wrong."

Of course.

"You were right." She shrugged. "He can't be defeated. My own *dorcha* betrayed me, and you barely annoyed him."

"How did you get away?" Ryanne asked.

Kara shrugged again, a movement to hide her disappointment. Her innate frustration. No wonder. She'd been adamant about killing Edward and like she said, we'd only annoyed him.

We were far from annihilating him. Ryanne and I were becalmed.

"Once you were gone," Kara said, "the rest of the bradaís left. Sergei and I followed on their heels after we noticed Edward staggering inside. Vulnerable as he seemed though it didn't last long." She eyed me. "How did you managed to disable him?"

"Without the coin, I was able to pour more *dorcha* into him," I lied.

"Did you?" Kara asked in the same tone I used. She wasn't fooled.

"Enough for Ryanne and I to get away."

Not a complete lie, though. My *dorcha* was more powerful than hers, most likely due to the fact that Anord created me in the same way as Edward: with pure black magic. For the rest of the bradaís, my creator had borrowed power from dark beings from Tír na Vraoichta, thus Kara had some of Odin's energy in her. I'd been saved from being mindlessly evil like Edward thanks to my touch of fae.

What a gobshite thing to have, and yet, it'd saved my life.

It let me feel. I reached out and squeezed Ryanne's hand.

"Now about Sergei," I said, leaning back on the bench and casually glancing around. "Are you certain he didn't lead Edward to my place?"

"Sergei used a PI. From what he told me after the altercation, he believes Edward knew about his movements, so he already knew about your places."

Ryanne interrupted. "Edward can only find you guys at sea, right?"

Kara gave a slow, thoughtful nod. "Yes and no. He can find us presto"—she snapped her fingers—"at sea, right. He can also pinpoint us on land but it's harder for him. Think of a crocodile."

"And you both were there," Ryanne said, pensive. "Two bradaís are easier to pinpoint than one."

"She's a keeper, this one." Kara winked.

A keeper, aye, if only we could manage to kill Edward.

Something as easy to do as daring a tsunami with a skiff. Thwart him, aye. Kill him? I met Ryanne's eye, who was certainly thinking the same.

Could our combined *préachtas* do more than nullify him?

More importantly, could Ryanne deliver a killing blow if required? Her gentle nature cringed at blood and killing.

It should be up to me.

"Time to split," Kara said, rising to her feet. "I utterly despise acting like a sitting duck."

"Wait. What are your plans?" I asked, my hand lifted.

She sat again and seized the empty tumbler. "I'm squiffy already and plan to be three sheets to the wind."

"Squiffy?" Ryanne asked, confused.

"Slightly drunk," I explained without taking my eyes off my sister.

Kara nodded. "Edward wants to tear me apart limb by limb and send me to Davy Jones's locker with stones tied to my feet. So I'll spare him the trouble and vanish from his sight. For good."

"How would you feel if you could be out of his radar?" I asked nonchalantly as though I was proposing a raid.

She leaned toward me, with that fire in her eyes I'd missed so much. "To whom should I sell my soul to?"

"You don't have one," Ryanne said with the same coldness as the fae, something she kept doing lately.

Kara signaled a waiter and requested, nay, demanded, more tequila shots. "That doesn't matter, love. Now, little brother, you have my full attention."

I smirked and signaled the pixie, who zoomed outside to call Gally. "We have a proposal."

"Say what again?" Kara glowered at me and then at the fae, who sat beside Ryanne.

"It's simple, pirate," Gally said, elbows placed on the table.

Kara rolled her eyes at the pirate moniker, an odd reaction from her. She would usually stab and laugh.

Gally continued, unabashed by her reaction. "I wound you until you cross the threshold of the living although not entirely dead, and you are free. What is it you don't understand?"

"Of course, sweetie." She bared her teeth, and her old self peeked out for a brief moment. "Now that you phrased it *exactly as you did a minute ago*, it makes so much more sense now." She snorted and eyed me. "Can you believe this bozo?" Not waiting for an answer, she emptied her tequila shot and slammed the glass on the table. Three more shots awaited her.

The pixie flew to where the booze was and sniffed it. Beside it, platters of Norwegian fare cluttered the table. Ryanne snatched a piece of pork knuckle and mumbled something about the wonderful mustard sauce. Bricius tried some and made a face.

"You don't seem to understand the implications, pirate."

"Look, Pretty Boy—" Kara started.

"Not another," Gally snarled.

"That's my line," I said, amused. "To everyone else, he's Gally."

"Gally. Whatever." Kara waved a hand in the air. "I'm not going to let this fae touch me"—she leaned forward and lowered her voice in a husky tone—"unless you're willing to share my bed tonight. What say you, pretty fae?"

"I give up." Gally slammed a hand on the table and stood up. "I need some fresh air. Tell this pirate what you want to tell her so we can leave." He gave the bar's customers a contemptuous look then left.

Ryanne waved at Bricius and jerked her head toward the stubborn fae. After giving her a worried look, Bricius zoomed after him. She then gulped the gin I ordered for her and sighed in delight. I made a mental note to order gin when possible.

"I know you told us this," Kara said and took a swig of her tequila, "but I can't wrap my head around it. Did he really kill you?"

I emptied my whiskey, and slammed the tumbler on the table in a similar fashion as Kara.

"Is that a bradaí thing?" Ryanne mumbled in annoyance. "Slamming things?"

Kara and I dismissed her.

"Hurt like hell. But here I am"—I spread my hands—"feeling better than before."

"And she helped, huh?" She glanced at Ryanne.

"All the way," I answered proudly.

"What about the coin?"

"Fé Erie has it," Ryanne said.

"Who?"

"She's the spirit of Tír D'aois," I said.

"Ah. Like the nádhúrthas."

"Not exactly," Ryanne said. "Nádhúrthas have several levels, from dark to light, while fae only have two settings: normal and Eadroms, and there is no darkness in fae."

"But there is a top level with nádhúrthas," Kara said.

"Well yeah," Ryanne answered. But she's at the top of all of them. Way top."

"You seem to know an awful lot about the nádhúrthas. And here I thought humans were completely oblivious." Kara winked to take the bite off.

Ryanne was forgetting about the Guardian, the equivalent of Fé Erie in the human realm. Not to mention Fé Erie also reigned over Tír D'aois' darker side. But it was not the time to start a nádhúrtha-fae discussion.

"Well, I haven't seen any nádhúrthas here," Ryanne said.

Except for Amriel. I craned my neck around the noisy bar, almost expecting to see the dark-skinned nádhúrtha at one of the bar stools drinking an espresso shake. He loved coffee, if my memory served.

"Of course not." Kara shrugged. "You humans have devastated this dimension like the virus you are and have stripped the nádhúrtha of their presence. I wouldn't be surprised if they fled to another dimension and left you guys on your own." She glanced at the darkened window.

Sullen eyes, drinking to oblivion, aye, she was depressed. An immortal robbed of her purpose.

"So," I prodded, "are you in? This will get you off Anord's radar."

She leaned back and drummed her fingers on the table. "Anord can't track you now. You sure?"

"Aye."

"Well, I'm sick of Edward knowing where I am all the time. By Odin's balls, let's do it."

"I thought we were going to have to buy another round of tequila," I said.

"That you will, love." She downed the rest of the tequila. "Once that fae skewers me. Whichever way he prefers." She winked in a mischievous way then shouted at the waiter for more drinks.

"I'm going out with Peter," Ryanne said, standing. "I need some fresh air while you two catch up."

Without waiting an answer, she headed to the exit, both Kara and I appreciating the way she swayed her hips.

"She *is* a keeper." Kara whistled with admiration. "Don't lose her, little brother."

"I don't plan to." Not ever. "Now, where are those drinks?"

TEN

Ryanne

I went outside to find Peter strolling on the nearby path. January in Oslo should have made me freeze, even with the full moon offering its glowing approval. Yet, I only wore a cardigan and was completely comfortable. Peter certainly didn't seem affected by the low temperature.

We were at a quiet intersection of streets; Kara had chosen a pub off the beaten path, one that catered more to locals than to tourists. Nearby, a cluster of trees stood as a quick gateway to Tír D'aois.

Bricius zoomed back to me and sat on my head, his favorite place. I glanced back at the noisy bar. Something bothered me, something about Titus lying to Kara. I frowned. Why had Titus lied to her? Why did bradaís lie? Didn't they know the truth was more powerful? *Préachta* swirled in me and agreed.

Snow fell in a white dance while the nearby trees boasted their winter ochre clothing. Peter and I remained still as silent statues. Normally I would talk, wanting anxiously to fill the silence, but I didn't feel it necessary now. It felt good.

Part of me yearned to be inside a taigh, by myself, but that was the icy fae part. Humans had helped me to root. Would going to Tír D'aois root that fae power and balance me, or make me more fae?

Even if it made me colder and more detached, there was no other choice. I padded my chest; if only that pooka wouldn't have stolen my locket, it would have helped me as an anchor.

I itched to go sightseeing around Oslo, but this was a business trip, which was a shame. The good news was that I wasn't feeling dizzy or snapping at Titus every time something didn't sit with me—mostly. Bricius's proximity had helped. I only hoped it would stay like this, though I still felt shaky at random times.

"It is time for you to tell me about the Erlking. It puzzles me," Peter said as if we had been chatting a moment ago. It didn't bother me. Each thing had its time and place.

Kara and Titus came out of the pub, both still in conversation. I narrated about how the pooka took us to the Erlking, and the conversation we held with him until Titus and I dashed out of the main cave.

"Have you met Pan, Peter?"

"That little self-anointed king of nothing?" Peter glowered. "I found out recently that, alas, he escaped from the Erlking's clutches. It was quite surprising and unnerving." He cocked his head in thought. "How did you know Pan was there?"

"He is a spoiled, horrible, horrible creature!" Bricius exclaimed.

"Well"—I lifted my chin–"actually, I released him."

"You did what?" Bricius exclaimed, terrified.

"How, pray?" Peter asked, his eyes widening slightly in surprise—the kind of expression fae wore that I used to not understand but was now getting pretty good at picking up on.

By then, Kara and Titus had joined us. She retrieved a cellphone and stepped away while she checked whatever she needed to check.

"Are we good?" I asked Titus, scanning the surrounding. Two bradaís and one Eadrom were more than enough to discourage anyone, but no one wanted to engage in a fight.

"Aye. Kara is precisely reviewing security, though all looks well."

"You're just in time," I said. "Peter wants to know how I released Pan."

Without waiting for his answer, I told Peter all about the escape.

"By the stardust, that settles it," Peter said, deepening his tone.

"Bound to his promise, the Erlking could not do it himself. He tricked you into releasing Pan."

"He must be something for the Erlking to capture him," I said, thoughtful. "The Erlking wanted us to release Pan. The old nádhúrtha, Amriel, told me to trust my heart, which I did by following the pooka to get my locket back."

"A locket." Peter cocked his head once again. It seemed he was assessing me under a different light.

"My grandmother's gift to me."

"Oh was that the one we used to play with?" Bricius asked in his shrill voice. "I loved that locket, yes, yes, yes. *Mo thiarna*, it has the power of family and memories. Very powerful. I'm sorry, Ryanne, that the pooka kept it."

"Stole it," I said, annoyed at the recollection.

"It was wise of your mother to return it to you," Peter said, thoughtful. "Such items often possess their own unique power. Do you think it is possible to acquire another?"

"I'm afraid not. It was a gift from my grandmother when I was a child." I sighed.

"Where does Pan come from?" Titus asked.

"You don't know?" I asked.

"*Acushla*, you'd be surprised, but there are many things I don't know." Unlike Peter, Titus was alert, scanning the surroundings.

"He's a nádhúrtha," Peter explained.

"That little brat?" I exclaimed. "He must be at the bottom of nádhúrtha hierarchy."

"Not quite. Nádhúrthas rule the human land the way fae do in our land, yet they have all but vanished in the past couple of centuries."

"Not all of them," Titus interjected, clearly upset that Peter had the lead.

Like Quintus. Maybe he'd vanished too, and we had been chasing ghosts. "Why would the Erlking want Pan free?" I asked.

"I do not know." Peter stressed the words.

"You don't?" Titus arched both eyebrows in obvious contempt. "I thought you knew everything."

"The Erlking's matters are as clear as troll's teeth," Peter spat.

"Pan is horrible!" Bricius interceded.

"Why the ruckus?" I asked, confused. "He's just a naughty boy. What harm can he do?"

"*Just* a boy? What *harm*? He—he is a menace!" Peter's face reddened.

Titus looked quite smug over Peter's discomfort. I elbowed him.

"This is splendid!" Titus said. "If just for this, I'm bloody glad we went to the lair and rescued the annoying brat. I should take a picture and put it on my ship as wallpaper. Your annoyed face is pure gold. Come on, what did he do?" Titus grinned wider.

Peter spat, barely restraining his anger. "He cut the nymphs' hairs, made them all bald, and used the strands to create traps to trip ogres and trolls."

"Nymphs screamed like banshees until their hair grew again," Bricius said.

"You fae complain too much," Titus said, smirking. "You sound like a whiny baby."

"He was warming up," Peter answered, annoyed. "And try sleeping with nymphs wailing. Impossible."

"He glued the mushrooms to the ground and the gnomes couldn't harvest them," Bricius said.

"Hid the ogres' maces."

"Peed on the Erlking's throne."

"Skinned his dire wolves' hair until they looked like undernourished puppies."

"Now *that* impresses me," Titus said, whistling low. "How did Pan come out unscathed without anyone demanding to skin him?"

"We had a council, and every creature clamored for his head," Peter said. "We had to stop him, but he's as slippery as a pooka."

Kara had joined us so silently I had barely noticed her. If she was indeed drunk, it didn't show at all.

"The Erlking had to step in," Bricius added. "Pan is resilient to fae magic, but the Erlking is cunning, yes, yes, yes."

"But Pan couldn't do a thing." I was confused by their anger. "He relied on us to escape."

Except for the hellhound, which obeyed the brat.

Peter pinched the bridge of his nose. "No one escapes from the Erlking's lair. Perchance not even Anord himself—we would have trapped Anord there if there wasn't a heavy price to pay."

No one escapes? But we did. *I* did, even if the Erlking let us escape. But . . . what if I imagined it? What if he was amazed at how I escaped and decided to let me go?

The idea was crazy, so I pushed it aside for later.

"Now that Pan escaped back to his land"—Bricius shuddered—"*mo thiarna*, he cannot return to Tír D'aois."

"If he does, then we would have to request the Erlking to trap him again," Peter all but snarled. "We would owe him a favor. But let us put that matter to rest." Peter's expression showed a struggle between staying calm and letting out the rage his eyes shouted. "The important issue here is your pirate friend. What say you?" he asked her.

"I'm in," Kara shrugged, "but I strongly advise that we leave this place. Now."

"Very well," Peter said, clearly struggling to be with not one, but two *bradaís* in such an amiable encounter. "Let us go to my taigh." He started walking toward the park at the end of the street.

"Wait." Kara frowned. "No one mentioned a stinky fae hole. I'm not going to no fae place. No way."

"My home is the safest place for you to undertake this, pirate." Peter clasped his hands behind his back, though I wondered if he itched to take his sword and force Kara. That was a very Peter thing to do. "There is also my Lady's taigh, but for the time being, mine will suffice."

Kara placed her hands on her hips. "Sweet boy, I'd love to go to your place on some other occasion. Not for my death, though."

"Could you possibly talk without the innuendo?" Peter all but growled.

She grinned. "Not a chance."

"Come on," I said in an attempt to convince her before she got cold feet. "Taighs are awesome and fun."

"For you, little one. Not to this girl."

"You must." Peter stood as straight as someone could be, and I knew all would be lost if Kara didn't give in soon.

Kara opened her mouth, her expression as stubborn as Peter's. Oh, goody.

"I know a place," Titus interrupted.

We all looked at him.

"There's this place in Switzerland, a hippie retreat—"

"Hippie?" My lips twitched in amusement but also, a little part of me, the human part, did a small jump.

"Whatever you call it nowadays. New Age, hippie. They believe in auras, energy, and aliens coming to scoop up humans." He exhaled. Hard. "They were interested in you before Mr. Wataru."

"Oh."

When I was a prisoner of my own making on his ship, Titus sold me to a Japanese lab that thought I was a key anyone could use to get into Tír D'aois. The creatures in Tír D'aois didn't let any humans in—smart guys, those—but I could thanks to the visa inside of me, the touch of fae. Those guys wanted to replicate my power and get in.

Like Sanders had wanted to do.

Hot anger took me by surprise at the memory of that man. That odious man had tried to do the same, but not before making me feel fear as I'd never felt from humans. Fear almost akin to what I'd felt toward Edward.

I was not sure whom I feared and disliked more.

"That is out of the question," Peter said. "It doesn't sound like a safe place. My taigh, on the other hand—"

"Your place, fae, is the equivalent of Davy Jones's locker after being flogged," Titus said in a hard tone. "My recommendation is better."

"That is not acceptable."

Again both faced each other with that distrust and feistiness that was getting on my nerves.

"I'm in," Kara said. "I trust him. I don't trust *you*, fae. So it's where my brother says or nowhere."

Titus gave her a smile, a kind one, the one that seldom showed itself but lately I'd seen more and more of that smile. "And what better neutral place than Switzerland?" he said with a satisfied grin, this one with a challenge at Peter.

Peter's jaw twitched and for a moment, I feared he would not accept, but then he sighed. The second coin certainly was an allure.

"If there is no other option, I shall place a protection around the place. It should be small, though."

"With my help, yes, yes, yes." Bricius shot into the air. "I'll protect her with my life!"

"There are cabins there," Titus said. "They'll serve our purpose."

"Are those people a threat?" I asked, remembering Haru and Squatty, the woman who'd run the tests once Wataru had left. And Sanders's guards, those who sneered and were mean to me. Hot swirled in me, anger coiled in my chest at the memory I'd tried to erase.

I reached out and snatched Titus's hands, entwining my fingers in his and attempting to find an anchor. As suspected, my forehead throbbed. What had the Erlking done to me?

Bricius landed on my shoulder, his familiar weight reassuring me.

"They're harmless," Titus said. "You'll see."

Kara clicked her tongue. "Frau Engel?"

"The same."

"She's a hoot. All right." She looked at me and winked. "You'll love her!"

The predatory grin she gave me left me doubting it.

ELEVEN

Ryanne

A devastated land splayed before me. Fae dead, their limbs in awkward positions, their once beautiful faces disfigured with missing eyes, terrifying rictus, and black thorns pulsating beneath their skins as tar veins.

My vision closed up without me wanting it to, and I saw the details in full. I wanted to close my eyes, to run away, but I couldn't. There were other creatures: humans, gnomes, even goblins. All dead. All destroyed.

All but a silver-haired nymph, who staggered and fell, panting. Maybe I disliked Zadora—for that was who she was—but her pain was too much, and I reached out to her, only to find myself glued to my spot.

Who did this? I wanted to scream, but nothing came out of me. I was a ghost, a spectator. Frantic, I searched the ground to see if it was a vision and the symbols Bricius had pestered me all my life to find were there.

I found a little gnome, which didn't seem to be part of what I was seeing. He frantically pulled my hand, his eyes fearful. But he had no runes.

A woman appeared in my line of vision, but only in profile. Long black ringlets hid her face from me. She wore leathers, and her skin glinted with a metallic sheen under the bright sun. She swayed her hips in a languid and sensual manner.

She crouched next to the nymph, who widened her eyes in fear and tried to escape. With a careless gesture, the leather-clad woman latched her hand on the nymph's throat. Her bloodied hands.

"Ryanne," Zadora said, "help!"

Heat throbbed in my forehead, and I glowered at the nymph, while images of her drowning me came to mind. I shivered; she didn't deserve this.

Let her be, I screamed. *Mercy!*

Zadora gurgled blood, and I screamed more, alongside the gnome.

I was still screaming when I bolted straight up in bed, my hands clutching the sheets.

Bricius came zooming in, sword in hand. "What is it? Where is the enemy?"

"*Acushla!*" Titus woke up and hugged me. "Another nightmare?"

"Leave me alone!" I scrambled out of bed, breath hitching and heart thumping wildly. A nightmare, but now I'd been able to remember those snippets that had bothered me.

Bricius hovered next to Titus, who'd already rose to his feet.

"I'm sorry," he said while approaching me as if I were a wild animal. "Do you need something?"

He stood there in his naked glory, and worry etched on his face. After looking in every corner for the invisible enemy, Bricius returned to Titus's side and sat on his head. Titus didn't flinch.

And I laughed, perhaps out of hysterics. A pixie sitting atop a pirate's head?

"No, I'm sorry." I launched myself to Titus and hugged him tight, trying to scare the nightmare away, to forget about the bloodied hands. He embraced me as well. "I was so scared in that . . ." I choked on the word. I didn't want to say it.

"Vision?" Bricius asked softly.

"There was that little gnome, but he was scared and didn't have runes," I said, voice breaking. "It felt so real."

"A seer-dream," Bricius confirmed.

I looked up to my little friend, befuddled.

"Sometimes seers have those dreams, and it's so powerful the rune-gnome cannot help." He scratched his head. "But it is not frequent, no, no, no. What was it about?"

Not frequent, which didn't surprise me; most seers ended up dead before reaching their full potential. "Peter said the fae killing was bad, but I saw them dead, and it was terrifying. And not only fae. I saw goblins, too, and other creatures." Who could do this to a nymph, even a bully one?

Titus sighed and brought me closer, his hands over my back in an attempt to calm me. "My kin are focused on fae, but anything can happen, now that things are getting out of control. That might be what your nightmare—"

"Seer-dream," Bricius corrected.

"I'm confused about the difference," Titus said.

"It's like visions," Bricius explained, "but while the seer is dreaming. Visions alert the bearer of danger, yes, yes, yes, but seer-dreams are more powerful and if not careful, the seer can be lost in them."

"What do you mean, lost?" I asked.

"You could stay there for a long time."

"The gnome was scared, and he was pulling my hand." I scrunched my brow. "Was it alerting me?"

"Yes!" Bricius nodded. "If you are able and if it is not too dark, take his hand, and he'll lead you out of the seer-dream."

"So"—I released myself from the embrace—"was this a warning about the bradaſs killing? But we already know that."

"Perhaps it's another clue," Titus said.

"Pirates are evil, yes, yes . . . not all pirates!" Bricius quickly added. "You are not bad, no, no, no."

"I'm starting to think not all bradaſs are evil," I sighed.

"Only Edward is evil by birth," Titus answered. "The rest are pushed into it, but I wouldn't trust any of them. Some don't understand the difference and act accordingly."

"Except Kara and Sergei."

"Except them. Possibly."

"When I had that seer-dream of you, before you were killed by Peter, I was scared. But this was different. I was terrified."

Titus wiped the tears from my cheeks with a tenderness that I still had to get used to. "I died, but I came back a better version of myself. Stronger."

"You are," I conceded. "You think that seer-dream—"

"It's not what it looks like, aye. Your nightmare showed me fighting over sharks' fins, by the Morrigan!"

"It did."

"Which one?" Bricius asked.

"Oh, it was one I had before Titus was killed. Peter and he were fighting over sharks' fins—"

"That doesn't make any sense, no, no, no."

"Precisely," Titus said. "This new vision, or seer-dream as you call it, might be something else, although it is something we need to be cognizant of."

I sniffed and went to the bathroom to blow my nose. For a second, I stood there, staring at the bin with my crumpled tissue. A lonely piece of paper, forgotten. I shook my head, that wasn't me.

I wasn't forgotten. I'd escaped from the fae to avoid being held behind walls, and they'd come for me, not to take me back, no, but to help us in our quest, somehow.

But your family will forget you, a little voice nagged me. *You might not come back, and they might shed tears over your lost body. But then they'd quickly move on.*

Images from that seer-dream came with force, and I retched.

"Are you well, *acushla*?" Titus asked to my back.

"Yes, yes." I reached out for another tissue, which followed the fate of its predecessor. "I'm still bothered by the images."

"Pixie," Titus said, "give us some privacy."

"Please," I said. "Remember to say *please*."

Titus scoffed but did as I asked.

"Very well," Bricius said, "but if something happens, call me." And with that he flew away into the streets of Oslo.

We'd decided to spend the night here before going to Switzerland, us three, since Kara and Peter would arrive tonight as a couple, to Peter's everlasting chagrin and Kara's everlasting amusement. But since it was a retreat, it was better that they arrived before us to avoid suspicion.

"*Acushla*, there's something I haven't told you, and it's time, before we go to Switzerland."

"Don't scare me. What is it?"

"I do feel stronger. Not only because I don't have that gold lure any longer, but because you're with me."

"I know, I numb the beast."

"Not only that." He brushed my messy hair out of my face. "I walked alone for centuries. I am not alone anymore. And that makes me stronger. You being with me."

"Aww." I reached for his hand and squeezed it.

"I don't want to lose you ever, you hear?"

"You won't. I'll always be here."

I couldn't believe this was the same Titus I met a few months back. Just a few months. How could everything change in such a short span of time?

How could *I* have changed so much? Half fae, with a touch of the Erlking that we still didn't understand why or what would be the side effects, besides feeling a bit hot at times and my mood swings.

And anger at those who'd bullied me in the past.

Titus took a deep breath, the type you use to deliver some godawful news, and I tensed. He reached out for my other hand and held both close to his chest.

This must be bad.

"I might be mortal."

"Mortal!"

"Aye. I won't know for sure unless a fae or one of my kin tries to kill me. But I'm different. I feel different."

"Is that such a bad thing? Now we could age together."

"If we make it that far."

He kissed my hands, his brow softened. Nightmare or seer-dream, it didn't matter. We were stronger together, and we'd find a way to defeat Edward, together.

"We're still here," I said, lovingly. "So let's seize the moment, shall we?"

I reached for him, for his kiss, for his touch, for the glorious feeling of skin against skin. For that electrifying sensation of knowing you were loved, you were cared for.

It was never enough with him. It would never be enough.

TWELVE

Ryanne

itus and I arrived in Switzerland at the edge of a copse of evergreens. Snow-capped mountains enveloped the bright, soft green grass of the Engadine Valley like a postcard. He'd teleported us to the forest next to Frau Engel's resort, a charming place of scattered wooden cabins surrounding a central building with a lake in the distance.

The plan was Titus would "lend" me to Frau Engel. While humans usually didn't spot Bricius, Titus was a bit concerned here some might, due to their work with energy. I wasn't sure I believed him, but I wasn't willing to sacrifice Bricius or our mission to find out. Bricius had proposed a solution: to hide in the trees like he did among the sails in Titus's ships.

I hadn't felt unbalanced since we met Peter, and only the Erlking's touch bothered me. Whether I could vanish it like Peter thought, that was to be seen, but I'd been attempting to erase it like I did Titus's dorcha a lifetime ago, back in Japan.

A short chubby woman with a big smile on her ruddy face waited for us at the entrance of the resort. Her flowered dress fluttered around her plump legs, more suited for a day at the beach than for a winter hike, though it hardly felt like winter in the valley. She looked north of fifty, but her face was devoid of wrinkles, so I couldn't be sure.

"Herr Doyle!" she sang, raising her pudgy hand in salute. She stood next to an open gate. A wooden, rustic gate with steel reinforcements for cars to go through, nothing more.

If she was surprised we were on foot, she didn't show it.

"Frau Engel," Titus greeted, offering a charming smile. "Allow me to introduce Miss Evans." We'd agreed to change my surname for privacy.

She beamed at me as if she were in front of a celebrity and giggled like a schoolgirl. "The seer, of course!" A little more and the good-natured lady would start bouncing with joy. *"Wilkommen!"*

"Er, thanks," I said with a tentative smile.

"You vill be quite at ease. Herr Doyle, your visit fills us with unlimited joy. This veek ve have several guests, and ve'll be enchanted for you to join us for dinner."

"I'd love to, Frau Engel."

Frau Engel closed the gate after us and led us down a path surrounded by trees with gnarled trunks. Evergreens dotted the landscape.

A flutter of gossamer wings appeared for a moment, just to disappear into the trees the next.

I turned toward a distant lake after advancing a few dozen feet. Azure suspended above cerulean while a path of fluffy clouds embraced the snowed mountains like children stuck in their mom's skirts. It was midday, and what a glorious day!

Frau Engel followed the direction of my gaze. "It's vonderful, *ja*? But I'm certain you've seen more beautiful things in Faerieland."

"Faerieland," I repeated with a straight face. No human so far knew its real name, Tír D'aois, as far as I knew. "What do you know about it?"

The lady's fine skirt danced with the cold breeze coming from the lake. "A magical, vonderful place, dear. A place I've vanted to see for a long, long time." She took my arm in a gesture of familiarity then gestured to Titus. "Come, Herr Doyle, don't dally. Our beloved guru told us of that vonderful kingdom, Faerie."

"Guru?" I stole a glance at Titus. He shrugged.

"*Ja*, he is connected with the energy of the Earth," she said reverently, bringing both hands to her broad chest. "Ve have decades connecting with our inner center and vork every day to feel the pure and beautiful magic of faeries around us."

I coughed into my fist. "Faeries here." There were no hawthorns in sight, so I couldn't see how fae could actually live here. "Yeah. Ah, what do you guys do with that?"

"To see beyond, Lady Seherin."

"Beyond what?"

"Ah." She winked at me like an old grandma discussing an important kitchen secret. "You'll see."

"*Seherin*?" I whispered to Titus.

"Seer," he explained.

Lady Seer. I liked that!

We walked under the trees, the layer of dry leaves crunching under our feet. It was like part of me was draining down my soles, but at the same time, I felt recharged. I had no idea what was happening through my body thanks to my bizarre-acting *préachta*: like a torrent of waters that suddenly found a dam, then forgot where it wanted to go or why it was there.

And since it was engraved in me, I felt the same way. Though this place, with all its beauty, calmed my aching soul.

"I thought it'd be snowy," I said, glancing at the green surroundings. My pixie guardian hid above in the trees, invisible. He was getting better and better at that.

"It vas all white a few days ago. But veather has been avfully inconsistent. I believe it knew about you. Ve learned a few months ago a seer" —she winked conspiratorially at me—"had an open channel with faeries, and that she vas on a tour."

"A tour." She thought I was on a tour promoting my, er, visions . . . well! Titus was in for an earful tonight.

"But your rates are so high, Lady Seherin!" she complained. "And ve couldn't afford them, so vith all the pain in our hearts"—here the lady let out a rather dramatic sigh, placing a hand on her chest—"ve vithdrew our request. But our beloved guru meditated and requested us to ask in humility to the divine energy, to cleanse us and change the bad vibe."

She smiled, as if I'd understood the string of nonsense she'd just spouted, then stopped and spread her hands wide. "And the energy replied, balancing our chakras. And last night, Herr Doyle called and asked me if you could stay with us for a few days. Vithout asking anything in return! That you were tired and vanted to settle down before moving on vith your tour. You didn't know you vouldn't gain anything vith your visit?" She looked as if afraid I would demand my fees.

"Herr Doyle handles my, eh, itinerary. I was just curious." I shrugged.

Titus winked at me with a shadow of a smirk, one I'd grown accustomed to. At this point, it was part of his sex appeal.

"Ve'll feel the energy around us tonight, connecting with the universe so you can share your experience," she said as she resumed our walk. "You don't know how happy ve are to have you here tonight, Lady Seherin.

"Ve have tried for decades to connect with that kingdom, and to have you vith us fills me with joy. But don't fear," she quickly added when she saw my horrified expression, "it'll be marvelous. I'm so excited!" She clapped several times.

I coughed on my fist, and Titus strangled a choke. *Yeah, strangle all you want, buster.* And here I thought I only needed to look pretty.

"You said *we*. How many people are here?" So much for a calm retreat with Kara and Peter.

"Oh, not many, about a dozen. Ve are in a retreat, and you came at perfect time since ve just started it. Although I'm not surprised; the divine energy knows vhen things should happen."

I glared at Titus, but he walked beside me with a straight face.

"There is only one requirement," Frau Engel said in a serious, businesslike tone. "Ve do not allow any communication with the outside."

"Hence why this is a good place," Titus whispered in my ear.

"And no cellphones are allowed. I'll safe keep yours with all the rest."

"Fine by me," I said.

We arrived at a wooden construction with sloped ceilings, large enough to accommodate several rooms. Surrounded by lush trees, the huge hut seemed to be lost in them. Inside, the ample space was decorated with rugs, the smell of wood, a touch of eucalyptus, and fire burning around us.

"It's gorgeous," I whispered as if we were in a house of prayer. Maybe staying here a few nights wasn't such a bad idea, after all.

Frau Engel smiled widely, evidently satisfied with my praise. "And vait until you see your cabin. Herr Doyle requested privacy." She did that happy wink of hers. "And I made certain you have the best."

One of the conditions for Frau Engel to have access to my, er, celebrity schedule was to have my own cabin and far away from the rest because I, of course, loved solitude while I connected with the faeries.

Thank Cuidi.

THIRTEEN

Ryanne

The food area was in a large room with two long wooden tables and benches on each side. About a dozen people sat there, and they all stood as we entered, clapping as they smiled or whooped. I stopped and looked behind me, but there was no one but me and Titus.

Hey, what do you know? I'm really a celebrity. A seer walking down the red carpet with a bradaí at my side. It didn't get better than that.

Kara was there, slouched on a chair and acting bored, but I couldn't see Peter. My skin tingled but ever so softly.

Those who'd stood approached us with bright smiles. They reached out to touch my arms and my face. Most were dressed in light-colored, loose-fitting clothing; Frau Engel's floral dress was highlighted as a speck of color.

"You've visited an enchanted kingdom," a long-haired man said, his hands joined in prayer.

"You've had contact with beings from another world," said a small, plump woman, stroking my hair.

"They're not from another world," I tried to explain, but they wouldn't let me, all speaking at the same time and surrounding me as if I were a rock star.

Titus stepped back and stifled a chuckle. He'd explained before we arrived that it hadn't been him who told them about Tír D'aois. These people somehow knew beforehand, and he'd taken advantage of the fact.

Which wasn't surprising given his pirate-y self.

Bricius had agreed to remain in the cabin. Now, where the hell was Peter? Not only did my skin tingle, but my being vibrated like a tuning fork, which always happened when I met with fae. Meanwhile, the crowd continued with their praise. It was starting to get annoying.

"Your chakras are aligned with theirs?"

"Did they touch the sixth, and opened your third eye?"

"You must have astral dreams. What do they tell you?"

I took a couple of steps back. *What the heck?*

"Calm down," Frau Engel cried. "There'll be time for your questions, *ja?* Now ve all need to eat and let our special guest settle."

One of the guys who'd remained seated stalked toward us. Tall, with a strong jaw shaded by a beard, attractive despite the long hair covering part of his face and the round glasses, which hid bright brown eyes. He wore tight jeans and a fringed leather vest, shirtless, showing well-marked pectorals on a hairless, tan chest. He smiled at me.

My skin tingled stronger. The glamour shifted, and I could see Peter behind it. I almost choked in laughter.

"Oh," Frau Engel exclaimed, her hand in the air. "Meet our new friends for the retreat. Miss Kleven and her partner, Mister Atkinson."

Everyone greeted enthusiastically, and Kara rose languidly, a simper on her face. Yet there was something else about her, something I couldn't quite put my finger on. She sashayed toward us, and I knew what was different—she looked more like her old self, the seductress on board.

"The seventies called," I whispered to Peter, "they want the John Lennon glasses back. And the vest."

"I beg your pardon?"

"You're a few decades late."

He glanced around. "I seem to fit in, though."

His left arm was full of tattoos, and both his ears were pierced. "Glamour," he said at my incredulous look.

"Well you look hot. You're the sexiest fae I've ever seen!"

Kara touched Peter's ass. "Isn't he?"

I gaped, mostly because Peter didn't react. She squeezed and winked at me.

"Are you looking for more?" Peter asked Kara, unperturbed.

"Hell yeah," she answered, almost giddy.

"Eh," I stuttered. "Did you guys . . .?"

Kara leaned toward me with a wicked gleam in her eye. "I'm never going for a human again. Fae is the new sexy. So good!"

Peter remained unperturbed.

"Really?" I said, surprised. "I thought . . . well, I didn't think anything. But, really?"

Kara laughed. "We fought," she said, "because I wanted to shag this human last night. You know, I might end up dead today. And then it happened. Crazy wonderful."

"Enough," Peter said, stern.

Oh no, nothing of the sort. I grabbed his arm and made as if he was just accompanying me, but instead I whispered, "Sex with Kara? Don't you hate her kind?"

"Hate is not a deterrent for sex. It even spices it up."

"So?"

"So what? It shall not be repeated."

"One night stand, huh?"

"I do not understand your meaning, but it was only this time. Perhaps once more." He glanced to Kara, who blew him a kiss. He scowled. "Indeed, once more."

Titus pulled me to him, eyebrow raised. "Hot? Sexy fae?"

"Oh c'mon," I said, winking, "you know you're the sexiest pirate ever."

"As long as I'm hotter."

"You'll always be."

Dinner was delicious, the fondue exquisite, though it was hard to enjoy with everyone staring at me and smiling as if I were a deity who had deigned to share food with them. Kara, Titus, and Peter were huddled together and left me alone for me to "enjoy" the spotlight.

To make matters worse, the plump little woman sat next to me without speaking, just stroking my hair with awe shining in her stooped eyes. I scooted away discreetly, closer to the long-haired man on my left. What would they say if they knew about Titus and Kara? Peter? Would they be shocked or enchanted? I was certain the latter.

The plump woman scooted right next to me, obviously not offended. "Did you have sex with the faeries? How was it?"

My cheeks matched Peter's reddening from before. With the fae? Heck no! "Uh, no, no sex."

She pouted, but her disappointed expression vanished as her next question burst out from her full lips. "Did you see them naked? Can you describe them for me?"

"Ah . . ."

"How did you receive their gift?" asked someone across the table.

Preferring that question over the naked one, I gave my stock, short answer.

"I received a light from a pixie, but it was a fae who gave me his touch of power."

The shower of questions started. At first, I spoke hesitantly. But then I grew amused watching their expressions as the story progressed and was even encouraged to speak more freely. So, like in Japan with Haru, I told them the whole experience, from when I saw the pixie to how the light entered me. About how they rescued me from the freezing river and when I saw Peter.

At that point, Peter leaned forward and listened attentively. We'd never talked about that time, and his eyes brightened, those weird brown eyes from his glamour.

Before I knew it, I was telling them anecdotes of my stays at Cuidi's dwellings, how I had to address her, and Bricius's oddities.

"So only you can see the pixie?" the long-haired man asked.

"In theory anyone with a connection to Faerie could, but I understand only a handful have that ability." I was silent for a moment, wondering if these people so open to these experiences could indeed see my little guardian. Perhaps they would.

"Do you think I could?" the plump woman asked, so absorbed with my story she even forgot to stroke my hair or ask awkward nudity questions, thank Cuidi.

"I don't know," I said with complete honesty. "No human adult in my experience has been able to."

A discussion started, and they quickly became engrossed in discussing who could see Bricius or who couldn't, and I felt glad he was hidden in the cabin. Where they agreed was that their—thankfully absent—guru would, since he was connected by his chakra from who knows where to the aforesaid energy. Strangely, they didn't seem so rare or peculiar now.

I found myself smiling, not the Special Fake Ryanne Style smile, but a genuine one.

I wasn't seen as weird, and all these humans believed me. They weren't stories for them; they believed it was the truth. I wasn't odd. My *préachta* filled me, but it wasn't confused or icy.

I felt belonging.

I beamed at Titus, and he raised his glass of wine. Titus was drinking wine? It seemed I wasn't the only one feeling cozy. Peter, after the faery discussion finished, looked uncomfortable but he remained, even as he was sitting as far away from the group as possible.

Kara? She now looked off, like someone who was trying too hard to show everyone she was cool and not worried. I scuttled by her side to see if I could make her feel better, but she waved me off.

"Shouldn't we go?" I asked Titus, worried about Kara's superficial hype.

"Not tonight, *acushla,*" Titus said nonchalantly. "Hot guy and I," he nodded his head at Peter, "agreed to wait until tomorrow since we are the center of attention. Better to wait to cool it off."

"I'm fine," Kara said, waving a careless hand.

A blonde woman with a long face approached and handed me a drink. "I thought you were thirsty."

I thanked her while stepping away from Kara. A *bradaí* could be unpredictable, and more so while about to undergo a dangerous surgery.

"What other beings have you seen?" the blonde asked. She waved a hand toward a seat, and I sat next to her.

"Well, pixies, fae of course, gnomes, trolls and some ogres." The

Erlking flashed in my mind, his odd attitude making me shake my head. "Oh yeah, and nymphs," I said, grimacing.

"Nymphs," the blonde said, an ecstatic expression on her face. "The most magnificent creatures—"

"No!" I slammed my hand on the table, and she started. I cleared my throat. "Nothing of the sort, I tell you. They're crazy."

"But—but," she stammered, "our Guru made a ceremony earlier this year and assured me that my spirit was benevolent because I had a connection with them." She clenched her hands, leaning a little toward me as if wanting me to retract what I said and assure her those nutty nymphs were as she thought. "I swim a lot, you see? I have mermaid blood."

"Sorry to disappoint you," I said with compassion. "But nymphs aren't like you imagine. Believe me, if you ever see one, run as fast as you can, in the opposite direction. Don't even get close to the shore because there's nothing more amusing to them than to drown the unwary."

Everyone looked at me like I'd just ruined their Christmas. Some even whispered among themselves, "Can't be," "Impossible," and other exclamations of disbelief.

I sighed. The possibility of them ever seeing a nymph was remote, anyway. While they loved to drown humans, they'd become lazy and rarely traveled to human lands. It was that or because they'd been hunted in the past century whenever they showed their scaly faces.

I decided to throw the kind woman a bone. "They *are* beautiful, with dewdrops entwined in their tresses, and their hair ranges from bright pink to blue and purple."

"Oh," the blonde said, "that's my favorite color!" She turned to the short plump woman, who'd joined us. "I knew I should have dyed my hair purple."

"You should do that," the plump woman said with awe.

The blonde brought her hands to her face, emotion taking over. Some hugged her, and they all laughed in joy.

I no longer insisted on the nymphs' deviousness, to the obvious delight of the audience.

"I'm Birdie," the plump woman said, her awed expression not leaving her eyes. "I'm connected with that land too, and it whispered my name when I meditated. Have you heard my name in the wind of the fae realm?"

"Uh, yes," I lied. "Birdie, yeah, sounds like a name from Faery."

She beamed and lay her head on my shoulder, sighing. "I knew it."

"I'm Mila," said the blonde with mermaid blood, obviously not wanting to be left behind.

"Come, children, come!"

Frau Engel directed us to another large room, this one without furniture but full of rugs and cushions. Sandalwood incense and candles burned in the corners. We all sat down in a circle and joined hands, the, er, *energy* apparently flowing with a good, ahem, *vibe* around us. Or so everyone said.

As soon as I could, I excused myself and went to my cabin with Titus and Bricius, glad of solitude, but mostly of the silence. I was lucky enough to escape before the group hugging began.

FOURTEEN

Ryanne

The locket, that gift from grandma, dangled from the mirror, exactly as I remembered from my childhood. I was sitting on my bed, smells of home invading my nostrils. My short legs swung, and I smiled, happy. Streaks of light flooded my bedroom.

Something was missing, and I scrunched my nose, trying to remember.

Mom and Dad's conversation reached my ears. Mom made breakfast, and Dad talked about the news, while Mom played deaf and pumped up the music.

But that wasn't what was missing in this bedroom. I hummed a tune and looked around, certain that what I was missing must be here.

Sudden darkness covered the room, and a chill settled on my skin. I stood up and knew I had to reach for the locket. It was important, but I didn't know why.

The window opened before I reached it, and a woman crawled inside, long black ringlets hiding her face. Even so, I knew there was something sinister about her, and I took a step back.

She slithered inside, like a worm, like a huge serpent dressed in leathers. She turned her back on me, as if I was unimportant. Darkness clung to her curves.

"Who are you?" I managed to say, terror gripping my limbs—terror of this strange woman, terror of the darkness in her.

Still with her back to me, she lifted a hand. No, not a hand—a claw, a deformed one—and picked up my locket.

"That's mine!" I squeaked. "Leave it!"

The locket dangled from her claw, and she crushed it, then threw the remains on the floor.

"No!" I yelled, sobbing, attempting to reach her but so afraid I was rooted in place. "Why did you do that?"

Darkness swirled and engulfed her. Then she was gone, but I was on my knees, sobbing.

I was alone. No more conversation drifting from below, no music, no laughter. Just a desolated landscape stretching to the horizon.

No humanity left in me.

"*Acushla*! Wake up."

I sat on my bed, yelling like a banshee. Titus's arms promptly circled me, and I sobbed on his chest.

"Another nightmare?" he asked tenderly.

"Seer-dream," I whispered. "She took the locket."

"Who?"

"That woman. Serpent woman. Warrior."

"It was a dream, a bad one," he cooed. He was getting better at this boyfriend gig.

"I-I don't know. The locket was important, and she destroyed it. It was—" I sat down straight and pushed him away to think better. "That's why I was in my childhood bedroom."

He frowned, clearly not understanding.

I patted my chest. "It's a symbol, Titus. Of me not losing my humanity. It reminds me of when I was just a human. But that woman destroyed it."

"Dreams are full of symbols. She might represent your fear."

I gasped. "I was terrified."

"See? Nothing more to it. Now, let's pretend all is well before doing what we came here to do."

I smiled, glad to be distracted from that awful nightmare. And nightmare it had to be since the little gnome was absent.

"Do you think Kara and Peter—"

"Aye, for sure."

We took a quick shower, grabbed some fruit from the welcome basket Frau Engel left us, and took the path toward the main cabin.

It was only a matter of time before we met with the good-natured lady.

Frau Engel greeted me with effervescence at the end of the path. "Lady Seherin, ready so early? Excellent!" The rest of the group was walking out of the main cabin. "Ve'll do our sun salutation, come, come."

I sighed and followed her. To the right of the main cabin, there was a clearing, surrounded by evergreens, where everyone awaited us. Kara and Peter, surprise surprise, were nowhere to be seen.

"Never leave your tequila behind," she'd said last night when we split to our cabins, followed promptly by Peter. Strong spirits were not permitted on the premises—only beer and wine—but she was a bradaí. She'd laughed, he'd grumbled, but didn't complain when she grabbed his behind once more.

Birdie promptly positioned herself to my right to my everlasting chagrin, and Mila at my left.

"I dreamed of you last night," Birdie said adoringly. "You had an aura around you, and faeries threw pixie dust at you."

"There is no pixie d—"

"I dreamed of you as well," Mila said, getting closer to me. "You were a goddess. You *are* one."

"I am nothing of the—"

"Bright energy surrounded you, and the fairies put gifts at your feet. What gifts do you like?" Mila asked adoringly.

"She likes faery gifts, of course!" Birdie said, glowering at the blonde. "Pixie dust and faery gold."

Mila took a step forward, and I was sandwiched between the two wackos.

Frau Engel clapped. "Everyone, attention, please!"

Oh, thank the gods!

Birdie whispered, "Who's your friend? The yummy one with the fringed leather vest. His energy feels familiar but he is so shy!"

"He's just a fan." I almost choked on that word.

"Oh! Can you introduce me to him?"

"Uh, he's with"—about to say *Kara*, I recalled her new name—"Kleven."

"That's a shame." She pouted.

We stood in a circle with Frau Engel conducting the breathing exercises, speaking with a calm voice. *Préachta* hummed and filled me like a peaceful river.

I had to say it did me good, feeling strangely at peace, rooted.

Maybe the energy *did* change our vibes.

FIFTEEN

Ryanne

The scent of pine filled the crisp mountain air as we headed to our cabin. Delicate wildflowers—which shouldn't be thriving in January but hey, crazy weather—scattered among the wonderfully tall evergreens that reminded me of some areas in Tír D'aois.

"This is such a beautiful place." Peter sighed. "Aghna would have loved this."

I shuffled my feet over the cold pavement. I'd always thought that Peter was a stick-up-his-arse fae, but he'd held pain for centuries after Edward tortured his wife, who eventually died, even as Titus had tried to save her in an odd show of mercy.

I couldn't wrap my head around someone being so in love and hurt after more than two hundred years.

Kara kept whispering to Titus while we strolled through the grounds. Both had joined us after the exercises. Titus looked calm but his eyes kept focused on Peter, and his expression turned darker the more we approached the cabin.

After being skewered by Peter's sword back in Tír D'aois, it was no surprise to anyone why Titus felt wary of my fae mentor in this particular instance. Well, in any instance, but this was worse. Or why Kara seemed to be having cold feet, which I couldn't blame her. But if we couldn't convince her, then we wouldn't be able to help any of the bradaís. And we needed bradaís on our side in the battle against Edward or it would turn into a slaughter—of us, not him.

Kara, as Titus's older "sister," wanted their little family to be free of Edward. She'd fought hard for them to be as they were before. Now this was the chance to take the first step. The question was would she do it willingly?

We reached the cabin, where Bricius hovered over the sturdy wooden door, adorned with intricate carvings that reminded me of the taigh. The exterior featured a steeply pitched roof covered in weathered wooden shingles.

Kara stopped in her tracks and wiped her palms over her clothes.

"Where's the basket?" I asked.

"I have it." Kara opened her bradaí portal and retrieved a wicker basket with everything required for her healing and extract of her coin. She handed it to me right away as if holding it burned.

"You'll be fine," I said reassuringly.

"You won't be the one dying, sweetie." Her tone carried a hard edge, her eyes fastened to the door.

"Titus survived."

"He had a fae-spirit aiding him."

"Actually, I did it all. My fae power helped him, and now you'll also have Peter's."

My fae mentor nodded. "It is unusual, but Ryanne explained what happened with Doyle. How her *préachta* was peaceful and non-intrusive. We'll do the same with you. Your life is in good hands."

"Easy for you to say," Kara snapped as she entered the cabin.

Peter's glamour washed away once he stepped over the threshold, as if a strong wind blasted and stripped him of his ridiculous clothes. He now wore his usual robes and dark tights, and his lovely, pointed ears peeked from his now longer reddish-brown hair. A sword dangled from his belt; he'd left his sword in his cabin to avoid scaring Frau Engel's people. Fae didn't have those handy dimensional pockets like the bradaís.

Timber-clad walls covered wherever my gaze roamed. A stone fireplace was located on one side, and there was a small kitchen and dining room for four on our right. Titus and I had removed all the cozy rugs, now tossed over our bed. The curtains on the large windows were closed to avoid any peeping Toms checking us out. Or weird fans.

"By Odin's balls," Kara exclaimed, her long strides taking her to the center. "Is this really necessary? Having this fae," she spat, "touch me to get rid of whatever shit Anord put in us?"

"*This* fae?" Peter said without batting an eyelash. "After having sex with me thrice, I hoped you would call me differently."

She faced him, hands on hips pushed to the side. "Sex, cutie tush, is another matter."

"You won't die," I said reassuringly. I placed the basket on one of the chairs.

"Not by you, but by my treacherous kin," she spat. "Once that coin is taken out, they'll come here in a frenzy. What was I thinking?"

"It's not too late to proceed to my taigh." Peter laced his hands behind his back, his trademark teacher stance. "You'll be wholly safe there."

"That's not happening. I can't be in a place I don't know how I'll get out. No way. You said you could safeguard this place."

"By all means, I was only anticipating the possibility of a revision in your decision. Bricius."

The little pixie zoomed by the window. "Yes, *mo Thiarna*!"

"Let us fortify this location with additional protection. Come with me."

Both stepped out of the cabin. Kara slid her hand up and down and retrieved her sword from her bradaí pocket. "Need this." Kara let herself fall to a chair and placed the sword on her lap. "What's next?" she grumbled.

"Your Name," Titus said.

"The beast is yelling not to say it." She pressed her fingertips to her forehead as if she was having a migraine. "It's hard."

"Maybe if you write it down?" I provided.

"Same thing. I've tried it before and believe me, the beast controls our movements when our Name is involved."

Titus gave her a curt nod. "Take your time."

"I need a drink," she said.

It was not yet ten a.m., but she could have whatever she needed. "There's only wine or beer in the kitchen."

"Tequila," she demanded. "That's what I need."

Titus shook his head. "The fae is prepping. It wouldn't make sense for any of us to go out."

Préachta swirled in me, energized. That was when I noticed the other energy circling us, surrounding us with a zing. Peter's. It started slow, like an ornamented vase pouring water over a bed of rocks.

"Gin," she sighed. "That'd be great. Or whiskey. You always store something in your pocket, don't you?"

Titus lifted his hand and slid it down. He frowned. "I can't access my pocket."

"Odin's balls," Kara cursed.

Both looked like prowling ogres that had been recently captured. I didn't feel trapped, because the fae energy building up energized me, made me feel alive.

That combined with the energy from Frau Engel's group offered the perfect kick. The best cocktail that tamed the icy *préachta* or the Erlking's touch.

Peter stepped back inside, without Bricius. "It's done. Bricius is making certain there are no energy holes, though we did comprehensive work." He stared at Kara. "You are safe."

She threw her head back and gave a sharp war cry, her sword in hand. "Fine. If this helps prevent Edward from finding me—"

"And Anord," Titus provided.

"Yeah, him. Fine." She shook her shoulders and rotated her head, then took a deep sigh. "My Name is . . ." She choked. "My . . . Oh, Odin take everyone to hell!"

I reached out and touched her arm. "You can do this."

"No way, little seer."

There was no *préachta* I could feel inside her like with Titus. According to what the fae told us back at Cuidi's taigh, Anord had to create bradaís with a sliver of borrowed power from powerful beings from Tír na Vraoichta, the dark dimension. All but Edward, who had only Anord's dark energy in him, and Titus, who had a bit of fae energy mixed in. And Kara had something of Odin's.

But there was something else inside if I focused.

"What are you doing?" Kara said, tense, but not making any effort to push me away.

I reached out with the other hand to the fae power encircling the hut, making a circuit with my inner *préachta* and Peter's. "Helping you."

"I can help as well," Peter said.

"No," I whispered. "I'm the bridge. Let me."

"Keep going, little seer," Kara breathed. "This feels good."

It was like that time with Titus when I sent my energy as a soft intruder so *dorcha* wouldn't feel threatened. While she wasn't wounded, her *dorcha* remained still, but little by little it relaxed to an inert state.

"Try again," I said.

Kara took a deep breath. "My Name is . . . Yrsa."

It sounded like "ursa" to me.

"She-bear?" Titus asked, pensive.

"Wild. Very fitting," Peter said.

"It is, isn't it?" Her eyes twinkled.

"Thank you for making Kara feel at ease. You did well, Ryanne," my ex-mentor said, stiff and detached, as always.

As all fae. As that icy feeling.

Before I thought it over, I hugged him tight. He stiffened more, if that was possible. He didn't liked to be touched.

Too bad.

My *préachta,* unlike before when it purred, pushed us away—like two magnets with the same polarity.

"All right, where's my coin?" Kara all but demanded.

Peter seemed grateful for the distraction and released my embrace. He stood beside her and moved his hands around as if measuring her. "I cannot find it."

"How did he find yours, little brother?" Kara asked.

Titus didn't seem upset by my show of affection with Peter, but he understood by now Peter was like a dear uncle. Well, a hot dear uncle.

"The redhead fae-spirit saw my creation," Titus answered. "She knew where Anord inserted it."

"I cannot feel it," Peter said.

"Come, sweet boy, let me help. These obnoxious clothes get in the way." She gave him a mischievous smile as she placed her sword on a chair then removed them. I was surprised to see she wore lacy blue underwear.

Bradaís didn't have an issue with shedding clothes, it seemed. Kara stood naked in all her glory beside Peter, who kept frowning and moving his hands around without touching her.

"Let me try," I said. "I'm more used to this."

I stood before Kara, who spread her feet apart, her arms resting at her side. I'd done this several times with Titus, trying to discover his connection to Anord. And I'd felt the place where his coin used to be— it was like the tissue there was tighter, denser.

So I felt Kara's body with my hands hovering barely an inch from her skin, my eyes closed and my senses alert. My palms prickled and my instinct tried to remove them, but I kept them there. Oily energy swirled inside her, angry at my intrusion—this time it wasn't docile like I just did, but more like probing. "It's like an ultrasound," I said.

"An ultra what?" Kara scrunched her face.

"Sorry, forgot you guys have never had one. I can sense your inner energy."

"She's definitively a keeper, this one," Kara said.

And there it was, under her rib cage. "Here," I said. "Just below her left breast."

Peter placed his hands next to mine. "You're right. It's subtle, but I can feel it now. Now, put on some clothes."

"They'll get stained with blood." Kara shrugged.

"That makes sense," I chirped.

Kara beamed. "Think of it as an encore from last night."

"Make no jest, pirate," Peter said as he unsheathed his sword. "Now, be prepared," he said, pointing his sword at the point where the coin was.

I flinched. Kara had her fists clenched but her gaze was steady. She was ready.

"Hold," Titus said. "Perhaps it's better if I wait outside."

"Too late, little brother," Kara said with her usual simper. "You put me here, you stay put like a good bradaí."

Titus grumbled and leaned on the wall, but his hands clenched into fists. Of course he was worried. He was about to see his big sister wounded by a fae, and not just any fae. The same one that did this to him.

I stood close to him, but his brooding expression made me want to stand on the far side.

Peter tightened his grip on the sword, his knuckles pale against the hilt. A single drop of sweat traced his temple. "This will only hurt for a moment," he said, voice steady but eyes flickering with doubt.

He lunged forward—swift, precise, deliberate.

But Kara moved faster.

With a sudden, predatory grace, she dove for her sword, snatching it from where it leaned against the chair. The blade hissed as it cut the air, now poised between her and Peter. Her eyes glinted, but something unnatural swirled in the depths, darker and fiercer.

"You think I'd stand here looking pretty while you *skewer* me, fae?" she snarled, venom dripping from the last word.

Peter froze, momentarily startled by the malice in her voice.

And then she lunged, a whirlwind of steel and fury.

"Anord's balls!" Titus cursed. "Kara, fight it!"

"What's going on?" I shouted, stumbling back as the clash of swords reverberated through the hut.

"The beast is taking over," Titus growled, shoving the table aside with a sweep of his arm. "Ryanne, help me clear this mess. We need space."

I did as told, moving chairs and anything breakable out of the way. But my gaze kept snapping back to the fight—a deadly, mesmerizing dance of blade against blade. My gaze found the wicker basket, and I clutched it to my chest.

Kara moved like a storm, all raw, unrelenting force. Peter countered her with calculated precision, his movements almost too quick to follow. Sparks flew as their swords clashed, the sharp ring of steel cutting through the air.

"No fae will touch me," Kara hissed, her voice guttural, barely human. Her sclerae darkened, black as a starless night. She faltered for a breath, clutching her temple, and a guttural sound escaped her—a retching, choking gasp.

"I—I can't stop it," she rasped, her voice breaking. "It's too loud in my head." Her shoulders heaved, and for a fleeting moment, her sword dipped.

But then her head snapped up. Her expression twisted into something wild and unrecognizable, and she charged Peter again, a cry tearing from her throat.

"Doyle!" Peter called out, his focus never wavering from Kara's blade. "What's your play?"

"Do it," Titus commanded, his voice grim. "The sooner, the better."

Peter's jaw tightened, and he surged forward, steel meeting steel in a ferocious clash.

I couldn't look away, though every instinct screamed at me to run. They moved like forces of nature, Peter's calm precision against Kara's unbridled fury. The hut shook under the force of their struggle, the walls creaking as they slammed against them. Dust and splinters filled the air as Kara twisted and shoved Peter back, only for him to roll and regain his footing in one smooth motion.

"Kara, stop this!" Titus shouted, his voice raw.

Kara faltered, her breathing ragged. She lowered her blade slightly, her eyes flitting to Titus. For a heartbeat, her expression softened, the feral intensity giving way to something vulnerable, almost broken.

"Do it," she said, her voice trembling. She held her gaze with Peter's. "Do it now, before I lose control again."

Her sword clattered to the ground.

Peter raised his sword. His movements were slow, deliberate, like the weight of the moment pressed down on him. The air grew thick with tension, each second stretching unbearably long.

And then he struck.

Peter shouted Kara's name. Kara was now against the wall, sweaty, Peter's sword embedded in her body. She wailed in agony.

"What the hell?" she screamed. "This hurts! Bollocks!"

"Hang on, Kara!" I said encouragingly.

She locked eyes with me. "Easy for you—"

"Yrsa," Peter repeated, striking for the second time. His eyes were haunted.

"Odin's balls in boiling water, what is this?" Blood poured from her wound, and her knees buckled.

"Hold on," Peter said soothingly.

I turned my head away. While I knew it wasn't fatal—*real* fatal, that is—and she'd live, it still hurt seeing her so vulnerable and in pain.

It felt like watching someone die.

Titus stood his ground, stiffened, eyes on her as if he couldn't tear them away. Was he seeing himself back at Tír D'aois forest?

Peter's brow was damp with sweat. Back then, he thought he was making Titus pay for allegedly murdering his wife, Aghna, something we both found out later that Titus didn't commit, but Edward. Now, Peter was playing a part he wasn't finding as enjoyable as the first time with Titus.

"Yrsa," Peter said for the third time, his sword deep below Kara's breast.

Kara's head lolled to one side. If someone were to peek inside, they'd think Peter had just committed murder and Titus and I were his accomplices.

I rushed to Kara's fallen side. There was so much blood! "The blood'll taint the wood."

Peter squatted and sat on his ankles, damp hair plastered to his forehead. "Bricius will call brownies after this. They'll clean up everything, don't worry. Let us retrieve the coin. Now."

Titus had placed himself by Kara's side and held her bloodied hand. "You'll be fine." His jaw was locked, and he was avoiding looking at Peter, who accepted the basket from Titus.

"It hurts like hell. Doyle, it hurts too much." Her gaze kept trying to stay focused. "I—I . . . I didn't think . . . it'd hurt . . ." Her lips quivered, her feet attempting to find purchase.

Titus's face was strained, his eyes steady on her wound. Kara's hand was pressed against it, blood seeping through her fingers.

"Hey," I cooed. "You'll be fine in no time. The pain will go away. I promise." I removed her hand and pressed one of the towels we brought for this. It was tainted red in no time. "Hurry, Peter!"

Peter retrieved the fine dragonskin gloves we kept in that basket full of goodies and handed them over. I left the towel for Peter to press and took the gloves. It had to be me. Fé Erie had explained that fae's energy was too strong and could kill the bradaí.

Kara's lips were purple and trembling, her skin as pale as death.

"You'll be fine," I whispered to her. "I promise."

"You shall," Peter said, eyes worried.

I closed my eyes and jabbed my hand inside her wound. It shouldn't be possible, but I had done the same when Titus had been on the verge of death. Back then, it felt like his body contained void fillers. Now, I was more sensible to the *dorcha* energy which licked around my fingers and pushed whatever was inside them apart for me.

And I felt it, hard and round.

Carefully, I retrieved my hand. A gold coin rested on my gloved palm, in its center a skull. Without taking my eyes off the coin, I stood up.

"Place it here." Peter had donned gloves as well and accepted the coin, his palms up as he cradled the precious object.

Titus growled low like a wounded wolf.

"Easy, Titus," I said, worried. "Remember this is for Kara's wellbeing."

Titus roared, and launched after Peter, his face disfigured, his jaw locked and saliva dripping from his lips.

Crap.

That was when I realized he was tempted by the power.

Kara's power.

SIXTEEN

Titus

K*ill. Maim. Take.*

The bloody pointed-eared fae held one of our coins. By the Morrigan, this was not acceptable. I tried opening my portal to retrieve my sword, but it was like cement. The fae had tricked us into this.

"You're cheating us!" I roared.

The fae stepped back, the power beacon hovering in his hand. Everything had darkened except for Kara's golden coin.

It is yours. Take it. Her power would make you stronger.

Aye, it was mine. The coin shone bright and called to me. I should take the power. But the bloody fae had it.

Yes. It is your right. Take it. Kill him.

"Titus!"

Someone grabbed my arm. Snarling, I curled a fist and prepared to strike.

Moss-green eyes peered up at me with that softness I'd come to appreciate and love. Her touch soothed me.

No. Kill the fae. Take the coin.

I exhaled hard. Nails dug into my palms.

"Don't listen to it," Ryanne said in a commanding tone I'd never heard from her. "It's trying to control you."

Control.

Hell.

You are better than her. She is only—

"Shut up!" I clenched my teeth, but Ryanne's soothing presence activated *préachta*. She placed a hand on my chest and looked into my eyes. Her *préachta* clashed with mine and together they drowned the beast. My heartbeat returned to what I'd learned was its usual rhythm. I let my shaky hands fall.

"Are you feeling better now?" she asked. "I really need to check on Kara."

Kara.

Hell.

"Aye. Go."

"Are you sure, pirate?" the fae said.

"I thought we were on a name basis now."

"Are you in control, Aódhan?"

"That's not my—never mind. What now?" To avoid eyeing the coin I turned my back on the fae, something I wasn't comfortable with. Though the bastard couldn't kill me twice. On second thought, aye, he could. I placed myself so my back was against one of the walls and Gally on my left.

Ryanne knelt by Kara's side. "Peter, give me a hand? I need her on the bed."

"I'll do it," I said. "He has her coin."

With Ryanne pressing the towel firmly on her wound, I lifted Kara's inert form and carried her over to the bed where I placed her with utmost care. Ryanne took charge and ordered me to bring the stuff she'd brought beforehand—basically first aid for cavemen. Herbs and shite like that but only to clean the wound superficially.

"It's time," Gally said.

"For what?" I'd consciously avoided looking at him, though I kept him visible in the corner of my eye.

"I will give this to my lady."

"And how—?"

A luminescence blinded me. The fae-spirit, Fé Erie, stood next to Kara, her long fire-red tresses swirling against her body akin to a gentler Medusa.

My first impulse was to fight them all and protect Kara. But Ryanne was there, and I trusted her. I didn't trust the spirit creating an energy flower in the air. Gally deposited the coin in its petals, which vanished along with the coin.

"Is that what happened to mine?" I asked.

"By the stars and the storm, yes," Fé Erie answered with a crone-like tone, matching her aged face. "Worry not, Aodhán."

"Don't call me that," I snarled.

"Your Name doesn't have power anymore," Gally reminded me with a tired voice.

"Fine," I grunted, fists clenched. The beast didn't complain anymore when they said my Name. Though I as sure as hell didn't like it.

Fé Erie acquiesced with a nod. "Both coins are now out of your kin's reach."

"They will come for Kara," I said. "She's vulnerable. Can you take us to that cave?"

"Alas, I cannot. We are not in my kingdom, but Gallchobhair's protection will do. She shall be as protected as you were, Aodhán. Remember, you can find the way into the Alpha's being. You and you alone."

My heart thumped. Bloody organ. "Because of that thing you put inside me?"

Her ageless eyes shone bright, whether in amusement or a warning, I was not sure. "My power, not a thing. A full-fledged bradaí could not do it. Only thee have what it takes to finish him."

A half-bradaí. What I had always feared.

What I had always despised.

And yet, it was the key to destroying Edward and finding my happiness. What an irony.

Though with all the murdered fae, it was clear why they wanted Edward gone. It was like killing polar bears at a faster rate than they could procreate. At this rate in a decade, perhaps even less, Tír D'aois would be for Anord's taking.

He could certainly afford the wait.

"What about Kara?" I asked. "Could you infuse your power into her? If she accepts, that is."

"Alas, I cannot do that either. She cannot handle my power at this stage."

Grand. I was the one who had to finish Edward. Which was fitting too: the Omega terminating the Alpha.

The lady vanished in a flurry of sparks.

Ryanne repeated what she did to me in the cave. What she told me she did; I'd been unconscious at the time, like Kara was now. Her touch was gentle and her voice bossy.

I liked that.

Gally joined her and together they placed their hands over Kara's body. Ryanne explained to me in a soft voice that Kara's *dorcha* needed to reactivate in order to heal her, and *préachta,* oddly enough, would help.

The only way to do that was to convince the dark energy that the fae wasn't a threat, by being gentle and friendly. *Dorcha* would be fooled, and *préachta* would only be coaxing it to help with the healing.

"*Préachta* is the nurse aiding the surgeon," she cooed, "which is Kara's *dorcha.*"

I positioned myself next to the window and looked outside. Nothing but trees. This was certainly like my own experience, and if so, Anord would not be aware of Kara's removal of her coin until she stepped outside of the fae protection.

She was safe, and that was all that mattered.

After a couple of hours, Ryanne and Gally stood and stretched. Kara's breathing became stable.

"It's done," Ryanne said. "Now it's up to her. She'll be awake tomorrow."

"It was impressive how you coaxed the pirate's Name," Gally said to her.

"Oh. Well, I did something similar: I just sent my *préachta* as a friend, nothing threatening."

The fae gave a slow nod, as though processing how those two energies worked together. By the Morrigan, I couldn't understand it either. It was good that Ryanne had thought of that.

A bridge. Aye, she was.

"Perhaps we could do the same with Edward," I said, pensive. "Use both energies as one."

Gally straightened his back. "That might work." His usually cold tone hinted at excitement.

This cold fae was someone I could never hang around. Aye, never.

"No, no," Ryanne said with a tired voice. "Kara was willing, and I felt that. Edward would never."

I cast a glance at my sister. "I need a word with Kara. Alone."

Gally didn't discuss the point, being that Kara was unconscious and the coin gone, and strode out, followed by Ryanne.

I sat next to her for a few minutes in silence. "Sister," I finally said. "I let my beast take over me, despite the fae power. Despite Ryanne's proximity. This is too big of a thing to do to Edward."

Kara looked anguished. Pale. I wiped away damp hair from her forehead.

"You can't hear me, I know. I was in the nether world. Perhaps you're there too, strolling alone, wondering what the hell happened. Though you have previous knowledge."

I rested my forearms over my thighs. "And this is what we need to do with Edward. Without knowing his Name, all this feels like gobshite. We're landlubbers left alone in a ship."

And yet, that was our job. There was no escape from it.

No turning back.

SEVENTEEN

Titus

Ryanne took good care of Kara in the following two days, though she kept visiting Frau Engel and company and found true enjoyment with them. That rooting she'd been aching for was surprisingly achieved with this group of strangers. Those group hugs Ryanne had fled from on our first night now were the highlight of her day. By night, she held me tight and wouldn't let go. It balanced her, she'd said, and I felt her calm, without those weird mood swings.

Still, that seer-dream returned, and her forehead beaded with sweat. The same one, she'd said. Fear lurked in her eyes, fear of that strange warrior.

"I'm not sure she's just my fear," she'd whispered.

"Perhaps. But for now, let us assume it is."

Those evolved visions turned nightmares were difficult to understand if we didn't have a clue what they meant, so I'd calmed her down as much as I could. Perhaps we'd have more clues later.

Frau Engel had provided food and anything we might need—she wouldn't hear of me paying expenses. It was an honor to have a real seer on her grounds, and all the rest of the group would follow Ryanne as though she handed them gold in heaps. Although it was only her smile and presence that made them swoon.

Gally's power kept my kin at bay as the spirit-fae promised, so none of my kin bothered us. Anord was indeed oblivious of the fact, for now. Ryanne loved to talk about the fae lands and even about the Erlking to Frau Engel and her retinue, to the delight of her new group of fans. Gally used his glamour to accompany Ryanne at times, and made certain she was safe, which she was—the retreat enforced a no-contact policy with the outside world because the aim was to connect with oneself. No interference of any kind was allowed, but none of the guests wanted it anyway.

Ryanne confessed that Gally avoided interacting with anyone. After briefly peeking inside wherever they were, he would retreat far from the group, preferring to keep to himself.

If they were to know there was a fae on the grounds, or even one of us, I could not fathom what they would do.

I was left with a weakened Kara, and I talked to her during the day, and sometimes at night, like Ryanne did with me, even if Kara couldn't hear me.

On the third day, she finally awoke, and was resting near a window, propped up with several pillows. I sat next to her.

"I feel like a goose without gravy," she grunted.

"You'll be fine. Look." I retrieved a gold coin from my pocket. Too small to generally care, but once it was in our sight, we couldn't stop until we took it. It was our nature. Or rather, the nature Anord imposed on us to do as we were told, like good puppets.

"Hm." She eyed the gold coin. "Feels odd. Like . . ."

"Like you don't crave for it?"

Kara reached out for the coin and played with it between her fingers. She'd always been good at that. She threw it back at me and leaned back on her chair, her gaze lost to the outside.

"I can't hear the beast," she whispered. "Is it . . .?"

"Gone? No, I'm afraid not. It's the fae power around us that protects us from the gold craving."

Which hadn't stopped me from trying to go after her internal gold coin, just to show how powerful that call was. I kept silent though, not wanting to upset her.

"Have we gone soft, Doyle? Are we going to be the fae's marionettes now?" Her jaw clenched. "I'm tired of others controlling us. Of following this bloody voice and being the perfect bradaí by killing and creating mayhem."

"And here I thought you were proud of that." I smirked.

She snorted. "You'd always thought you should try harder. For our Creator to feel proud of you."

"I want out," I said. "I don't want the voice inside."

"But you told me it's not controlling you anymore."

I evaded her inquisitive gaze. "Only when Ryanne's with me. She numbs it."

And by Anord's balls, it was high time I found a way to control it without her. I couldn't rely on her to numb it every single bloody time.

Don't let it control you when she's not around, the nádhúrtha Amriel had said.

Easier said than done.

"Like Phil did." Kara sighed.

"You still remember him?"

"Sometimes. He was the only partner I'd been comfortable with. I can't even remember the faces of any other."

"It seems you have a new one now," I said with a straight face. "A bloody fae, who would have thought?"

She threw the cushion at me, and I caught it, laughing.

"Gimme a break. He's just there for the taking. No way I'm getting involved with a fae." Her mildly amused expression turned sour. "We're getting soft, Doyle."

"Aye. Next thing we know, we'll be behind a desk and—"

She threw the other pillow at me.

"We have the mercenary job," I said. "It's still exciting."

"And now Edward can't pinpoint us to beat our arses." She tried a smile.

"There won't be any Edward, Kara. We must kill him. One way or another."

Her gaze unfocused, she pressed a hand below her completely healed breast, where her coin had been. "Would Sergei do this?"

"I doubt he'll be able to stand a fae more than you. And he won't bed them." I winked.

"By Odin, bring your arse to anchor!"

With a snicker, I was about to stand when she lifted a hand.

"Get him. Bring Sergei to me." Her voice didn't leave room for contradiction, as when she used to be our leader.

"Aye, we'll both do that, once you're safe."

"No, I mean get him *now*." She straightened, a fire in her expression. The fire she always had before we faced Edward.

I liked that. I didn't like her command though.

"That's not a good idea. We both should go."

"I want both of you here, Doyle. *Now*. I just got both of you back when bloody Edward intruded, beat the crap out of us. I haven't seen him since."

"Where's he?"

She shrugged. "Last time I heard, he went to Taiwan to have a little chat with Shen. I have his number, though. I'll call him."

"Not here. I don't want our kin to pinpoint you until you're better. We should wait."

"Since when are you so cautious?" She threw me an askance look. "Get him, little brother, while we have your woman and that pretty fae. I'll convince him, and he'll undergo the same. For me. I know it."

"We don't have our phones. Frau Engel has them." What a lame excuse.

She laughed. "And since when has that ever deterred you? Steal them back."

By the Morrigan. I raked a hand through my disheveled hair. "Very well."

EIGHTEEN

Titus

Gally and Ryanne entered the cabin, Bricius flying above them. This was as good a time as any.

"A word, fae?" I asked.

"I thought we were on first-name basis, Doyle."

"Old habits. Kara wants another of us here."

"When she's up and about," he said, "she can go find them herself."

"You don't understand. We were united, us three."

Gally cocked a reddish eyebrow. "I find that quite hard to believe."

"Really? After all you've seen?"

Gally shook his head. "I don't believe it's a good idea."

"I want Sergei here, fae!" Kara yelled from behind me.

Gally turned to her. "Don't you think I deserve to hear my name from your lips?"

"Those nights deserved I call you by many names, pretty fae. But that's not the point. I need him here. You'll have a third coin."

A struggle crossed the fae's eyes.

Ryanne placed a hand on his arm. "I think it's a wonderful idea. Sergei is Titus's best friend."

"*I* am his best friend," Kara yelled. She seemed to be in the mood to yell. "That Russian douchebag is second."

"That's to be seen," I said, frowning. "But if he agrees, I'd feel more prepared to fight Edward. I already called Sergei, and he's waiting for me. It won't take longer than a couple of hours."

"How did you do that?" Ryanne asked, befuddled. "We don't have—"

"I stole them."

"Of course you did." Her eyes took that emerald fae hue, hardening.

Gally's expression attempted to be flat but his eyes shouted distrust. Of me, of the bradaís. Which was no wonder, after centuries of fighting us.

"Hell," I said. "We let you do this." I waved at Kara. "She's in a weakened state, and you distrust *me*?"

"You are a bradaí, Doyle. It is not an uncommon sentiment."

"Don't be a twit," Kara said. "I put my life in your hands. Now let me have my friend."

Gally glanced at her, then at me. He seemed to be trying to cope with having *friend* and *bradaí* in the same sentence.

"You have my word, Gally. Ryanne can vouch that my word is good."

"It is," she said with earnest. "He is trustworthy when he gives his word."

"Who is this bradaí?" Gally asked. "Why should we trust him?"

"There is no *we,* fae. I trust him. Kara trusts him."

"That is not enough," he said. "I need to know more."

"I don't need your permission." I took a step toward him. We were almost the same height, but I used the extra couple of centimeters I had on him.

He took a step forward until we were almost touching. "I am afraid you do."

"You can stick it where—"

"Guys!" Ryanne eased between us and pushed both away. We only took one small step back but the glare remained. "Talk to Peter about Sergei, Titus, tell him of that time you both found Ivan. That'll do."

I was about to refuse when I looked down at her. Her mossy green eyes were full of fire, though at least they weren't bright fae green.

"I haven't heard that story either," Kara said with amusement. "Tell it, little brother."

I pinched the bridge of my nose. "Very well."

NINETEEN

Titus

London 1852

Thievery pumped in my blood. Stealing from thieves added an extra layer to the fun.

A group of quite successful English robbers had managed to stop a gold shipment heading to the Continent barely a couple of hours ago. Sergei—my brother in arms—had learned of their plan beforehand, and we were about to relieve them of the booty. Gold to us bradaís was the ultimate aphrodisiac; we could never get enough of the precious metal.

London had grown beyond anything I could have imagined since the last time I was there. Not only in size but in the number of souls bustling about, some of them wealthy and lucky enough to receive my attention. Yet for all its growth, only rats seemed at ease in other parts of the city, where humans dwelled in squalor and disease.

More often than not I covered my nose as we walked, the air heavy with sewage. Horse manure was scattered everywhere, thus I was careful not to soil my boots. Soot covered every inch of this forsaken place, making the city even blacker at night.

Sergei and I arrived at a busy corner, dimly lit by a lamp post. Fog surrounded us, although it was light enough to see several yards ahead. This area was less gloomy.

"Are you sure their lair is around here?" I asked.

"You're not patient, Doyle." Sergei raised his hand, and we stood still. The big man blocked my view, but I trusted him.

Two policemen crossed our path. We let them pass. No need to attract unnecessary attention. Right behind them, a gentleman strolled while a pick-pocket relieved him of his purse. I grinned; the boy was certainly brave. He started when our eyes met and scurried into one of the dark alleys.

"Let's go," Sergei whispered. Blond strands of hair brushed his wide shoulders.

We crept in the shadows. I could do this much easier if I were alone, but Sergei brought me here. It had been his idea to plunder together, and why not? Annoying Edward was a bonus since the Alpha couldn't stand it when two bradaís worked together. And if those bradaís were friends, he might even fume. My grin widened.

Sergei stopped at the next corner, opposite the house where the thieves were booked up: a shady three-story townhouse. I lifted two fingers then thumped his back. Two lookouts weren't even worthy of one bradaí.

Blood. Destroy.

Aye, we would.

We turned the corner and strolled aimlessly, shouting and laughing while we embraced. The two men outside the three-story townhouse tensed. The taller one lit a cigar, reddish embers the only color discernible.

"Got vodka?" Sergei asked, slurring his words and leaning toward them in a drunken manner.

"What the Dickens are you doing, foozler?" spat the taller man, taking a step back and thrusting his hand beneath his coat. The other man did the same.

I straightened and retrieved my sword from my bradaí pocket, the humans were none the wiser at our quickness. The thieves raised their pistols. Sergei and I scythed their bodies before they could fire. Stupid humans and their guns—they didn't have the beauty of the clashing blades.

The men fell dead on the street, and we dragged their bodies to a nearby alley.

Clip, clop. Clip, clop.

We pressed our backs against the cold wall and waited for the horses to pass by. Our hands gripped our bloodied swords, ready to hack any fool peering into the alley. Easy killing wasn't something we cared for. Not worth our effort.

Once the way was cleared, we stepped out.

The entrance to the townhouse was locked. Sergei rammed his shoulder against the door several times, and it clicked open. We found the gloomy foyer empty, though we had made enough noise to alert anyone in the house.

Sergei pointed above, and I acknowledged with a nod. The gold was close, I could feel it. A yearning in the pit of my stomach pulled me toward it like a demanding lover's call. Calming myself, I followed Sergei up the narrow, dirty stairs.

A gun went off at the top of the stairs, the bullet hitting Sergei's shoulder. I pushed Sergei aside, jumped the next steps, and buried my sword into the burly shooter's chest. He fell and rolled down the stairs. Sergei groaned and leaped over him.

Sergei stuck two fingers into the wound then pulled out the lead and tossed it. Not even his blond mustache twitched. He concealed pain better than me.

Two more men waited for us at the end of the hall. The first man aimed at my chest, firing at close range. The bullet burned like a sword of fire and a buzz rang loud in my ears. I clenched my muscles, keeping the pain inside. Unlike Sergei, I'd rather let my body dissolve the bullets. The man grinned.

No pain. Kill them all.

I bowed my head a notch, slowly lifting one corner of my mouth. The armed man cursed and aimed again. In a couple of strides, I reached out and broke his neck. His lifeless body fell over the second man, already dead. Sergei was not one for theatrics.

I picked up the pistol, a Colt from across the Atlantic. Perhaps I should go there again. Another man burst into the narrow, dingy hall, and I shot him, trying to understand the allure. The man stumbled at my clumsy shot, and Sergei finished the job. I flung the gun over my shoulder—definitely not for me.

We grinned at each other and stepped over the bodies.

Destroy them. Let the blood ink the wood.

I sang to my beast's tune. Not five minutes had passed before the rest of the thieves in the house could not tell tales anymore.

We stormed into a room on the second floor, facing the back street. Only a wooden table sat in the center. A candle cast a feeble light, shining upon gold coins and ingots stacked in beautiful columns.

Take it all and disappear. You are faster.

My hands clenched as I tried to control myself. I could not betray Sergei. The gold beckoned me. My whole being cried out to grab it all, to leave Sergei behind. I was faster, I could—

Sergei's hand fell heavily on my shoulder. He was struggling too; his sullen eyes told me everything, unfocused and lost for a moment, narrowed the next. But I trusted him, as he did me. The beast might try to pull our strings, yet we fought it with all our strength. When we could. I was sure that, of all the bradaís, only my family was able to do so.

I breathed deeply and nodded. Thumping my back twice, he handed me a heavy-duty canvas bag with reinforced leather straps. We collected the coins and ingots, distributing them evenly.

Shouts wafted from the street whence we came, and we both looked down to the worn and stained floor. The police had noticed the bodies. I cared not; he and I could dispatch them without breaking a sweat.

Sergei pointed at the window on the other side. "Better leave this way; I'm tired of blood."

Stunned, I stood still. Tired of blood?

He lifted his hand in the air and slid his fingers down, a silver line appearing on the path—the bradaí pocket. He dumped his share inside.

I shrugged as he disappeared over the ledge. Before I followed him, I dropped the gold into my pocket.

Someone gasped behind me. The pickpocket boy lingered near the door, looking at me wide-eyed. I winked at him and jumped out the window.

I landed with my knees slightly bent, next to Sergei. We walked into the dark, foul-smelling streets of London.

"This calls for whiskey," I said, wanting nothing more than to sit on deck and empty a bottle.

"Whiskey? *Nyet*, vodka!" Sergei guffawed, thumping my back like he wanted to break it. A warm, brotherly show of affection. An odd thing for us bradaís, not so odd for us friends.

Brothers.

Behind us, the sound of running footsteps. The sound didn't come from soldiers' boots. The uneven rhythm belonged to a loner.

Sergei cracked his knuckles, ready to deal with the new threat. The pickpocket burst from behind a corner where a lamppost futilely attempted to dispel the night. He stopped short, then wended his way toward us. He was thin, too thin for his ten or so years, wearing worn, torn clothes. His cheekbones protruded—the boy was familiar with hunger. His uncertain gaze and trembling hands told me he was familiar with fear too.

"What are you looking for, boy?" Sergei asked.

The boy gulped, alternately staring at the dirty ground and us. He took a deep breath. "Take me with ye." His accent was thick and Eastern, like Sergei's had been when I first met him, more than a hundred years ago.

Sergei and I looked at each other. "Our life is hard, boy," he said. "We're pirates."

"I'll work 'ard." His face was set with determination, yet his eyes mirrored his agony.

"What is your name, boy?"

"Ivan Antonovich." His tone was firm and punctuated with a small nod.

He is weak, useless. Kill him.

No, he was yet a child. I did not have trouble killing a grown-up, but children were off my list. I had to face opponents with at least the strength to hold a sword and wield it properly, otherwise, where was the challenge? I stepped between them. If Sergei's beast told him the same—

Sergei shoved me aside. My fingers curled into a fist. He was stronger, but I had learned a trick or two.

"You Russian, boy?" Sergei asked.

"*Da.* Came with my papa." He twisted his torso to the thieves' lair. "They killed him."

His tone was flat, emotionless. I had seen that before on those who had lost what humans called hope.

"I'll take you." Sergei shook hands with him, relief flickering on the boy's gaunt face.

I unclenched my fist.

"I need hands on my ship," Sergei said, winking at me.

No, he did not, much less a puny and untrained boy.

Faraway noises took us out of our immobility. "Time to go," I said.

Sergei ruffled the boy's dirty blond hair. "You will now be Ivan Sergeivich. You can call me Papa."

The boy's face lit up, and Sergei smiled. I looked at him askance. "Anord's balls! Why do you want a *son*?" We bradaís could not produce offspring. Thank the Morrigan.

Sergei's smile faded, and his eyes hardened as he straightened to his full height. "You say nothing, Doyle."

I clapped the big man's shoulder. "I'll always have your back. Hasn't Kara jabbed us to death with that family shite?"

Sergei cracked a wide smile. "Then let's celebrate with vodka, brother."

No brothers. No friends. Kill the boy.

"Vodka it is." I shivered but held my smile. The beast might protect his crew from him, but not from the rest of us. Though trust was all we had, and I would never betray my brother.

No matter how much the beast insisted.

TWENTY

Titus

"A son."

I thought Gally couldn't be more distrustful. I was wrong. "Aye, he adopted Ivan."

"What happened to him?" he asked.

"You should know. Ivan had a touch of fae."

His eyes hardened. "I remember him. That human left us since he'd developed a bond with your kin, and he was murdered by your friend."

"No. Not by Sergei. By Minho, who . . ." My words trailed. I didn't want to go there.

"Who what?" Gally asked.

"Killed him for fun," I said deadpan, hoping Kara wouldn't correct me.

"You're lying, Doyle," Gally said, "but—"

"I'm not telling you the full story, aye, but it is irrelevant. You wanted to know more about my brother. Now you do."

"Brother." His tongue rolled the word slowly, as though attempting to fathom the meaning.

That was when it hit me. It wasn't us. He'd been alone. Pretty Boy didn't have a real family.

"Peter," Ryanne said, her tone showing the platonic affection she had for him.

I could not feel jealous anymore. I trusted her.

"I think you should let Sergei come," she continued. "He wasn't taken by the call as strongly as others, and he's more like Titus and Kara than any other bradaí. And Kara's right," she said louder when the fae was about to talk, "if you can convince him to give up his coin, you'll have three."

Gally lowered his head in thought, then said, "I'll go with you."

"Hell, no," I said. "Ryanne and Kara would be unprotected."

The fae glared at me.

"You don't trust me," I said deadpan.

"You are a bradaí, Doyle. We might have joined for Ryanne's sake, but do not mistake our temporal partnership with anything else."

"I wouldn't dream of it."

"Okay you two. Enough." Ryanne grabbed my hand and then grabbed the fae's. "You are going to shake hands and stop this. Now."

"Hell no," I said.

"There is no need," Gally said at the same time, his gaze reflecting horror, which was ironic given the couple of nights he'd spent with Kara.

"For me. You obstinate mules. C'mon." She pulled our hands. "Shake."

Begrudgingly, I reached for Gally's hand. Just for Ryanne. I could see in his eyes the same reluctance, but whatever feelings he had for her, seemed to do the trick and he shook mine.

Power electrified our hands and something else lurked in the energy combined.

"The Morrigan take me!" I pulled my hand back at the same time as he.

He didn't curse but surprise reflected in his eyes.

"What?" Ryanne asked, glancing at each of us alternately.

"Nothing." I swiped my hand over my trousers. Definitively not a good idea. "Stay here, Gally. I can do this on my own."

"I am quite certain you can," he answered. "But let us assume for a moment this pirate is held under surveillance. Perhaps your Alpha is nearby thus you need someone to protect your back. I do not wish to take any chances." He gave Kara a brief look.

He could not care for my sister so soon. Bedding for the sake of bedding wouldn't do that, and he already had her coin. Perhaps he'd been alone for far too long, and he wanted more. I could relate to that.

And the fae might be right about Edward having Sergei under surveillance. The Russian was smart, though, and knowing Edward had been following him would make him extra careful—Kara thought he was in Taiwan, but Sergei had already moved.

But the fae was right. If Edward was lurking nearby, having him would be a powerful deterrent. Edward would not dare fight an Eadrom.

"You said it wouldn't take more than a couple of hours," Gally said. "This is a place as safe as we could find in this realm. They shall be alright."

"Very well," I agreed.

Bricius flew around us. "I'll protect them, *mo Thiarna*, yes, yes, yes!"

Gally jerked his head toward the door. "Come."

I addressed Ryanne. "It's better if you keep to the cabin. We'll return shortly."

She laughed merrily. That odd attitude of hers while in Rome had subsided, and she looked like the Ryanne of old. Frau Engel and retinue must have helped. I smirked, proud of myself since it'd been my idea to come here.

"I'll tell Frau Engel that I need to be in touch with the 'divine'"— Ryanne air-quoted—"and 'want solitude for my meditation.'"

"And I'll protect them!" the pixie repeated, sword in hand.

"Contact me right away if you sense something," Gally said to the hyper excited pixie.

"Yes, *mo Thiarna*!"

"Don't you two worry," Ryanne said with confidence. "We've been here for days and they adore me."

"And it'll be good for the pretty fae to see Titus and Sergei in a different venue." Kara winked while sipping hot cocoa with tequila, her new favorite cocktail—she'd hidden a bottle in her bradaí pocket.

Anord's balls. Taking Gally to meet Sergei could be the worst thing I'd done.

Anything for Kara. And Sergei would come running down to remove his coin if he was really on our side. At least he would like to see Kara.

TWENTY-ONE

Titus

Y ou're deluded, Doyle, *da nyet.*"

The big Russian folded his muscular arms. We were in a live band restaurant in Singapore. It seemed Sergei enjoyed this type of venue, something new to learn from whom I used to consider my best friend. It was quite eclectic, electric colors on the ceiling and chairs, shiny wooden floor, and interesting furniture. Ryanne would have loved this.

Or perhaps not. She'd seemed off in the last places we'd been.

"Come with us," I said. "You don't have to agree, but you'll see how Kara's faring. How I'm faring."

"I can see how you're faring, Doyle." He glowered at Gally, who had retired to another part of the bar per Sergei's request. "You're getting too cozy with the fae. Remember that time in Corfu? Everyone called you a fae lover. What's next?"

Fae are our enemies. Kill him.

The beast had been absent, but now it surged its ugly head. It felt confused though, and I'd been pondering about that since we arrived here. I had a fae by my side, but there was no hatred in me.

"That was a manipulation from Edward. You see that now, don't you?"

The tension was still there. Sergei had finally believed I didn't kill Ivan after Minho had confessed to the crime and blamed me.

Bloody Minho, always at Edward's shadow. But then, where else could a fae-turned-bradaí be? I threw a quick glance at Gally. No way could I tell him about Minho and how he came to be.

"I don't like it. This strange fae spirit has your coin, you say, and now Kara's. What if they have another plan, Doyle? Have you thought about that?"

"All the time. But Ed can't pinpoint me now. Hell, Anord can't, either. I'm off the grid. Don't you want your freedom?"

"Does the beast still speak to you, Doyle?"

You should return to the Alpha. Obey him.

Since I'd arrived here, it'd been pounding hard, calling me, upset by the fae proximity. The beast at its best, and I forced myself to not heed it.

Was Anord aware of this? He was after my head but couldn't pinpoint me. Yet the beast was part of Anord's power, a recording of sorts if Anord couldn't find me.

Was Anord disappointed in me? Aye. Like an abusive father.

I swirled the glass and chugged the beverage. "Aye. It does."

"Then we're not free. We're still puppets. Anord or fae, who cares? Tell me it's not there. Tell me it's gone for good. Then I'll believe you. But right now, all I can see is bradaí befriending fae. What's next? You residing in their taighs?"

"We need to put those prejudices aside, big guy." By the Morrigan, I almost choked at this. Aye, Kara was right. I must be getting soft.

Gally chose this inconvenient time to return. "Will he be accompanying us, or will he not?"

Sergei lifted his menacing gaze and bored it into the fae, who sat next to me. Now it was Gally and me apparently sitting on one side against Sergei. Hell.

"You didn't feel the call, did you? About Kara," I said.

"If this is like with your experience, Anord is not aware of the fact yet. Unless the fae tricks her." Sergei glowered at Gally.

"We are not like your kin," Gally said, glowering back.

Sergei dismissed him and addressed me again. "If you've been on the run, you don't know what happened to your ship, *da*?"

I stiffened. "What about it?"

"Minho took it. He's got Homkar."

"Homkar's in Tír D'aois."

Sergei shook his head. "Minho bragged on the bradaí network a couple of days back. Since you're now off the grid, your head has a price."

I sprang to my feet. "By the Morrigan! I'm taking my ship and my first mate back from that gobshite."

Sergei slapped his mug on the table. "Now we're talking, Doyle. In that, I'll help you."

I pondered about why Homkar returned to the human world instead of keeping safe in Tír D'aois. Perhaps he returned to the ship to review it with the crew, something he did on occasion.

"Is this a subterfuge?" Gally asked, glancing at me and at Sergei alternately. "Because you're going nowhere without me."

"Then come, fae," Sergei said, smirking, "and watch how we bradaís work."

"No," I said. "First let us check on Kara, let her see you because that's what she wants. Then we check my ship and recover Homkar." I was skeptical about Minho being able to trap Homkar. Perhaps Sergei was setting me up, though I would go anyway.

"Impossible," Gally said with a shake of his head. "You'll put her, a bradaí, before your ship?"

Even Sergei seemed curious.

"Aye. She's family. Like you, Sergei. You're my brother."

The fae kept his stony expression, but he looked at each of us like he didn't believe what he saw.

"This is no trick, fae," I said. "Kara comes first."

"Let us go, then," Gally said. "I'm troubled regarding the fact that our work could come undone thanks to your not-so-kind kin."

"You heard Sergei. Anord is not aware of what we're doing."

I wasn't worried about Frau Engel, and the energy circle felt akin to what I felt back in the cave with Ryanne. Gally assured me his power would hold while we were away since Bricius was holding it together.

And while Ryanne wasn't the best at following orders, she knew what was at stake now. I checked my watch—it'd been two hours since we'd been away.

Thank the Morrigan for portals.

"We could find out where my ship is once we check on Kara, analyze the situation and return to the cabin before an hour is gone. You can rekindle your energy circle there." I turned to Sergei and hesitated. Back in the day, I'd count on his help without asking. But we'd been apart for decades, and things were not as clear as they used to be.

"*Da*," he said, amusement twinkling in his eyes. "I'll help you get your ship and beat Minho good while we're at it. The bastard went away last time before I was able to complete my vengeance. Nothing will give me more pleasure."

I clapped a hand on his massive shoulder. "Thank you, brother."

He grinned back. "Let's get him, Doyle. Make him pay for Ivan. For what he did to you too."

Sergei extended his arm, and we grabbed our forearms. A strong bond. A family bond.

The fae jumped to his feet, his eyes glazed. "There's trouble." His eyes cleared and he stared at me. "We need to return to the cabin. Now."

TWENTY-TWO

Ryanne

Kara groaned, and I fetched some water. She eagerly drank, her face pale. It reminded me so much of that time in the cave when I had to take care of Titus, though being in the human dimension gave a different kick. I could always go to the kitchen for some food, or head to the meditation group. Or I could join in my favorite, the morning salutation.

Of course, back there at the cave, I didn't want to be anywhere else but with Titus, not to mention I couldn't know for sure back then whether Titus would respond. With Kara it felt so much easier.

"Is this what you did for Titus? By yourself?" Kara laid down her head with a grunt. "I bet he was an arsehole all the time."

I chuckled. "No, actually we bonded very well. It was weird, but nice."

"Ah, yes. That bradaí and human with fae power type of thing. Doesn't end well, though." She looked away.

"Philippe, right? I'm sorry."

She propped herself up with her elbows and gave me a steady look. "Not just him. Ivan. And others too. Like Luc's lover."

"Titus told me about it. That it never went well."

She scoffed. "That's the *bradaí* understatement of the year. Ed kills them all. *Every one of them.* Didn't you hear my warning, little human?"

"Didn't you see me thwarting Edward's attempt to kill Titus?"

Kara let herself fall again. "I was a bit busy feeling lousy while fighting my kin to notice. Tell me all about it; my recollections are fuzzy at best."

I hugged myself, remembering the darkness looming behind those shark-eyes. I settled down with my hot mug. In another time, this would be a wonderful moment. The Engadin mountains loomed outside in the cold, crisp spring weather despite being winter. Here I was in a gorgeous cabin in the middle of the woods, all for free. Well, with some Ryanne performance at dinner and a couple of creeps wanting to touch me all the time. Thankfully Birdie and Mila had been at a silent retreat, though that didn't stop either whenever they saw me.

But a horde of bradaís would be bloodthirsty for Kara's power the moment she stepped outside. If this was remotely like with Titus, they should be confused while searching for her like a pack of mad hyenas without knowing where she was. Outside Peter's ring of power, she'd be advertising her position *and* her vulnerability. I glanced at the wooden door, hoping Titus and Peter brought Sergei back soon.

Besides, how much could they tell Kara? It might not have been a good idea to brag about thwarting Edward's attempt.

"Edward was trying to kill Titus by getting his coin," I said.

"Which he didn't have."

"Right. But Edward didn't know. He was using his *dorcha*."

"It's Luc all over again. And Thomas. Titus has been telling the truth all this time, and no one believed him. Not even his closest friends." She grimaced and reached out for the water again.

"Edward said it was one of the guardians."

"Eadroms, yes."

"It's confusing," I said. "Cuidi said fae weren't involved in those two first killings."

"Who?"

"Lady Cuidigtheach. One of the Erdom—"

"Eadrom. *A-drom.*" She smiled.

"That." I smiled back. She was easy to get along with.

"So how did you thwart Ed's attempt to kill my little brother?"

"Remember the goblin's blade?"

She squinted, then recognition lighted her eyes. "Ah. Yes, the one you found on the floor during the skirmish."

"Minho's. He jabbed Sergei with it."

"Ouch."

"I used it against the Alpha. I jabbed him—"

"Liar." Her eyes hardened as if I was indeed trying to trick her. "You can't just jab the Alpha."

I sighed. "I used my power."

"You must be very powerful." She lifted her blond eyebrows in disbelief. "Fae can't resist him. He's the Fae Terminator."

"No, I couldn't defeat him by myself. Titus has power of his own. Combined we were able to defeat him, if only for a moment—"

Kara all but jumped. She crouched atop the bed in a predatory pose. I jumped back, mug and coffee sloshed over the floor. She snarled.

I was alone. At the mercy of one of the most dangerous creatures who walked the Earth.

No. Not defenseless.

Préachta jumped within me, and I got ready to shape it into a fierce creature.

"You and Titus can kill him," she hissed, her muscles tense. "You *can*."

I opted for the truth. "We're not sure. We might but—"

She launched herself toward me, and I thumped my back against the wall. But I'd been able to shake off a nymph. I curled my fist and got ready to strike.

She hugged me. Tightly.

"By Odin's sacred balls," she whispered, still glued to me. "You're what Titus needs. What all bradaís need. If that arsehole leaves you, I'll kill him, I swear to Odin."

"Is Odin real?" I blurted. *Some legends were real, some weren't. You never knew.*

She guffawed and let me go. Thank Cuidi.

"Oh, he is, little human. He's from the same place as our dear

Creator, Tír na Vraoichta, the dimension of darkness. He's not as obnoxious as Anord, though."

"Have you met him?" I discreetly arranged my clothes.

"Oh, yes. Quite charming, he is. His fame isn't ill-founded, you know?" She winked. "Quite a hunk who loves Norway, where I'm from." She sat on the bed and placed her hands below her left breast, grimacing. "Remind me not to move like that again. I can't wait to walk away from here and not feel that stupid tug ever again."

I picked up the chipped mug, went to the closet for a mop, and started to clean the spotless floor. Brownies—summoned by Peter—had done a marvelous job of removing all the blood after Kara's injury. They might come in handy after we finished here, as payment for Frau Engel's lovely attentions.

"I could use some meat right now. Do you think that crazy gal still has some? I'm starving."

I reviewed the basket they'd left us earlier today. "There's tofu and salad."

"Ack, I can't stand any more of that organic food. I need something more solid. The bloodier the better."

"I can get some food from the kitchen."

"Aren't they going to fall all over you? But you're a dear. I'm really hungry."

"Sure. Just stay put. As long as you're inside, they won't pinpoint you. Peter's power protects us."

"I adore that cute fae. He does wonders in bed." She simpered at me. "He has the loveliest tush I've ever seen."

"Oh, please. Don't," I said, grossed out by the comment. "He's like my big brother."

"And you're like my sister now. You are dating my little brother. I like that."

Tingling washed over me, and I gave her a warm smile. "I like that too. Just call me Ryanne instead of little human."

"You're good, *Ryanne*. I take back what I said in Doyle's ship. Now, off you go and bring me some food. Don't let the whackos detain you."

I laughed and opened the door. The crisp cold mountain air welcomed me along with the usual pine smells, and I picked up one of the sweaters next to the door, a cardigan, since I couldn't bear to have something warmer.

Bricius guarded the outside.

"Where are you going?" he asked, wings perked. "Peter said not to go out."

"Just to get some food. Our patient is hungry."

"I wish I could go with you, yes, yes, yes."

"No, Kara's more important right now." I checked my watch. "They should be in meditation. Perfect! I'll raid the kitchen and be back before you know it."

"Don't take long, no, no, no."

Bricius's words were devoid of his usual worry. It was no wonder since this place was so peaceful. And yet that seer-dream kept coming. Last night, someone called that warrior woman's name, someone big and scary and yet the creature had not appeared. It'd been behind me all the time.

What was the name? It'd slipped the moment I woke up, but I knew it wasn't a name I'd ever heard before.

And that gnome who'd tried to make me go away hadn't appeared again. I should ask Bricius why on the way back.

The pathway was gorgeous to walk on and dispelled any bad vibes from troublesome nightmares. Funnily enough, I wouldn't have minded being in the meditation group. It helped my fae power, and most importantly, meditation helped me root my human side. I hadn't felt that rage or hot-like fever since Frau Engel guided my breathing and inner peace. Once Titus and Peter returned, I'd rejoin those meditation sessions.

Cuidi knew I had to increase my *préachta* if I ever had to fight, like back at the cabin with Kara, though Titus and I were at standby with our powers. Perhaps I should take Titus's offer to train with the sword and—

I frowned; I was no warrior, what was I thinking? The sword and I weren't friends. It hated me and I hated it back. Even as it felt good punching Zadora back at Cuidi's lake, that wasn't something I looked forward to.

Sander's face came into focus and my fingers stiffened. If I were to see that bastard again . . .

That hot-like fever took over, my forehead throbbing. No, I wouldn't let it take over. I pressed the heel of my palm and guided *préachta* like Peter said, then closed my eyes and performed one of the breathing exercises I learned with Frau Engel. The cold breeze, smell of wet grass, and chirping birds soothed that weird anger.

My fae power. That's what I need to focus on.

Let it grow, as Peter said. That was the answer with me and Titus enhancing it. Peter had been right—I couldn't face one of them head on. Not by myself. Not yet.

A golden eagle soared the bright blue sky, and I kept on, my feet light.

The kitchen was empty, and I picked up some cheese and bread for Kara.

My vision splashed with sepia, and sounds faded. I saw Minho walking next to a cabin, a Swiss, all too familiar cabin. I sucked in a breath. And the red circle at the bottom of the vision let me know he was here *now*.

Reality returned with a *pop*. How could he be here if Kara hadn't left the cabin? Had there been a hole in Peter's protection ring? No, he and Bricius checked it, and my pixie friend would have noticed something amiss.

Or did Kara leave the cabin by herself? Bradaís didn't follow rules, even if those protected them.

The sound of footsteps made me tense up. I didn't want to have a conversation with anyone. I had to return to the cabin and alert Bricius and make certain Kara hadn't left.

Birdie came inside. I stifled a groan, not her! Her eyes twinkled.

"Miss Evans! How lovely you're here. I've been dying to ask you something."

"I'd love to, but—"

"Oh this is going to be quick, I promise!" She smiled sweetly at me.

I smiled back. What terrible timing! My heart thumped fast and my eyes wanted to roam about. Where could Minho be?

"How can I become a seer? I'm dying to be one."

"Well"—I glanced through the kitchen window but saw nothing but trees—"I can tell you all about it later. I want to take a restoring nap. A seer's nap, you see? And I'll—"

More footsteps. Heavy ones. The hairs of my nape bristled, and I seized Birdie's arm.

"Or maybe now if you can keep quiet," I whispered while dragging her to the ample larder.

"Here?" she squeaked.

"Shh!"

Whoever it was, was now in the kitchen. It could be someone else, but I couldn't risk it. *Oh, please, let it not be Minho.*

"Is this a game?" Birdie whispered in my ear adoringly.

I nodded and pressed a finger over my lips.

She giggled, both hands over her mouth.

I couldn't call Bricius since he'd come zooming here and Minho would see him. So I tried to be as calm as possible to avoid alerting the bug. But I could call Peter. I scrunched my eyes and called his name, his fae one, three times.

"Are you doing a seer thing?" Birdie asked in a low voice. "I think you are. Can you teach me?"

My shoulders tightened into a knot, and I bobbed my head. Anything to keep her quiet.

"I like this game," Birdie whispered. "I feel I'm your favorite now."

Something was off with her, but I couldn't pinpoint what. Her whacko smile. That's it. She was crazy. Her meditation retreat hadn't helped stabilize her one bit.

I pressed a finger again over my lips. Why was Minho here of all places? And how?

Like that time in the woods when Titus and I walked out of the cave. Minho had appeared, and no one knew how he'd managed to reach us so fast. Titus and Peter should be here any moment. Oh gods, let them be back soon.

The footsteps receded, and I let out a relieved breath. Minho was outside the kitchen now.

"So?" Birdie prodded in the same hushed tones we'd been using. "Am I?"

"What?"

"Your favorite."

"Ah, sure. Yeah."

"I love that!" Birdie clapped her hands together. "I knew it!"

Birdie's face blurred.

"What the heck!" I stepped back and bumped into the shelves.

Thick dark ringlets fell over her shoulders. Brown-yellowish eyes stared at me like a puma. She was no longer plump but taller than me by an inch and lean.

I gasped and pressed my back against the pantry. My seer-vision flashed for a second. The woman in my nightmare had been here the whole time!

"I—I know you!" Oh, Cuidi, what was this? Was she one of the bradaís?

No. Titus and Kara would have recognized her and besides, bradaís couldn't use glamour. Only fae. But it couldn't be.

And how could glamour hide her height and size? Peter couldn't— or didn't—do it.

"You can't remember me, I see," she said, pouting. "Of course, I was in the shadow of someone powerful, so I'm not surprised."

"Who are you? What powerful person?" I asked in my most calmed voice, a hand clutched to my cardigan in a silly attempt to hide my terror. Edward? No, only Minho had been with him.

That powerful creature in my nightmare, the one I couldn't see.

Bricius, Bricius, Bricius, I called in my head since Peter was nowhere to be seen.

She tapped a finger against her chin and pursued her lips. "Hmm, it was dark. That could be it." She beamed at me. "Oh, little darling. You might not remember me, but I'm sure you remember my lover."

Minho stepped inside the larder, and I strangled a scream. He looked exactly as I remembered him–cold feral eyes, black hair tied at his nape—except he was dressed in jeans and a leather jacket.

"You were right, Birdie. You keep surprising me."

"I told you, dear boy. My dreams never fail." She tilted her head and displayed her yellowed, pointed teeth in a smile. "The Irish's woman is all yours, love."

Part Two

TWENTY-THREE

Titus

Sergei, Gally, and I stepped out of the portal and into Engadin Valley. Snow-capped mountains surrounded us, and cold air whistled through the trees.

"Fast way to travel, *da*?" Sergei said, his body alert and hand ready. If he was still carrying the same weapons as before, then he had several daggers concealed in his belt and boots—possibly in his leather jacket as well.

"The only one," I said, distracted. "What is it, fae?"

Gally had kept silent about his distress and seemed focused on returning to the cabin. His jaw was set, and his eyes roamed about.

"Something's off. I cannot describe it for you, nor is there time to do so. Follow me."

Sergei and I stepped behind him like a bloody pair of bodyguards. He looked the part of a rich, spoiled junior, his glamour in place. If Frau Engel or any other in this retreat spotted him now, they wouldn't recognize him from his previous glamour.

We reached the area where our cabins were in no time.

The little pixie bobbed up and down the front of my cabin. He looked relaxed, so I loosened my shoulders. Had Gally had a premonition? It made sense, if Ryanne could see glimpses of the future, then her fae mentor could as well.

The trick here was not to let our guard down.

"All well?" I asked.

"Yes, yes, yes. Who is the big man?" the pixie asked, brow furrowed and wings flapping furiously. He pointed his sword at Sergei. "The bradaí Kara is under my care."

I had to give that to the little pixie. He was brave.

"He's my friend," I said. "Now move."

Sergei clenched his fists. "Reeks of fae."

"Just get in. It's fine," I said.

"You've certainly changed these decades, Doyle." He gave me an askance look. "Fae lover, *da*?"

Fae lover. A moniker Edward gave me to have all suspicions on me and avoid questions. It was the worst thing you could call a bradaí.

When I opened the door, I saw only Kara. She was humming, lying on her bed.

"You're back!" She sat upright. "I thought you were Ryanne."

"What do you mean?" My heart seemed to stop. Was it gone now? "Where is she?"

"She went to the kitchen for some food. She should be back by now."

"Why did she leave the cabin?" I all but yelled. "Was it too much to ask to stay put for a few hours?"

"Hey! I was hungry, all right? Chill. She's fine." She beckoned Sergei. "Come, *dorogoy*. Let me tell you about something fun you should do. You'll love it."

"I'm getting her," I said, turning on my heels and ready to slaughter anyone standing in my way. Why couldn't she heed one bloody instruction?

Sergei greeted Kara, but their words got lost on me. If the fae hadn't had that premonition, I wouldn't mind having Ryanne outside the protected cabin. As it was, I disliked the idea of having her unprotected.

The pixie gasped, his wings perked up. "Ryanne! She's in trouble." Without waiting for us, he zoomed away toward the main cabin.

"Anord's balls!" I dashed after the pixie, that thing inside me beating furiously. Obviously it wasn't going away.

Gally matched my pace effortlessly.

"I don't need your help, fae." Where was that bloody pixie? I slid my hand in the air to retrieve my sword from my bradaí pocket without breaking stride.

"If it's one of yours," he said without breaking a sweat, "you'll need it."

"Suit yourself."

Albeit he was right. A fae by my side while I fought one of mine. Anord be damned. How did they find out about Kara? She was supposed to be safe from Anord's awareness. And if one of my kin dared to touch one of Ryanne's hairs . . .

The grip on my sword tightened.

What went wrong? Sergei hadn't felt Kara's change of situation. So how did any bradaí find us?

"Where is Bricius?" I yelled in anguish.

"He's over there," Gally said, pointing at one of the adjacent buildings that housed the kitchen. The pixie flew around a copse of trees. The lack of human voices reminded me the group was in a meditation session. Grand.

No noise inside the buildings and, extending my awareness, I couldn't sense anything off. Gally was exploring in the gardens, his element.

I approached him and said, "I'm going inside to look. You keep an eye out here."

"Agreed."

"I'm coming with you, yes, yes, yes." The pixie dashed inside.

I followed him with sword in hand and senses in full alert. Inside, a whimpering short woman stood next to one of the kitchen tables. I recognized her right away—it was the crazy plump one who kept stroking Ryanne's hair. Bricius glided from object to object, sniffing everything.

"Where is she?" I grunted, ready to behead the first foe in my sight.

"Oh, thank goodness you're here, Mr. Doyle!" the woman wailed. "He took Miss Evans!"

"What? Who?" I itched to leave the premises, but I needed information. Sword still pointed at somewhere in the kitchen, I looked for clues. Anything that could help me.

"I don't know," she shrieked. "An angel!"

Bricius and I shared a skeptical glance.

"An angel?" I asked to obtain more information while I lowered the sword. Had a nádhúrtha taken Ryanne away? How?

"Yes!" She was crying and tearing her hair. The woman was on the brink of having a hysterical attack. And I was *this* close to shaking her senseless. "He—he opened something in the air, like a window into another dimension"—her eyes widened and her voice lowered to a whisper—"and he flew with her among gold rays. It was so beautiful." Her hands joined as if in prayer, and she closed her eyes. "An angel."

"What did he look like?" I asked.

Her eyes flew open. "He looked like one of those K-pop stars, but grown up. Cute, very cute." She tapped a finger on her double chin. "His black hair—so shiny!—was tied at his nape. What a hunk! Do you think he'll come back?"

Minho. I cursed under my breath. But Minho couldn't open portals. "Was someone with him?" The Morrigan take me. I felt my heart thumping in dismay. Minho would take her to Edward.

Curse all my kin to eternity!

"No. He was so beautiful," she sighed.

"Did he say something?" I asked her, attempting to tone down my anger but by her frightened expression I wasn't successful. "Where did he take her?"

"I can't believe I saw an angel," she whispered, my questions lost on her. "So gorgeous. I wish he'd taken me too, but I'm no seer."

There was nothing more I would get from the lunatic. "Stay here," I snapped. I left the kitchen, sword drawn and looked for the fae. Perhaps he found something helpful.

The pixie flew around, sword in hand and looking anxious. We found Gally in no time, and I filled him in, all the while extending my senses but with the fae so close, his energy interrupted my sensory search.

"Let us return to the cabin and form a plan," the fae said.

We strode back to the cabin, the pixie zooming around us like a bloody fly. But he would do anything for Ryanne and for that, I didn't swat it away.

Ryanne gone. Blood-red spots swarmed in my vision. Minho, or Edward, had taken her away from me. Without her, I'd soon be shark bait.

Was that Anord's intention?

Luc's and Thomas's fates came to mind, the two bradaís Edward had killed and taken their power. My heart clenched as though hit by six pounders. Not just them, but their partners: those I used to believe were killed in the crossfire. But I knew better.

"Do you trust that woman?" Gally asked.

"I don't trust anyone, especially not some crazy woman who was fixated on Ryanne. But Ryanne's not here, and she described a portal. Same thing happened when Ryanne and I walked out of the cave: Minho was there. I'm going to kill that bastard son of a whore." All I wanted was to find Ryanne. Nothing else mattered.

Edward wouldn't take her from me, not even bloody Anord.

"Minho?" the pixie gasped. "He has Ryanne?"

"Minho," Peter said in an afterthought. "The one who murdered Ivan."

"Aye. Edward's left hand."

Bricius wailed and clutched his hair in despair. My jaw muscle twitched, and my grip on the sword tightened.

"Somehow," I said, "Anord knew about Kara and sent Minho. He was the first one to arrive when I went through the same."

Why would Minho of all my kin know how to get me? I would tear him limb from limb, then toss that half-bradaí into the ocean with lead as Edward had wanted to do to Kara.

The fae grew serious.

Sergei stepped outside of the cabin, brow furrowed. "Kara's not well. What did you do?"

"She'll be fine," I said deadpan. "Are you certain Anord didn't send the call?"

"Completely." Sergei tapped his forehead. "It might be thick, but I still hear him."

"Then it's not because of Kara." I frowned. Aye, it was not about her, it was about me. "Anord doesn't know about this, not yet. I need your help now."

"She better be all right, Doyle," Sergei grunted. "Or we'll be back to where we were before Edward."

"Ryanne's not here. Minho took her. I need to know if I can count on you to get her back. Edward will kill her." Darkness engulfed me, but I grit my teeth. Emotions, even those I'd relished on, clogged the mind, and I needed my head clear.

Gally grabbed my arm then released it immediately as though the electricity that shook us before would return. "Kill her. Are you certain?"

"Aye." Again that deep emotion that sent my heart to kiss the gunner's daughter shook me.

"Your woman. *Da.*" He cracked his knuckles. "I'm in, but I won't leave Kara on her own."

"Bloody hell. I need you *now.*"

"No, Doyle, you don't understand. Kara needs me."

The fae watched us intently. By the Morrigan, who would have thought we would be planning something with one of his kind?

"I'll go," Gally said. "I don't want her hurt, and I'd do whatever it takes to get her back."

A fae. Aye, even as I would prefer to go alone, he would be a good asset. "Very well, fae. You come with me. But we're going to need my ship first."

"I'm going too!" Bricius exclaimed.

"Not you, Bricius," Gally said, brow scrunched.

"*Mo thiarna*, I would like to help to rescue Ryanne, yes, yes, yes." His pixie face showed anguish and, knowing how much he cared about her, I was about to say aye, come with us, when Gally beat me to it.

"I need you to handle a special task."

"Yes, *mo thiarna*." The pixie's wings pointed downward.

"But you," the fae said to Sergei, "you look like someone who can help us in our quest."

"My sister—" Sergei began, his fists clenched.

"I understand."

The fae looked like he still didn't, but I kept quiet to see where he was going. I needed Sergei with us even as I itched to retrieve my ship on my own.

Patience, aye.

"Or rather," Gally continued, "I do not understand how bradaís can be so fiercely protective of each other, but I respect that. I also want Kara safe." He scrunched his face as though he was surprised at this. "The best place is my taigh. Allow me to send Bricius directly to it."

"Can you do that?" I asked, surprised.

"I am the rightful owner. The taigh answers to me."

"I don't trust taighs," Sergei snarled.

I placed a hand on his shoulder in a feeble attempt to placate him. Time was running out, but I needed them both, as ironic as it would seem.

Anything to help Ryanne.

"She trusted the fae to retrieve her coin," I said. "She will be safe there."

"I shall talk to her." Gally gave me a considerate glance. "It will be but a moment. Come, Bricius."

Cumbersome thoughts about Ryanne with Minho made my heart twitch.

Hurt.

As though it had been chopped by a fierce ogre then stomped on by a dragon and set on fire. I needed her back. I needed her whole or the Morrigan help me, I would set every bradaí on fire.

TWENTY-FOUR

Ryanne

Minho removed the bag from my head, and I sucked in a breath.

I took in my surroundings. I was in a wooden cabin, but not one tucked into the Swiss mountains. The roll under my feet and the smell of salt and water told me we were on a ship at sea.

A growl erupted from my gut. Once again I was captured, a pawn in the bradaí–fae struggle. No, not a pawn. My fists clenched.

This was the path I took with my eyes open. I was not a pawn but an active subject in my own decision.

"You can't open portals," I said, breathing sharp.

"Who says I did?" he snarled.

"The woman. Who's she?"

He latched a hand over my jaw and dug his fingers in my sensitive flesh. I grimaced. "You're more concerned about her than me, yah. You'll forget about her soon enough."

"What's her name? Her real one."

He gave a cruel smile. "Birdie."

I frowned at him.

I'd already decided I wouldn't show fear, no matter what. Predators feast on fear, and I'd seen that too much with Titus and Sanders. Minho's issue was with his own kin, Titus or Kara, not me.

He had been searching for Kara and found me instead. So I was bait.

And I needed as much time as I could get.

Minho released me and approached a desk, where he opened a drawer.

"Is this your ship?" I asked then remembered he didn't have one as Edward's first mate.

He tensed.

Maybe I could use that. "It's odd you don't have one of your own. I'd always thought bradaís couldn't stand being next to each other for long."

"That's none of your business, seer."

How odd that label still hung to me when I was now much more than that.

He pulled out a black velvety bundle and placed it on the desk.

"It must be quite an important role to be second to Edward."

Before I could blink, he slammed me to the wall. I grimaced, his hand latched against my throat. "I *am* a bradaí," he snarled. "I respond to no one. Do you understand, seer?"

"Y-yes."

I coughed once he released me. He unrolled the bundle exposing a collection of knives.

Minho, that crazy knife whacko, Kara had said, long time ago. Oh dear Cuidi.

I slapped my hands over my throat. No fear, no fear! My knees buckled, and I leaned on the wall. I called *préachta* and let it loose in my body. Strength returned to me like brownies to a dirty kitchen, filling me up.

"Were you, were you a . . . hunger? Hunter!"

"Hunter." He stopped what he was doing and lifted his head. "Yah. We all are." He reached for one of the knives. A pointy one.

A *very* pointy one.

I wanted to scream in fear, but I didn't want to give him that pleasure.

Not for the first time, I recalled Cuidi's words about this situation being over my head. Totally over it. I was at the bottom, flat as a pancake, and the situation was the roof of Dubai's super-high tower.

And yet, I wanted this. *So suck it up, Ryanne. You've already defeated a nymph. You can do this.*

Préachta stirred and expanded like a rubber ball. Calm. I had to be calm and call the ogre.

Red points floated on a sea of mist, a vision I had while I jabbed the knife into Edward. That warrior woman flashed briefly in the desolated land with corpses at her feet. I blinked to dispel the unwanted recollection.

"So Edward is captain here?" Any information I could obtain might help at the end. "How powerful is he?"

He lifted the knife against the light. "Our Alpha is more powerful than any of us. Even famous Doyle." With a disdainful gesture, he waved a hand. "Famous. I'd seen him dozens of times under my captain's boot, never able to touch him."

Where was the Minho who'd wanted to be out of Edward's shadow? Perhaps he'd been lectured. Brainwashed and deluded.

"Don't you know what Titus and I did to your precious captain?"

He glared at me. "Barely a scratch. You two pulled a nice trick, but it won't be repeated."

Minho had been outside when Edward staggered, weak after what Titus and I did. Surely Edward put up a good front, and no bradaí was the wiser.

Minho stood before me, the knife glinting. "I don't agree with my captain. There's a certain beauty in you." He pressed the cold edge against my cheek. I tried to hold his stare, empty like that of a shark. "Not perfect, yah. But I can make you perfect." He pressed harder and a white point of pain erupted.

I pushed his hand away, my other hand on his chest, but he held on. He was quite strong.

A sharp pain as the metal slid down. Something wet on my cheek.

I bit my lips to trap my yell and pushed harder. The knife kept its path of hurt.

"Oh, yah. It's a shame your pale skin is now tanned. Red goes very well against pale skin. But it would do. Beautiful," he murmured.

The whimper came unbidden from my lips, my chest heaving.

"Cry. Ask for mercy. Beg for it on your knees." He kept sliding the knife over my throat, ever so slightly but deep enough for the pain to follow the path. And the blood.

My hands shook from the effort of pushing him away, but my human force wasn't a match for his *bradaí* strength.

I pulled my lips tight. *Préachta* had covered my chest and thumped against it. It was looking for a way out.

Out.

I stared unblinking at him. My cheek and neck stung, but it was forgotten when he pressed on my collarbone. More pain, like a burning metal, but I managed to bite back the yell and pressed my shaking lips tight.

He pulled a sad face. "No! You have to beg. Whimper and do those silly things humans do. Move so my knife creates a work of art on your body."

I seized his wrist, and he laughed.

With my intent and direction, my fae power burst from within and into him. He took a step back like someone who'd been electrocuted, his face contorting.

The knife thumped to the floor.

I poured more, my eyes narrowed, my focus on pushing *préachta* out of me and giving it direction—a purpose.

I embodied the very essence of an ogre. While it happened inside my head, I felt it was true. I felt myself stronger, taller. I growled and punched his face.

Minho recovered fast, beads of sweat trickling down his nose. "That's not how it goes." He punched my face back to prove his point.

My cheek stung, and I pressed against the wall, angry and fearful. Angry at myself, for not being a warrior. Fearful of feeling I could be one.

But it was that or bust.

Red points floated before me, and anger took over. Hot fever erupted.

"You're not touching me again!" I snarled. One of my hands found a way to latch against his throat and the ogre took control.

I was powerful.

I was Ryanne.

I knocked the knife from his grip, and I hit him. On his face, on his side, while I yelled and felt stronger. He staggered, surprise reflected in his cold lifeless eyes.

That heat inside me grew and fed the ogre. Blood spurted from his mouth, but he reacted and hit me so hard on my stomach I gasped for breath and crumpled to the floor.

It was then when roles were reversed. Minho latched his hand over my throat, and I gasped for air, frantically scratching at his hand.

A sharp pain hit my ribs, then the sharp point of a dagger pressed against my collarbone.

My head was about to explode with the pressure, and panic gripped me. I felt about to faint, my ears ringing, white dots covering my sight. My nails dug deeper, but he kept throttling. Was he going to kill me? Was I going to die?

Then he released me, and I coughed, my lungs coveting the precious air. Oxygen rushed to my brain and for a moment, I felt elated. Futile information about how that feels after being strangulated. How long had that been? Too long and it would be fatal.

I coughed more and *préachta* roamed my body, filling it, healing it.

Minho smirked. "No, little bee. You act like a fae, and I'm surprised. But make no mistake." His eyes hardened. "Don't try that trick again or you'll feel the bite."

He pushed the dagger harder, and I whimpered. "Stay put," he said, and proceeded to tie my hands above my head.

I struggled against his weight, but there was nothing I could do.

Blood seeped from my cheek, from my collarbone, and my ribs throbbed.

But I was bait. Only bait. Minho wouldn't kill me.

Just torture me.

He forced me to stand up and pushed me against the wall. "Look, I have a full repertoire." He waved a hand toward his utensils, and I glued my back harder to the wooden wall. I felt the chips behind it, its unevenness. And we were at sea. Titus said he had never been able to pinpoint

Edward while at sea. And Peter couldn't either. So they wouldn't find me until Edward wanted them to.

My knees buckled under me, and I had to press my back to the wall to avoid falling on my face.

"Ah, much better!" He seized a chunk of my hair into his fist. "Beg."

"No," I snarled.

"They always do. Be brave now, little bee. But you'll beg, I can guarantee it. There is a way for you to stop this." He lowered his head a notch and watched me under his lashes. "Yah?"

"What do you want?" I spat.

"Nothing much. Tell me about Doyle. What makes him special?"

"What?"

"I want to know how he moves so fast. How he escapes from impossible situations." He squeezed my jaw. "I want to know"—he squeezed harder, and I whimpered—"how can he submerge in the sea for so long without coming up for air. What is his relation to the sea?"

His breath roamed my lips, fingers painfully digging deeper.

"I won't tell you," I spat again.

"Oh, you will. It's just a matter of when and how much pain you're willing to handle." He released me and fetched a different knife. "I've always wanted to try this one."

Hate erupted from my gut. Hate of being manhandled like this, not only with him but also that time with Sanders, where he'd left me down to my skivvies in the middle of that dingy room. My teeth clenched so hard it made me forget the pain in my body. I struggled against the ropes on my hands to no avail.

Don't let them get to you came Peter's voice from a memory, from that time in the taigh.

The door opened wide, and the warrior woman with curly black hair sashayed inside. I pressed more against the wall, my hands trembling.

"I told you to wait outside," Minho snarled.

"You'll want to know this piece of news, love." Birdie stood before me and lifted my chin. "The bradaí is coming here to find his ship."

"What?" Minho cursed. "How did he know?"

"That huge friend of his. The Russian. Why is there blood on your face?" she said to me in a purr, her fingers caressing my cheek.

I cringed, remembering how she effortlessly murdered people in my seer-dream.

"I'll take care of him," Minho said, brows pinched.

"Why so worried, love?" she said, turning her attention away from me, thank Cuidi. "My big friends are here. They'll help."

"They better," he said. "The ship is not yet mine."

I put it together. We weren't on Edward's ship; we were on Titus's. Though I was still under the control of two psychopaths, I felt enormous relief.

The transformed Birdie pouted. "This is your big chance, don't spoil it."

"I know!" Minho threw me a damp towel. "Wipe your face. But don't look so relieved. The Irish will never have you again. You're mine now."

"Like hell," I spat.

He bared white teeth against brown skin. "Oh, little bee, you have no idea what's in store for you."

"I'll take care of her." Birdie winked at him. "And no need for this little bee to be tied up, is it?"

Minho snickered as he stepped out of the cabin. I doubted it.

I was certain Minho was lying and didn't have Titus's ship. Wasn't that what Titus said, that all bradaís were a bunch of liars?

TWENTY-FIVE

Titus

Fae and bradaís never mixed, not for hundreds of years. Not ever. And yet, here I was, with the one who used to hate me the most.

Admittedly, having a fae could be handy while getting my ship and recovering Ryanne.

It hadn't been hard for me to sense my ship, even easier with Sergei's information narrowing the area down. The *Scáil Dragún* was mine, and as long as she was in any body of water, I could pinpoint her. Besides, there were few places Homkar would have docked her, and I'd been lucky to find her in the second place we looked: a deserted island in the Pacific.

We were on a vantage point, hidden behind some bushes, the tranquil and deserted cove some twenty meters below. Gally was at my right and Sergei at my left; my friend watched with distrust at the fae, and the fae paid him back in kind with contemptuous looks. The only reason Sergei had accepted the fae was the same reason I did; besides Sergei could have what was left of Minho when I was done with him.

I looked past the beach at my ship. I squeezed the pommel of my sword. Humans strolled on deck, looking at ease.

Kill them, burn them. They took away your ship.

I closed my eyes, calming my breathing. I needed my head cool right now, not the beast dominating me. Ryanne would have helped.

That half-bradaí's corrupted energy stained my ship. The nerve.

My eyes scanned for Minho. If he was here, Ryanne was too—bradaís always kept prisoners in our ships. At this thought, my heart thumped faster. It was odd, but I was getting used to its displays of affection or distress.

"It surprises me the ship is docked," Gally said.

"The *Scáil Dragún* won't sail away with just any captain. Our ships never do—if Minho plans to sail, he needs to own the ship. That is not an easy endeavor."

"What is your plan then?" Gally asked.

With the coldest look I could muster, I replied, "Kill them all."

I smirked at his shocked look while Sergei chuckled. But it didn't last long. His eyes turned as cold as mine, but in his case, the cold looked like an iceberg.

Tie him up now that he is distracted. Control him.

My hands twitched and, for a moment, I thought of doing so. Bloody beast.

I needed to control the beast, or this mission would end faster than a ship sinking in Cape Horn.

"It's getting to you, isn't it?" the fae said, deadpan. "Your darkness."

I growled, my gaze fixed on the human crew who dared to tread my ship. I only had to hold out a few minutes more. Ryanne would soon be back to me.

"Aye," I admitted. "It's telling me to kill you."

His quiet laugh made my blood run cold.

"I'd like to see you try. Give me an excuse, just one."

"I almost beat you once, if not for your spirit protector. Remember that."

"You did?" Sergei asked in surprise.

"Almost one out of many, many times where I triumphed," Gally said in an amused voice.

I narrowed my eyes at the remembrance of the last time we crossed swords when he buried his sword in my side, dealing a fatal blow that would have cost me my life if it weren't for Ryanne. My heart trembled at her memory, of her sweet touch. What an inconvenience to have a heart when I needed to focus. I couldn't afford to think about her now.

And yet, all I could think about was her in Minho's hands.

"Let's—" I started.

"Fomorians!" Sergei growled.

"This is unbelievable," Gally spat under his breath.

The Morrigan take me! Two of the gigantic creatures roamed the beach. Hideous-looking deformed monsters who came from the darkest parts of the ocean, places not even I dared to go.

It was uncommon to see them outside Tír D'aois in this century, but creatures from that realm were able to come and go as they pleased, creating havoc among humans and birthing legends.

The human crew weren't looking their way. Technology and modern times made them skeptical and blind to anything, even if it was right in front of their faces. Despite the fact that the monsters walked just a few meters away from them, their brains didn't process the oddities and discarded them.

"I thought they only obeyed the Erlking," I said quietly.

"They do," the fae answered, obviously annoyed to see them guarding a ship.

"I can handle one," Sergei said. "I've fought them before."

"I'll handle the second," Gally said. "They're formidable fighters, but I believe we can do it."

"Hold." I placed a hand on his shoulder then removed it right away when my fingers prickled with energy. "Don't show them you're an Eadrom. You're my bow chaser."

"I beg your pardon?"

Sergei explained before I did, "His wild card. You understand that, fae?"

Gally dipped his chin.

Minho emerged from the cabin. From *my* cabin. Ryanne was here. My heart thumped in what I was starting to interpret as hope.

"Is he the bradaí?" Gally asked.

"I'll take care of him," I said.

"Leave me something before you reduce him to a pulp," Sergei grunted, his body about to launch forward. He was itching to fight and possibly maim Minho instead of the monster.

But it was *my* ship. It was I who would take care of Minho first.

"What about the crew?" Gally asked.

"Didn't you hear me, fae? I'll kill them all," I said.

"No shedding blood. They have no part in this," Gally said.

"They did since they set foot on my ship," I said, my voice dry. They wouldn't even know what hit them.

Yes. Kill them all. No mercy.

Gally patted my shoulder quickly as though I was radioactive. "Ryanne is here, Doyle, isn't she?"

I blinked at his touch, at the small exchange of energies neither wanted to dwell on, and the blood lust subdued. "Aye."

"Let us focus on her, then."

As much as I loathe accepting it, he was right.

Stealthily, we approached the beach covered by vegetation. We had inspected it previously, making sure no one would appear in the middle of the attack. Not to mention I knew this place quite well.

Take your ship back. Kill.

The muscles in my arms tensed as my jaw clenched from the tension. There would be no more pointless killing, no more blood. Shoving away the beast intrusion, I concentrated. This hit was vital.

I couldn't afford to fail.

Ryanne couldn't afford me to fail.

Gally and Sergei were already ahead, blending into the undergrowth. The fae knew how to ambush, I had to give him that.

The fomorians stopped, their beady eyes scanning around. One had one leg and the other only one arm, both had a large humped back and purple gray skin. They wore scraps in lieu of clothes as was their wont.

Knowing I could count on Sergei and Gally to take care of the monsters, I took a deep breath and blended with the Shadows. Sepia and blurred images took over, coldness seeping through my clothes, my hair, my skin. The shadows around the trees became thicker, darker. Sounds from the ship became distorted, as though I was underwater.

I slipped unnoticed through the underbrush then across the lowered plank. My focus on the real world, I left the Shadows and colors poured in, breaking through the sepia tones. Warmth returned to my limbs.

I boarded my ship, thirsty for blood and vengeance.

Minho started at my sudden appearance, his usual hatred reflected on his expression.

With my sword tight in my hand, I let loose a war cry and aimed a killing blow at Minho's skull. With a speed he didn't use to have, he blocked with his own sword. We glowered at each other. He was barely a few centimeters shorter than me, our faces contorting with the effort, the veins in his arms standing out under the light-brown skin. Beads of sweat ran down his forehead.

"Where is she, you miserable half-bradaí?"

His coal eyes, dark as the pits of hell, gleamed.

"Where?" I shouted, pressing more.

"Oh, Irish, Edward has her now." He laughed. "You've lost her."

"You're lying, you son of a whore."

"Am I?" He smirked. "Perhaps I am, or perhaps she'll be dead before you find her."

Images of Luc's lover reaching out to him, dead but with Ryanne's features, came to me.

Dead. Gone.

With a scream coming from my gut, I released the pressure and kicked him in the stomach, causing him to stumble. Before he scrambled away, I put the sword to his neck.

No mercy.

Before I could deliver the blow, he contorted his body like a Cirque du Soleil performer, though back in my day, we'd call that courting the devil himself. Minho screamed a name and jumped overboard.

"You bastard!" I yelled. "You don't cut and run!"

I dashed to the rails and caught some movement above the waters: a flash of thick ringlets and a female face. There was no splash. What the hell?

I threw my sword to the deck, retrieved a dagger, which I placed between my teeth, and jumped into the sea, blood boiling in rage.

But I found no Minho. I swam around, the waters murky to the normal eye, but then, I was no normal being. I could see clearly in a wide radius.

The waters embraced me in a welcoming hug, and I felt my muscles relax. It had been so long since I'd last submerged in the ocean. If it weren't for Minho and the need to find Ryanne, I would have stayed here all day. But I couldn't dally.

Where in Anord's hell did the bastard go? From the strange creature I glimpsed, it was certain he must have used a portal, as there was no bradaí around.

Vibrations covered my body like a wounded Yell, and I whipped my head, just to see one bloodied fomorian cutting through the water. It was escaping.

The second one followed suit, both disappearing before I even blinked. But no Minho.

How? Frustrated at his disappearance, I focused on the dragonwood and used the anchor's chain to climb back.

The human crew was in total disarray, screaming in terror. It took me a second to notice the cause of their fear—a bánánach erupting from below deck. The shrieking demon was too close for the humans to dismiss it; even if they couldn't see its goat-like appearance, they certainly sensed its violent energy.

A demon and fomorians. What was Minho playing at?

The bánánach and I stood face to face while the crew jumped into the water.

"This is my ship, hellish demon," I declared, standing my ground with my sword gripped tightly in my hands. These creatures were among the scariest to humans, but not to us. They reveled in death and violence, but so did we. Unlike my usual gusto for the fight, I hesitated. I could be mortal. But this was not the time to test whether I was or not.

The bánánach shrieked and lashed a hand at me. I ducked. Under other circumstances, I would not hesitate to engage the demon, but Ryanne could be below. Minho had lied, I knew. Why else would he have had a demon like this?

The demon shrieked and pierced my ears. I took a step back. Heart thrumming, I winced. When had a bradaí shied away from a demon?

Sergei cut its hand with a sword strike. The demon hissed and focused on his attack, deeming me no threat. After Sergei successfully parried his attack and sliced through the creature's other hand, it retreated into the ocean with another piercing shriek. Two soulless bradaís might have been too much for a demon who collected souls.

"Another Erlking creature," the fae said, his chest heaving and clothes damp.

Both of them held bloodied swords.

"Why didn't you use your power?" I demanded the fae. "The bánánach could have skewered me if not for Sergei."

Gally stood, rigid, less than two meters away from my friend. "Water."

I'd forgotten about that detail, the safety net of my kin against the fae in our element.

Normally I'd make fun of Gally's impotence, but all I could think about was Ryanne. My heart thumped painfully, and I looked for her in my cabin and the captain's mess. The fae and Sergei searched as well.

"She's not here," I said, attempting to put my emotions in check.

I dashed below deck. She should be there, and safe. Minho would not have killed her . . . only tortured.

The Morrigan take me! I ran faster.

TWENTY-SIX

Titus

"Careful, Doyle," Sergei warned as I reached the bottom of the stairs. "There could be more traps."

I extended my senses, resisting the urge to charge headfirst into every bloody door. Sergei was right; it was better to be prepared.

"I don't sense anything. You?" I asked Sergei.

He shook his head. I glanced at the fae.

"Alas," Gally said, "we creatures from Tír D'aois have our senses dimmed in this dimension. We cannot sense others, I'm afraid." He looked almost sick, perhaps from the feeling of being trapped in the ship.

In another time, I would have smirked. Instead I exchanged a look with Sergei. No wonder fae had a hard time finding us here.

Perhaps that was why Anord created us here rather than in the fae realm.

Grunts and muffled cries came from the crew's mess to our left. I jerked my head down the hall, signaling Sergei to search. Gally was behind us. I signaled him to follow Sergei while I entered the mess. It reeked of human waste and foul odors.

Some of my crew were tied up, bruised, and gagged—Stephen,

Mouse, and four others. I glanced around but couldn't sense anything off.

"Where's Ryanne?" I asked, nay, demanded, while I untied them.

"We saw her with the pirate," Mouse said, shivering, "but we couldn't see where he took her."

"Captain!" the redheaded Stephen, my helmsman, said with relief. "Homkar escaped to alert you. There was a demon. Is Homkar safe?"

"Where the bloody hell is he?" I yelled.

Stephen didn't wince, used to my bad temper. "We don't know. We were thrown here. Minho said he would untie us only if we pledged to him. We didn't, sir, not one of us wavered."

Something raspy lodged in my throat as I acknowledged them with a nod. Those bloody feelings could overwhelm me if I wasn't careful, and they made me want to shout even more.

Sergei peeked inside and said, "Doyle, you want to see this."

The rest of the crew gave me thanks I hardly heard. Some retched and most staggered. They would have to work hard to clean this mess.

Sergei pointed at the cabin, the one I was going to place Ryanne in, so many months ago, when I thought I'd kidnapped her from the taigh. Fae's games.

"Ryanne!" I exclaimed with relief yet terrified of what I would see.

"No," Sergei said. "Your first mate."

I glanced behind, where the crew was standing at the foot of the stairs. "Search the berths and engine room for Ryanne. Leave no place unchecked."

"Yes, sir!"

"And all of you take a bloody shower once you're finished. You stink."

"Yes, sir!"

I doubted she was on the ship. There was an emptiness in me I hadn't had since Gally took her away from me, that time in Rome when Sanders captured us both. Despite my orders to search the ship for her, I knew she was far from here.

The Morrigan curse Minho for all eternity.

Gally was inside the prisoner's tiny cabin, crouched next to a bruised and bloodied Homkar who lay on the cold floor. A gag was below his chin. The fae was working on the bindings.

"You look bad," I said, fists clenched.

"Not worse than when we first met," Homkar said, his voice hoarse.

"Get some water," I said to Sergei.

I waved the fae off when he finished. Understanding my request, he moved aside, and I crouched next to my loyal first mate, who barely moved from his initial position.

"Never thought Minho would be able to bring you down, my friend."

Homkar glared, and I smirked. If he could still be upset then he wasn't so hurt.

"Minho would have gone down quick if he hadn't brought that demon. It took me by surprise." His lips twitched in disgust, briefly like lighting striking the sea. "But I would have defeated it if not for the fomorians."

We grasped our forearms, a fierce smile on my face. By the Morrigan, seeing my friend and loyal first mate somewhat safe brought peace to my being.

Emotions swirled in me, and I pulled him to hug him tight. Homkar, unfazed, thumped my back in brotherly affection.

"Careful, Doyle," Gally said, that surprised tone of his present. "Your first mate is wounded."

I released from the embrace and arched an eyebrow at the fae. He had that same puzzled expression when Sergei and I were worried about Kara.

"He's tougher than you think," I said.

"Nevertheless," Gally said, "I'll heal him. Move."

Despite the curt order, I obeyed. Homkar came first.

Gally placed a hand on Homkar's chest and another on his own. My first's mates expression softened, and he closed his eyes, releasing a long sigh.

"I thought your power was inhibited." Yet, I felt oddly grateful that he was healing Homkar.

"Not my healing powers," he said softly, "those come from within. Nothing can thwart them."

"What are your orders, Captain?" Homkar said, still with his eyes closed.

"Heal. You are no use to me wounded."

Homkar smiled again while Gally turned his head slightly toward me, as though reassessing his judgment, still uncertain despite what he'd witnessed.

Fae.

After helping me move Homkar to his cabin and leaving him to rest, the fae and Sergei followed me up on deck. Stephen, the one who knew my ship as good as I, had searched high and low, but no Ryanne. Those pesky emotions, the ones attempting to take over my body, my reasoning, my inner peace, clogged me, and I could barely breathe.

Gally glanced at the waters with distrust, making certain he was far from the railing.

"You won't be of much use against Edward," I said with a note of steel in my voice.

"Is that where we're going, Doyle?" Gally asked.

"We're after Edward," Sergei said at the same time. "In the ocean." His voice denoted distrust.

We'd never been able to hunt Edward here.

"Minho said Edward has Ryanne," I said.

"He's lying," Sergei said. "He was taunting you."

"Perhaps. But I see it this way: she wasn't here, so Minho might have been trying to lead me astray. And he had Erlking's creatures, although the Erlking let Ryanne go. If the Erlking truly wanted her, he wouldn't need Minho. Thus, Edward."

All paths led to Edward.

I glowered at the ocean, at the point where Minho had vanished. Those creatures, the fomorians and the bánánach, or perhaps that strange woman who snatched him, they were the ones opening portals for Minho for him to vanish like that. No wonder I could not detect him before.

"And if he wasn't lying," Sergei said, "he knew you'd never catch Edward."

"He wants me to despair. To know I've lost." I turned to Sergei. "Did Minho see how we beat Edward, back at my apartment?"

Sergei stared at me. "You haven't told me how you did it." He waved a dismissing massive hand. "You'll tell me later. Edward only looked mildly discomforted once you two vanished. If you indeed beat him, Edward would never show it."

"So Minho believes Edward's untouchable," I said, pensive.

"Then I'll wager he won't expect you chasing after him," Sergei said.

"Or she's bait," Gally chimed in.

Sergei and I looked at the fae.

"There was a witness, the human who saw Minho take Ryanne. Why would Minho leave a witness?"

"To let you know he has her," Sergei mused.

I glanced at the ocean and its waves, begging them to tell me where Ryanne was. Did they miss her like I did? "It doesn't matter, whether she's bait or not, he's expecting me to chase Edward."

"Then we'll go after her," Gally said, defiance in his eyes.

"You won't be able to help much," I said, sighing.

"That's why I'm here," Sergei said happily as though he hadn't been forced to come and leave Kara at the fae's mercy.

If it weren't for the dire situation, I'd laugh. Kara would never be at anyone's mercy.

"I can still fight," Gally said, defensively. "My power is the only thing constrained."

"We need to set sail," I said. "But first, I need to take my ship back. You two stay away from me."

"Aye, Captain," Sergei said with a gleam in his eye.

I forced myself to relax, remembering those early years when I started my training. Finally, control came to me. That control that had cost me so much work since I left the cave.

The cave Ryanne had taken me to save my life after Gally's sword blow. The cave where everything changed . . .

I shook my head. *Concentrate.*

I took a deep breath, feeling the energy return to me.

My ship.

I ran a hand over the rail, feeling it creak under my touch. My brow furrowed—Minho's disgusting mark contaminated my ship. It was time to cleanse her.

With a couple of strides, I jumped over the space that separated me from the helm. I grabbed it and closed my eyes. A dark feeling took possession of me, the bloodlust crying out for Minho.

Bloody half-bradaí. If he thought he was going to be able to take Ryanne away from me and that I was going to let him get away with it, he was wrong. I would hit him back so hard he wouldn't even know where it came from.

But first, I needed my ship back—one step at a time. I concentrated on the ship, on every part of it. First on the mainmast. Mizzen pole and ratchet pole. The forecastle where Ryanne and I watched sunsets.

Bradaís were lone creatures by conception. Our *dorcha* never interacted well with others of our kind, as Kara and I experienced first-hand when we tried to attack Edward.

When any of us obtained our ships—after decades of attempting to find the Valley of the Dragons in Tír D'aois for the dragonwood and stealing sea nymphs' tents for our sails—our first task was to imprint our ship with our *dorcha*, to avoid another bradaí stealing it.

And that was what I was doing now: sensing each part of my ship and using my *dorcha* to remove Minho's.

I continued with the bowsprit, the stern gardens, and the poop deck, intentionally sweeping Minho's footprint. I'd been prepared to sense resistance from Minho's *dorcha,* thus making this process long and tedious. Instead, it was as though he'd slapped his *dorcha* on like a crappy painter who'd been in a rush and didn't take the time to do it right.

I allowed myself a satisfied grin; the idiot didn't even know how to properly take over another pirate's ship. This would be much easier than I thought.

Once the surface was cleaned, I concentrated on the castle, the batteries, the rudder, and the keel. Minho's last footprint disappeared, and my ship responded to my touch, to my thoughts.

The *Scáil Dragún* was mine again.

TWENTY-SEVEN

Ryanne

Once Minho left the cabin, Birdie lifted her fingers and wiggled them, silver sparks flying out like I'd seen Titus do. Who was she?

More importantly, *what* was she?

"Come, sweetie," she cooed. "There's a surprise waiting for you. You'll be so comfy there."

I barely had time to open my mouth when she grabbed me in a bear hug. After wisps of fog and whispers in a strange language, my breath was knocked out of me, and I was in another cabin.

"What happened?" I asked, dizzy and terrified of her.

She clenched her raised fist, those sparks flying around it, and smiled. "You're now home, sweetie. Where you belong."

"You don't know where I belong."

"Oh, I know more than you think. One thing is sure, you're far away from your lover's hands." She blew the sparks in my face. "Sleep now, sweetie. You'll need your strength against the Alpha."

When I awoke, I was on the deck of a strange ship, while sea nymphs sang a lewd sailor song in the water below. I frowned. Since when did they sing *those* songs?

Their music and joyful expressions vanished, and terror reflected in their eyes. Blood blossomed all around them, tainting the waters crimson. Black threads stitched closed the empty orbs where their eyes should have been. Suddenly they vanished into the churning waters as if the Kraken pulled them to the depths.

I stiffened, hands clutching the rail. What happened?

"They deserve it," a woman croaked next to me.

She was wearing the leathers I'd seen her in before, her sharp nails tainted in blood and her long ringlets hiding her face in disarray.

"I—I don't think they did."

I took several steps back, my heart thumping wildly while the breeze turned into a gale.

The day turned night, and it was pitch dark. Lightning struck, and the warrior woman turned to me, her face obscured by her unkept hair.

She terrified me more than before.

"What do you want from me?" I screamed over thunder.

She lifted her clawed hands, blood dripping from the wicked points.

Darkness fell again; the ship rolled under my feet. When the next lightning struck us, there was no woman, no one on deck but me.

Thunder shook the ship, and I screamed.

"Wake up, sweetie," someone said. Loud.

I woke up with a scream, Birdie's face next to me, her ringlets falling down her face, obscuring it like my nightmare.

"You," I breathed, scrambling backward.

"By the Erlking's horns," she said, scowling. "You scream louder than a banshee. It is time. Edward is ready for you."

TWENTY-EIGHT

Titus

I stood at the entrance of my cabin, memories hitting me in the pit of my stomach as my legs jerked. I took a deep breath, my hand resting on the door frame.

Bloody Minho. *You'll pay for this. For every hair of hers you touch.*

My eyes swept the place, from the table where we ate our food to the bed where we slept. An intense desire to have her here again, on my ship, assailed me from the depths of my being.

My heart throbbed furiously at the memories. To run my fingers again among that silky curtain of hair, her tanned skin, and her tempting lips . . .

Cursing under my breath, I strode outside to the deck. Sergei, on the other hand, was glad to be aboard a ship and was shouting orders as my temporary first mate while Homkar convalesced.

The fae stood alone next to the mainmast while my crew made certain to give him a wide berth. His hands were clasped behind his back, his perfect red-brownish hair showed his ridiculous pointed ears, and he was now clad in his usual tights and robes. What a gobshite.

"Everything all right, pirate?"

"Perfect, fae," I replied, baring my teeth. "If you're going to be aboard my ship, you have to exchange your absurd outfit for a real one. I'm not keen to have landlubbers on board."

Gally sighed.

"How's Homkar?" I asked.

"He'll be fine. He is certain he will be up in no time to help with the quest."

Our quest. An impossible one, Ryanne would say.

"Sir!" Mouse said, the only woman in my crew. "So happy to be above and see you well." She beamed at me, as did the rest of the crew. "Are we hunting for Ryanne?"

"Aye," I said. "Stephen! Hoist the sails and man the decks. We're in a hunt."

"Aye, aye, Captain."

The sturdy redhead shouted orders, and they all went to work on the sails and lifting the anchor.

Gally looked thoughtfully at my crew. "Your crew is happy to see you."

"Surprised to find we have a heart?"

"This loyalty grew before you gained one, wasn't it?"

"You'd be surprised," I said with a flat tone.

Centuries of experience crossed his seemingly young countenance. "I suppose it will be very enlightening to spend time with you. Now, what did you do when you boarded your ship?" He stared into my eyes. "You vanished into a shadow."

"Not now, fae." Enough chatting with him.

He took me by the arm, stopping me short, but released me when that odd energy peaked. "We won't leave until I understand what you did. The shadows. You walked among them. None of your kin can do that, I'm sure."

He is not your friend. Kill him.

Aye, he wasn't. Pinching my nose, I took a deep breath to quiet my beast. Although I didn't like him, the fae was useful.

"What I'm going to tell you, no one outside of Ryanne knows."

The fae's gaze was impassive. Hell, this wasn't a good idea, but I needed to have him on my side. Sergei had climbed to the crow's nest and seemed content there.

Sails deployed, and we headed out to sea. It was a calm day, and the ocean showed us mercy. I welcomed its embrace and the wind's favor, but mostly, the taste of salt on my lips, the roll under my feet, and the *kee haw* of seagulls circling above. A good omen.

"How much do you know about us?"

He opened his mouth, arrogance in his countenance. Then he looked at the ocean, and his expression settled to something different, one I'd hardly seen: humility. "Alas, I know little of your kin."

"Aye, I knew that." I smirked. "But mostly they're all arrogant enough to believe they have nothing to learn from humans. I'm different in that regard."

And Sergei now. Perhaps Kara as well.

"I learned shadow-walking in Rome," I said. "With someone called Quintus."

"The *scáth* Quintus?" Gally said in surprised recognition.

It was my turn to be surprised. "You know about the Umbra Gente?"

"Not by that name."

Scáth. Shadow. The fae knew them by another name, which was no surprise. "Ryanne said you didn't know about them. Or the Shadows."

He seemed to ponder about that before answering. "She had asked me about them, indeed, but it was not knowledge she ought to have. The *scáths* are not beings who should be in contact with humans, nor should humans have any knowledge of them."

"And yet, Ryanne is not a normal human."

He grabbed the rail and again kept silent while the shouts of my crew surrounded us. The ship was now underway, and despite the fact that my heart was riddled with a different type of shadow, lightness seized my limbs and a weight lifted off my shoulders.

"She is not," Gally said, though the way he intoned it made me think it was more to the wind than me. "I must admit her growth has surprised me." He turned to me, worry etching his gaze. "And troubled me as well."

He'd noticed her imbalance, her lack of root. I gave a slow nod.

"I'm surprised Quintus took you in. He exhibits discerning selectivity in deciding whom to allow to approach."

"Aye. We reached an agreement, Quintus and I."

"And your Alpha is not aware of said agreement?"

"None of my kin. Ryanne is the first one to know, now you."

"And yet, your Alpha is more dangerous than you."

"He's powerful, stronger. His connection to Anord is flawless, and he knows where all of us are. Except now Kara and I, but he used to know. And he's the only one who has another bradaí subdued as his first mate, Minho. That makes him twice as dangerous."

"Has he ever caught you?"

It was my turn to set my gaze on the placid waters and the way the waves rolled as a song, a sight that always elated me. Having a normal conversation with the fae did not, and this temporary truce was lasting longer than I would like. Alas, it was needed.

"As said," I replied, "he knows where all of us are. And he loves nothing more than to assert his Alpha position. This hunting will not be easy."

Gally seemed to ponder this. "No, it won't. I wish I could use my powers in this realm of yours."

I looked up to where Sergei was, comfortably standing in the crow's nest despite his size. "I have Sergei."

"You trust him that much."

"My old self wouldn't. It's thanks to Ryanne that I'm open to it. I believe I can trust him." I needed to trust him. On the other hand . . . "Is Kara really safe behind your taigh's walls, fae?"

"I gave you my word."

I cupped my hands around my mouth and shouted, "Sergei! Take Stephen and take inventory of what they left behind. I hope there's some food."

Without waiting for his answer, I stepped off the poop, heading toward the forecastle. I wasn't ready to lock myself in the captain's chamber. I needed to feel the scent of the sea on my face, the saline scent in my nostrils. It'd been too many months since I'd set foot on my ship, since I saw the sea again.

Since I left the cave.

Once in the castle, I jumped and landed on the bowsprit, swinging without a problem. The wide sea displayed in front of me and filled my lungs with what I longed for most.

I'd make the bloody bradaí pay dear for daring to take my ship.

And my Ryanne.

TWENTY-NINE

Ryanne

The first time I met Edward I almost peed myself, terrified of him. The second time I'd conquered my fears, and while still terrified, I'd been able to thwart his attempt to kill Titus.

But back then, Edward's focus had been on finishing Titus by removing a coin that wasn't there anymore. This time, I was on his ship, in his place of power.

There was no Titus, no Peter. No Cuidi or Bricius with me.

There was only little old me—a human with fae power enough to fight back. But against the Alpha, all I could do was play along until Titus found me.

The wound on my face and neck throbbed, and I tried hard to conceal the pain behind it. I wiped the sweat—mixed with some blood —off of my cheek and collar and got ready to meet Edward. Since I stabbed him the last time I saw him, he wasn't going to be happy to see me.

Birdie led me above deck, her sharp nails digging into the skin of my neck, sometimes pressing harder, guiding me wherever she commanded. And I, like a puppet, silent and eyes downcast, obeyed.

I couldn't feel what type of creature she was. While my seer-dreams, or nightmares, were quite present in my mind, somehow I was not as frightened now as I was in those dreams. *Self-preservation stifles many emotions*, I thought.

It was night, that much as I could tell, and besides the roar of the ocean, the cracking of the wood, and the whistling of the wind, all was silent as well. As if ghosts roamed the ship.

Finally she released me and opened a door. "Come, sweet girl, don't dally." She pushed me inside.

The captain's cabin was a temple to bad taste. Dense red velvet curtains covered the windows, tied with shiny golden cords. A golden Persian rug with silver piping cushioned my footsteps. Golden chandeliers dimly illuminated the place. An intense aroma of incense swirled around paintings with images that made me blush. A huge bed took up the center of the room with four golden posts and crimson blankets and cushions.

Edward sat behind a baroque desk. He looked pretty much like when I'd first seen him—white pants, an expensive-looking blue jacket, boat sandals with no socks. His rich brown hair was loose and brushed his shoulders.

He looked like your typical billionaire yacht owner if it weren't for those cold, appraising eyes—for the darkness behind them.

Don't show your emotions, Peter had warned. *Let them guess.*

"We meet again, Irish's woman," Edward said. His soft voice made me shiver, but not as much as his shark-like eyes.

"I'm not just someone's woman," I said, strangely calm.

He smirked, in a way that reminded me so much of Titus in the first days aboard his ship. "Leave us."

"Your word is my command," Birdie chirped in a sarcastic manner and closed the door behind her.

"Take a seat." Edward pointed at a chair.

"I'll stay here," I said with intent. Predators only feared other predators.

Predators never feared prey.

"I wasn't asking."

There was power in his voice. The type of commanding power that made you do things without realizing it. I was sitting before I finished processing all of it.

"Here, clean your wound. I apologize for Minho. He can get quite passionate about his art."

He handed me a clean handkerchief. I thought it impolite and absurd to refuse it, so I cleaned the throbbing wound.

He snapped his fingers. A side door opened, and two gorgeous, runway models stepped in. Both wore provocative clothes and swayed their hips. In unison, they smiled suggestively at Edward.

But there was something wrong with them. Their gazes were empty and didn't reflect the smile on their full lips.

He snapped his fingers again and both stopped. "What do you think about them?"

This was some sort of test. Then it hit me what was off. Their skin was not a natural human color: one was slightly tinted blue and the other green. Tiny iridescent scales reflected the candelabra light. Their hair wasn't dyed, but that shade of blue was common only in . . .

"Nymphs," I breathed. What were nymphs doing *on* a ship? And without their usual spark and craziness?

Edward regarded me, this time more intensively. "Very good! You're not so useless, it seems. Yes, they *used* to be nymphs. Now they're mine. Anord's, I stand corrected. He only wanted us to kill fae but then I thought, why waste our gift on fae only? If these creatures can serve us, why kill them?"

I sucked in a breath and gripped the edges of my chair with my palms.

Oh gods. Fae could infuse their power into humans like me to give us gifts like my foresight. Bradaís injected their darkness and killed fae—and humans—that same way.

I thought back to the strange creature Pan and I saw when we were escaping from the Erlking's lair that Titus stressed was a goblin.

If Edward used that darkness to taint other creatures, things were worse than we thought. No wonder the fae were in a hurry to stop the bradaís. The seer-vision came to me again, the desolate land and the corpses at Birdie's feet.

"But they stop being fun after some time." He clapped his hands, and the nymphs retreated the same way. "I underestimated you. Now, I'm curious about that little trick you and the Irish did last time we met each other." He poured himself a glass of wine, then took his time to savor it. "There's something about you."

He left his glass on the table then dragged a chair over and sat before me. "The Irish knows it too, yes? Tell me, does he feel when he makes love to you?"

"What?" I leaned back, the further from him the better.

"We had this chat, him and I. He said he only felt emotions when bedding a woman and when killing. You knew this about us, yes?"

His shark-like eyes never left me. I bobbed my head, my hands latched to the chair.

"You know a lot. And you both pulled a pretty trick. Does he love you?"

"What?"

"You're not the smart type, no? I wonder. Not gorgeous, not smart. What does the Irish see in you?" He cocked his head, analyzing me.

About to deny that Titus loved me, my *préachta* reacted, and I almost said that he did.

"Your kin don't know how to love," I said with a straight face.

Not lie, just skirt around the facts.

He reached for my hand and patted it. "You're not a good liar. I know he can't be away from you. Something about you makes him crazy, Anord knows what. And you, you love him, yes?"

"Yes," I said before I could help it.

"And he loves you."

"Yes." His voice commanded me to obey him, and it was a struggle to lie between his power and the fae energy in me.

He squeezed my hand, and a current hit me. I gasped. It was the same I felt back when I met Titus.

"Oh, yes, little human. You're now marked. You're now *mine*."

THIRTY

Titus

The Morrigan take me. Someone was strangling me. I couldn't breathe. We were deep underwater, and my limbs were tired from the struggle.

That didn't make sense. I was stronger there. But they had me trapped and all my efforts were for naught. My portal was unreachable here, and I had no sword.

Tentacles tightened over me, rubbery and slippery. Not a person but an octopus.

That didn't make sense either. Sea creatures had always accepted me. They'd never judged me or been afraid of me. I'd always let them be.

My body felt broken. Soon, it would be over.

The answer is within you.

The creature released me, and I stood atop a mountain. That voice wasn't my beast.

A dark-haired man in bright white robes stood nearby with his back to me. The nádhúrtha, Amriel.

"You have answers," I said and sprinted toward him.

But no matter how fast I ran, I couldn't reach him.

"I can't," I said, panting. "I can't find Ryanne."

The man turned. It was Edward. And he had Ryanne in a chokehold, his dagger pointing at her collarbone. Her eyes were blank and her limbs limp.

"I will kill you," I yelled, reaching for my sword.

There was no sword, no bradaí pocket to reach.

He grinned and said, "The answer is within you."

I gasped for air, my forehead beaded with sweat, and then, everything vanished and my room was in sight.

A nightmare. A bloody nightmare.

With a jerk, I pulled the covers off, donned my trousers, and left the cabin in the black of night. The stars were shining above my head and lightning struck in the distance, but no light shone within me.

Ryanne was away from me in Edward's hands. How was I supposed to find him?

How in Anord's hell was I supposed to kill the Alpha? The Unkillable?

Everyone expected me to kill him because I was different, special, the bridge between my kin and the fae. But the Morrigan take me if I knew what the hell was inside me except for that obnoxious *préachta*.

Obnoxious, aye, but it'd helped us thwart him.

The wind picked up and the sails flapped, releasing a sad tune. They missed Ryanne as much as I did.

And again, the unspoken question rang loudly in my head.

How was I going to find Edward's ship? The one that no bradaí could ever find?

I leaned my elbows on the railing, gaze fixed on the wide sea. The full moon reflected on the churn water and the salty air reassured me, but didn't fill the hole in my chest.

The answer is within you.

What in Anord's hell did that mean?

Below deck, my loyal first mate rested, healed, thanks to the fae. We had a conversation, and I talked about everything that had happened since I last saw him: how Ryanne and I were able to temporarily defeat Edward, how the three Eadroms, Ladies Cuidigtheach, Tuiren, and Gally, insisted on fae and bradaís working together. How Ryanne and I escaped from them and fell into the Erlking's hands, only to free an annoying brat.

Light footsteps told me the fae wasn't sleeping either.

"Troubled dreams?" Gally positioned next to me, his hands on the rail.

I frowned. Did Gally also read thoughts? "I wanted to see the sea."

"When still the stars shine and the sun is yet to appear?"

I gripped the railing. "What's that to you?"

"I'm worried about Ryanne, pirate."

"I thought we were on a first name basis." I gave him a sideways smile.

"Call me Peter, then."

"Hell. Never."

He chuckled, the type of unbidden laughter one does not seek to give. We were united in our quest to find Ryanne, nothing more.

Only Ryanne thought to call Gallchobhair by a name from a children's story. Though granted, she'd been eight when she confused him with Peter Pan. How surprised she had been when she found the real Pan back at the Erlking's cave.

Surprised and delighted.

My grip on the rail tightened. All our plans were thwarted, and we had no Quintus to hide us. Edward had Ryanne. Gally couldn't use his fae power at sea to find her.

The beast tried to break through, I could feel it like a bloody tumor contaminating my body. I forced *préachta* to drown it but it was as hard as crossing the Darién in Panama.

"Your body is balancing," the fae said. "You're like an addict in withdrawal."

"You're familiar with that concept?" I asked, surprised.

"I possess a deeper familiarity with human affairs than you may realize. Not having your coin is unbalancing you. Let go of your control."

Control. I straightened and watched the swell of the ocean, increasing in size and speed. The octopus chocking me.

"The ocean. Control," I said quietly.

"What is that?" Gally asked.

"I had this dream. There's something I can do," I said, removing my trousers.

"Strip naked on deck?" Gally cocked a reddish eyebrow.

"Well, what do you know? Tight-arse fae has a sense of humor." I picked a coiled rope and tied it around my waist. I reached out to the nymph-woven sails and focused.

Feihnum, they sang.

The ship lost speed, and I jumped on the rail. "When I pull, tug me back."

"What did you just do?" Gally asked, for once not recriminating but oddly curious.

"Tell you later, Pretty Boy," and jumped into churned waters.

All pirates had a connection to the sea, but none of them had the skill that I acquired through dozens of years of patient training. I closed my eyes, allowing every part of who I was to blend into the ocean. My kin were terrified of letting go of their control, but I was not.

Usually.

So far, I'd only been a spectator, relishing the calm sensation and peace the water brought me. The octopus coiled around me could have been a warning that it was time to change that. The ocean was everywhere and knew all that happened. What if it could pinpoint us? I had to reach out further than I had ever done to find Edward's ship.

For that, I needed to forgo my control, as the fae said. Abandon caution and let myself loose in the ocean. Be part of it. Nay, more than that.

I allowed the ocean to control me, to possess me in such a way that my own thoughts vanished. Not someone different, but part of it.

My hands were not my hands anymore, but a creature in harmony with the sea. My heart slowed its steady beating, and I felt my body melting into the water.

My conscience pulled me apart, but it was not painful or harmful. A ghost, nay, squid ink spreading in the water.

The only thing connecting me to reality was the constant tug of the rope at my waist.

Schools of fish, white sharks and small sharks, octopi, even plankton, flowed inside this wonderful complex world. I could sense each of them as part of this magnificent opus.

But this was not enough. I needed more.

I needed Ryanne.

I focused on those times with her inside the ocean, her bright energy next to me.

Where are you? I asked in my mind, searching.

And then, I could feel something different.

Not contaminating like human ships, yet not belonging here, like dark spots in my consciousness. Bradaís energy.

A bradaí ship, somewhere in this vast interconnected ocean.

Those dark spots engulfed a bright spot of energy: Ryanne's. She was there. The Morrigan take me! How to calculate that spot in nautical miles?

It attempted to slip away from my focus, and I reached out further to that point, but I felt thin like sea foam.

No, no! I wanted to yell. I must know where Ryanne was. I must find her.

But the spots vanished and so did she.

I regained my control, an implosion of my consciousness in my body. Anguish covered me. I'd been so close, and I'd lost her.

Again. And again.

The tug to my waist was constant, a tug that brought me to my present situation. I pulled back and almost instantly felt someone retrieving the cord. I reached my ship and braced my feet to the side. Pink broke the darkness in the east.

Feihnum, the wood sang.

Gally pulled the rope and, soon, I landed on deck. Stephen was at his side, muscled arms folded across his broad chest.

"How long was I in?" I asked.

"Long enough for this one to snarl at me."

Stephen nodded at me and returned to the helm. Sergei was asleep and Homkar still recovering in his cabin.

And I stood on deck, alone but for the fae, frustration ringing in every part of my body.

I'd been so bloody close.

"What is it?" the fae asked politely.

"I felt a ship," I said. "A bradaí ship, but I don't know where it is or how far away."

"You don't know?" Gally asked again with that curiosity that reminded me of Ryanne. "Why not?"

Three hundred years of mistrust demanded me to keep silent. But I'd trusted Kara, and it'd paid off. I trusted Ryanne. And Ryanne trusted this fae. Maybe I could give up a bit more control.

"This is the first time anything like that has ever happened."

"That you went into the water?" Gally leaned over the railing then as quickly he retreated, face pale. Lightning struck again; a storm was brewing not so far away. Grand, perhaps it'd evolve into a typhoon.

"No," I said, annoyed. "That I sensed other ships. I've never done that."

"How did you do it?"

"You sound like one of those human brats. If you want to know, jump into the ocean." Perhaps that way he'd stop his incessant questions and drown.

He peeked over the rail but remained on his spot. "I can swim, but you know my energy will be trapped."

Trapped. Like I was.

I dared the ocean with my glare. Where is he? Where is *she*? Did she feel abandoned by me?

Did I fail her?

"Are you certain your Alpha has her?" Gally asked.

About to snap at him, I forced patience into my tone. Something useful could come out of having him here. Perhaps. "We bradaís always take our prisoners in our ships." My back straightened. "Of course. If Minho had a ship, he'd have her there. He might have tried to take my ship and, when thwarted, he somehow sent her to Edward's ship. It all makes sense now. I was right."

That woman creature could have transported Ryanne the same way she had Minho.

"Always?" Gally insisted.

"You know we destroy. We kill our enemies, but some we keep, especially if we're going to sell them. And water makes us feel safe. It's part of who we are."

He wasn't surprised but in another time, I would have stressed how we killed and maimed our prisoners. This wasn't the time.

"Is there another way to find your Alpha?" Gally asked.

I took a bloody deep breath to avoid yelling at him. "No."

"How are we going to find him, then?"

"I, fae, not we."

"I am aware of my vulnerability in this realm of yours. My hands are tied, Doyle, and . . ." He pinched the bridge of his nose. "I am deeply worried about her. I failed her."

He let his hand fall, and I saw tears welling in his eyes. Those tears hit me. Something happened within me, something unfamiliar that was choking me. My heart felt squeezed and trampled over.

"You didn't fail her, Gally," I choked. "I did. I failed her. I should not have listened to Kara and gone to find Sergei."

Images of Edward with Ryanne hit me, and I staggered. He was going to hurt her. He was going to hurt her so badly. "I can't do a thing," I said, voice strangled by that strange emotion.

"What did you say?"

"I can't do a thing," I sputtered. "I can't find Edward's ship. I don't know how."

He didn't reprimand me. But emotions swirled on his face. Those welled up tears began to break free over his cheeks.

I fell on my knees and broke myself. My chest, once bereft of emotions, now drowned by a maelstrom of turbulent dark waters. The worst tsunami, the biggest storm condensed within.

Perhaps that was what the octopus meant.

"I failed her," I cried. "He's going to kill her."

"Don't say that."

"He will. He always does. It doesn't matter if she's bait, or not, she'll be dead by then because . . . because I can't bloody find his ship!"

It was then that I couldn't hold myself anymore and cried. "I love her, Anord help me, I love her and now I lost her."

The fae grabbed my arm and helped me to stand up. Bereft of strength, I staggered, not minding his energy pricking my skin.

"We'll find her. *We*, Doyle. By all that's mighty in this world, we will find her. Alive. You hear me?"

He was also crying, his face no longer stony. His pain, echoing mine, reflected on his anguish.

"I don't know how."

His hand still grabbed my arm, as though he knew I'd fall on my face. That odd feeling burnt my arm, but I didn't care. I, Titus Aodhán Doyle, a pirate, allowed himself to be vulnerable before a fae.

What a bloody irony.

And yet, I couldn't care less.

"Is this what you felt when you saw me with Aghna?" I asked, voice cracking, remembering that time where I saw him cry over Aghna's feeble body.

"Yes. No. Different. But I know you are feeling as I did."

His gaze found mine, and here we were, pirate and fae, arms locked, on my ship. The energy in our contact crackled and hissed, oil and water refusing to mix.

Footsteps sounded over the planks, and I stood and let go of the fae's touch. I could be vulnerable before the fae, but not before my crew.

But it was Homkar. He looked better, albeit weak. He looked at both of us with that serene, deep gaze of his. His stare was unfathomable, and it alternated between us and the wood planks.

Silence but for the keening of the wind and the thunder in the distance.

Then, Homkar spoke. "I have an idea, sir. A crazy one. But I believe I know how you can find Edward's ship."

Ryanne

Months ago, when we first met, Titus had marked me. Which basically means that he infused some of the darkness all bradaís have within me: their *dorcha*. The real purpose of the marking is to kill fae, their true purpose and the reason why Anord created them. But they also found that they could pour some of that thick, oily energy into a human and pinpoint their location.

Some sort of Find the Seer app. Or rather, Find the Marked Human since they could do that to anyone. Pour a little, the human will be fine and easily located. Break that balance and the human will die. Now that I think about it, that's *exactly* what they do to fae; bradaís infuse their putrid essence into fae and little by little, the fae's immortality ceases. They are no longer connected to Ard-Beight. And Anord's goal was achieved—bradaís killing fae, and fae not able to kill them back.

But one bradaí successfully crushed a fae's orb, the spark of creation that connected them with the Supreme Being, Ard-Beight, without killing the fae. That bradaí had been Titus and the unfortunate fae, Minho.

Edward and Titus had attempted to do the same to another fae, Aghna, Peter's lifelong partner and the main reason Peter used to hate

Titus so much. Titus had repented and rescued Aghna, only for Peter to see Aghna die because of Edward's dark essence infused in her.

Now, Edward marked *me*, the bradaí bastard.

When Titus squeezed my hand in that joke of a date, I felt electricity coursing through my veins, like a soft electrocution, if that was possible.

Now that I was more attuned to their energies and to my own fae energy, what I felt with Edward was like a small snake striking, its venom finding its way to my fae core. *Préachta* reacted and tried to nullify the threat, but the snake recoiled into itself, a capsule of dark energy surrounding it like a corrupt cocoon. The fae power enveloped it but couldn't destroy it.

Like some sort of virus attacking my immune system.

That was how they marked us. And when trapped in that lab in Japan, I'd been able to nullify the *dorcha* since Titus only infused a little. Edward had been murdering fae since he took his first breath and had been quite successful. Unstoppable.

I snatched my hand back and stood up so fast the chair fell with a clank.

"Now, now, dear . . ."

Edward's words got lost. I focused on that energy burrowing within me and shaped my fae power into a sword. It cut through the cocoon and two capsules of darkness floated inside me.

"Sit!" Edward said from far away.

I kept focusing and cut the capsules over and over until they dissipated. It was gone.

"What?" In two strides Edward reached my side and grabbed my wrist, then twisted it painfully. "What did you do?"

"Nothing of consequence," I said with the most inexpressive face I could muster.

"You're a very bad liar," he muttered. "Show me that trick again."

He poured his energy again, and I held my breath. His shark-eyes bore into me. But they weren't challenging. No, there was curiosity in him.

I let the power within. Maybe later I could try that trick and . . .

"Do it," he snarled.

"I—I don't know what you're talking about." Which technically wasn't a lie. "It" could refer to many things, and *préachta* let me get away with fact-skirting.

Whatever curiosity held him vanished. Darkness swirled around us and my vision dimmed.

"Do it, or I'll give you to Minho. He loves to play until his victims bleed to the point of death."

It wasn't a threat. It was a statement casually said. And I couldn't refuse it.

"I'll try," I said, shakily, "but step back."

He did, and I repeated my internal actions, though it took me longer because I found my ability to focus very shaky. My throat was raspy, and my body weakened as if I was sick.

"Interesting. I wonder what you could do if I pour more. Have you been practicing with the Irish?"

I took two steps back and bumped against his desk. Where could I go? Even if I were able to bypass the most dangerous of the bradaís, Minho and Birdie were out there. Could I jump off the ship myself? I glanced at the almost black porthole. Swim at dusk?

I had to try. Anything was better than being in this ship.

Edward seemed to be patiently waiting for me to arrive to a Oh-my-god-I-can't-do-anything-and-have-to-beg-on-my-knees   conclusion.   I gave him the Ryanne Sweet Smile, trademarked, and offered my hand.

That threw him off. Just a second, but enough for me to dash around him and head to the door. My hand flew to the doorknob, and my fingers slid over its bronze-smooth surface.

And my head jerked back, my hair pulled by a strong hand.

"Sneaky. I like that."

He threw me to the wall, and I snarled a grunt. What was it with these bradaís and throwing people against walls? His steel fingers clasped onto my already-bruised jaw.

"I do love a challenge dearly. Fight. Resist me."

Energy snakes slithered from each of his fingers and, before I felt them inside, I racked my nails over his face, screaming.

"Bloody woman!"

He let go and, heart bursting, I rushed to the closed door. A shark-filled sea at night sounded better than remaining here.

He seized my arm with a claw of steel. "You're getting on my nerves."

"You said you wanted a challenge. Or is your definition of challenge for me to stay put?" I spat.

He blinked. Then laughed.

Grunting, I tried to remove myself from his grab to no avail. I yelled and kicked him.

Tried.

My fist clenched, and I threw a punch.

Tried.

Edward trapped my punch as easily as swatting a fly. "Challenge, little woman, isn't about you trying to pathetically fight. I'm not in the mood to oblige you. Use your power."

"I am not little!"

He snickered.

A vision interposed, an old man looking back at me, though only pitch black remained of where his eyes should be. That vision was important, I knew. There was something about that old man I should understand.

Understand.

This could be the chance to gather knowledge about Edward. I was being used as bait, so he was playing with me.

I'd thwarted his first attempt to mark me, didn't I?

"Let's play, then," I said, offering him my hand again.

"Good girl, I'm liking you better now."

Corrupting creatures might be Edward's ultimate goal. Understanding him was mine. I'd tried before and it'd been stupid. A child's play.

But I wasn't *caílin* anymore. I was *bean*.

Game on, Edward.

THIRTY-TWO

Titus

Gally and I stood face to face on deck, Homkar at my side. My first mate was recovering, although, if he still hurt, he didn't show it. The roll under my ship increased as well as the strength of the wind.

"Now what?" I asked, fists clenching and unclenching.

Homkar placed each of his huge hands on our shoulders, in a way that connected us through him. He closed his eyes, head slightly bowed as though in prayer, and I let him be.

While he followed my commands, he was also an advisor and friend. Gally also closed his eyes, his face relaxed.

Homkar suddenly thumped our shoulders and took a step back.

"Are you going to explain now?" I asked, brow arched.

"When you two knelt, I felt something through the dragonwood." He pointed at the planks then at both of us. "A circuit." He looked at me. "You said you're supposed to work together, pirate and fae."

Bloody hell. "Aye."

"I felt it," Homkar continued. "A connection."

Now it was Gally who scowled.

And despite the fact that I wasn't keen in working with the fae,

Ryanne's fate was on the line. "Why the face, Gally?" I said, tense. "You said the same basic thing."

He sighed. "Indeed we did. I assume it is easier to say it than to accept it. But . . ." He scrunched his brow and glanced at Homkar with a pensive stare. "How will that help us to find Ryanne?"

Homkar nodded as though approving his question. "You fae, you can't use your energy in the water. Captain, you can, but it is not useful to pinpoint Edward's location. Nor can the fae pinpoint any bradaís location."

I sucked in a breath, understanding where he was going. "But if we join our energies—"

"—then we might be able to achieve what we cannot separately," Gally finished, his expression awed.

"Let's try it." I removed my clothes, ready to submerge once again.

"It might not work," Gally said as he removed his.

"Perhaps. But I need to lose my control, and what better to lose control than with a fae?"

I jumped on the rail. Homkar would keep the ship nearby, so there was no need for the rope. The fae jumped next to me with grace.

"Now what?" he asked, eyeing the stormy gray waters with distrust.

"You said you could swim?"

"Indeed. Water does not nullify *me*, it just contains my power."

"Fair enough."

I dove headfirst. He dove right after me, so we were floating in the ocean while waves increased in size. Marvelous.

"Now what?" he asked, spatting water and struggling to keep next to me.

"Hear me out. Your power is contained. When I submerged with Ryanne, we held hands and our *préachtas* joined. She was able to feel what I was feeling."

"Shall we, then?" He offered me his hand.

The Morrigan take me. The idea of holding his hand nauseated me so instead I grabbed his forearm, that oil and water feeling prickling my own, and we submerged. Unsurprisingly, his fae power was quite strong, and my beast yelled in despair. I could feel it cornered—a torrent of waters pushing the filth away.

But unlike before, I was glad the bloody beast was dimmed. It only interfered with what was important. His fae power felt like an invasion, and my body tensed like an anchor thrown to sea.

I shook my head and released him, then swam to the surface. He followed suit.

"That was unexpected," he said, sputtering water.

"Your energy is too strong. It was trying to control me."

"Was it?"

"Aye. You need to control it. Don't attempt to conquer my own. It needs to be subdued for me to help you."

Gally's head cocked, the waves bobbing us up and down. "Subdue it."

"Aye."

"Let's try here."

I gave a curt nod and he grasped my forearm. It didn't feel as awkward though the energy prickled.

"Steady," I said. "It's still strong."

"I'm making an effort." He scrunched his brow.

"I am not someone to defeat," I warned. "We are to work together not suppress each other."

"I understand, Doyle. I am endeavoring."

It took us quite a while, but finally I felt his energy akin to Ryanne, even as it was still quite strong. No wonder it was almost impossible to eliminate an Eadrom.

"Ready," I said. "Now we submerge."

And so we did, forearms clasped.

The fae and I were suspended in water. Like me, he could hold his breath and sense his surroundings. Hell if I knew how. But I felt the synchrony of his energy and how he pushed his fae power out. Perhaps he was adapting on the go.

Unlike me, where sea creatures glided by, those nearby reached out to him. Schools of fish surrounded him, and dolphins nudged him to play.

Focus, I wanted to yell.

Instead, I nudged his back then pointed at the relative position of the ship. He acquiesced with a nod and closed his eyes.

Our *préachtas* balanced—I could feel his cowering at the water energy, but mine enveloped his and I pushed it away, toward the black spots of energy.

My energy was the carrier, his was the agent.

Again that light, shining weakly among the darkness.

He lifted a fist then slowly lifted a finger. Then another. Then all five fingers and lifted another fist. He scrunched his face, then smiled. Eyes now open, he jerked his head up and we both broke the surface a moment after.

"Did you—?" I started.

"Yes! I was able to pinpoint it."

"How far?" I asked.

"Quite far, I sense a big land mass between that light and us."

"How. Far."

"I'd say around two thousand *mullachs*."

"What the hell is that?"

He glowered at me. "They're used to measure length at sea. They don't serve on land."

"Aye, like nautical miles."

"I don't know what those are."

"By the Morrigan! We just wasted valuable time." I swam back to my ship and climbed it.

Gally climbed after me. "Doyle, wait. We can figure this out."

"Grand. Can you give me a time estimate?" Wind whistled with force. Once on deck, I reached out and picked up my clothes.

He mulled over it while picking up his. "Perhaps ten or fifteen days, if not for that humongous land impediment."

I nodded, absentmindedly. He might be referring to the American continent. It wouldn't surprise me if Edward was in the Atlantic.

Sergei emerged from below deck and stared at us. "What are you two doing naked? Having some fun?" He grinned.

"We've pinpointed Ed's ship."

"You have? And you had to be naked to do so?" He grinned wider.

"I have an idea," I said, glowering at Sergei while waving at Stephen.

"We make a good team, Doyle," Gally said. He was in no hurry to don his clothes.

"You certainly do," Sergei said, still grinning like the mad Russian he was. "A fae and a bradaí . . . naked."

"Shut your hole," I said, annoyed.

Sergei grew serious all of a sudden. "It is all good if you want your fun, Doyle. But he *is* fae."

"I know," I spat.

Sergei continued, now addressing Gally, "And I am still hoping, for your sake, that Kara is safe behind walls, fae."

"She is, pirate," Gally said while donning his clothes. "Safer than anywhere."

"Let's go to the captain's mess," I said. "We need to discuss something."

Sergei stared at Gally, then headed to my cabin with Stephen. What Homkar did wore him out, so he was forbidden from coming up on deck until he rested. Not that he followed my orders in that, but at least he did at times.

Gally was smart not to mention that had we heeded him before and went directly to his taigh, Ryanne would have not been captured.

The image of me launching after Kara's coin twisted my guts. But it was nothing compared to what I felt about Minho taking Ryanne. That pain flew to my heart; it was like the organ seeped all the hurt like a bloody black hole, and I staggered.

"Something's troubling you, Doyle."

I leaned my shoulder on the mast and took deep breaths. "I'm fine."

"You're not. It hurts you."

I glowered at him, but there was no mockery. There was concern about Ryanne, and something else.

It was then when I understood Gally's pain. I sensed the despair looming behind his stone gaze. He hadn't forgotten what Aghna had gone through at Edward's hands.

At my own hands as well.

"Come," he said. "Your friend's already ahead."

We headed aft to the captain's mess, where Sergei and Stephen waited. My friend was scowling as though he had a fierce headache.

"Anord's upset," Sergei said, wincing.

"How do you know?" Gally asked.

"I don't like you wanting to know so much about us," I said.

Sergei leaned toward us. "But you certainly like to join energies with the fae. Is that what this is all about, Doyle?"

Dismissing the annoying Russian, I said to the fae, "It's time to put our differences behind. And work together."

"Fae and bradaí. This is unheard of. What's next? The Erlking with one of the Ladies?" Sergei scowled.

The fae looked unfazed. I wondered if he had friends who would bully him. I didn't think so. Lucky him.

"Anord lets us know his displeasure," I said, "by infusing more darkness in us. It's like his power enhances in those brief times."

"Is that what you feel?" Gally asked Sergei.

"*Da*. But I'm usually good at dismissing him. Better than anyone else."

"Are you?" Gally arched his eyebrows.

"His skull is thick. Now . . ." I waved at Stephen, and he approached the table.

I showed them the map, and we discussed the whereabouts per my understanding of latitude and longitude and whatever the hell Gally talked about. Stephen called Mouse and, once inside, the hacker on ship did some calculations and finally we were able to convert the fae's unit of measurement.

Sergei and I exchanged a look.

I knew where that ship was.

Sergei leaned his big frame over the map. "Sardinia."

"Tirreno," I said, thumping a finger next to the Italian island. "Near San Teodoro."

"Very well," Gally said. "But we aren't better than before. It's still more than ten days away and an ocean apart. Aren't we in what you call the Pacific?"

I smirked. "Fae, yo"re about to see something you'd never seen before."

"Oh? What?"

"I'm calling the Dragon."

THIRTY-THREE

Ryanne

The first time Edward sent his energy, I felt them like little snakes the width of veins. This time they were thicker, pencil-like tiny rams trying to batter down my defenses.

Edward grabbed my crossed forearms with both hands. My breath stirred as his amused shark-eyes bored into mine.

Somehow I split both realities, not unlike a computer with split windows: in one we held a staring contest and in the other our energies fought.

Something told me he was probing, sending his artillery a few at a time. Seeing how I reacted.

Fae before me, creatures with far more power than mine, had died at his hands. But it was not instantly. And I was no fae. I was human. Well, mostly human.

The nymphs' blank stares mocked me, but I pushed that thought away. An ogre would do.

I only had to hang on while Titus found me. Titus and Peter. As an Eadrom, Peter would kick Edward's ass.

I'd been using the same strategy: my power as tiny swords that decapitated his energy snakes.

But it was time to do something more. I managed to split another reality, one where *préachta* turned darker. I pictured an ogre, and thick green skin covered me. Muscles sprouted within me.

Edward dug his fingers into my skin and smirked. "That is a nice trick, human, one I had never seen in a fae. But you're stopping that right now."

His *dorcha* overpowered me, and I gasped, that ogre attempt fizzling out. Once again, I called the ogre, but Edward's darkness swallowed the attempt.

"What do you feel?"

The sudden question startled me, and *préachta* recoiled. He wasn't seizing the opportunity to send more energy but was genuinely curious.

Sarcasm was my only escape. "I'm good. Wanna call a break? I'm all for coffee."

"What are you feeling, human?" he insisted.

Darkness engulfed us, and I felt the power behind his words. They compelled me to answer, to please him.

Feel.

I commanded my free will to avoid his compulsion. "You want to feel, Ed?"

"You don't get to call me Ed," he said, apparently calmed but I sensed something else beneath his tone. He was upset.

"You want to feel like a human, *Ed?*"

I might pay dearly for my spunk, but I didn't care.

His fingers dug painfully, and his eyes darkened.

Bullseye.

"Wanna feel loved? That's why the nymphs. I bet they don't ca—"

"Shut up!" The veins on his forehead throbbed in a way that I would have taken a step away if not for his tight grip. "Shut up, human. What do *you* feel?"

It was then I realized snakes slithered throughout my body. They'd bypassed my defenses without me even realizing, like a flea infestation.

"Afraid," I answered without realizing.

"Show me your fear."

He framed my face with his hands and overpowered me with his body. My spunk vanished, and that fear shook my being.

"Yes," he said. "You're afraid. Describe your feeling."

More snakes shot from his fingertips and the darkness pressed on me.

He was a virus, and I'd been cocky.

"My chest is tight."

"Go on." He tightened his hold more, my hands tense at my sides.

Pain burst inside, and I bucked his invasion. "Let go of me," I said shakily.

My *préachta* didn't know where to turn. Like the hydra, with each snake my tiny swords decapitated seven more swam by, invading my body from my toes up to my tongue.

"What else?"

His voice amplified, and it was the only thing that mattered. I had to answer. I had to obey him.

The snakes were all over me, and my fae power was an overwhelmed, tired army. The corrupted enemy snapped and bit. The gummy things were frantic, searching . . .

Searching?

"I'm not bait," I whispered, the effort making my head spin. Cold-drenching fear numbed me.

"Oh, no, little woman. You never were."

The nymphs came to mind with their vacant glazed eyes.

"You want to turn me." My throat was raspy as if I had a strong infection.

"I'm turning you, yes. You'll be my third prize. And the Irish will see you by my side. My puppet."

I choked; tears tried to reach my eyes, but they dried before even getting out. His fingers weren't digging anymore but instead, he caressed my head, as if I were a favorite pet.

"I'm no challenge," I managed to say.

"You never were, dearie. Give in. You're mine now."

My vision turned dark, and I saw him from afar. His voice potent inside me, commanding me.

The snakes reached a door and many of them congregated there. They chewed and gnawed.

The door to my spark of life, to my connection with Ard-Beight.

Edward was after it.

THIRTY-FOUR

Titus

Fae energy sprouted from the wooden boards as though in celebration, and that energy gathered around the sails.

Feihnum, they both sang.

Then the colorful sparks took the shape of a dragon's head, its maw ready to devour the ship.

The Dragon energy engulfed us, and the hair at my nape bristled. The portal to Tír D'aois opened, and we sailed through. The horizon shifted as the ship rolled and dipped into dark troughs between waves. Those waves sounded different than the dimension we left, as though creatures whistled and shrieked from the depths.

Gally was in awe, I could tell.

"Never thought I could do this, did you?" I said, smirking.

"I never thought anyone could do this," he said sincerely. "this is quite a feat."

"By the Morrigan. A fae giving a compliment. Don't let anyone say a bradaí is left behind." I acknowledged him with a slight bow of my head. "Thank you, Gallchobhair."

He bowed his head back. "You even pronounce it correctly. Perhaps I was mistaken about you, Doyle. You're full of surprises."

"And that makes you like him more, *da*?" Sergei came between us, threw one arm over each of our shoulders. "A fae liking a bradaí. That's a first. What comes next? Peace for the world?"

Sergei hadn't stopped his stupid fae-bradaí jokes. The fae removed Sergei's arm, and I remembered how Ryanne said fae didn't like to be touched. No reaction from Sergei, so there had been no energy exchange, which wasn't a surprise; I was the only bradaí with *préachta*.

"The fae's right, Doyle," Sergei said, now serious. "Why did you never tell me you could do this?"

"I'm a fae lover, am I not?" I regretted the words as soon as they came from my mouth.

"You certainly are. But no worries," he winked at Gally, "he is also a bradaí lover. What comes next?"

"Please. Stop," I said, deadpan.

"You living in a taigh, that's what comes next!"

"Anord's balls, how old are you, fifty?"

His guffaw overpowered the creak of the wood and the roaring wind. Saltwater sprayed us as Stephen battled at the helm. He, along with the rest of the crew, had never witnessed the Dragon Portal, and I sensed their awe distracting them. But I needed all hands on deck.

Once Sergei's laughter subsided, I said, lips tight, "Finished? Let's focus. Ryanne's in danger, and we're about to board Ed's ship."

Sergei and I exchanged a glance. No bradaí ever had been able to do it. Ever. Edward had always been a step ahead of any of us. Would two bradaís and an Eadrom who could not use his power be able to defeat him? And he would have Minho at his side.

But then, no bradaí had ever been able to kill an Eadrom, or even hurt them. Not even Edward.

And yet, no fae had ever fought in a pirate ship, as far as I knew. Gally could use a sword, but not his fae power. That, however, could still be an advantage—no bradaí could be certain of an Eadrom appearing on their ship.

Many things could go wrong, and yet many others could turn out all right.

Gally was still in awe, hands clasped behind his back. I frowned, pensive. For this to work, surprise had to be on our side.

I turned to Gally. "When you fought the fomorians you didn't reveal yourself as I requested?"

"No. I fought like a fae would. There was no need to show myself to them."

"Grand. Edward will expect a fae, not you."

"*Nyet*," Sergei said, shaking his head. "Minho might have told Edward about a fae fighting alongside you, but he lost your ship. He will downright lie to Edward—"

"—and tell him I had fae help, hence why he lost. Edward *will* expect a fae."

"I still say *nyet*. Even if Minho told him that, no fae has ever been on a ship. They know fae energy is suppressed by water. Why would a fae ever be in one of our ships?"

I gave a curt nod. "It might be as you say, but we need to be prepared for anything."

Sergei cracked his knuckles. "We will. He won't. And speaking of the Alpha, how did you fight Edward back? Kara said you and Ryanne thwarted his attempt."

"You fought the Alpha?" the fae asked. "With Ryanne?"

Both zeroed on me. Hell.

I opened my mouth and shut it. Glanced at the sea. At the sails. The sea breeze soothed me and perhaps because of it, I spilled the beans.

We were in this together, Anord help me.

"I did. We did. We used our *préachta*." I told them what had happened.

"That's the key," Gally said, thoughtful. "That is why you can eliminate him. I understand now how important it is for Ryanne to be with you. We were wrong, back at my lady's taigh."

"I know," I said.

Sergei caressed that powerful, square jaw of his. "Your woman is more important than I thought. She's feisty."

"Ryanne," I said, annoyed. "She's Ryanne. Call her by her name. She's earned it."

"*Da*, she has."

The ocean splayed before us. The immense, powerful ocean, its song a lullaby, its waves the carrier of its thoughts.

Water. What Ryanne feared, what I relished the most, and now it would play against us.

"Since you have never fought on a ship before," I said to Gally, "why don't you practice now against Sergei?"

"My pleasure." Sergei cracked his knuckles.

Gally lifted a hand, closed his eyes and breathed. That was when I noted what Homkar had said. The dragonwood vibrated under my feet, and I could sense the fae's energy anchoring to it.

"Get ready, big guy," I said.

"Always am."

Sergei did what he did best—threw a punch with all the power his enormous frame could muster. His fist cut through the air like a ballast, but Gally was quicker. The nimble fae slid past the hulking Russian, a blur of motion, and drove a sharp jab into Sergei's side. The impact barely registered on Sergei's massive form, but Gally was already moving again.

The next few minutes were a dance of power against agility. Sergei's fists kept swinging, each blow strong enough to blow the man down, but Gally was always just out of reach, slipping away like a fast dolphin. His quick feet carried him around Sergei, dodging and weaving as if the ground were made of ice, his every movement frustrating Sergei's attempts to land a hit.

The fight ended as abruptly as it began. Gally sprang into the air, using the momentum of his lithe body, and delivered a solid punch to Sergei's face. The force of the blow finally made Sergei stagger, a look of surprise flickering in his eyes as he registered that the fae had managed to break through his defenses.

"What did you do?" Sergei asked, caressing his jaw.

"Learning what Doyle showed me." Gally knelt, his fingers brushing the planks. "I'm surrounded by dragonwood and nymphs' sails here. They belong to Tír D'aois as I do. You said all bradaís use dragonwood and nymph-woven sails."

"Aye."

The fae looked up, pensive, then slowed his breathing, his fingers stretched out, lightly touching the wooden planks beneath him. He released the breath, and with it, blue sparks flew from his fingers. He rose to his feet and gathered the energy between his hands, molding it into a glowing orb. With a graceful motion, he released the energy ball, sending it soaring toward the sails.

"While I would not be able to use my power, I can borrow the dragonwood's energy for a bit of a show, like you did with the Dragon Portal. Mind you, it won't last long so we don't have time to put on a big fight. Now, do you have a plan?"

"I have a plan," I said.

"Good," Sergei said. "I was worried we'd end up with our arses kicked."

I jutted my chin toward Gally. "If you can beat Edward temporarily without your power, we can rescue Ryanne and get out of there in one piece. Make sure to use all the tricks you can, like that flying ball. That might fool him enough for us to get away."

Gally nodded.

"Ryanne is who matters here," I said, emphatic. "We're not here to defeat Edward. Not yet."

As long as she's not dead, a voice said inside me, a nagging voice I'd been trying to suppress. She wasn't dead. She couldn't be.

"Have you fought him before?" Sergei asked Gally.

The fae took a step forward, hands clasped behind his back and staring at the ship. "I have never fought against him before. He is the most slippery fiend. But after the fight training with Sergei, I am confident I'll be able to hold him long enough for you to rescue Ryanne."

"He won't even know what hit him." I jerked my chin toward the captain's cabin. "Go and hide, Gally."

"I do not like hiding, Doyle. It isn't in my nature to hide."

"And that's why you've never beaten us. Now, do as I say. You're on my ship."

The sparking waters of the Tirreno's sea welcomed us. And about thirty nautical miles away, a ship navigated across its deep blue waters.

"Stephen," I said to the helm. "Ask the lookout about the sails' color."

"Lookout! What color are the sails?"

"Blue," the lookout shouted.

"It's him." I gripped the railing, excitement and dread coursing through my body.

Homkar placed himself next to me. He limped but barely. Sergei stood on my other side.

"Are you fit to fight, Homkar?" I asked without taking my eyes off the ship.

"Yes, sir. To death if required."

"No need. I want you alive."

"If Minho expects us, then it's a trap, Captain," Homkar said.

"If Minho expects us," Sergei said, somber, "I'll beat the crap out of him."

"It might be a trap," I said, "or not. But it doesn't matter. Edward is not one to act coy."

Edward's ship had always been faster. I'd never wanted to show the Dragon Portal before to any of my kin, but all hands were on deck. Either he knew by now or someone from his ship noticed the disturbance.

Hard to miss a magical dragon appearing out of nowhere then coalescing into my ship.

They wouldn't kill her, not yet.

I couldn't afford to think about anything else, especially since Ryanne had a vision of us, together. She was fine, I knew.

She would be fine. She had to be.

And Gally was here. Aye, we had a good chance against Edward, if not yet killing him, at least to recover Ryanne.

That was what mattered.

Waves continued to hit the hull of my ship while she danced across the waters, shrinking the distance between us. Sergei and I waited on deck, both eager to face Edward and Minho.

As suspected, the *Thunder* awaited. She wasn't used to being pursued, always the hunter.

But not this time.

Minho stood near the deck, and Sergei growled.

A growl from the big guy would worry anyone. But Minho was not looking at him. He was glaring right at me.

I seized my sword and stood straight. Darkness engulfed me, and all I could see was Ryanne taken by him.

Please, I beg thee, he'd said, two hundred years ago when I killed his fae essence and turned him into a bradaí. A hatred that hadn't diminished in centuries.

A hatred that was now paid in kind.

"Look at the crew," Sergei grumbled. "I don't believe it was a trap."

The *Thunder*'s human crew looked worried and even exchanged glances among them.

"Nay," Homkar said. "They weren't expecting us."

"The Morrigan take me." Something akin to fear wrapped around me like the Drakken's tentacles.

Ryanne wasn't safe.

THIRTY-FIVE

Ryanne

I was doomed.

Soon, Edward's energy snakes would open the path, and I'd lose my connection to Ard-Beight. I'd be like those poor nymphs, a showroom of another type.

Creepy showroom from bradaí hell.

My will focused on that last bastion of defense, but Edward's power was too much, too intense. What could I do? I wasn't a full fae, and mighty fae had fallen to this sort of attack before me.

The defense faltered, and the snakes gnawed with renewed intensity.

But I wouldn't give up without a fight. Edward said I was no challenge. I had to prove him wrong. There must be something I could do.

"Yes," Edward whispered in my ear. "Give in, little human. You'll show me how you make the Irish feel. You'll make me feel, too."

That again. That emptiness Titus had told me about gnawed at Edward as his slithering power was doing to me.

Feel.

Feel!

I *could* feel. A human with a whole range of emotions, different from the fae. Light and darkness, the reason why I was able to call Erlking's creatures unlike the fae. But this was *not* about calling them, it was not about my fae side, so I shut my eyes tighter and focused on my memories. My very *human* memories.

Of when I found Bricius the first time and found the portal myself, even though I was only eight years old.

The snakes kept going and chipped part of my defenses.

Of that time I met Santa Claus. And he'd laughed. Oh boy, did he laugh! Ho ho ho.

When Mom baked me cake, and when my sister Evelyn pulled my hair when I told her I saw Santa Claus.

A few snakes trailed behind.

When Titus had laughed with me back at the lake, when he was prisoner in the taigh.

Titus.

My heart focused on him, for those times we were together. When he showed me in the sea who he was. That beautiful connection of his, of his love for creation, for life.

Some snakes faltered. Others renewed their attack. Words outside my brain—surely Edward's—held no meaning. From afar, I felt cold sweat and my body shivered.

That time in the sea with Titus. I felt renewed. I felt love.

Our first lovemaking in the cave. Titus's hands over my body and his mouth covering mine.

When he said he loved me.

I renewed my defense, and it grew as if an invisible construction worker reinforced the entrance with mortar and bricks. The shivering stopped.

"You can't be fighting back!" he yelled.

"I will," I answered. "I always will."

I could hear Edward's angry words and feel his fingers tightening on my jaw, attempting to break my connection.

Perhaps I did need some fae memories too, so I went deeper.

I found the taigh.

Cuidi's patience at explaining what my visions were. Where the fae power came from. Of Peter training near the Hawthorn. His smooth movements, how he was one with the sword.

Peter stopped and smiled at me, a bright smile that lifted a weight from my chest.

Don't give in, he seemed to say. *Fight with all your might.*

Of Bricius, dear Bricius! Always at my side and making certain no harm came my way. Yes, yes, yes, dear friend. You have always been there for me and taken care of me. My best friend.

His memory zoomed happily in my mind, his gossamer wings reflecting all the colors in the spectrum.

Don't give in, Ryanne, no, no, no, I could hear him say. *You can fight him, I know you can, yes, yes, yes.*

The walls thickened and, even as Edward sent more snakes, it held on.

The pathway was closed. As thick as an iron door within a bank. As safe as a taigh.

"Aha!" I exclaimed in victory. "You can't get in!"

I was safe in this place, whatever it was. Those thickened walls loomed around me, and I did a three-sixty. It looked powerful. Unbreakable.

"You'll give in," Edward said from faraway, like he was dozens of feet away and he was shouting at the top of his lungs.

Hot fever covered me. How dare he? Icy *préachta* took control, and I wanted to squish him down. How dare he try to take away everything I'd worked on!

"I won't let you," I snapped and lifted my arms, focused on strengthening those defenses. "Never!"

The walls turned to a dark sepia color, so high I couldn't see over them. I gave a full turn but it felt safe here, as safe as I could be from his attack. I sighed in relief, leaning over, hands on knees, while I recovered my breath.

The walls held any attack coming from the outside.

I was safe. Safe from Edward and his attack. He couldn't get in here. Somehow I felt his frustration and anger from far away, his shouts about how I should give in and be his.

"Never," I seethed, "Never! You hear me, Ed? I'll never be yours!"

Ryanne, a different voice climbed inside my head. Red eyes pinpointed in a shroud of velvet darkness.

Red points in a mist.

"Who's calling my name?" I asked, haughtily. This was *my* place.

Ryanne, the cavernous voice boomed again, but not outside like Edward's. No, whoever it was, was inside with me. *You'll come to me.*

Anord!

I wouldn't . . . no. Wait. The voice was familiar.

That was not Anord.

Mocking laughter echoed inside the walls. *I'll be waiting, Ryanne. Don't take long.*

Darkness wrapped me, and my forehead throbbed, but I knew that voice.

Gods, I *knew* him!

THIRTY-SIX

Titus

"I rish! Come, the captain's waiting for you," Minho said with that cheerful confidence those who have the upper hand possess.

"I bet he is," Sergei mumbled next to me.

Ryanne came first. Alas, to find her, I must go through Minho. It was I who must confront him. Then Sergei and Homkar would reduce him to a pulp.

Aye, they would.

Minho smirked. "You're looking for your little pet, yah? She's now the captain's pet. They've been locked up in his cabin for hours. Having lots of fun, yah?"

The darkness inside demanded me to take his head. My knuckles turned white.

"Doyle," Sergei whispered, "remember the plan. Don't lose your head."

Aye. Emotions screw up plans. In order to succeed, they should be kept in check.

The crew, bold at Minho's confidence, whistled or cursed at us, fists in the air.

And yet, all I could think of was wringing Minho's neck. He'd dare to take Ryanne to make me despair, to sink me down with an anchor wrapped around my neck.

Hatred never won battles. Emotions always made you trip. I couldn't give in on either.

Edward was nowhere in sight. No surprises there. He'd come out from his cabin looking bored once I stepped on his ship, I was certain.

No bradaí might have reached the *Thunder,* but he wouldn't break a sweat either. He wouldn't show any kind of vulnerability.

Boarding ships with grappling hooks, and jumping with a rope, only happens on screen. In reality it was a stupid idea since ships part ways, hooks loosen, and the boarding party falls into the sea.

But none of those were bradaís ships.

"Clear the decks!" Sergei boomed.

I jumped on the rail, Sergei next to me. Stephen and Bill threw the grappling hooks, and Mouse handed us the cords. We swung and landed on Edward's deck, boots firmly planted.

The crew surrounded us, though Sergei and I already had swords in our hands. The blasted humans looked cocky with the confidence of being part of Edward's crew.

"You coward," I roared, my sword leveled at Minho. "Face me instead of vanishing, you piece of shite. Where is she?"

No human would dare to challenge me. Not unless they wanted to die a swift and merciless death.

"Anord will make you pay." Minho gloated, his sword pointed back at me. "Edward is taking care of her. You've lost her."

His words struck like a cat o'nine tails, stinging deep. I remembered Luc and his lover, their corpses bloodied after Edward slaughtered them both.

Something boiled within me, emotions churning stronger than any maelstrom. I couldn't lose her.

Not now, not ever.

"Where is she?" I roared, my voice slashing through the air. "Give her back to me or I'll blast you to hell!"

Minho snickered, and the crew's laughter echoed like mocking chimps.

I lunged at him. No time for games. Darkness engulfed me, and all I could see was the bastard half-bradaí in front of me. Each strike of mine was fueled by pure rage, each blow aiming to destroy.

Hatred might not win battles, and emotions often led to mistakes, but not this time. This time, my fury made each swing of my sword stronger, each shout more deafening. Minho's cockiness drained away with every cut, every step that forced him back.

"You touched her, you'll die, you miserable rat!" I screamed, my sword slashing through his vest, tearing his trousers.

"Stop!" he cried, but there was no mercy left in me.

Blood seeped from his wounds, and he found himself trapped between the railing and the full force of my wrath. His sword clattered to the deck, forgotten. I switched from my sword to my fists, savoring the satisfying crunch of bone beneath my knuckles.

"Irish!" a voice called out, distant, almost drowned by the roaring in my ears.

"Where is she?" I demanded again, but my voice was raw, nearly gone.

Minho whimpered, a pathetic sound that only fed my fury. I hauled him up by the front of his shirt, ready to smash his face into pulp.

"Irish!" The voice cut through the fog of my rage, more forceful now.

Sergei stood at my right, his hand on my shoulder. "Doyle. Look."

I followed Sergei's gaze aft—toward Edward's cabin.

Edward stood there. His powerful presence making everyone cower. Everyone but for Sergei and me.

"Did you come for this, Irish?" Edward said. He reached out for something inside and then pulled Ryanne in front of him.

"Ryanne," I croaked.

She looked odd, gaze vacant and limbs like a puppet without cords. Black veins crisscrossed her face, neck and arms. A fresh wound marred one side of her face and down her neck. My heart clenched.

I roared and lurched through the crowd, my hand tight on the sword.

"She's mine now, Irish."

Her eyes reflected fear, anger, her lips trembling. The Morrigan take all Alphas to hell and let them rot there.

Then she crumbled into a heap.

Hell broke loose around me, but I couldn't care less. I skewered two who came after me, their faces unimportant. Edward crossed his arms and leaned on the door frame, his countenance showing that boredom when fighting us.

He straightened and suddenly his sword was in his hand, pointed at something behind me, his shark eyes first showing surprise, then anger.

"An Eadrom! You really hit the bottom, Irish, by joining forces with the likes of them. You traitor. You fae lover," he spat.

"Aye, that I am," I growled.

The fae had kept to his word, not appearing in the fight until Edward showed his face. It was time for his show, and we had precious minutes while he drained energy from the dragonwood.

There was now fear in Edward's eyes. Grand.

I jumped the last couple of steps. Edward stepped over Ryanne's inert form and pushed me aside, his strides confident despite that fear I saw. Instead of facing Edward, I crouched to Ryanne's inert form. Gall-chobhair would distract Edward while I got her out of there.

Ryanne came before my vengeance.

Thick black thorns covered her face, neck, and arms. Her lips were purple and her body limp.

I checked her pulse. Faint. I almost collapsed and exhaled a shaky breath. She was alive.

Carefully, I scooped her into my arms. The clamor of the fight rushed to my senses: the cries of Edward's crew as they lay wounded, Sergei's roar as he hacked against the rest of the crew, the hum of the wind and seagulls circling above us, Gally fighting with Edward.

My eyes searched for Minho, but the bastard was gone. Again.

No sound came from Ryanne's lips.

I stood straight, knowing I had to do something. But not here. I had to get Ryanne back to my ship. Homkar caught my eye and strode toward me, a path of destruction for anyone daring to oppose him.

Homkar stopped at the base of the stairs. "I'll clear the path for you, Captain."

"Thank you, my friend."

Gally fought fiercely, perhaps not with the same intensity as when he faced me back in Tír D'aois, but enough to make Edward wonder what other tricks we had up our sleeves.

Edward never liked situations he couldn't control; he always needed the upper hand. Facing an Eadrom on a ship, when fae were never supposed to be there, was something he couldn't be certain he could win.

In other circumstances, I'd enjoy Edward losing ground to Gallchobhair. He'd never faced a fae like him. Hell, none of us had if we could avoid it.

But Gally would not last long. It was time to leave.

All I cared about was using that *préachta* I had within me to help Ryanne and counter Edward's dark energy. I just had to figure out how.

With the utmost care, I held her in a fireman's grip and got ready to swing back to my ship.

Then, something happened.

A whoosh, a stirring in the energies, and suddenly, the woman with thick dark ringlets appeared behind Edward. She wrapped herself around him, and before I could blink, they vanished.

Another whoosh, and another crew member disappeared in the same way. Even Gally, usually unflappable, looked confused and tense, his sword raised and ready to strike. But the woman reappeared, only to vanish again, taking a different sailor with her each time.

It was over in less than thirty seconds. Besides those on my side, no one else remained on deck

"Cowards!" Sergei roared. "Come back here!" He looked around, frantic. "Where did they go?"

Gallchobhair's sword dripped blood, his chest heaving.

This could be a trick. "Let's go back," I said with an urgency I'd never felt in my life.

"How is she?" Gally asked, his face pale. If I didn't know better, he sounded worried and even fearful.

"I don't know. But we can't stay here."

It was a chore, but I was able to swing back to my ship, Ryanne close to my body.

"Let's get the hell out of here," I said, now on deck, eyes wary toward the *Thunder.* "Gally, sails."

The sails flapped above me at Gally's command. He'd understood what I'd been doing and now could handle sails as I did. For better or for worse, my fate was now linked to the fae.

Not wanting to understand the consequences of such a partnership, I placed Ryanne's inert form on deck. "Homkar, get us away as fast as you can."

"Yes, Captain."

"Where did the crew go?" Gally asked above me.

"Cowards," Sergei said, face reddening. "Vanished. Cowards!" He roared again.

No time to go to my cabin. With my hands on her chest, I focused on her energy, *préachta* a battling ram.

There was nothing now but total silence from her side.

A silence that frightened me more than ever. I tried again, eyes closed and feeling *préachta* flowing from me into her, but instead of meeting her own *préachta* as before, that dance I'd been used to, there was a wall erected between our powers—a thick, impenetrable wall.

"Let me try," Gally said, crouched on the other side.

"No," I said. "I can do this. I can . . ."

But nothing responded. The thorns on her body hadn't diminished. In fact, they looked bolder.

"Doyle."

Sergei pulled me to my feet. I tried to resist, but Sergei weighed four stones more than me.

"Let the fae do this thing. This falls in his category."

"No."

"Doyle," Gally said with a drained voice. "You're not the only one who cares for her. I've known her since she was a child. I beg you, let me try."

I grunted, reluctant, even if he was right.

Gally closed his eyes, his lips slowly moving, hands hovering over her body. The memory of when we first met, me carrying his almost dead lover in my arms, he trying to save her and believing I was trying to kill her, burst in my mind, and I choked.

Aghna had died in his arms after Edward, and I treated her much as Ryanne had just been treated.

Gally hadn't saved Aghna. She'd died days after but only because I'd been able to thwart some of Edward's poison. Otherwise her demise would have been almost immediate. I wasn't there for Ryanne. Would she make it? She had to.

The fae puffed, his eyes showing a worry he shouldn't have.

"Gallchobhair," I said. "Is she . . .?" I choked, and thorns pierced my heart. Cold sweat beaded my forehead, and my breathing came out forced.

Gally stood up, his gaze focused on her. "I stabilized her."

"You saved her." Relief made my knees fall to the deck. I was trembling so hard I did not know if I could stand up again.

"I'm afraid not. I've only postponed the inevitable. Your Alpha poured in too much of his dark energy into her, and her life is ebbing away," he said, his voice cracking.

"No!" I reached out and tried again to feel her. But the silence and the dark wall erected in her being was the same. Except now, I felt something else. A power I couldn't even fathom that was keeping her alive, similar to the energy surrounding our cabin back in Switzerland. That much I could understand.

Fae energy.

This was out of my depth. All my years of experience, all this dealing with the alien energy that she had been able to reactivate, it was all for naught.

The heart she helped reactivated.

There was a bloodied wound on her cheek, the one I'd barely noticed when Edward pulled her in front of him. I traced it with my finger, from her cheek to her collarbone. Anger should be all I felt toward whoever did this. Minho, surely.

But I felt nothing.

I covered my face and wept.

A sad song came from the sails, a wailing that struck a chord within me. The wind whistled, and the waves crashed against the keel.

"Doyle," Gally said, firmly. "Get up."

"Let me mourn in peace. Leave me alone."

"All is not lost. There is a way."

I looked up, my face wet with tears. "What way?"

"It's not an easy one, although it is the only way for her life to be spared. But we need to reach my taigh first. I'll explain everything there." His face darkened.

By the Morrigan. Not another taigh.

Sergei's face mirrored my own. "The one Kara is in?"

"The same," Gally said.

"Very well, Gallchobhair," I said, scooping Ryanne's limp form into my arms and standing up. "Show me the way. I will follow."

I held her tight, her lifeless expression a contrast to the liveliness I was used to.

And then, I wept again.

Part Three

THIRTY-SEVEN

Titus

A stormy sky reflected my inner turmoil. Hell, if it were up to me, there would be lightning striking the barren land before us.

Gallchobhair strode beside me, one hand on my shoulder as though to restrain me while Sergei walked on my other side and Homkar covered our rear. A part of me was grateful for their protection, but I itched to go faster, to arrive to Gally's taigh and find out about his plan. But with Ryanne in my arms, I could not allow to stumble. He'd claimed she would remain stabilized with his touch, although I suspected he cared about her more than he showed. I'd pushed my pride aside and had to admit his touch worked: his fae power made a circuit between us three.

Since that immersion with our powers combined, my *préachta* acted weirder. It had connected with Ryanne's right away, but Gally's power was on a different level—I felt like the Panama Canal, bridging two mighty oceans that stood at different heights.

Hope had kindled within me, despite the fact that Gally didn't look so happy with whatever proposal he had in mind. Any sliver of hope kept me sane.

My boots trampled over dried long grass, and even the air was stale, devoid of the vibrancy I would have expected in this kingdom. The other two taighs kept immaculate lawns outside its walls, while this place was anything of the sort.

I'd transported us through a portal directly from my ship to a point in Tír D'aois, then Gally had used another for us to arrive within the borders of his taigh. That was the only way to travel here. As a bradaí, I could not make a portal to his property.

He was the rightful owner, and therefore he was able to transport us directly before his home. I used fae power to open my portals, but his portal felt different. The bubble-wrap Ryanne mentioned came to mind, though instead of plastic it was flexible. I had traveled through his portal once, when he defeated me back when I attempted to kidnap Ryanne, although I'd been hurt enough not to realize the difference.

My crew had remained with the ship and were in charge of taking her to one of the safe spots, a hiding place near Lough Swilly in Ireland.

Ryanne wasn't completely still. She would gasp or twitch every now and then, and I resisted the urge to cradle her closer to my chest.

"You're not stabilizing her correctly," I finally snapped.

"This is as best as we can do, Doyle," Gally said in a tired voice. "Unless you would rather let me carry her."

"Like hell. She's fidgeting too much."

"She *is* stable."

I forced myself to trample beside him.

"Is it true that ogres and trolls have taken over your taigh?" Sergei asked.

"We wouldn't be able to head there, would we?" the fae answered, his gaze focused ahead.

"Your Hawthorn died, didn't it?" Sergei insisted. "We've heard rumors that it was there for Anord's taking."

Gally sighed in exasperation. But he wasn't as upset as I was with Sergei's questioning, which hadn't stopped since we'd stepped off my ship. By the Morrigan, if he weren't my longtime friend, I'd stab him and leave him to rot.

"Darkness took over," Gally said. "But it's been pushed back."

It seemed I wasn't the only one sharing secrets of my trade.

"An abandoned fortress," Sergei mused, now by my side. The wind resembled that in the Highlands and whistled through the plain like a banshee.

I lifted my eyes, not realizing I'd been more focused on Ryanne's gasps of breath and the way her body trembled.

The taigh loomed before us. Three turrets rose from the main building, where daighs patrolled. A five-meter wall encircled it. A closer inspection showed some parts of it partially collapsed. Vicious creatures worked the repairs, beings I'd never seen: some as tall as the wall, some so small I had to squint to notice. Not one of them resembled any other, varying in shapes, number of arms or legs, or even whether they had heads. The creatures were fast and deceivingly strong. One of them rose up from the rest, a massive furry black body with eight legs attached to it, its giant and thick fangs snapping at the wall—a humongous arachnid. An involuntary shiver crossed my back. Immortal or mortal, those fangs would snap me in half without a second thought.

Daighs protected the creatures, their backs to them and hands on their swords.

"Is it safe?" I asked, wary, cradling Ryanne closer to my chest.

"It is," Gally said without breaking stride. "I recovered it recently with Lady Tuiren's help and some other beings. You shan't worry."

"The wall is destroyed," Sergei said, stating the obvious.

"That is only the physical part. It is almost repaired."

"What are those creatures?" I asked, curious despite my haste to be behind the walls.

"They're the guardians of the wall."

"The ones residing *inside* the wall?" I said, stumbling. Ryanne moaned, eyelids fluttered and I rearranged her. Gally's hand pressed harder on my shoulder.

"Yes."

Sergei and I shared a look. So many legends about the creatures but I never thought they could have a physical body. I recalled Ryanne mentioning how the thick wall in Lady Cuidigtheach's taigh seemed multilayered, like a beehive's. How it was hard to focus on it since her vision blurred like a mirage in the desert.

She also mentioned she thought she could see beings inside the wall and eyes followed her—the guardians. Those who protected the taigh per an agreement with the fae, if my memory served me well.

"Don't look at them," Gally said nonchalantly. "They might think you will threaten the wall and attack."

"They do look dangerous," Sergei mused. "I wouldn't want to step closer to any of them. Why are your guards protecting them if they're so mighty?"

"I said, don't look. Heed me, pirate. And my daighs aren't protecting *them*. They're there to steer away any other creature casually bumping into them and being horribly killed. Keep straight to the gate."

"But—" Sergei started, obviously wanting more.

"Save your questions for later," Gally said, waving for us to enter through the huge metal-reinforced doors.

Before I turned away, I noticed they weren't building the wall as a mason would. Nay, they were shedding their physical vessels and those vessels were glued to the wall and became part of it, while their translucent . . . being? . . . was absorbed by the wall. And yet, their numbers didn't seem to diminish.

"Let's go, then," I seethed, fists clenched.

Sergei thumped a reassuring hand on my shoulder.

Each taigh reflected their owner. Whereas Lady Cuidigtheach's home reflected peace and calm, this one had war etched on every gray stone. Even the hard-headed daighs, both the ones giving their backs to the wall guardians and the ones guarding the gate, looked more combative and wore armor from head to toe instead of the loose robes of the ones who had held me captive.

We reached the huge metallic doors, and Sergei stopped in his tracks. The daighs had opened it for us. Nay, for the fae, although they had no choice but to let us in as well despite their sour faces and upturned noses.

"Never been inside one?" I asked.

"*Nyet.*" He gave me an askew glance. "What are we doing, Doyle?"

"Surviving. Now, get inside."

My brother grunted but complied. When we crossed the wall, I noted Ryanne had been right on point regarding the beehive simile. Not only that, but my vision blurred and couldn't focus on details. Those eyes she spoke of followed us.

"I feel their energy," Sergei mused. "Those guardians . . . The wall is their domain, *da*?"

"Yes," Gally simply said.

It was when we crossed the doors that I realized something. "Oh, fae?"

Gally stopped, not bothering to look behind.

"You're not asking us for the oath." An oath to conduct ourselves as guests and make sure we don't murder the owner of the taigh in his bed.

He turned around, surprise on his face akin to mine. As a bradaí, being able to enter a taigh without any oath, would be ideal. But it didn't feel right. Ryanne needed to heal, and I needed all the protection I could get.

"Say it."

I didn't kneel as custom dictated. I was no stinky fae, even as some of their power was imbedded in me at my creation.

"I, Titus Doyle, promise to behave in your taigh and be a respectful guest, as long as my host respects me and mine as well."

I nudged Sergei and Homkar to do the same. Both grunted but complied and repeated my pledge. Gally accepted it and granted his protection to all of us.

Kara was waiting for us in the gloomy courtyard, Bricius flying around. It was clear Gally had always had his taigh in mind as our place of reunion to sketch a plan for bringing Edward down.

It was also clear I could not avoid the fae. All roads converged here.

"Brothers!" Kara beamed at me and Sergei and hugged each of us tight. "You're here."

"I don't like here," Sergei mumbled, evidently not happy at having accepted the fae's hospitality.

Kara didn't seem to mind. Perhaps she was indeed softening. That or sharing a bed with the fae helped. She beamed at him and, oddly enough, the fae cracked a smile at her.

A fae and a bradaí together. Anord must be having a seizure in his dimension.

Homkar glanced around. He'd never been inside a taigh before either, but his demeanor didn't show what he was thinking.

"Don't dally, Doyle." Gally snatched my shoulder and pulled me.

If it weren't for the deep worry eating me, I would have been ecstatic to have all those I cared about in one piece.

The fae took us through somber hallways, barely illuminated by the sconces in the wall.

"Cheerful place," I said.

"It's been like this since you and I met for the first time," he answered deadpan.

Aghna's death had certainly changed him if the taigh changed as well. Perhaps as much as Ryanne had changed me, unknowingly. My distressed heart couldn't take this any longer.

I couldn't take this any longer.

THIRTY-EIGHT

Ryanne

I stood in a small, darkened room. Edward sat on a couch, nostrils flaring. Other people crammed the windowless room—sailors by the look of them.

What was this? No one looked at me and—

I sucked in a breath. This was another seer-dream, like with the warrior woman, Birdie.

Edward's hand trembled. "Bested by a fae!" he roared.

A gust of red wind hit me, and anger made me clench my teeth.

A bloodied and beaten Minho limped his way into my vision; he was clutching his shoulder with a bruised hand. "That wasn't any fae, Captain, but one of them guardians of the Hawthorn."

"What is the Irish doing with the likes of them? An Eadrom, of all fae!" Edward spat on the floor.

The red wind caught my eye—it was like translucent red smeared in my vision. How odd. It scattered around until only dots floated, like crimson dust in a light beam.

Birdie stood among the crew. The rest had obviously been in a battle, but not her. She leaned on the wall and filed her long sharp nails with a carefree attitude. Dark ringlets spilled over her shoulders, obscuring her face like in my previous dreams. Curiously, I wasn't terrified this time. No, just empty. How odd indeed.

"Your Irish likes the fae," she said, the only one not showing fear of Edward. Yet she looked exhausted, like someone who just spent a lot of energy. "And that fae was spent, did you not see how he was extracting energy from the planks? I told you it was possible, but you don't listen." Her sharp canines pierced her full lips.

"Shut up," Edward growled.

The wind turned into a gray smear and swirled around me. Curiosity about the woman and her strange powers washed over me.

"Captain," a sailor said, "it's thanks to 'er, we're safe."

Edward strode toward him and slammed the burly man against the wall. His nails bit deep into the man's flesh.

"Beg for your life," Edward said, calmly.

"Please, Captain," the man stuttered, eyes widened.

"Never beg!" Edward released him and, with a swift motion, embedded a dagger deep into the man's guts.

Really, these bradaís love to smash things and throw people to the walls!

The man crumbled into a heap, eyes blank. The colored wind turned to green and hovered above the corpse. Even as a pool of blood coalesced around the man, I felt detached. Uncaring.

"Captain," Minho croaked. "We need to recover our ship."

"*My* ship, Minho, not ours."

Minho narrowed his eyes but only for a moment. He bowed curtly, stiff. "Yah, Captain."

"I can go back," Birdie said, shrugging. "They'll never see me coming."

That gray wind circled her.

"Yes." Edward did a careless wave of his hand, but that apparent coolness was absent from his eyes. "Do that."

She grinned with sharp, yellowed teeth, then strode out of the room.

She returned in no time.

"Well?"

"It's empty except for your dolls," Birdie said.

"Are you certain?" Edward's eyes were murderous. The kind of look that would make a full-grown man pee in fear.

Birdie waved a hand. "See for yourself." She opened a portal, his ship on the other side.

A blue gust of wind circled us. Yearning.

"Ah. It is deserted indeed. Let's go."

They returned to the ship—me trailing after them without even thinking about it—which was empty as she'd said.

"Curious," Edward said as he pressed a hand on the rail. "The Irish didn't care for my ship."

"He came for his woman," Birdie said in that same bored tone.

"All this trouble for her? Curious indeed. He only wanted his toy back. What an oddity."

Toy? But no emotion circled in me. Besides the initial anger, I was truly empty. It should frighten me, but the void took away that emotion too.

A smirk crept to his face. "It's a shame I didn't finish the job and crush her will to mine, but I can track her. She can still surrender her will to me."

Blue specks of dust floated around me, but no one seemed to care about them. Perhaps it was something they were used to.

Edward glanced at the sea and murmured, "Oh, yes. The Irish's woman will be mine. To feel," he murmured so softly only I heard.

Feel. Edward was obsessed with that. The blue had turned to gray, and I cocked my head. Curiosity was the only thing I felt.

He strode to his cabin and said, "I don't want any interruptions."

I didn't have to think about following him. My seer-vision form trailed after him as if we were attached by a cord. He poured a glass of wine, emptied it in one gulp, and thumped the glass on the table.

"An Eadrom on a ship," he grumbled for himself. "I should have known he wouldn't last long. Blasted Irish."

He then removed his shoes and sat on the bed, back straight and feet pressed together. With eyes closed and palms over his knees, he slowed down his breathing.

Meditating? Edward?

That was as odd as watching the Erlking doing a tango.

Energy rippled around the room and everything blurred.

What the heck?

The room vanished.

We now stood near a cliff, a strong wind messing with his clothes, but not with mine.

Despite the lack of runes, it occurred to me this was happening now, not in a future vision.

How curious.

Near the cliff, a man had his back to us. Long dark hair reached his mid back and wore clothes of yesteryear: long boots to the knee, a long leather vest, and puffed white shirt.

Edward strode to the man with confidence. The man turned.

That red gust of wind circled us again, and anger returned.

Titus?

"Irish?" Edward seethed.

The haunted eyes of the man reflected his own surprise. Long sideburns framed the gaunt face.

Not Titus, just similar.

"He was Irish, yes," the man said in a deep voice. "I created him here," he pointed to the cliffs, "believing he would be as powerful as you."

No more red wind but magenta. Something flickered inside of me. Awe?

I tried to understand but my brain, as my body, seemed to be glued to Edward.

"My lord." Edward bent one knee to the ground, head bowed.

Anord!

Attached to Edward indeed. I lifted my hands, but they looked smooth, not marred with the dark energy he'd infused in me. Maybe since I was not really here, this was not really my body.

"Arise, Alpha," Anord said with a careless gesture.

"Why am I seeing you like this?" Edward asked with deference.

Instead of answering, Anord returned his gaze to the turbulent waters below. "I pushed him to the water right after I created him." He pointed below. "Did you know that?"

"I did not. Is that why he can stay underwater for so long?"

"Can he?" Anord remained silent for a few heartbeats. "There are so many things I do not know about my last creation. The fae queen took that away. And he was going to be the most perfect, even better than you."

Edward's jaw twitched but he remained silent. Obedient. Angry red swirled but only briefly.

"Now, I cannot pinpoint him. He is out of my reach, as well as the Norwegian, the one with Odin's touch."

"Kara?" Edward asked, surprised. Gray specks floated around us.

Oh, so Minho was not in Switzerland because of her. It was because of me. Birdie knew. Who is that woman?

"Is that the name my Norwegian goes by?" Anord nodded in deep thought. "I used to favor her. I had such big expectations for her. Now, she's out of my sight."

Anord waved his hand, and an old, yellowed map appeared, floating in the air. I could almost smell the paper's crispness. Several ships appeared on the map, each with a named flag. Some flags were on land but those flickered in and out.

Edward leaned forward while gray specks of dust hovered in the air. Curious, I leaned as well.

"Shen's in Singapore," Edward mumbled, then touched a flag. "Ntombi in Africa. Good. They stay put."

Oh! It's a bradaí map! That's how Edward can locate everyone. The ones inland are not as defined. Curious indeed.

"Not only Kara's flag is missing, like the Irish's. A third one is gone," Edward said, stroking his chin.

"Yes, three," Anord said. "The Russian, but I still can feel him. Fae power hides him from my sight. Why have my children abandoned me?"

Sergei? How? Were they all in a taigh? That was the only way bradaís vanished from Anord's sight, if they still had their coin.

"I was going to request their positions, my lord. I am after the Irish's lover. She's—"

"One of the favored by the fae, yes," Anord said distractingly. He waved a hand. "Do what we previously discussed. I found the missing piece."

"My lord?"

"Yes," the god said for himself, "that piece fits perfectly well in my master plan." His eyes darkened as did his expression. His figure changed to a bulky, taller one, and armor strapped to his body, a black cape shrouding him. Titus's face changed to one blue-skinned, long and scarred, without eyebrows, and the cliff vanished.

"But the Irish lover—" Edward started.

"You have but one task, my Alpha. Abstain from endeavors devoid of substance, and do not call me until you have fulfilled my bidding."

THIRTY-NINE

Titus

After crossing an inner courtyard, guarded by more stone-faced daighs, Gally led us to a chamber on the first floor to avoid climbing stairs with Ryanne.

I placed Ryanne carefully on the bed. Gally crossed her arms over her chest. Bricius and other pixies laid flowers around her.

"What are you doing?" I waved my arms to shoo them away. "She's not dead," I stressed.

"I know, yes, yes, yes," Bricius said while he zoomed around as he was wont to do, "but she's always loved to entwine flowers in her hair."

Kara sat next to her and decorated Ryanne's chestnut hair with the flowers. "Look, she's sleeping like that woman in that kid's story." She looked at me, a mischievous twinkle in her eye. "Perhaps she's waiting for her pirate in shining armor to kiss her."

"She's not sleeping either," I all but yelled.

Homkar placed a hand on my shoulder. "Captain, they're celebrating her in their own way."

"No celebration," I grunted but acquiesced Homkar's attempt to soothe me with a curt nod. "Fae, tell us what this solution is you spoke of."

Gally waved a hand to the chairs. Sergei slumped into one. Kara remained seated next to Ryanne, while Homkar, Gally, and I remained standing. The pixie sat next to Ryanne's head and lowered his wings.

Despite Kara's apparent nonchalance, she looked worried about Ryanne. Perhaps they both bonded back when her coin was removed.

"This is not strange to us," Gally started. "Your kind contaminating us."

"Skip the backstory, fae," I snapped. "Our sails are down."

"Not to mention we're at your mercy in your house," Sergei said, shifting his massive weight and clenching and unclenching his left hand as if wanting to have his sword there.

Gally waved a hand. "I don't mean that. I'm only setting precedence. We'd seen this, your power so embedded in us that we can't take it and die. It is inevitable."

"You're not improving my mood. You said you have a solution."

Gally glared.

Kara said, "Little brother, let him speak, for Odin's sake."

I acquiesced with a curt nod.

"We'd tried many things to avoid this fate. To endeavor to purge our bodies of this dark energy. We'd infused our own, but the only thing we accomplished was that our friends died faster. We couldn't counteract the poison. Then Aghna—"

"Who's that?" Kara asked.

"Don't interrupt him," I hissed. I was so close to losing any patience I might have had.

"I felt the same type of power in Ryanne as in Aghna," Gally said. "Each bradaí has a particular way of poisoning us."

"We do?" I asked, surprised.

Not only me, but Kara and Sergei looked confused as well.

"Indeed. Your signature, if you will. Aghna discovered that. She devoted many years to understanding your darkness not only in our kind, but in humans too."

"That's when Edward captured her," I said. "Haiti. 1792. She was helping humans."

Gally gave me a leveled look. "You'll have to tell me that story some other time."

I gave a slow nod. Something was happening between us. Perhaps not friendship, but the partnership seemed to have taken a step further up the ladder. The strangest thing of all, it wasn't bothering me.

Gally continued, "Aghna was quite intense and focused, trying to find the cure. And she found it."

"What is it?" Kara asked.

I pinched the bridge of my nose before I exploded. Every second counted and I was itching to find out what the cure was.

"Aghna found it wasn't with light that we could cure us, but with darkness."

"That makes no sense," I said. "I tried using *dorcha* against Edward's *dorcha* to no avail. It was with light we'd thwarted him."

"In any other situation, I'd agree with you," Gally said. "But not when fae are concerned. You fought the Alpha with your dark power but his was stronger. You used light to confound his darkness and you succeeded. Momentarily."

He took a long look at Ryanne. "We fae are made of light. Your darkness devours it and no matter how much light we infuse, the darkness engulfs it and snuffs it out. With fae, only darkness can fight darkness."

"Wait . . ." I paced around, something clicking at the back of my mind. I stopped on my tracks and stared right at him. "Aghna. When we arrived in Tír D'aois, that night back in 1792, I tried something. I started to pour *préachta*, and she reacted well."

"What is that? A different kind of energy?"

"Nay. It's my fae energy."

Gally took a step forward, his eyes wide. "What happened with Aghna when you did that?"

"You appeared and I had to pull back."

He bowed his head as though attempting to contain an unfathomable emotion, then waved a hand. "Try."

"I know you said it doesn't work, but we'd practiced together. Her energy responds well to mine. Perhaps . . ."

I latched my hands over Ryanne's throat with delicacy as I did with Aghna back then. Her skin had a light gray tinge.

"Doyle." Gally's voice sounded from afar. "It's a gamble. Be careful. Infuse only a little."

"I will."

I closed my eyes and willed a little *préachta* into her. *Please, work.* In my mind, like I was watching a different dimension, the wall I'd felt last time stood before me and it reinforced itself with steel, like a defender against its enemy.

The wall looked imposing, but I knew she was inside. She wasn't recognizing me though. Would *dorcha* work?

As before, I sent just a wee bit of *dorcha*, but the ground shook and a palisade burst. It was then I noticed snakes—dark, pulsating snakes—swarming around the wall, attacking it with renewed energy. The more I watched, the more they grew, like they were multiplying.

Hydras from hell.

"Stop!" I heard, and I stepped back.

Ryanne whimpered and stirred anxiously. Sweat beaded her forehead, and the gray tinge turned darker.

"Those walls," Gally said. "I saw them, felt them, when you tried with both energies. They're different from what I'd seen."

"Did you see the snakes?"

"Yes, and yours shaped differently—some shape resembling crows. I saw those snakes with Aghna. This is your Alpha's work, for sure." His gaze bored into me. He might have seen inside Ryanne's mind that I didn't kill Aghna, but this piece of information solidified the notion that it'd been Edward's *dorcha*, not mine, which killed Aghna at the end.

"What if I try with more?" I asked.

"You could suffocate Ryanne." He placed a hand on my shoulder and something happened between us. An understanding.

"Then what is the answer?" I whispered.

He latched his hands behind his back and gazed outside as though recalling a memory, a painful one. "Aghna was what you would call a researcher. She—she wouldn't stop until she found the answer. And dragonblood was the answer." He shut his eyes closed, and I could see myself in him. The pain of losing someone so dear, so close.

No. I was not losing her. Morrigan's crows could peck me for eternity, but she'd remain with me.

"Dragonblood," Kara said from her place on the bed. "What the hell is that?"

It took Gally a moment to answer, his eyes still shut tight. He bowed his head, and silence but for Bricius's flapping of his wings.

"Exactly what it sounds like," Gally whispered as though in prayer. Then he lifted his head to look at all of us. "We need the blood from a dragon."

"What if it doesn't work?" I asked.

His expression turned somber. "There's nothing more, Doyle."

A shock hit me. My chest ached so hard I doubled over. That pain of losing her—no. That was *not* an option.

"Then let's go find a dragon," I managed to say. "What are we waiting for?"

"Wait." Kara rose to her feet. "If Aghna found this solution a couple of centuries ago, why are the fae still scared of us?"

"My Aghna . . ." The fae's eyes were haunted, and I recalled that time when he found her, almost dead at my feet, the same pain.

Would that happen to me?

Kara faced the fae. "I had one I cared about, and I saw him die before my eyes. The pain never goes away." She squeezed his arm in something akin to understanding. "But it diminishes."

And it was then I saw it happening. If before both found comfort behind the bedroom door, now their gazes softened in mutual comprehension, of two people going through the same.

"Well?" I prompted.

Gally sighed and took a step back away from Kara and composed himself. "It's not as easy as it sounds. Yes, dragonblood nullifies your poison, but it remains inside the cured fae. You must understand. We're beings of light. Darkness has no place within us. And the dragon has control over whoever has their blood."

"Like the beast," I said.

"I beg your pardon?" Gally asked.

"Anord's darkness in us. What controls us and compels us to obey him, so we can be good bradaís."

"Something like that," Gally answered. "Not as strong, though. But dragons belong to the Erlking, and we have never seen eye to eye."

"You guys seem to have many foes," Kara said. She'd retreated to her place on the bed, as though the moment she shared with Gally had never happened.

"The Erlking is our natural enemy," he said. "You are not. The Erlking and his creatures are part of the balance of this land."

"Continue," I demanded.

"The Erlking is unpredictable. And so are his creatures. Dragonblood coursing through our veins made those of us poisoned unstable. Rogue."

"Rogue fae," Kara said as she patted Ryanne's sweaty forehead with a handkerchief. "I like the sound of that."

"Not to us," Gally said. "They stop belonging to us and have strange moods. There is no balance anymore."

"I've never seen a rogue fae," I said. "You?" I glanced at Sergei and Kara, who shook their heads. Homkar scrunched his brow but didn't answer.

I knew his expression though. He might have seen them but dismissed them as some other creature. Tír D'aois had sections like the depths of the sea, places no sane living being would enter and where powerful and ancient creatures roamed about, creatures like the wall guardians.

Like that woman with the thick ringlets who'd snatched Edward to safety.

"They hide deep in the heart of Tír D'aois," Gally continued. "Nomads. You'd never see them if they don't want to be seen. But their lifespan is cut short since they turn into mortals."

"Is that what happened to your Aghna?" Kara asked. "She went rogue?"

Perhaps talking so much about her softened him but anguish was barely present now. Perhaps Kara smiling at him helped as well.

"No," he said. "Before that fatal day, she made me promise I would never infuse dragonblood in her. She requested to die instead; that she would loathe being unbalanced. And even as my heart was broken, I honored her request. She died in my arms, and we gave her a fae funeral —her body laid on a mound, covered with flowers of the sacred hawthorn. Her energy vanished soon after."

Bricius's wings perked. "That's how we're born," he whispered. "The fae energy returns to land, and a pixie is born."

"Not when the fae is tainted," Gally said. "There were no pixies born from her energy."

"I'm sorry," Kara said.

His jaw clenched. "It is done. I cannot hold to the past anymore. Hatred has blinded me for so long, and thus, I didn't honor my guardianship. I am thankful to Doyle for returning me to peace." He glanced around. "I can feel the change in my taigh, if not outside, deep in its foundations."

"What would this dragonblood do to Ryanne?" I asked, glancing her way. Her whimpering had stopped, though she was restless like someone having nightmares.

"It'll help her fight corruption and drive it away. What would happen later"—he glanced her way as well—"I cannot say. No human has undergone this procedure, and the results can be unpredictable. She's not a being of light like us, not in the strict sense of the word, so mayhap being a human would help her."

"Or not," Kara mused.

"Or not," Gally agreed.

I considered the options. "Humans have darkness and light within them."

"She can call an ogre!" Bricius provided while he zoomed excitedly. "And she turned into a nymph too."

"Did she?" I asked surprised. "You must tell me that story another time."

"Yes, yes, yes."

Gally continued, "The light didn't help Ryanne, as you noticed. There is a barrier within her that doesn't let the light come through. This barrier is different from what I'd seen in tainted fae, thus your *dorcha* makes her feel attacked and makes her worse, as we just saw. Though I must say it's speculation. I do believe dragonblood is the lesser evil here."

"And you believe the human dark side might help to balance the dragon's power?" I asked.

"I can only speculate," Gally said.

"What's the other option?" Kara asked.

"She dies."

"That is not an option," I said.

"Then we go find the dragonblood," Gally said.

"Very well," I answered.

"Unfortunately . . ." Gally glanced at the pixie, who was wringing his little hands.

"What?" I snapped.

"We cannot approach dragons. Not as fae."

"By Anord's balls! You and your light and dark issues. Wait a minute . . . Ryanne told me she rode a dragon with you."

"No." Gally waved a hand. "You're talking about a different kind of creature. The dragons I'm talking about are the Erlking's offspring, as you might well know. The one I called to take Ryanne and I to my Lady's taigh, is a lags."

"A what?" I asked.

"A *Snámh Laghairt*. We call them lags. They're not winged like a dragon, but they can fly, and their scales are usually in shades of red, yellow, sometimes green. They're nocturnal."

"Ah," Sergei said, "I've seen them, but they're shy creatures."

"Quite," Gally agreed.

"You told Ryanne it was a dragon."

"No, she said that. I did not correct her." He sighed while looking at her. "She asks too many questions."

"That she does."

We both smiled, then I dipped my chin in thought. "But we bradaís can approach dragons, can't we?"

"You should know," Gally said. "You all tried to bypass them to get the dragonwood for your ships, isn't it so?"

"Aye, so what?" I said.

"Were you able to approach one?"

Kara, Sergei, and I looked at each other, wary. "No," Sergei said for all of us. "They're tricky and—"

"Dangerous," Gally said. "Too powerful a creature to confront."

"There was this time," Sergei said, "when one of us was cocky enough to face one. He got burned so badly he took fifty years to heal!” He guffawed.

“Who was that? Cedeño?” Kara asked.

“*Da*. He had to hide from Edward, who knows where.”

“Ah.” Kara clicked her tongue. “That’s why he didn’t go to the summoned bradaí council, so Edward beat him good and he had to hide for ten more years.”

Both she and Sergei grinned, to my everlasting exasperation. This was no time for tales.

“Then how did Aghna approach them?” I asked.

Gally shifted his weight, the first indication of uneasiness I’d seen from him. “She had help.”

“From whom?” Kara asked.

If I didn’t know the fae, I would bet my ship his eyes reflected fear.

“Pan.”

FORTY

Ryanne

It was all dark but for a pinpoint of light stories high.

I stood alone in an unfamiliar place. Walls erected around me until their edges got lost in the luminescence above.

"Hello?" I called.

There was no noise here. Where was I? There was no cold either. I pressed my hands over my stomach, but no hunger beset me. Dimly I recalled that I'd dreamt about Edward, but for the life of me I couldn't remember the specifics.

I reached out to one of the sides of the wall and pressed my fingertips against it. Pain rushed to my body like a swarm of water pixies armed with poison, and I doubled over, shivering—a familiar disarming pain.

Edward.

"Stop this," I croaked and lifted a trembling hand to the walls. They couldn't come down—*shouldn't*. So I willed all of me to stand the attack.

Memories rushed to me: Minho's capture, Edward's ship, he pouring dark energy into me.

The red eyes. Pinpoints of crimson in the mist.

"You remember," a cavernous voice said around me.

"Who are you?" I asked. "Let me out!"

"I am not detaining you, little one."

The seer-dream with Anord on a cliff. But the voice didn't sound like the godlike dark creature.

"You're not Anord," I said, annoyed. "And stop calling me little."

A booming laughter deafened me, and I fell to my knees, hands over my ears to stop that laughter.

"I am not retaining you, so you should be asking yourself who is."

Walls. I'd erected them, didn't I? I eyed the wall, not wanting to touch them again to avoid the pain.

I turned in a circle, all four walls were slightly different. It was hard to tell, but the materials varied from one to the other in texture and shade. All shook from the attack except one. Wait. It was shaking except for a rectangular area the shape of a door, a door as tall as me and barely wide enough to pass through.

Tentatively, I reached out, tense and expecting it to hurt. The moment my fingertips reached the area, they went through, as if it wasn't there.

I took a hesitant step forward, still with my arm raised and fingers stiffened, but they touched nothing.

I repeated the steps, and I had a familiar feeling, like when I walked through the taigh's gate while millions of eyes followed my movements, making every single hair in my skin stand. The guardians in the wall.

It was not exactly like Cuidi's though. It was denser, a barrier of thick smoke that could be felt.

Still I kept on, step by tiny step.

I was in a barren land. My hand fell to my side, my mouth agape. A yellowish light covered it, yet there was no sun, no stars, nothing but that sick light.

I turned back, but there were no walls, only the land everywhere I looked.

This place looked familiar, but I couldn't remember from where.

I walked without direction, wanting nothing more than to get out of here. But if I didn't know where I was, how could I get out?

Was I in my mind or was this place real?

Everything around looked the same. I could be walking on the moon or a desert at night, but then there were no animals, no flora, no sounds. No wind. Thought there was something ahead, and I trotted toward it.

The hunched form of an old man.

"I've seen this before," I breathed. "In a vision."

Fog covered the place in seconds.

"This isn't where you're supposed to be now," the cavernous voice said.

"Then where am I supposed to be?" I yelled.

"At my side."

Red dots floated before me. Eyes.

The face of an older man with a mask covering him except his long beard, with antlers that came from a helmet.

I sucked in a breath. The Erlking!

"Yes, it is I," he said, still shrouded in the mist.

"You helped me. Back when I helped Pan out of your lair."

"Ah. Yes. You owe me. The *Wilde Judg* didn't capture you, did it?"

"You helped the fae. To set Pan free."

"I help no one!" he boomed. "No. When you appeared in my lair with that pure heart of yours and the power of the fae within you, I knew I wanted you by my side."

"Why?" I asked, confused.

"You are not fae but close."

His entire form appeared, and I stepped back. What a weird notion that the creature I'd feared the most in my life didn't provoke binding fright. Though neither did Edward.

Perhaps I should revise that. Both creatures warranted fear.

The Erlking waved a hand, and a woman appeared next to him. Thick dark ringlets fell over her shoulders and yellowed teeth peeked from her full lips.

Birdie, the warrior woman. But again, I felt no fear of her.

"Who's she?" I asked. "I saw her before."

"My daughter."

It was then that I recalled her, back in his lair, surrounded by goblins. "I've never heard of you having one. The fae never told me so."

"The fae don't know everything, little one. But she's gone now, grown up and left the nest. I miss her. I need a new daughter." He waved his hand again, and the woman's form vanished into rivulets of smoke.

I blinked. "Why?"

"Life in the lair can get lonely."

"You have your goblins."

"It's not the same." He grinned. "When you wake up, you'll be one of mine."

I pressed my hands on my breast to try to feel *préachta*, but it was empty. "I am with the fae."

His grin grew wider. "And they'll send you to me."

"No they won't." I frowned and turned around. "I don't know where they are."

He guffawed, a harsh laugh that rattled my brain. "They're set to find Pan. He'll lead them to the dragon, and you'll get its blood." His red eyes shone deadly. "Dragons belong to me."

"I don't understand. Why do I need the dragon's blood?"

He jabbed a finger in my chest. "You have a deadly poison coursing through your veins."

Poison.

When he said that, I started to be acutely aware of my body. Of that pain coursing through my veins, of something dark clogging them.

The snakes. Ed's power.

I retched and fell to my knees, my hair falling at my sides. Suddenly I couldn't breathe.

"Don't worry, my child. If the fae does his job well, you'll be cured, and I'll welcome you with open arms."

I curled in a small ball and my fingers dug into the hot rocky soil, wishing for this harsh pain to go away.

To leave me alone.

FORTY-ONE

Titus

The Morrigan take all fae and their stupid plans.

"Pan. That little brat," I said, a vein on my forehead throbbing.

"Who is this Pan and why can he help?" Sergei asked.

"Nitwit," Kara said. "He's the god of the wild and has the legs of a goat."

"No," Gally said, annoyed. "He's a shapeshifter and certainly not a goat. He doesn't look like that at all."

"Just the legs?" she asked with a small smile.

"No, he did that in ancient Greece for fun. He wanted to scare humans and create mischief, which he certainly excels in. But for centuries he's adopted the form of a—"

"Brat," I said. "A boy in rags who loves to create mischief."

"What is he then?" Sergei asked again.

"There is no time for history lessons." I cut short the conversation, the walls of the room closing in, sucking my breath out. "Let's go find him."

"It's important for your friends to understand who we shall be dealing with," Gally interjected. "And Ryanne is stable."

Kara glanced at her. "She *does* look like that sleeping woman in that kids' story."

I took a step toward Gally, fists clenched. "No, fae, she cannot hold forever. We need to move."

"Worry not. I can explain to them as we head out."

"Who'll take care of her?" I asked, barely restraining myself.

"Me!" Bricius exclaimed, chest puffed. "*Mo thiarna*, I'll make certain that she's safe, yes, yes, yes."

"There is no one I would trust her to more," Gally answered.

The little pixie's chest puffed. "I shall make you proud, *mo thiarna*!"

"Go and fetch some of your friends. You'll need them," Gally said.

The pixie zoomed outside.

"A few pixies won't be enough," I spat.

"There'll be more than that," Gally said.

"A hundred. A thousand. Not. Enough."

"You are wrong, Doyle. They are quite brave, as you are aware, besides my guards will also make certain no one bothers her."

Homkar stepped forward. "Captain, I can keep an eye on her."

"No," I said. "I need you. This journey can be unpredictable."

"Say no more, Captain. I'll go wherever you need me."

"Call me Doyle. You're my friend, Homkar. Not to mention there is no ship here."

Homkar thumped a hand on my shoulder. "You'll always be my captain, Doyle."

I thumped one hand on his shoulder as well and brought his forehead close to mine. "I can't thank you enough, my friend."

Gally said, "She'll be safe here, Doyle. My taigh might look vulnerable, but it is nothing like that. It stands strong, and foes can't bring it down."

"Thank you, Gallchobhair."

"There is another thing." The fae addressed Sergei. "Have you made up your mind, pirate?"

"You call my brother Doyle, you call me Sergei, Gallchobhair."

Gally smiled. "Fair point, Sergei."

"And no," the big man shook his head, "not letting you near me."

"Then you cannot come with us, I'm afraid."

"Why not?" Sergei scowled. "I want to help. I've been away from my friends, my family, for far too long. Not anymore. We're a team again, *da?*"

"Because, nitwit," Kara said, cutting in front of the fae, "you'll put us all at risk. With that coin of yours," she jabbed at his chest, "Anord knows where you are. Hence . . ." She lifted her eyebrows at him.

"Edward too." He let several Russian expletives out. "But if I stay to protect Ryanne, Anord would know I'm here."

"Hence," Kara said again, "you should remove your coin." She turned to me. "Does Anord know when you're in a fae's taigh?"

I furrowed my brow. "Fae energy tampers with the beast. There is too much around here."

We all three bradaís looked around us as if said fae energy would come down on us like an anchor. The pixie zoomed inside in that moment, followed by too many of his kind. Gally requested for the others to wait outside so they left, except Bricius, who sat next to Ryanne.

"Per what you've said," Gally said, "I would assume not. But we cannot take any changes, Sergei. Whether you come with us or not, you need to remove your coin. If you do not wish to perform the operation, you would need to leave us."

I brooded. I was counting on Sergei, but the fae was right. It was a risk. And even if he'd wanted to take his coin out, time would not let him. He'd have to recover, and I couldn't afford that.

Ryanne gasped.

We all stared at her. Her eyelids fluttered, and she let out a moan of pain. In two strides, I was by her side. The scar on her cheek and neck throbbed and was still red, and the black thorns over her grayish skin were as present as ever.

"The thorns. They're not receding," I said, holding her cold, limp hand.

"They won't," Gally agreed. "Not until we get her the drag-onblood."

I kissed her cold, sweaty forehead. "I wish I had protected you better."

A thump, then a sharp pain on my arm. Kara had punched me.

"What was that about?" I scowled.

"You're an arsehole, Doyle. She wants to stand by herself. Can't you see how she's fighting Ed's control?"

Ryanne's expression was far from being unconscious. She would frown at times or wince in pain.

"She's not giving up. And you'll help her better if we bring her that blood instead of playing all macho."

"Didn't you say I was her pirate in shining armor?" I arched an eyebrow.

She rolled her eyes. "I was jesting, nitwit."

"No more talking," I said. "Sergei, are you in or out?"

"You know what's next?" Sergei's eyes gleamed.

I pinched the bridge of my nose. Patience . . .

"I'll do it," Sergei boomed. "If that's what it takes to help you, brother, I'm in."

Brother. I felt full. I used to walk alone, but I was not alone anymore. I had my family with me.

"The problem, as I see it," I said, lowering my voice so as not to disturb Ryanne's fitful rest, "is how to locate his coin. Ryanne managed it because we've been practicing."

Sergei cursed in Russian, loud enough to make me wince.

I shot him a glare. "Keep it down."

He raised his hands in mock surrender. "Sorry," he muttered.

"What did it feel like for her?" Gally asked, stepping closer.

"She said it felt denser than the rest of her energy—almost oily." I gestured for him to approach. Trusting a fae with this still felt unnatural, but I had little choice.

He came forward, lifting a curious brow, hands spread in question.

"Here," I said, pointing to the right side of my torso. "Feel for yourself."

His hands hovered over the spot, his eyes slipping shut. His expression shifted to something almost serene, an unnerving contrast to the moment.

"Now here." I waited for him to open his eyes, then directed him to the left, just above my hip—where he'd pierced me through months ago.

His brow furrowed as he focused, lingering longer this time. Finally, he nodded. "I think I understand."

"Good." Kara bounced forward, practically vibrating with impatience. "Do me next."

Gally gave her a bright smile, then repeated the same process, his hands skimming various parts of her body until he paused just below her rib cage.

"Ah." His eyes lit with understanding. "I see. Sergei, I'll try to replicate this with what I did with your kin."

Before Sergei could respond, Ryanne whimpered from across the room, her movements restless and erratic.

I glanced her way, my stomach knotting. "Can we do this somewhere else? She needs rest."

"Of course," Gally said smoothly, already moving toward the adjoining chamber.

The rest of us followed without a word, leaving Ryanne to her uneasy dreams.

Once inside the room, which was bare and utilitarian, Gally placed himself in front of Sergei and touched his forehead with one hand and placed the other over the Russian's ample chest. Sergei spread his feet apart and clasped his own hands behind him.

I wasn't sure if it was because of my own fae power, but I felt in my body what Gally was doing to Sergei. He was infusing *préachta*, like we did to corrupt fae, but it was different here. Instead of an oily and thick energy, his was light and effervescent.

"I believe I know where his coin is," Gally said, eyes still closed. "I located the darkest part and isolated it." He took a step back and looked up at Sergei. "Ready?"

Sergei cracked his knuckles. "Let's do this."

"Who shall help?" Gally asked. "I cannot retrieve the coin myself, and Ryanne was essential for the task."

"Why not?" Kara asked.

Gally filled us in about the requirements and why his fae energy was dangerous to us. Ryanne was the one to do so because her energy was gentler and purer.

We stood confused, and Sergei looked distraught. Ryanne's pureness of heart was not something any of us had, for certain.

"I can help!" The pixie shouted. "I can retrieve the coin, yes, yes, yes."

"That will work," Gally said, pensive. "We would have to cover your hands in dragonskin. Mayhap ask another pixie to help as well."

"Yes, *mo thiarna*! Cassie will do." He zoomed away.

"I'll help in any way I can," Kara said.

"Are you sure you're up to the task?" Gally asked Kara.

"Love, I'd do anything for my brothers. Don't worry."

Gally's expression softened as though he liked what she said. "Then come here. I will pour energy in you to tame your beast. I cannot take any chances. The idea is that your darkness—"

"The beast." Kara smiled.

Gally smiled back. "The beast will be subdued under my energy."

He had the grace not to say it, but he was not taking any chances after I launched at her coin.

Kara stood before him as Sergei just did. Bradaís accepting fae energy—certainly Anord would have a stroke at this. Gally pressed a hand on her forehead and another over her chest.

What an oddity indeed. Accepting the weird *préachta* energy to encapsulate the beast and tame it temporarily.

"Let us do this," the fae said.

"I'll go next door," I said.

Homkar followed me while the rest remained with Gally.

I was glad to return to Ryanne. And gladder that, besides Homkar, this place was empty.

I sat next to her and brushed her face. "Hang on, love. Resist. We're coming."

FORTY-TWO

Titus

Four daighs were positioned already in the room to counteract any issues with Sergei's surgery. As soon as Gally deemed it necessary, they closed the door behind them, and a tinge of envy washed over me. Aye, it could have been me, but I'd hesitated when the fae brought it up and Kara didn't hesitate. Didn't waver.

Kara had stepped in for her brother.

I watched the closed door, impatient, then returned to Ryanne and whispered words of encouragement. But I couldn't stay still and returned to the hall.

"It's done!" Kara came out of the room, dragonskin gloves covering her hands. Bricius, along with another pixie, zoomed outside and grinned.

"So fast?" I asked, relieved.

"Love, it was amazing!"

Gally came behind her, with an awed expression. "You should have seen her, Doyle. She was magnificent. Bricius and Cassie struggled with the coin, but Kara caught it and handed it over to my Lady without a blink."

"He's in love with me," Kara said, winking.

Gally sighed. "Sex is not love, pirate. I have no qualm with sharing a bed with you, nothing more."

"Oh, you want us to play that pirate and fae role again?" She laughed. "I'm in!"

"How's Sergei?" I asked.

"Unconscious," Gally answered, seemingly glad of the turn in the conversation. "But I have a couple of dryads looking over him. He shall be fine. Let's go."

Thank the Morrigan.

Per Gally's explanation, we had a week before the fae's power withered and Ryanne was left to her own devices. Even as time was different in this land, for Ryanne that didn't matter. The countdown was on, and the Morrigan could take me if I let it reach zero.

Two bradaís, one dannan dubh, and a fae on a quest to find a godling with a goat's brain. And said godling was the only answer to cure Ryanne.

Morrigan's crows.

We crossed the wall and avoided looking at the guardians and walked out of the plain spread around his taigh. This area resembled the highlands of Scotland with its high mountains, brass-monkey weather, and rural roads. A cloudy sky over our heads reflected the color of my mood. The whistling wind was a banshee to my ears.

Doom.

"Tell me more about those guardians," I said to Gally to avoid thinking about doom.

"They're ancient ones," he said. "They've always been defenders, and we reached a pact, fae and them, thus they made the wall their domain. It's the ultimate barrier."

"Then why is it destroyed?" Homkar asked.

Gally took his time to answer. "When I departed from the taigh, its guardians no longer felt compelled to defend it and withdrew to a remote area, the dark corner of Tír D'aois. In their absence, other dark creatures invaded and partially destroyed my home. I searched tirelessly for the guardians and was fortunate enough to bring them back. They missed their home deeply and were grateful to return."

Kara turned her head toward the receding taigh. "Creepy creatures. I'm glad they're confined inside. So where are we going exactly?"

"I assume you know where to find Pan," I said to Gally.

"I always have eyes on him. It's in every fae's best interest to know his whereabouts and avoid his coming back to this land. He is forbidden to return, but he's more resourceful than a gnome hunting for mushrooms. As nádhúrtha, he should remain in his dimension, but he's been crossing that line for centuries. Dimensions mean nothing to him."

"Pan is a nádhúrtha?" Kara asked. "I know little of them. Enlighten me, pretty fae."

"Humans have destroyed most of their land," Gally said, "what used to be the most powerful of dimensions. It is in a sorry state, and the nádhúrtha's power has dwindled over the centuries. The most powerful of them are holding Tír na Vraoichta closed to avoid powerful beings like Anord or Odin from returning to create mayhem. Many nádhúrthas have flown to other realities once they realized they couldn't contain humans, as much as they want to cure that dimension. Others are unstable, trying to balance Tír na Donna back to what it was, but it's all for naught."

"Odin is awesome," Kara said in awe. "I'd love to see him again."

"You've met him?" Gally asked, curious.

"Long ago, before the portal was sealed." She sighed in yearning. "I'd follow him anywhere."

"He is not welcome here," Gally said, frowning, "nor the likes of him."

"You were saying about Pan?" I asked, curious for once.

"Pan used to reign over some of the creatures on land like wolves, bears, squirrels, and pumas, among others, but we believe humans drove him to the edge when they all but wiped out his creatures. He also flew to other dimensions. But love of his creatures made him come back, and every time he would go berserk. He began playing tricks back in Ancient Greece, first to trick humans and hoping they would leave his creatures alone."

For the first time, I felt sorry for the little brat.

"As you know," Gally continued, "it didn't go well. Humans took over the natural world and haven't relinquished control since."

"So where is he now?" I asked, itching to know. The cold wind and the somber area matched my mood.

"When I found out Ryanne let him escape, I asked someone to watch over him. The *scáth* Quintus."

"*You* know where Quintus is?" I said, attempting to keep my voice under control.

"Yes. As one of the Eadrom, I ought to do so."

Morrigan's Crow. Ryanne and I spent weeks looking for Quintus in Italy, and all this time Quintus had been in charge of looking out for Pan.

"I'm surprised you're really one of them. I'd always thought Eadroms were wise, level-headed people."

Homkar choked in laughter, and Kara snickered. Gally didn't react.

"When you and I met," I said, "I'd only seen you as impulsive and hotheaded."

"It was because of Aghna. I was made an Eadrom with her by my side." His expression darkened. "I always thought I'd live with her within these walls"—he jerked his head toward the shrinking fortress—"for eons. She was my everything, my sun, my stars. But she was too obsessed with finding the cure for the poisoning."

Kara and I glanced at each other, uncomfortable. We'd tainted fae in the past. Killed some. Hell, I'd tried to corrupt Aghna, bent on fulfilling our creator's wishes and not minding the trail of pain we left behind us.

The nádhúrtha Amriel came to mind. That nightmare had plagued me right after the encounter where I faced my nameless victims. His words, about not giving in. How I almost gave in when I saw Kara's power for my taking back at Frau Engel's. If I didn't find a way to cut off the beast, I'd never be free for good.

I glanced around the plain to dispel those thoughts. First, I had to find the dragonblood to cure Ryanne. A cure that would drive our poison away, but with secondary unpredictable results.

"Your taigh is impressive," Kara said, looking behind his shoulder. "I'd never thought it would be like this. Like a human fortress."

"Have you seen other taighs?" I asked, glad that my mind was occupied with these tidbits of information.

"I've seen Tuiren's taigh," Kara said. "Once, and from afar."

"You have?" I said. "Why?"

"Long story. It reflected wisdom. It's perched on a cliff, and waves constantly seem to salute it, celebrate it."

"Cuidigtheach's taigh reflects calm," I said.

We all looked at Gally.

"Each taigh reflects the inner state of the guardian," Gally said. "When I took residence, it was mine for the taking. It was a different place with Aghna at my side." He looked over his shoulder, the taigh now a blur. "When I lost her, it transformed."

He stopped. "We're far enough to open a portal."

"And this would take us to Quintus immediately?" I asked.

Gally opened the portal by waving his hands, and we stepped through it. It was nighttime in Tír na Donna. We'd reached somewhere rural, lights ahead indicating a village. It was warm enough, and a few stars scattered above our heads. I sniffed the humid air—no sea nearby but it had recently rained, not more than a day.

A waxing gibbous moon was set in the horizon, faintly illuminating the tall, leafless trees around us that reminded me of the titan trees that dragons liked, back in Tír D'aois, in the Valley of the Dragons, a place we would see soon enough, Pan or no Pan.

"Madagascar," Homkar whispered.

That was when I recognized the trees. Baobabs were giant thick trees, nearly twenty meters tall, some even more, with a wispy network of thin balding branches. Marvelous trees.

"Gorgeous," Kara breathed.

"They are amazing, yes," Gally said, hands behind his back as we walked among the baobabs. "One of my favorite places in this human dimension. Aghna and I used to camp under the stars," he whispered, nostalgic.

"Camp?" Kara asked, amused.

"Indeed. She was amazed by this dimension, hence why she was always trying to make it better. Helping humans to be free."

"Aye," I said, pensive. "She was helping humans when Edward and I found her."

Gally furrowed his brow, and I opted to keep silent on the subject.

And here we were, two bradaís chatting amicably with the one we used to hate the most, with someone that our beasts demanded to kill, to maim.

What an irony, my beast always demanded to be far away from them unless it was for the kill. Now that I'd allowed the proximity of one, it was numbed and let me think in peace.

What I'd always wanted.

"Weather's off," Gally observed.

"It was also like that in Italy and Switzerland." I stared at the darkened sky. "Shouldn't there be a myriad of stars here?"

We all stopped and looked up.

"It is weird," Kara conceded. "But weirder is that I thought I saw a strange creature behind. Like a goblin went wrong."

"Ryanne and Pan saw something of the sort when we were running away from the *Wilde Jagd*."

"There's something off, indeed." Gally frowned. "The sooner we find Pan and cure Ryanne, the better. Let us go."

Something pricked the back of my neck, and I glanced around, the land swathed in shadows. But it wasn't the type of energy Quintus or any of his Umbra Gente exuded.

It was an awareness.

"How do you know where to find Quintus?" I asked.

"I simply know. Fae and nádhúrthas have always been allies, so it is easy for us to find each other."

"Ryanne and I roamed Italy in search of him."

"Whatever for?" Gally asked. Kara seemed curious as well.

A faint prickle in my senses warned me we were not alone, but whoever it was, was too far away to know what kind of creature it was.

"We're being followed," Kara whispered while we kept walking.

"Yes," Homkar said, "for five minutes now."

"Friend?" I asked Gally.

"Not Quintus but could be one of his. Let us be on guard but keep walking."

"It is not one of his," I said.

Whoever it was, it might alert someone else. Too foolish to attack the four of us by themselves.

Here wasn't Rome, when Ryanne and I had been ambushed, but I wouldn't take any chances.

"Bradaí," Kara said all of a sudden, taking her sword from her pocket and pointing it toward one of the baobabs.

The awareness swept the area, but it didn't quite feel like a bradaí. It was like Anord was searching, scanning the area, so I hunched my shoulders in reflex.

A hooded figure stepped out from behind one of the giant trees. "Well, well," it said in a hoarse female voice. "Doyle and Kara. What a surprise."

FORTY-THREE

Ryanne

Edward's cabin. I watched everything, while something nagged at the back of my head. I'd been somewhere else, but I couldn't remember where.

Maybe I'd been here all along, in the captain's cabin.

He was sitting at his desk, writing something. He snapped his head and looked around, those cold eyes searching. He seemed to look my way but then he stood.

Again, that emptiness engulfed me.

Colored wind billowed around until it settled on red. My fingers brushed the crimson specs and anger fevered me.

Anger must be red.

I sucked in a breath. That emptiness was what Edward was feeling, if emptiness could be called that. And that colored wind was showing me his emotions. Those non-sappy ones bradaís felt, like anger. Curiosity, anger, even yearning.

Why?

He clapped his hands twice, and the back door opened. The nymphs strolled out, all empty eyes and smiles.

"Sit," he ordered.

The women complied, but I couldn't feel anger at that. Edward was not feeling anything, and this seer-dream was connected with his moods.

Bits of blue dust hovered, and I trailed my fingers over them—yearning. Did he yearn for these women?

Edward paced around. "It's time to find out where the Irish is or any of his so-called friends. Friends." He stopped and addressed the nymphs. "What is that strange word that holds no meaning?"

"Yes, Alpha," both said in unison, flat tone.

He looked at them in contempt. "Pretty heads with nothing but my will in you. But you both listen."

"Yes, Alpha."

Red wind blasted but briefly.

"Minho is my puppet, but he is soon to be gone. And I'd be alone. Alone is good. That's what it means to be a bradaí."

"Yes, Alpha."

"Then why had I never been alone? I like to be surrounded by bradaís. Shen at first, then the Irish, now Minho."

"Yes, Alpha."

Nothing stirred in me as I glanced at the poor creatures. I knew they were strong beings with wills of their own. Were they struggling inside, against Edward's will?

"It's odd," he said as he poured himself a glass of wine, "I've been questioning things since the Irish somehow cut his connection to Anord. His powers should have gone to Minho, per our god's request." He paused. "He failed, so I was meant to be the recipient." He paused again, fingers curled tight against the glass. "And I failed as well."

He placed himself next to the porthole and savored the wine.

"What did Anord mean by having a piece of the puzzle? I'm the puzzle. I'm all he needs. He needs me to take care of a situation. Two, if I'm precise, yes?"

"Yes, Alpha."

"Shut up!" He took a deep breath. "No more talking, just listen. By Anord, I'm starting to miss having the Irish's lover here." He took a sip of the wine. "She's more interesting than I thought."

Huh. And he keeps talking, so he's more alone than I thought. That yearning. For a friend? The poor nymphs sat on the bed like creepy dolls but again, nothing stirred in me.

Why was I connected to him? The power. *His* power in me.

A snapshot flashed before my eyes—the barren land, the old man. Red eyes in the mist.

But Edward's words brought me back to this seer-dream . . . or connection.

"Our beloved creator, Anord"—Edward gestured widely as if he addressed an entire room of spectators anxiously waiting for his wise words—"wanted Minho to have the Irish's ship since the Irish was supposed to be blasted to oblivion. Now, he wants me to forget about the Irish and his lover and focus on the new task he gave me."

A thought struck me. Edward was envious of Titus and wanted to experience the world more like Titus did. That was why he'd kidnapped me and tried to make me his.

Edward sauntered to the nymphs. "What say you?"

They kept silent with that creepy empty smile.

"Good, good." He paced around. "Perhaps it would be best if you were to talk, but there is nothing in you, yes? I wonder if the human I tainted would be like you. She put up a pretty good fight."

Edward stepped right in front of me, and for a moment I thought he saw me. He cocked his head and reached out to me.

His hand went through my chest.

Gray wind swirled around us. Curious.

"I cannot forget about the Irish and his lover," he whispered, not to the room this time, but to himself as if trying to assert his purpose. "But Anord wouldn't mind while I obey him in that task, yes? I'd do as he says, but I'm also—"

A knock on the door.

Edward stepped back, his eyes attempting to pierce what he wasn't seeing.

"Come in," he said, gaze intent.

Minho stepped inside. Edward glowered at him but signaled the nymphs to go away.

Something in me wanted to feel more at seeing them retreat, but I knew I was in for the non-emotional ride. My fae mentors could be cold, and yet I knew they had feelings, emotions, sensations, and reactions at the beauty around them, at situations where they needed to readjust.

Edward's coldness was devoid of everything I'd ever known or felt. I could not feel any type of emotion in Edward besides anger and envy. Titus once said they were filled with other powers: Titus with the fae power, and the rest of bradaís with stolen power from other creatures. Edward alone was only filled with *dorcha*.

"I need another opportunity," Minho said with deference. "To capture the Irish's ship."

Edward gave a dry chuckle. "You had one job. Anord handed you the ship and you blew it."

Minho bowed his head, but not before I noticed how he clenched his jaw. "Our revered Anord certainly would help me again. I was to have his powers!"

"Ah. Yes. But you blew that as well, yes?"

Images hit me, of that blue-skinned god and Edward chatting in different places.

Emptiness housed in my chest.

"Our revered creator," Edward continued, "as you put it correctly, has given me all that I have ever desired. You were to step out of my shadow and be like the Irish should have been."

Edward furrowed his brow and glowered at the bed where the nymphs had been.

"The Irish took a fae like you. Ran away with her."

"I'm not fae," Minho growled, his dark eyes set on Edward.

"Whatever." Edward made a careless gesture with his wrist. "I believed the Irish did it to take a prisoner from right under my nose and then brag about it."

He was talking about Aghna. I remembered that tale.

Edward paced around, pensive. "But then, the Irish never bragged and instead, looked uncomfortable when I graciously forgave him. I thought then he must have taken her for more nefarious reasons. The fae was fine to look upon."

Minho looked confused. Maybe he wasn't used to Edward being open like this or maybe he truly had no idea what he was talking about.

"Now," he continued, obviously not minding Minho's confusion, "he has one of those fae-touched humans as a lover. Despite her not being graceful or interesting, he's kept her for months. And joined forces with an Eadrom to rescue her! And he didn't even try to take my ship.

"What bradaí would refuse to keep the Alpha's ship as a trophy and brag about it? The Irish, that's who. An insurmountable mystery."

"What is your next order, Captain?" Minho asked. "Are we to finish our task with those bradaís?"

"Not yet. I want that fae-touched human. There's something about her."

I knew Minho was upset with this interaction, perhaps because Edward knew Minho was upset.

And Edward was enjoying this.

"She's not going to survive after you tainted her."

"Oh, she will." Edward glanced about and dark tendrils shot out of him, probing. They passed through me and I stifled a gasp. "Such a riveting feeling."

"Feeling?"

"That's what makes it riveting. Now, take your creature friend—"

"Birdie."

"—and find the Irish's lover."

Edward started to blur. The last thing I saw of him was a smirk, right at me. One of the tendrils grew as thick as a troll's leg and twined around me.

Darkness rushed over me, and sudden pain made me retch. A weakness I'd never known engulfed me. I gasped for breath and tried to scream, my nails scratching a dry surface.

The snakes rammed and chipped away. I was back in the walled room and the walls were crumbling.

I was about to die.

No, worse.

I was about to succumb to Edward.

Forty-Four

Titus

Ntombi, one of the lesser bradaís. A vibrant gele of rich, shimmering fabric framed her dark, luscious hair, emphasizing her high cheekbones—sharp and striking. But tradition ended there. She wore sleek, white leather pants that clung to figure and a matching cropped top that gleamed under the light, radiating modern defiance. Her dark eyes sparkled with mischief, the kind that hid dark secrets.

I positioned myself between Kara and Ntombi. "You," I said to Gally to avoid naming him in front of her. "Cover our backs."

Kara pushed between us. "I don't need you to defend me." She pointed her sword to Ntombi. "You want my power; come and get it."

"After you, Iron Maiden?" She tilted her head. "Why would I do that?"

If I'd learned something from my kin, it was not to trust them, although I was good at reading them as well. Many centuries helped with that. And Ntombi's confusion felt real.

Looking more closely, Ntombi didn't have that crazed frenzy look.

I shared a look with Kara. "He doesn't know."

"Who?" Ntombi asked, her expression flat.

"Isn't Anord demanding my head?" Kara asked.

She laughed quietly. "Ah. Our Creator *is* throwing a tantrum." Her beautiful lips sneered. "He can't pinpoint the Iron Maiden, nor Doyle, but he's not sending the Call." She glanced at us, her face puckered. "Not even our Russian friend. That is quite remarkable. I'm guessing it has something to do with that handsome fae over there?" She craned her neck to see Gally behind us.

"If you're not after her," I said, "what are you doing here?"

"Ah. I was looking for you, *a mhuirnín*."

"Here?" I arched an eyebrow, dismissing her Irish endearment.

"I was following you when Anord gave us the order last fall to destroy you. But then, he was confused and didn't know where you were. It was as if you'd vanished from Tír na Donna. Word was you were in Tír D'aois, so I headed there.

"I know people there. The dannan dubh." She beamed at Homkar. "We share some common things, and I found something very interesting. That you were in a fae taigh. I didn't want to believe it unless you were taken prisoner. So I waited outside the taigh, and saw you escape with a human.

"By then, Anord's call had diminished. You still had a price on your head, but he wasn't pulling us toward you. That made me curious, so I've been tracking you. I saw you in Rome, in the catacombs, looking for Quintus."

I remembered that odd sensation of eyes on me when we were in Rome. Maybe Ntombi's presence was why Quintus wouldn't show himself. "You know him?"

"Just by name. He's a slippery one. Very shadowy." Her head tilted back. "I did some research and found he was here, in my territory. Once I knew where, I waited."

"You're very resourceful."

She laughed. She had a deep laugh, throaty and sensual. "Do you think you're the only one who knows how to move around? I have a hundred years on you."

Kara chuckled; her sword was still tight in her hand but lowered. "He thinks he's special."

"Oh, he is." Ntombi's dark eyes glittered. "That is why I was looking for you, *a mhuirnín*."

I was getting impatient. Anord's balls, if I were to get distracted from my goal one more time, I'd behead the next creature before me. I couldn't feel the awareness anymore, but my instinct warned me it'd been Anord searching for me. And my instinct seldom failed.

"Lovely chat," I said. "We'll catch up next time."

"No." She stepped closer to me, her obsidian eyes reflecting the velvety night sky. "You are free."

"Not quite."

"But you are. Edward's jealous of you, and I want in, whatever"—she waved a slender, graceful hand toward me and Kara—"you are doing."

"Not now," I said. Whether she was genuinely curious or not, it had to wait until Ryanne woke. Alive.

Nothing else mattered.

Ntombi grabbed my arm, and if I didn't know better, I'd say she was scared. "He went for Shen."

"Edward?" Kara asked, stepping forward.

"Yes." She let go of my arm. "You were right all these years, *a mhuirnín*. He killed Luc and Thomas, and now he's doing it again. Not just Shen, but Edward also went for Cedeño's throat."

"Shen? Murdered? And Cedeño too?" It was hard to fathom I'd seen the Mexican only a few weeks ago.

"Shen was badly hurt, but he escaped. Word on the Bradaí Network is that Cedeño was able to escape as well, though nobody knows for sure. That Cedeño is as slippery as you. Edward's on the prowl. But something's off, Doyle. Shen and Cedeño had done nothing wrong, so this smells worse than a bloated corpse. And I want off the grid."

"Not now, Ntombi," I said, itching to get out of here but we had to shake her off.

"I can take you to Quintus. I know exactly where he is." She craned her neck once again toward Gally. "Oh, fae? He's getting quite impatient with the task you gave him."

I scowled. Ntombi knew too many things. What was her relationship with Quintus? Had she acquired the mastery of moving in shadows as well?

No, I knew Quintus only showed me because of my distinctiveness. Ntombi might be a lesser bradaí, but the woman was smart. We could trick her and lie as we were wont to do. She wouldn't be fooled, of course, but time was of the essence, and if she knew where Quintus was, by the Morrigan, she would help.

"Very well. Take us to Quintus."

"Are you sure, Doyle?" Gally whispered. "I could find him before the next sunset."

"The quicker, the better."

Kara pulled me. "What if Anord finds us with her here? Edward?" she hissed.

"But if she knows about Quintus, it's better to have her close." Keep your enemies close and all that shite.

Kara nodded curtly. I didn't need to utter words to ask her to keep an eye on Ntombi.

We followed Ntombi, swords at the ready. I was getting a bit lazy, knowing Gally was with us. The way he chased Edward away was making me a wee too confident, and I couldn't afford that.

Walk with family, aye. Rely too much on them, that could be my death.

And walk we did, for an hour or two under the baobabs until we reached a body of water.

She looked over her shoulder. "I believe you know how to call him."

"This is the end of the line for you," I said. "You kept your word. I'll keep mine. Be gone, and I'll find you. Make sure to keep your head under the radar."

Her onyx eyes narrowed to slits. "I'll hold you to it, Doyle. Trick me and you'll be sorry for eternity."

"I wouldn't dream of it."

She acquiesced and disappeared into the trees. I signaled for Kara to follow Ntombi. Gally stepped into a pool of shadows and raised his hands, but no words came from him.

Vibrations hit me. They were coming from the fae. The shadows swirled, and Quintus stepped from the thickest one. A shadow embraced him, then swirled until it turned into a cowl, hiding most of Quintus's eyes.

"Lord Gallchobhair. I have done as you requested and kept an eye on that . . . boy."

Quintus had always been nonchalant, unperturbed. In all the years I'd known him, his voice had never faltered. I sensed a touch of uneasiness now.

"I am grateful for your assistance in this delicate matter, Quintus," Gally said with a different voice. Graver. The type of voice he'd used when we faced each other again a few months back. I cocked my head at him. He'd dropped that recently. Since he found Ryanne and I, and agreed not to fight us.

"It is I who is grateful, Eadrom," Quintus answered in a formula-type tone.

Bloody hell. Could everyone drop the niceties and do what we came to do? Ryanne was waiting, and the sooner we reached her, the better. To hold her again in my arms, feel her warmth near me, her kisses and love.

To have her awake.

I had to focus. I wouldn't be of any help if this sappy emotion took hold of me.

Quintus bowed his head. "May I be dismissed from the task?" A yearning seeped through his otherwise calm words.

"Not yet," Gally said. "I might need you again."

Quintus removed his cowl. Shadows blurred his face, but like dust after a strong wind, they whipped away. Roman features shaped his pale face, tight cropped dark hair, and aquiline nose. His thin lips tightened.

"No. Release me from the debt I owe you and find someone else to take care of that *irrumator*," he spat. "Jupiter have mercy on me. If that *filius canis* pranks any of my Umbra Gente again, I swear to Juno . . ."

The last bit was a string of Latin curses that, despite all, made me laugh.

"What did he do?" Homkar asked, curiosity taken over him.

"He froze a few Umbra Gente when they were in their shadow form. Froze them." His voice quivered with anger. "Then thought it would be hilarious to paint rainbow colors upon them. Painted a shadow! How dare the little *irrumator*!"

Quintus's shadow pulsated as though it was a black hole.

Gally sighed. "Very well, Quintus. We're looking for him anyway. Point us in the right direction and I shall consider your debt paid."

Quintus threw his arm toward the west. "Keep walking that way for fifty *stadium*. You will find him there." He placed his cowl over his head, and shadows blurred. "You cannot miss him."

Once Kara returned and we were certain Ntombi wasn't nearby, we continued trekking through the jungle. We were able to shake off a possible follow up by Ntombi by opening portals. Gally and I seemed to be in a competition on who could open them faster, but in the end, we arrived where we wanted.

Kara and I discussed Edward's attack on Shen and Cedeño. Had they failed Anord? Then there was Ntombi, one of the lesser bradaís, bradaís that usually did what were told and remained the same.

I recalled the woman that Cedeño looked at with love. Love, aye. Now that I knew what it was, it was easy to see.

We could only speculate though.

"Why did that bradaí call you Iron Maiden?" Gally asked.

Kara answered, "Because I sell guns, pretty fae. And I'm tough."

Gally looked surprised. "Do you have a fondness for guns? I was under the impression your kin loathed them."

Kara laughed. "I don't need to love them to sell them. They are fun, though. One day I'll take you to a shooting range."

Gally paused and lifted a hand, and we all stopped in unison, wary.

A boy sat on a branch, looking wistfully at the animals around him: fossa with long tails trudging through the underbrush and lemurs in a nearby tree. Dawn was on us, and the gray land was starting to wake up.

Green reigned in this forest, where moss covered rocks partially submerged in a nearby stream. I couldn't feel that awareness anymore, but that didn't mean it wasn't around. Anord must be pissed off because he couldn't locate me.

"Look at him," Kara whispered. "So lonely."

"Perhaps he's just a hurt boy," Homkar answered.

"Let's not be hasty," I warned.

"Indeed not," Gally said. "Be wary."

We approached the tree, but the boy was still immobile. He looked the same as the first time I saw him, back at the Erlking's lair—dirty face, covered in rags, and dirty blond hair.

"Pan," I called. "We need to talk to you."

The boy looked down at us, then scooted to another branch. The lemurs screeched and jumped in place, but it sounded more like fun than fear.

"Bloody hell, we don't have all day."

The four of us stood next to the trunk yet not so close in case he pulled a trick.

"Pan," Gally called. "We have—"

A shower of something warm and odiferous fell on our backs and heads. Before we reacted, laughter came from behind us. At ground level.

"What the hell?" Kara yelled, drenched in the smelly water.

"The Morrigan take you, little brat!" I wiped the stuff from my eyes and glared at the real Pan, who'd just thrown away a bucket made of wood and branches. I glanced up and saw just a shadow instead of the boy we thought was Pan.

"What did you do, boy?" Homkar bellowed. He spat out foul liquid.

Only the fae stood apparently undisturbed despite being tricked like all of us.

The ragged boy was rolling on the ground, laughing his heart out. "You should have seen your face, Maggot Brain!" He wiped the tears from his eyes and stood, then snapped his fingers.

The figure above, dark and two-dimensional, crawled and reattached to Pan's body. His shadow.

"Now who's this?" Before any of us blinked, Pan jumped onto Homkar's back. "You smell. And you're a Big Idiot. That's your name."

Homkar grimaced. "I am not, you foul boy."

"Big Dannan Dubh Idiot. But that's too long. Hello?" He managed to jump from Homkar to Kara.

"Remove this . . . *thing* from me!" she screamed.

"What is this thing? Skunk scent?" I spat.

"You're not Potato Breath." Pan stuck his out tongue at Kara and jumped to the ground.

Despite his obnoxiousness, he remembered Ryanne. Perhaps all was not lost.

"And a pig-faced fae!" Pan turned around and farted.

"What did you drench us in?" Homkar growled, taking a menacing step toward Pan.

"Lemur piss, Big Idiot."

The lemurs above screeched again, a full ruckus echoing in other trees. It sounded like mocking laughter.

"There's a stream over there," Kara grunted. "I'm cleaning up. Someone tie that brat to a tree."

Pan puffed his chest, hands thumped to his waist. "No one ties the Greatest King Who Has Ever Existed to a tree, you bilge rat stick."

Homkar cracked his knuckles and stepped toward Pan.

Pan's eerie eyes reflected the uprising sun. "No one."

FORTY-FIVE

Titus

We cleaned up in turns to avoid being pranked again by the boy. Or god. Or filthy creature.

The stream lazily flowed, and Pan crouched on one of the moss-covered rocks, spitting into the waters, then laughing every time the spit splashed.

"Now," I said to Pan, "we're going to talk business. You owe us a favor."

"Not to you, Maggot Brain."

"To Ryanne."

"Who?"

I pinched the bridge of my nose. "The one you call Potato Breath."

"Ah! The human. Why didn't you start with that?"

"She's dying."

He shrugged. "That's great. I won't have to pay the favor back."

I seized the shabby shirt in my fist and brought his face next to mine. "Listen to me, you shitty brat. Ryanne helped you escape from the Erlking's lair, hid you from the *Wilde Jagd*, and now she needs a favor from you. Do you understand me?"

"Your breath stinks." He faked gagging.

"You are going to take us to the dragons and ask for their blood."

He froze in mid gag. "You want dragonblood?"

"Aye."

His face turned serious, so I released him and straightened. Perhaps I'd finally been able to put some sense into him.

"Did the pig-faced fae tell you what happens with dragonblood?"

Gally rolled his eyes. A strange reaction coming from him but totally understandable.

"Aye," I said. "She'll be unstable. But she'll live."

I'd seen killer whales attacking a seal. The water takes the form of the whale right before they break the ocean's surface. Pan's eyes held that same eerie quality.

"You should know, pirate, dragons are Erlking's creatures. Fae before have attempted this, but the consequences are dire. The Erlking is unpredictable, and no one understands why he does what he does."

I didn't know what surprised me the most. His serious speech, his warning, or the lack of insults.

"Ryanne's strong," I said.

"So are the fae," Pan answered.

"Pay the favor back, Pan, and help us with the blood."

Mischievous eyes replaced the previous seriousness. "If I'm allowed back to Tír D'aois without any consequences, yes."

"No, absolutely not," Gally all but yelled.

"Just a month." Pan shrugged.

"Not even a day," Gally seethed.

"I have to go in to give Potato Breath the blood."

"Just for that," Gally said.

"And a day."

"No."

"Then I won't." He sat on the mossy rock and whistled. "Also, now the smelly piggy fae"—Pan pointed at Peter—"must say all the great things that I am."

"It's going to be the shortest list in the world," Kara said, as she made it back to the clearing a bit less stinky.

"You must," I said. "You must return the favor back."

"The favor is owed to Potato Breath, and she's not here. Besides," Pan said in a whiny voice, "the fae won't let me in."

I glared at Gally.

"All right," he conceded. "One day free in Tír D'aois after you successfully deliver the dragonblood to us."

"And I want the Big Idiot to carry me." Pan lifted a smelly, dirty, callused foot that could pass as a baby elephant's. "I have delicate feet, and I can't walk much."

Homkar glared but acquiesced with a bow of his head.

"Pan," Gally said in his formal voice, "say the words."

He jumped to his feet and lifted a palm. "I, Pan, the Greatest Excellency That Has Ever Existed, the King of Human Maggot-Filled Land, agree to deliver dragonblood to Maggot Brain and the pig-smelly fae in order to fulfill the favor to Potato Breath"—he hung his head—"who's sadly dying." He mimicked flinging a non-existent tear from his eye.

"I, Lord Gallchobhair—"

"Lord of the pig-smelly fae," Pan happily provided.

Gally glowered. "Agree to allow Pan—"

"His Greatest Excellency and King of Human Maggot-Filled Land."

"Into Tír D'aois in order for him to provide dragonblood." Gally cleared his throat.

"And?"

"And allow him to stay in Tír D'aois for a full twenty-four-hour day in accordance with Tír D'aois' time."

"*Gamóto.*" Pan grimaced.

Gamóto. I searched my brain for that word. Greek. Aye, Greek for . . . ah, Pan and his filthy mouth!

He then snapped his fingers. "Very well. Now have Big Idiot kneel before me so I can climb him."

I felt like a huge weight had lifted from my shoulders and hope rekindled in me.

Ryanne had a chance.

She could be saved.

FORTY-SIX

Titus

Not wasting time, Gallchobhair opened the portal, and we stepped into Tír D'aois, where a place remarkably similar to where we just left awaited us: a forest with green-leafed trees, moss-rocks and streams crisscrossing the underbrush.

Pan inhaled deeply and sighed, his hands latched to Homkar's thick neck. If Homkar was bothered by the boy clinging to his back, he didn't seem to show it.

"I'm already picturing the lovely nymphs. Has their hair grown back?" Pan asked Gally, who deigned not to answer but instead trudged forward.

"This is odd," Kara said as we started to walk through the underbrush. "I'd never been focused on trying to save someone."

"Aye," I said. "We were created to destroy, not to build."

"Or cure," Kara said, pensive.

"Indeed it is a change," Gally said. "You are working as a team for a good cause. I never thought I would see this."

"Ack!" Pan made as if retching. We all ignored him.

"Ryanne's lucky to have me," I said. "Thanks to me, we are all here in this quest to save her."

"You surely are jesting," Gally said. "It was I who made all this happen."

"You're deluded, fae. I found Edward's ship."

"Which you wouldn't have without my help."

"You didn't even know we could find our ships at sea!"

"And who made your Alpha run away?"

"It was my plan, if you recall."

"And yet—"

"*Hése mas*!" Pan said. "*I* am saving her. Without me, you can't get the dragonblood. Now chop chop, Big Idiot. You're going too slow."

I glared at the brat, who was now using Greek insults, and so did Gally. Homkar grunted.

"I found you," I said to Pan.

"With my help," Gally intervened.

"Enough of this nonsense," Homkar said. "Neither of you are the one saving her. Pan is right. He's the one doing it."

Pan grinned his mischievous smile.

"No. It was I who requested Quintus to keep an eye on him," Gally said.

"And we're the ones who made him come," I said.

"You would never have done that if Ryanne didn't save him in the first place," Homkar said.

"Yeah! Tell 'em, Big Idiot!"

"And you, fae, you forget she's in this situation because of you," Homkar addressed Gally, "gave her *your* power so she could be in harm's path."

"We didn't—" Gally started.

"Yes, you did."

I puffed my chest.

"And you, Captain," Homkar said, "you took her along instead of leaving her with the fae."

"Aye, but—"

Homkar continued, "Because of her kindness you are not under Anord's control anymore. Because of her Kara isn't either."

"Of which I'm grateful," Kara said, obviously enjoying this exchange so much she hadn't even bothered to intervene.

"I helped as well, don't forget that," Gally said.

It was my turn to glare at him. "You tried to kill me for revenge. Don't feel smug."

"So all of you"—Homkar waved his hand to include all of us, including the little brat—"have lots to thank Ryanne for. For her kindness and selflessness, something not one of us can brag about."

Even the little brat had the decency to shift his gaze elsewhere.

We kept walking through the undergrowth, the scenery hardly changing at all. Gally would stop at times and move his hands as though painting in the air then carried on.

"You could be right," I conceded.

"Ryanne could have been out of harm if she stayed put as we requested last November," Gally insisted.

"Don't push it, fae," Homkar growled. "As my captain says, she's on this path because you placed her on it first."

"Free will is involved," Gally said.

"Free will my arse," Homkar replied. "You showed her the fruit, let her lick, then pretended she shouldn't bite too? I call bullshit."

Gally blushed. "I never thought of it that way."

"Are we going to walk all the way to the Valley of the Dragons?" Pan whined.

"You're not walking, little brat," Homkar grumbled once more.

"I'm older than you, dannan," Pan grumbled louder.

"We're not," Gally said. "I'm waiting for the right spot to open a portal."

"Then do it soon," Pan said. "I'm getting tired."

Gally nodded. "Wait 'til we arrive at the dragons' mountains. There's a steep climb there."

"Of all my luck!" Pan blew a raspberry.

Kara grinned. "I never knew traveling with a bunch of idiots would be so fun!"

Perhaps all of them were having fun. I wasn't. I couldn't wait to obtain that blood and hope for the best.

If all failed, I'd go to Tír na Vraoichta itself and find a way to kill Anord.

Dragons flew over the valley. Giant trees stood like Titans' arms protruding from the earth. Their colossal trunks were smooth, like polished marble—the first branches began dozens of feet above the ground.

It had taken Gally an hour to find the right spot. I wasn't aware there were energy tunnels throughout Tír D'aois; I'd usually just try to find a place where energy felt akin to where I meant to travel, but this was even better. If this went well, I could go anywhere in this huge dimension if I knew what to look for.

Albeit those tunnels didn't carry you over to the Valley of the Dragons, and we'd wasted a few hours climbing the mountain. While everyone yapped, I kept my mouth shut, focused on my task.

Focused on saving Ryanne.

Pan had explained dragons gathered at dusk, and it was the perfect time for our task. But it was better if only Homkar, who could fight alongside me if trouble arose, and I went with Pan, to avoid attracting too much attention.

Now, we three were ready to keep on—I at least. Pan sat, his back against the bark of a tree, claiming he needed all the rest—and all the food anyone could bring to him while he snapped his fingers.

He indeed acted like a rotten king, though whatever lurked behind his eyes made me wary: there was much more to this creature than a simple brat.

Homkar was talking to Kara and even smiling. Their easy banter only made me growl louder. I did not understand the levity of everyone else.

Except the fae. He at least was as concerned as I was.

Gally took me aside. "Take the phial." He produced a tear-shaped phial. "Pan should place the tip on the dragon's neck and blood will flow."

"Understood." I stored it in my bradaí pocket.

"What did you do?" Gally blinked his eyes at the lingering silver sparks.

Seemed I also had to share trade secrets. "It's a dimensional space, belonging to each bradaí. When we were ready, Anord let us use it. We can store some things there."

"I didn't know that."

"It's pretty handy."

He seized my arm and whispered, "Make certain Pan asks for a young, female dragon."

"What do you mean, ask? Wouldn't any dragon serve?" I frowned at the mountain.

"It is all about the energy. While females in adult form are as aggressive as males, sometimes even more, males are aggressive upon hatching. The older they are, the worse their energy is. This is of vital importance."

"Very well." I glanced up to the soaring dragons, some with a thirty-meter wingspan. "Is this really the only solution?"

"You cannot afford to have second thoughts now, Doyle. My power is temporal, but she still suffers nightmares from the poison coursing through her veins. To defeat such poison she should battle it herself, aided with the dragonblood."

"And her own power is not strong enough, I know. But I cannot help but fear the outcome. What she'll become."

Gally seemed to mull upon those words. "Indeed," he finally said, "that is most unpredictable."

"And she'll balance eventually." I stared at him.

"We can only hope."

And with those dreary words, I set up to find the blood.

"Let's go, you two," I snarled. My temper was running shorter the more time we were away from the taigh.

"We'll keep busy here," Kara said, winking at Gally. "Don't you lot worry about us."

Curiously, he didn't complain and almost smiled.

"So, Big Idiot, ready to carry me again?" Pan grinned at Homkar.

"Call me Big Idiot again and I'll call you Flat Pancake, if you get my drift."

"You're no fun."

"Shut up and climb."

The boy eagerly did. Homkar barely flinched while Pan adjusted his weight upon my first mate's back.

We left Gally and Kara at the apex of the mountain overlooking the valley.

A Dragon Gathering was something new for us bradaís—we hardly knew a thing about this place and yet we acted as if we did.

"Pan," I said. "You are to find a young female dragon for this task."

"Don't tell me what to do."

"I'm serious. This is imperative, do you understand?"

Pan turned his eerie gaze at me. "I know what to do, Maggot Brain."

If Aghna used him before and he complied, then we should be good. Still I couldn't breathe with ease. Not until I saw Ryanne awake and balanced.

The climb was steeper now, and I felt like a goat. There was an alpine vibe to the area, windy and cold. No fauna at all, or flora, only rocks and the whistling wind.

Empty, except for some of those odd gnomes-slash-goblins. They hissed at us, but one look at Pan and they scurried away. It demonstrated they weren't afraid of bradaís but of the nádhúrtha.

The climb to the top was unexpectedly quiet. Homkar was focused on finding the right spots on the rocky wall to climb. Pan held tight to Homkar's neck though I was certain Pan wouldn't hurt himself if he were to fall.

The perks of being an immortal brat.

Craggy peaks rose everywhere, and mist rolled around the silent place. No more odd creatures, not even small ones. The higher we climbed, the colder it got.

We finally reached the top. Boulders were scattered around, and we hid behind one. I retrieved the phial from my bradaí pocket in case I couldn't do it later. Dragon magic was strong; the flapping of wings, grunts, and heavy smell of smoke hung in the air. With a patience and carefulness I'd never expect from the nádhúrtha, Pan peeked from behind the boulder he was hiding. He lifted five fingers, and before I could nod, he dashed toward the dragons.

"Hey, pimple faces, you're uglier from up close. What, a worm ate your tongue?"

Homkar cursed, and I sighed. Knowing a sword would be of no use against dragons, I headed toward what could be our doom, Homkar trailing behind.

FORTY-SEVEN

Titus

A grinning Pan stood in the center of the rocky esplanade. Five dragons in a semicircle stared down at him. My steps faltered. It was one thing to fight fae, another to fight invincible creatures who could burn me to a crisp. I would heal, but it'd take me eons to recover my normal self.

It took Cedeño fifty years to heal back to his old self.

Ryanne couldn't afford to wait even one more day.

Homkar stepped into the clearing, and by the Morrigan, so did I. Pan was still grinning, hands on hips. So were the dragons, if such creatures could grin.

Homkar exchanged a concerned look with me.

Five humongous heads lifted, yellowish slitted eyes boring into us.

"It's rude not to answer," Pan said to us, furrowing his brow.

"Answer what?" I asked.

"Apologies, mighty lords," Homkar said, bowing his round pate at the dragons.

"Ah!" Pan said, dashing to our side. "Maggot-brains are stupid and ignorant. I forgot that." He jumped and slapped me. A migraine erupted in my brain,, and I winced.

I opened my mouth but then the migraine subsided. A myriad of voices erupted inside my head.

"They steal our wood."

"Puny little things."

"They are brave."

"Brave and stupid."

That last voice I recognized as Pan's.

"Let them speak," said the first voice.

"No, they do not deserve to be here. Let us eat them." An orange-scaled one leaned its head toward us.

"No eating," Pan said, *"you'll get indigestion, and your tummy will hurt for many moons."*

The dragons dipped their heads and agreed. Thank the Morrigan. I wasn't looking forward to spending eternity in a dragon's stomach anytime soon. Albeit what really surprised me was the ease Pan had with them. It sounded like a reunion of all friends.

"So, are we in agreement?" Pan asked.

The dragons whispered among themselves, then one puffed smoke at him.

"Very well, godling," one of the dragons said. *"You shall have the blood. But first, payment."*

I leaned toward Pan and discreetly pointed a green one, the smaller of the lot so possibly the youngest. "That one would do."

"Leave it to me, Maggot Brain. Potato Breath will have the best."

"Not the best, just young and female." I handed him the tear-shaped phial.

Pan shooed us. "Wait next to the boulders. Only creatures of great power can see this."

"No," I said. "I'm staying"

"You cannot," Pan said. Darkness shifted behind his eyes. "I'm serious. You are not allowed. Go and hide behind the boulders until I return. Off you go."

Pan retrieved the flute that was named after him from within his dirty rags and started to play and dance. The dragons lowered their long necks and puffed smoke.

I was in the dark regarding dragon body language, although it wasn't hard to see they were enjoying Pan's performance.

"He has good footwork," Homkar said.

I clenched my fists but hid with Homkar behind the boulder. I waited for as long as I thought was prudent and put a finger on my lips, then slinked my way around the boulder.

I could not see Pan through the backs of the dragons. One of the tails lashed at me, and I had to jump. From the cluster of dragons, a humongous head raised, and its eyes zeroed in on me.

Scales as dark as midnight covered it, slitted crimson eyes that gleamed with malice. Jagged horns framed the massive triangular face, etched with evident disdain for me. Or for any biped creature but Pan.

It exhaled, releasing billows of smoke tainted with the scent of brimstone.

"*Who are you? You dare!*" Its voice was rough and male.

It advanced and the other dragons parted for him. Crimson nested among its horns as if the fire in it consumed his body.

I lifted my hands in a peaceful attitude. "I thought you'd finished. I'm—"

The dragon opened his mouth, and a ball of fire formed in his immense jaws.

"*Wait!*" Pan jumped between us, his back to me. "*Pardon this stupid pirate, mighty Balzgroth. He's going now.*" Pan signaled with one of his hands for me to retreat.

Having no choice, I did, step by step without turning around. Doing so might make this seemingly old and powerful dragon forgo Pan's request. Homkar snatched my shirt and pulled me to him.

We were with our backs to the boulder on the other side of the esplanade, my heart thumping fast.

"Boy said to stay put, Captain."

"I know. I wanted to make sure Pan was following instructions. Ryanne's life is on the line and the fae stressed it should be a young female dragon."

"Why female?" Homkar asked. "Makes no sense. Why would anyone think females are more easily conquered than males?" He chuckled softly,

I scowled more, and Homkar sobered up.

"Sorry, Captain. I know you're hurting."

I gave a curt nod.

"He saved you."

"So it seems."

"That brat is something unique," Homkar mused. "Unpredictable."

"He's more than just a brat," I said, remembering the shifting darkness. Perhaps even more dangerous than dragons.

We remained like that for what seemed like an hour. When Pan finally strode back to us, his chest was puffed like a rooster and expression smug. The dragons growled and flapped their wings, then took flight, the one Pan called Balzgroth among them.

My heart eased. It would not do to be incinerated while Ryanne needed me.

"I told you I had this. Didn't you see how friendly and malleable they were?" He placed the phial inside his shabby shirt. "Now let's go. Potato Breath is waiting for us."

Without hesitation, Pan descended the mountain with purpose.

I looked up to the sky swarmed with dragons. Not in the many years I'd walked the Earth had one of mine been able to approach a dragon. No one had, in fact.

No one but Pan.

Not having another choice, I followed him.

"You worry," Homkar said.

"This is the first time I've felt impotent. Weak. What can a bradaí do against a dragon? Nothing. Absolutely nothing."

Pan was like a goat, not missing a step at any moment.

"Then why did he need *me* to climb up?" Homkar said.

"I have a crazy theory."

"Can't wait to hear it." Homkar continued the slow descent.

"He's fond of you."

"Growing fond of his mount, you mean."

"Perhaps."

Homkar kept silent and so did I as we continued our descent. There was nothing more to say.

Nothing more to do but hope this worked.

FORTY-EIGHT

Ryanne

Soft voices came from above, voices that sounded familiar, but for the life of me, I couldn't attach faces. I lay in a tight curl and tears were a faraway memory. My body spasmed from time to time. It'd taken me a while, but every time the dark energy—those slithering snakes—rammed against my defenses, my body reacted.

Or what I thought my body was.

It was inevitable that my defenses would collapse. The jerking was more often, and I tightened up. I was going to give in, and Edward would ram his way in. My connection would be severed.

I'd become a puppet. Glazed eyes with no will of my own.

I'd lose my friends: my darling Bricius, my beloved Peter. Cuidi. Would Edward send me against Titus? Make him hate me? Worse, Edward wanted me to make him feel. What if he took me to his bed, and I complied?

What if Edward commanded me to kill any of them? Deceive them?

Did I risk everything just to be the cause of Titus's failure? Of the fae being wiped out of their land?

Tears came back, so many I choked, along with a deep despair.

I grew ashamed at my show of weakness. Stop it!

I wiped the snot from my nose just to discover there was none. My body jerked. Another attack.

Enough!

I wasn't going to become a puppet with no will of my own. I would never go against my friends or my mentors. Against Titus.

Never.

Could I do something from here? Not curled up in a ball, that's for sure. Taking heart, I came unwound. Soft wings, like that of Bricius, caressed my cheek, and I turned around in a daze. For a second I thought I heard his voice from faraway.

"Bricius?" I called, desperate to see my little friend.

How I missed the bug! But he wasn't here, otherwise he'd be flying about.

Where was I?

As I had grown accustomed to, there was dense fog everywhere.

Before another spasm occurred, I stood up, legs wobbling. A memory came, of a pooka stealing something of value, something that could help me. I padded my chest, but the necklace wasn't there.

"Hello?" I yelled. "Anyone here?"

Even the Erlking would be welcomed. I started to walk without any direction because it really didn't matter. I only wanted to feel alive once more.

It was hard to feel here. Not fear, nor hate . . . nor even love.

It was like first waking up when my mind hadn't kicked into gear yet. Instead it insisted on mulling over the tragic events of the night before. Except that my mind felt sharp. It was only that *something* was missing.

Terribly missing.

"Hello?" I called again.

Snippets of a vision came to me. I'd been running in this same barren land, some time ago. When did I have that vision? Or maybe it wasn't a vision but a memory.

I started to run, just to remember. Run, run, run.

Just like the bug would have told me, no, *commanded* me to do. My chest hollowed, missing him so much. And someone else. My dark-haired pirate, with eyes the color of . . .

I stopped in my tracks. For some reason, I couldn't remember what hue his eyes were, and that troubled me so much.

Titus. Bug. Visions.

Barren land.

Edward.

They were connected somehow, but my head hurt with the effort of trying to figure it out. It was full of interference, noise, and anxiety.

I turned slowly, taking this nothingness in.

I'd seen this land when Titus and I fought Edward. When I'd jabbed a goblin's blade into his neck.

Yes! That's when I saw this vision.

And I'd seen Edward in his cabin back at his ship, in those seer-dreams. But I couldn't connect the dots.

A dark shape materialized in the fog. A figure. It strode towards me. I placed a hand over my eyes to try to discern its features.

"Lovely Ryanne," a woman purred, slightly taller than my own five-foot-seven.

Her voice was familiar. She came into view, dark thick ringlets falling from within her hood and partially obscuring her face.

"You're that woman who was with Minho," I said, lowering my hand. Not only Minho, but didn't the Erlking show her to me? "You're the Erlking's daughter."

And the warrior woman who killed everyone in my vision. I should be afraid, but I couldn't feel here. Not fear, at least.

She lowered her hood, and brown-yellowish eyes stared at me. "Oh, dear girl! To be classified as just someone's daughter isn't the way things go nowadays, is it?"

"Then who are you? And why were you at Frau Engel's?"

"Ah! That is the real question. Who am I?" She circled around me. "I was someone before. Different. But I woke up in the Erlking's lair. He was curious about me and decided I would be his daughter." She shrugged. "Then, one grows up and decides to come out from Daddy's shadow."

"You haven't answered my question. Why were you at Frau Engel's?"

"Who?"

"The Swiss lady?"

"Ah, yes. Sweet, sweet Frau. I had a dream of you. I saw Engadin Valley and Engel's place. I headed there, and you showed up next day." She shrugged. "Simple."

"Why would you dream of me?"

She looked around. "I am in a dream now. This is not me, as this is not you. And I dream dreams. Where are we?"

She said it casually, but maybe because of the time spent with bradaís, I felt something behind her words. While something in me compelled me not to lie, I could skirt facts.

Not to mention I had no idea where I really was.

"In a dream," I said. A seer-dream so there was truth in my statement.

"Hm. Where are you dreaming?"

Even if I knew, something told me not to tell her. "Birdie. That was your name. Did the Erlking name you that? Birdie?"

"Of course not," she snapped. "I am Birdie because I wanted to be named like that. Free as a bird." She scrunched her face. "He's inside my head, attempting to control me again, but I'm free. Free!"

She vanished. Not slowly, but one second, she was there, and then she wasn't. "Wait! Don't go!" *Why are you in my dreams?*

I shivered while the fog thickened. Red spots floated nearby.

"Erlking!" Anything but being alone again.

"You're warming up to me. Good. Everything is falling into place."

"Everything what?"

"You'll see, little one, once you're awake. I have a gift for you."

A necklace suspended in the air, a silver one with a locket, and I took it. It felt familiar but, at the same time, different. I put it on, and its coldness seeped into my skin. I knew it wasn't right, it should not feel cold, but I left it there.

"Yes, it fits you right," the Erlking said.

The red dots began to vanish.

"No, don't go!"

"I'll be back. Soon."

FORTY-NINE

Titus

The next couple of hours were as odd as a doubloon in modern times. We treaded through the underbrush at the base of one of the mountains, the Valley of the Dragons at our backs.

Since Pan descended, we only had time to signal the others and carry on. The fae had tried to talk to me, but I was in no mood to oblige him. Pan snapped at anyone who tried to interact with him and seemed focused on fulfilling his part. Perhaps his only motive was to pay the debt then create havoc; certainly his mind was occupied in the many things he would do once free.

Without meaning to, we were in a single line, walking through an endless meadow with a cold sun above us. No animals, no birds, except for dragons soaring high.

Worry ate at me. Would Ryanne accept this blood? What if she didn't? I could not have that, so she better accept it.

Pan strode forward, his steps never faltering. Homkar stepped behind him, but neither crossed a word with the other. Kara and Gally had fallen into some sort of camaraderie and talked amongst themselves at the rear. For a fae who had loathed my kin for centuries, he'd turned around fast.

Perhaps there was hope for us, as Ryanne said.

Ntombi waited for me, and she could very well be the fourth bradaí to turn away from Anord.

Shen and Cedeño might be persuaded as well, if they were still alive —although I still had reservations about Shen's motives. Cedeño had always been quite reserved, the most quiet of all, and seemed quite unfazed about anything related to the bradaís.

Now that I thought about it, Cedeño was a mystery. But we needed all the help we could get in order to face Edward. Though at the same, who could say my kin wasn't preparing another coup?

It had happened already. We'd tried to stir the nest, and the nest stung back and removed any leadership I could have had. Kara's reassurances that bradaís needed someone other than Edward to lead had fallen into the drakken's black pit of hell.

Ryanne I could count on, but now, she lay unconscious and nothing was certain.

I'd expected to have Ryanne and myself practicing our power together before facing the Alpha. Everything had fallen apart. We'd finally found Quintus but for a different reason, and not even Gally knew how long it would take Ryanne to balance. Or whether she would at all.

In any other circumstance, we could remain hidden behind Gally's taigh walls.

Behind a bloody taigh. Hidden.

If this wasn't a complete turnaround, I didn't know what was. Now a taigh felt like a safe place for us—though temporary. As long as Anord wouldn't start a hunt, his own *Wild Jagd* against me and mine.

That awareness I felt back in Madagascar, I knew it'd been him. He might have even sent Ntombi to bring back tidings of me and Kara.

"I believe it's time for you to tell me what happened," Gally said.

The fae had placed himself next to me while Kara was talking to Homkar.

"I was not able to see," I said.

"Why? I thought my instructions were clear."

"Tell that to Pan." I jerked my chin toward him, who was still striding in the front. I told Gally what happened and how the dragon made me retreat.

"Which dragon was that?"

"Pan called him Balzgroth."

Galley stumbled then snagged my shirt. "Do tell me Pan didn't use his blood."

"No." I removed his hold. "He said he did as instructed."

"But you didn't see it."

"I was not allowed."

"What did he exactly say?" Gally demanded.

"That he had this, is all." I glowered toward the front where Pan had already gained terrain. "Does he lie?"

"He's like a fae. He wouldn't lie directly, but he can skirt around facts."

We started walking fast again, attempting to catch up with the rest.

"Should we worry?"

He mused upon my words. "When Aghna used Pan before, the dragons had no problem with acceding to this request. And Pan, surprisingly, honored his word. So I believe we're good."

"What is it with him and the dragons? I also saw him controlling hellhounds when the Erlking sent the *Wilde Jagd* after us, and he's not even from Tír D'aois. And the dragons acted like friendly trained puppies around him."

"I'm not certain. We as fae have power in Tír na Donna, even as it is not the same as in our land. Nádhúrthas certainly have power here as well but like us in their dimension, it's dimmed. Pan, though, has the same influence on creatures here as he has in Tír na Donna. It's odd, but I've thought about this before. No one can contest his love for his creatures. They must sense the same. He cares for four- or six-legged creatures, not bipeds like us."

"Even dragons."

"Even dragons."

I jerked my chin at mysterious Pan. "What's he doing with us, anyway? I thought he wanted to cause mischief here. That he'd just hand us the phial and then be gone."

Pan had not said a word since he descended by himself. It had been us following him. And he'd taken us right to Gally's taigh through a portal of his own, though he couldn't arrive at the taigh's doors. He'd taken us right at the border.

"I've been pondering that question ever since he acquired the dragon's blood. Were I not familiar with his character, I might suggest that his intention is to ensure Ryanne obtains it."

The Morrigan take Pan. As if we would do something else with it. And yet, I would have done the same, not trusting anyone.

"Could he really care?" I said.

"I cannot fathom anything else. He has nothing to gain here. Is there anything else that happened I should know about?"

"I was able to hear everything because Pan activated something in me. Everything except the first exchange, but Pan was surprised I couldn't hear them. Homkar though was hearing from the start."

Gally sighed. "We should be good, Doyle. Ryanne should be good."

My heart constricted at these words. Aye, she *would*.

He stopped and told everyone to wait, then opened a portal. After we stepped through, we kept going in the same order.

"Did Aghna ever try with the dragons?" I asked.

I don't know who was more surprised about this conversation, me or the fae. Hell, we almost behaved like ship mates.

"No. But she was very sensitive to their energies and respectful to them, or any other creature, and that is why Pan liked her."

"Pan liked her. Aghna. And she liked him?"

"The only one who did." He smiled.

"Nothing to do now but sail with the wind."

"There is another matter I would like to discuss with you before we reach my taigh."

"What is it?"

"It is better if only I am present when Ryanne takes the blood."

"That's not an option."

"Are you aware of what happens?"

We hadn't discussed it even though I could understand the mechanics. "You push the blood to her body as we bradaís do with our energy. The dragon's energy does something with our *dorcha* and she recovers."

"With the dragon's energy within her."

"Aye. I gathered as much."

"Dark energy. Similar to what you have inside." He cocked an eyebrow.

"You're afraid I'll react like when you extracted Kara's coin."

"You're not over Anord's control. He cannot pinpoint you, and gold and destruction aren't your aim anymore, but you are still his creature."

"I won't hurt Ryanne."

"You wouldn't hurt Kara either."

"I launched after her power, not her."

"And you would have obliterated her."

I gritted my teeth. "I would have regained control before I snatched the coin."

"We cannot know that, can we? No, Doyle. If Edward's dense energy leaves Ryanne, I need to dispose of it. I don't want you anywhere near it."

"That's it?" I laughed. "No, Gally. We don't care about that energy. That's not power. It's only useful against fae or humans, not us."

"It is not? Are you certain?"

"I am." I gave him my predatory smile just for fun.

He scoffed.

"It's only the coin that Anord put inside us that matters. That dark energy is called *dorcha*. But it's useless outside of us. Is that what happens?"

Gally hesitated. "I am not sure. I was never present at Aghna's experiments, though she talked about them with me. To be honest, we do not know exactly what the dragonblood does to your *dorcha*."

"Do you have a guess?"

"I assume it pushes it out, but again it is pure speculation."

"As long as it deactivates Ed's energy, I'm good."

"I as well."

Aye. We were certainly changing and more comfortable with each other. And all thanks to Ryanne. Homkar was right. She was the catalyst for change here.

After the last turn, we reached the taigh, looming and menacing. The daighs, despite Gally was with us, glowered at each bradaí yet started at seeing Pan, their hands scrambling over their swords' pommels. He didn't even pay attention to them but kept walking as if on a quest. The daighs looked up at Gally, then opened the doors. Pan hadn't broken stride.

That was quite odd.

I said to Gally, "Could it be that he wants to make certain that the favor gets paid?"

"By the troll's bridge, that's it. Yes, that is correct. It all makes sense now. If we were to take the blood for ourselves or for another person, then the favor is not paid."

We both looked pensive at Pan. "Are you thinking the same as I?" I asked.

"Yes, he'll create havoc once he makes certain his favor is paid and complete. I'll have daighs after him." He sighed. "That would not be enough, I'm afraid, but I do hope the damage is minimized."

Pan turned around as if sensing we were talking about him. Yet his expression kept somber and dangerous.

"Where is she?" he asked, haughty. "Let's not waste time. Chop, chop!" He snapped his fingers and some of his previous self shone in his mischievous eyes.

Aye, he couldn't wait to repay the favor.

FIFTY

Titus

Gallchobhair led the procession, Pan finally stepping behind. Some of what the fae said glued to my thoughts: Edward's *dorcha* might disperse once it vanished from Ryanne's body. I cared nothing about it, and I was certain neither of my kin would. Yet, I'd never seen it fade away, only change places.

Sergei limped toward us, a daigh and two dryads behind him. He was pale and obviously weak, but his eyes showed determination.

"You look better," I said.

Kara grinned. "That's a quick recovery."

Sergei shrugged. "It wasn't so bad. Did you get the blood?"

I nodded curtly.

We turned a corner, and Gally requested us to remain outside for a moment.

"I need to prepare the place correctly, and I need no distractions."

We all acquiesced, but Pan managed to slip inside before Gally shut the door.

Sergei took me aside. "Your expression is more somber than a Spanish prisoner in an English galley. What gives?"

"The ritual. It's better that only the fae and me are present. You and Kara should wait outside."

Sergei nodded. "As long as we go after Edward and I can blast Minho to Davy Jones Locker, I don't care."

"Oh no." Kara stepped between us and glared at both. "I'm going inside. She helped me when I recovered and the least I can do—"

"—is helping her when she recovers," I said.

"Which I can do if I know what she goes through. I'm going in."

I folded my arms across my chest.

"You're hiding something," Kara said, menacing. "I thought we were beyond that."

"Anord's balls, when did you become an expert in reading me?"

"I've always been, little brother. I was there when you laid your first woman, wasn't I?"

"Outside the room," I said. "Not with me."

She shrugged. "I peeked. Now, what ails you?"

I pinched the bridge of my nose but told them what Gally warned. "It's his *dorcha*, and I know we don't care about it. But what if that energy behaves differently?"

Kara glanced at the door. "You mean like when we both fought him? You're afraid it can attack us?"

That was what I couldn't pinpoint before. "What if it does?"

"No worries, Doyle," Sergei said, expression firm. "If needed, I'll use the fae as a shield."

"I thought you weren't coming in," I said.

"If Kara's in, then I'm in."

"And once she recovers, we go after Edward." She grinned.

Sergei glanced at the closed door, somber. "I'll be ready to fight the moment we're out."

"The clock's ticking," I said. "I can feel Anord's eyes on the back of my neck, ready to pounce. The longer we dally, the worse it can be for us. Edward might be very well setting a council."

The three of us exchanged worried glances. Hell, of course the bastard would set a council. Ntombi could have been the scout, by all means. In fact, the more I thought about it, the more right I felt. They knew. They were following me. Even that Shen and Cedeño gobshite.

That time in Rome? Cedeño could have been a spy. I knew something had been off.

"But we have our pretty fae." Kara beamed. "He'll balance the odds."

"Not if we need to obtain Ed's Name," I said. "You know how the beast reacts. Have a fae nearby and it'll cry blood. He can't get near. It's up to us."

Sergei cracked his knuckles. "I'll get Minho. If I can't kill him, then at least I'll maim him for centuries. The bastard deserves it."

"We get Edward, *then* Minho." She eyed me. "You *know* how to get his Name, don't you?"

"No. Ryanne and I were going to practice and hope to the Morrigan that we could figure it out. Unless Edward tells us his Name himself, I don't see what else to do."

"And you both attack him," Sergei said.

"Does everything have to be about attacking for you?" Kara said.

"By all means, share with us that wondrous idea about how to obtain the Alpha's Name," I said.

"We force him." She lift a clenched fist. "We tried with *dorcha*, but it failed. But with that power of yours, you could subdue him."

"And hers," I said, jutting my chin to the door. "I need her. You should have seen her jabbing that goblin's blade into his neck, then sending her *préachta*. Then, maybe, we can subdue him."

It was extremely odd to talk like this, trusting them completely. Yet it felt right. No more boundaries among us.

"So," Kara said. "For this task to be successful, we rely on a human."

"Who has fae power," I reminded her.

"And soon, dragonblood," Sergei said.

We all stared at the door. So many things could go wrong in this endeavor. For us bradaís, there was no turning back. We either succeeded or were blasted into oblivion. Without a soul, there was no afterlife for us. We would perish like sea foam in the ocean.

I'd be in that nether world again, then disperse into the void.

That heart of mine seemed to shrivel and yell in despair. That hurt, that pain, echoed in every part of me.

Not seeing Ryanne anymore. To be apart for eternity. The torture of it almost broke me.

"Now we three are free of Anord," Sergei said, clutching his shoulder. "If we can't get to Edward, let's find the Guardian, that old *nádhúrtha* you told us about, and deal with Anord himself."

Kara beamed, and I bowed my head to Sergei.

My friend. My brother.

The door opened and Gallchobhair stepped out. "We are ready. Are you certain you shall not be affected by the dark energy?"

"Not only I," I said, "but my family as well. We're stronger together. We'll be fine, I assure you."

Gally nodded.

As I stepped inside, I could feel my beast retreating to the innermost corner. Thick fae energy dangled in the room, and my *préachta* reacted.

Blue curtains draped around the windows. The glass door to the inner garden was opened, and pixies sang outside with a few gnomes marking the rhythm. Dryads danced. Candles abounded in the room despite the light coming from the garden, while sandalwood burned in a corner. Gauzy curtains wrapped around Ryanne's bed.

And Pan perched on a stool, his mood dark.

Hell, with all this bilge water, I'd be as unhappy as the annoying brat. I strode to the bed and pushed the curtains aside. The black thorns taking over her body looked prominent against her grayed skin, her once shiny hair dull and tangled spread over the silky pillow. Her chest barely heaved, and her expression conveyed angst.

I took her limp, cold hand and massaged it, then leaned to kiss her sweaty forehead. "Hang on, love," I whispered.

"What's with the Cinderella mood?" Kara asked, glaring at the dancing dryads.

Gally clasped his hands behind his back. "I'm uncertain of what you are talking about, and I'd rather not know. I'm preparing this room with gentle energy. Ryanne enjoys watching the dance of the dryads and playing with pixies and gnomes. This will help in her awakening."

"That sounds to me like what a kid would like." Kara tilted her head, watching Ryanne's sleeping form. "She doesn't feel like one to me."

"She used to be *cailín* until recently, yes," Gally agreed. "Not anymore. But that doesn't mean she still doesn't enjoy these things."

"Enough." Pan stood and retrieved the phial from within his rags. "Pig Face, tell those mosquitoes to hush and the walking sticks to stop their convulsions." His eyes darkened. "This is serious."

Gally closed the glass door and nodded at Pan.

"I, Pan"—the brat dramatically placed a hand on his chest—"the King of Everything, will keep his magnificent word and return a favor to Potato Breath."

"Ryanne," I said, enunciating each syllable loud and clear.

"She saved me from Cow Head," Pan continued with his theatrical voice, "so I shall be gracious and do the same." He bowed to us as if expecting applause.

"Must he be the one to do it?" I said to Gally.

"I'm afraid so."

Pan lifted the phial and stared down at Ryanne for the first time. "By the goat's horns! She's uglier than a hellhound. Who tattooed her face? Goblins?"

"Just do it!" I yelled.

Pan placed a hand on Ryanne's forehead and lifted the vial. "This is for Aghna too," Pan whispered, then his face pinched in confusion.

"Huh." Pan removed his hand and stared at Gally. "I was under the impression that sweet Aghna died but—"

"What do you mean?" Gally interrupted, scowl deep. "Aghna *did* die."

Pan shook his head in obvious disagreement. "I saw Ryanne with her in a vision, but she was completely changed: think ringlets and yellow eyes. When did she strike a deal with the Erlking?"

Gally choked and sobbed. "What?"

"The woman in the ship," I breathed. "She . . . she's Aghna?"

Pan shrugged. "She's alive and has Erlking's energy in her. That's all I can say."

Gally placed a hand on the wall, head bowed, and Kara placed herself at his side, whispering soothing words. As sorry as I felt for him, and as many questions as I had about Aghna and Minho's partner being one and the same, Ryanne couldn't wait.

"The vial," I said.

At this, Gally recovered and, face ashen, stood next to the bed. He might be dying inside but he had a responsibility to Ryanne.

I nodded at him and he nodded back, swallowing.

Pan waved his hand then jabbed the sharp point of the phial into her neck. Ryanne recoiled and gasped. Seizures took her body while Pan kept administering the dragon's blood.

I took a step forward but, Gally stopped me short.

Foam came from her lips, and the seizures grew stronger. I stiffened while Gallchobhair chanted a slow song without words. Images of the sea, of the sunsets that Ryanne loved so much, of the time we were inside the sea and she saw that other part of me, came to my mind, and I relaxed.

The sea.

"Fjords," Kara murmured, and her eyes took a faraway look.

"Howling wolves," Pan breathed.

"Chicken Kiev," Sergei said, smacking his lips.

Ryanne sputtered more foam, but then her limbs relaxed. She became limp, her head lolled to the side.

Everyone stilled but Pan, who placed a dirty hand over her pale, beaded forehead. "If she doesn't accept the blood, then you better say your goodbyes."

"I beg your pardon?" Gally said, his body leaned toward him.

I stepped forward and shouted, "That wasn't the plan."

"That's why you're Maggot Brain and I'm the king. I know things. If she can't handle the power that comes with the dragonblood, she's toast. She'll burn into coals." His eyes took a black sheen.

"Did you know this?" I growled at Gally.

"No. Every fae who has undergone this has accepted the blood."

"Because they're fae," I sputtered. "She's not!"

"Chill, Maggot Brain. She has enough fae power to counteract the dragon's power. But she must know how to and not be swallowed by the dragon. If she's strong enough, she'll endure."

Pushing the issue aside, I went to her. I gently squeezed her cold hand. "Fight, Ryanne. Fight like you did Edward." I focused and sent *préachta* but nothing stirred. It met the same high wall.

Nothing answered my plea.

"Remember," I insisted. "The sea. It crashes and sweeps but there's peace within."

Her chest heaved as if relieved from pressure, and a breath came unbidden from my lips.

Pan stepped back and said in a macabre voice, "It's done."

FIFTY-ONE

Ryanne

Curled into a ball, Edward's energy clogged my arteries with its oily thickness, as if razors scratched against every inch of skin. I whimpered and knew I wouldn't hold on much longer. The fae power that had held it back weakened, and I shut my eyes closed, my body shaking.

A whiff of dampness and cold washed over me, and I was back at the Erlking's lair. Young, teary eyes watched me behind bars.

"Help me," the boy pleaded.

"I will," I said.

He grinned and red dots replaced his eyes and darkness engulfed him. As cavernous laughter boomed, a bearded hulking creature with a helm and antlers rising from his mask replaced the figure of the boy.

The Erlking grew and grew, his powerful legs encased in snow boots and his cape, made of dry leaves, fluttered about them. His eyes became burning coals, and I stepped back, heart thumping furiously.

Nothing was merciful in his expression; nothing remotely kind or friendly shone in those burning eyes. He was now as tall as a building, and stormy clouds swirled beneath a yellow sky.

He threw a hand, and winged arrows escaped from his fingers.

No, not arrows. They were mighty dragons erupting with fire.

The energy snakes hissed and launched at the flying dragons.

Instead of the razors now, I felt as if someone had dumped hot coffee over me. Over and over again.

They clashed, and the dragons burned the snakes. A fire that reached me, and I screamed in agony.

It burned. Oh gods, it burned so much!

The snakes recoiled and screeched. Tiny pinpoints of blackness engulfed by fire.

Then, everything vanished.

I was running next to the sea. Sweat dampened my armpits and my stomach, but the wind kept my face fresh.

"Faster, faster," croaked the creature perched on my shoulder. "Don't stop."

I kept running. Something cold pressed against my chest, and I padded at it—a locket. A burning cold locket that felt familiar and yet alien.

Something was missing from the landscape. There were no people around, no tourists, and there was no sound either despite the fact that waves crashed against the dock.

A yearning took over me at the sea memory.

There used to be mountains around here, but I couldn't remember their name, as I couldn't remember the name of the creature that sat on my shoulder. He was a friend of mine I sorely missed but couldn't remember.

What I did recall was it shouldn't weigh this much, nor did it have such thick claws piercing my shoulder.

"You're hurting me," I puffed.

The claws dug deeper into my flesh, and I winced. My body hurt from the creature's weight and its wicked claws. I'd been running for hours, and my thighs burned. My calves screamed in protest, and my throat ached.

"I need to stop," I pleaded.

"No, no," the creature croaked. "This is not over."

I stumbled and rolled over the hard heated pathway. The creature still clung to my shoulder, and its claws dug even deeper. I screamed in pain.

"I can't," I wheezed. "I can't move. It hurts. It hurts so much."

Wings flapped, and the creature finally lifted from my shoulder. "Look up, child."

And I did, despite the muscles in my neck straining, as if I'd never used them before, as if I was dead and those little strips were the remaining tissue over my skeleton. And then, I wished I didn't.

A huge dragon, with black glistening scales, stared into my eyes with his red slitted ones that didn't blink. Wicked horns adorned its head, and crimson dots spread across his face, as if a permanent fire resided beneath the scales.

"You're in pain, little one."

As if agreeing with its words, pain coursed through my body like an electric shock. I bit back the tears. "It's been like this for hours. I can't move well."

A memory of a past life burst into me, when I was young and fit and helped the elderly . . . somewhere. They couldn't move at times, pain in their joints. I felt like them, attached to a bed, hard to move without this forever pain clinging to my muscles.

The pain hit again, this time like rusted nails jabbing into my skin—like the ones Sanders wanted to use on me. That fat bastard should be the one suffering, not me. I cried and dug my fingers into the dirt. "I can't take this any longer."

"I will help you."

I lifted my face, tears rolling freely over my cheeks. The dragon's face was no longer frightening, but there was a welcoming feeling. "Who are you?" I croaked.

"Your new mentor."

It extended its wings so wide that they covered the sky above and engulfed the sun. Soon, all was darkness.

"Come, little one." It opened its maw and pulled me toward it.

"No," I managed to say.

I shut my eyes and whipped my head away from the dragon. Cold flickered inside me.

Cold. That was familiar.

"Come!" the dragon roared. Power like I'd never felt pulled me toward it.

I opened my eyes to a huge body of water before me. *The sea crashes and sweeps but there is calm within.* It anchored me.

Of course, that was how I'd fight back! I pictured the cold power as an anchor and sent it deep into the ground. Then I stood and faced the dragon.

The maw called me, but I kept my ground.

"No. I will stand." I lifted a hand in defiance.

"Then I'll devour you."

The dragon leaped and darkness engulfed me.

A shock ran again through my veins. The cold power within me struggled with the newcomer. Lava replaced my blood, and I shouted for the pain to stop. It burned, and the heat was unbearable.

As much as I tried to hose the fire down, I couldn't. It was like having a 110-degree fever and irons pressed against my skin.

I tried to gulp air, but it was as hot as scalding steam. I pressed my temples. Would this pain never end?

"Accept me," a voice said around me, a different yet familiar voice, "and it shall stop."

My heartbeat pounded. The Erlking's red eyes floated before me.

"I need a new daughter. My dragon will mentor you."

The dragon appeared instead of the red dots. "I can take your pain away," it said. "Accept us."

"No!"

I'd been lost, that much I could remember. My human self being swallowed in a sea of fae power. And now, someone else wanted to do the same, to erase who I was? I would not allow it.

I would never allow it.

I pushed the dragon outside of me with a defying yell. "I am me! I am no one's. No one's," I repeated.

The scenery changed, and the dragon and I were on a rock in the middle of ragged waters. The churning sea crashed in huge waves around us and droplets of salt water splashed my face.

From far away, the chant of pixies reached me, and it filled me with joy. My friend. My darling, loyal friend. Bricius!

Bricius must be nearby. The cold within me reacted, and I was able to calm down enough to focus. The energy expanded beyond me, and the dragon stepped back. Its slitted eyes changed to red dots that floated. Soon, it was all I could see.

Something warm prickled my chest. The locket. Someone gave it to me. It rooted me, didn't it?

I pressed one hand against my chest and felt the metal beneath my palm, a warmth that turned into scorching heat. The throb in my forehead, once forgotten, came with full force and a migraine took over.

My blood boiled. It was so hot inside my body that I feared a volcano would erupt from within. My skin hardened and puffs of smoke came out of my nostrils.

"I am me," I repeated. "You have no power over me."

The dragon roared, and I winced, then I realized it was laughing. "You have already accepted me, little one. Look at you."

I did. A metallic sheen covered my skin, and I recoiled. The heat inside me, it was the same as the Erlking's touch but enhanced. It covered me whole.

I was not me.

"Now look there." It turned his head toward the nearby shore, a shore that was now connected to the rock I was standing on.

A woman stood by the sea, a warrior per her stance. Her dark ringlets spilled over her shoulders and obscured her face. She was dressed in leathers, and some of her ringlets were as crimson as the dots in the dragon's face. The woman of my nightmares, Minho's lover. The one called Birdie.

"Birdie!" I called. "Help!"

The woman didn't react.

"She doesn't go by that name because it's not her," it said.

"What do you mean she's not . . ." Something cold pressed over my chest, a dreary feeling. If she wasn't Birdie, who the heck was she?

"Fiadh," the dragon called.

And I knew she was the dragon's creature. I just knew. Fear gripped me, a fear I hadn't felt since I had those seer-dreams with her. It was now I could see the difference between this woman with a metallic sheen on her skin and those crimson ringlets and Birdie.

Fiadh turned, her face full in view, and I screamed, scrambling back. "It can't be. This is a trick, a deception," I whispered, terrified.

The woman wore my face, my eyes, the same shape of my head, and she smirked with that smirk I'd always hated. My locket dangled from her neck.

She swayed toward me, with the confidence I'd seen in Kara, and I pulled back. Her nails elongated into claws, bloodied and sharp.

"No. You're not me," I breathed. "You can't be the woman from my seer-dream." And yet I knew she was.

She spoke for the first time, with my voice, with my own voice.

"Oh, but I am you. You are I. Say hello to the new improved you, sweet darling."

Epilogue

Balzgroth soared across the lands and circled around the Erlking's lair. And there his master was, standing before the opening of the cave, hands clasped behind his back. His cape, made of stitched leaves, clung to his thick neck.

The dragon descended, his huge wings slowing him down. He bowed before his master.

"Is it done?" the Erlking asked.

"Yes, master."

"Good, good. All is going according to plan. You need to infiltrate the taigh and teach her."

Balzgroth acquiesced with another bow. "The fae will never know what is happening. I am already in her dreams."

The Erlking grinned. "Well done, Balzgroth. The god Anord is planning his next bold move. His Alpha is doing his bidding, yet curiously, also has a plan of his own. Yes," he said to himself as he turned toward his lair, "all is going well, indeed."

Glossary

- A mhuirnín: *dear*.
- Aine: a dryad from Tír D'aois. Ryanne named her power after her.
- Becalmed: in naval terms, when there is no wind, and a sailing ship is unable to move because of it, the ship is said to be "becalmed."
- Blow the man down: to strike someone hard enough to bring him to the deck or to kill a man.
- Bradaís: Immortal creatures created by Anord with black magic.
- Brocach: *filthy*.
- Cáilín: child fae.
- Cat o'nine tails: a whip with nine lashes used for flogging.
- Catgut scraper: slang for the ship's fiddler.
- Dannan-dubh: a race from Tír D'aois. Homkar belongs to this race.
- Dragonwood: a special wood that comes from the Valley of the Dragons in Tír D'aois.
- Daigh: guards of the fae. The word comes from "flame."
- Dorcha: Bradaís dark energy, the one they use to kill.

- Dorogoy: *dear* in Russian (as Kara uses it).
- Dainséar: *danger*.
- Eadrom: Guardian of the Hawthorne. There are only three: Gallchobhair, Turien, and Cuidigtheach.
- Erlking: resides over half the creatures in Tír D'aois. He's the dark equivalent of the fae.
- Feihnum: a chord with Fé Erie's power.
- Goose without gravy: A severe but bloodless blow.
- Kiss the gunner's daughter: a punishment consisting of being hoisted over one of the ship's guns and flogged.
- Mo thiarna: *my lord*.
- Minho: the only fae turned bradaí and Edward's second.
- Nádhúrtha: human-like beings that reside in Tír na Donna. They are the fae equivalent.
- Pooka: a shapeshifter in Tír D'aois. They're considered neutral creatures but love mischief.
- Powder monkey: term for a crew member whose job during battle was to run back and forth from the ship's powder hold to keep the guns supplied with black powder.
- Préachta: fae energy inside Titus and Ryanne, both from Fé Erie's touch.
- Snámh Laghairt: creatures similar to Chinese dragons.
- Scáil Dragún. Titus's ship. This is inspired by "shadow" and "dragon."
- Tír D'aois: the fae's realm. Means Old Country. Pronounced "Tir doisch."
- Tír na Donna: human's realm.
- Tír na Vraoichta: the realm of darkness. Pronounced "vroishta."
- Taigh: where the fae dwell. Means "home." Pronounced "taigg."

Plea from the Author

Dear Reader,

Out of all the epic tales and swoony romances you could have chosen, you picked *Corruption of Faete* from the *Bradaís Pledge* series. I can't thank you enough for diving into Titus and Ryanne's world (and putting up with all their chaos). You've made this author's heart do a little happy dance!

Now, I must ask for one final favor. Could you leave a review on Amazon or Goodreads? Share what you loved, what made you scream at the book (hopefully in a good way), or even that one thing that made you roll your eyes. Long or short, every review matters more than you know.

Your words could be the guiding star for another reader to discover this story. After all, without your help, how will they ever get to meet Titus and Ryanne? And trust me, they need to meet them—just like I needed you.

Thank you for being part of this adventure. You're the true seer of stories, the keeper of magic, and the wind that keeps this ship moving.

With gratitude and a sprinkle of magic,

Ligia de Wit

If you're interested in being first in line to learn more about the fae and the bradaís, join my newsletter (https://ligiadewit.eo.page/bd8xf) and be the first to know about news of this series and more.

Thank you for your support.

Want more just like this one? Sign up for our newsletter so you don't miss out on the adventure. You'll get:

- A free book for signing up
- Advanced notice of new releases
- First word of books on sale
- Opportunities for free books
- Most up-to-date information on author appearances.

We're busy and know you are too. We won't send more than one newsletter a month.

Register below.

Acknowledgments

If I tried to write alone in a little bubble, this book wouldn't exist. I wouldn't survive without my crew of fellow writers, editors, and magical humans. At least this author wouldn't!

So, let me keep this short and sweet (but still full of love).

Tracy, Jessie, you two are the absolute best. The beach will always be our sacred writing retreat, and the snowy Springs our haven of hot tub inspiration. I'd brave sharks and snowstorms for you both (but maybe not at the same time).

Kelly, my yelling partner-in-first-draft-chaos—you get me. Somehow, between all the shouting (on page, on comments I then delete, thanks, Kevin!), you work your editing magic, and together, we spin something incredible.

Sara, my eagle-eyed grammar guru and secret superhero. Your younger eyes catch all the sneaky things my (ahem) "experienced" ones don't. Thank you for your dedication and for helping this bilingual brain stay on track.

CDS authors. Yes, I added a spider. Yes, it's big.

And finally, to my family, who patiently endures my "I need to write!!!" moments of madness. You are my anchor, my heart. Forever and ever.

Thank you all for being my constant in this wild adventure. You make the impossible possible, and I couldn't have done it without you. I know it sounds cliché, but I swear it's true!

With love and pirate-sized gratitude,
Ligia

About the Author

Ligia de Wit is a quirky bilingual writer, residing in Mexico City. An eternal romantic who's loved fairy tales and swashbuckling stories all her life, she blends both with fun language and a hefty sprinkle of romance while she's at it. Her stories are full of personality with endearing characters.

You can find her short stories with Palamades Publishing, Backchannel Magazine, and WordCrafter.

When not concocting stories, she works at a global leading distributor company. Chat with her at ligiadewit.com.

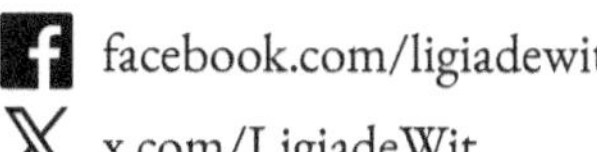

facebook.com/ligiadewit

x.com/LigiadeWit

instagram.com/ligiadewitauthor